I

BINARY SOULS

FORGIVING DARKNESS

CAT SIROTA

FORGIVING DARKNESS

To my sweet Manny boy.
You will be forever missed by us all.
May we meet again. In this life, or the next.

Forgiving Darkness is a fantasy romance with content that might not be suitable for some readers. Triggers such as violence, torture, death, reference to the death of a parent, reference to murder, reference to past abuse, animal death, profanity, and consensual sex.

If you feel that a trigger has been missed, please contact me.
I'll keep an updated list of trigger warnings on my website
(www.catsirota.com).

CONTENTS

NORDIA
OBERRETTA
SOLIAN
AGROSIS
THE DEAD TREE
ESTRID'S COTTAGE
THE DARK FOREST
N
E
S
W

CHAPTER ONE

Estrid's lungs burn and ache as she sucks in air. She wills her legs forward as the drumbeat of horses galloping pounds the ground behind her. The tall grass whips her legs as the sun beats down on her back. She needs to make it to the tree. He's waiting for her there.

"Get her!" a soldier yells.

Hooves beating, armor clanking—it acts as a guide to her of how far ahead she is. Closer. Louder. The soldiers are gaining on her.

Her muscles grow tired. Her chest feels like it's on fire. Grimacing, she lets out a whimper of pain. She wills her body forward. Just a few more meters. She needs to press on.

A flash of black and gold to her left draws her attention away from the trees ahead. A soldier flanks her.

"Gotcha," he says, throwing out a rope.

Without a thought, she draws her dagger and drags it across his horse's side. It lets out a whine of pain, throwing itself up in the air and tossing its rider to the ground. She needs to get to the tree on the hill's small crest. A lone oak tree, its heavy branches stretch out like a fan. The dense foliage from its leaves casts a shadow across the ground. Protection.

"Stop running, you wench, or you'll make it worse for yourself," another soldier shouts behind her.

Her heart races. They're closer. The horses' labored breaths become louder as they draw nearer.

Using her last reserves, Estrid picks up a little more speed. She reaches the oak tree, scrambling up its branches. The coarse bark acts as a steadying grip for her sweaty hands to latch on to. Up she climbs until she's high enough off the ground. She pushes herself hard against the side of the tree, using the thick foliage to hide in. *Gods, that was close. Hold your line, Rafe,* she thinks as she tries to calm her racing heart. The sounds of clanking metal come to a halt directly under her. Horses huff and snort after their sprint from the village.

"Come down, you Solian bitch!" one soldier with a bushy brown beard calls up to her.

Estrid peeks down through the dense canopy as they circle the tree. She watches them from above, evening out her breathing to avoid giving away her position. The soldiers remove their heaviest armor, the chain mail dropping with a thud on the ground. They're coming after her.

She smiles to herself. That twinge of darkness begins to rear its head, like a black cat opening one eye from sleep. She can feel it stretching in her. It starts to course through her body. Her fingertips tingle in anticipation.

The man with the thick brown beard is the first to move. He grabs a dagger from his boot, placing the hilt in his mouth. He climbs up the old oak tree, the others searching from below.

Estrid steadies her position, waiting for him. She takes a deep breath in, then another. In and out, in and out, calming herself as the scraping sounds of boots against bark reach her ears. *Come on, you stupid fool. Just a little further up until I have you.*

"There you are, bitch. I'm going to cut you down," the soldier says as he scales the branches toward her. She can see his blotchy skin as beads of sweat run down it as he hauls himself up. Her heart stills before a vicious smile breaks out across her face.

"You think I *fear* you?"

The soldier stops climbing, a look of confusion washing over him.

"It's you who should be scared. I will take *everything* from you."

Black tendrils wrap themselves around her wrists and arms. They're familiar and soft, like the caress of a lover's touch. A grin erupts on her face as she throws out her arm to the man. Before he can scream, her magic sucks everything from him, draining him and leaving a sand-colored husk the size of a dog.

The cocky smiles on the other soldiers fade as they watch, with wide-eyed horror, what's left of their comrade floats down. They stumble back from the husk as it lands with a soft rustle.

A branch snaps, chaos erupting as shouts to get their crossbows and kill her mix with screams to run. A menacing growl vibrates through the air. Horses whinny in fright at the vicious sound. Dirt flies as their hooves hammer the ground. Their riders curse them as they rear up and gallop back into the tall grass. *Perfect, Rafe! I'm coming!*

Estrid climbs down the tree to the sounds of flesh being ripped and the gurgling screams of the dying soldiers surrounding her. She lands with a thump on the ground to see her familiar, Rafe. The enormous black wolf tears into one soldier while another tries to crawl away. She calls on her magic again, walking to the fleeing soldier. His black-and-gold tabard glistens from the blood that soaks it. He holds up his hands in a plea.

"Please. Please don't—"

She unleashes her magic. Like a rope, she tosses it over the soldier, strangling him. It takes, as it always does. Behind her, Rafe crouches lower over a third soldier, a low growl coming from his gaping jaws. The man's eyes are wide with fear as he clutches the wound at his neck.

"You shouldn't have come here," she says in an infuriated tone, walking toward the man. "You shouldn't have tried to harm those villagers. You'll pay for that."

A gurgle replaces his words as blood oozes from his torn throat. She curls her fingers in the air as her magic pulls tighter. He goes silent as death wraps around him.

A twinge of guilt spikes in her chest. The memories of the innocent lives she took years ago threaten to overcome her, but then she remembers what she's here to do. She's here to stop him. Stop Rodden and his men from ever hurting an innocent again.

Standing under the tree, all is quiet again. No shouts. No screams. Just the whispering breeze that rolls through the trees.

"Come on, Rafe. Time to clean up," she says to her familiar sitting beside her, blood glistening on his black muzzle.

With a huff, Rafe pads around and starts picking up the husks of the soldiers in his giant mouth, placing them in a pile over the discarded tabards.

Estrid circles the tree, picking up the metal armor and weapons that can't be burnt and putting it into one of the pits she dug earlier. Satisfied that everything is accounted for, she strikes the flint in her hand, the sparks catching on the remnants of her enemy. Orange flames ignite as soon as the spark hits. Everything that can catch alight in the other pit she dug will burn.

Rafe comes to sit next to her as she crouches down. They watch the orange flames consume their enemy in silence. The warmth of the fire kisses her cheeks as she lets out a sigh. The day isn't over yet; more work must be done.

The pair trek across the grassy plains, back to where they first lured the soldiers. A village lies just over the ridgeline. Stone houses with thatched roofs belong to unsuspecting people going about their daily business. She watches children laugh and play, their parents scolding them as they get in the way. Screams don't follow the laughter as they once did.

Those memories are her penance—payment for all those innocent lives taken. A heavy debt she's not sure will ever be repaid. She walks closer to the village with a heavy sigh, keeping low in the grass.

Estrid takes a deep breath, closes her eyes, and focuses her energy. She reaches down to the ground, her fingers grazing the top of the damp soil. Buried beneath it, in a shallow grave, the smooth surface of a river rock grazes her fingers. She traces them over the cool stone, finding the hardened raised symbol from the blood she drew it with. Her blood.

With another deep breath, she funnels her magic into it. The symbol on this rock acts as a beacon to the others she placed around the village; each symbol in blood is a command from her magic. Like a lit fuse, the black coils of her magic cascade down the invisible line, connecting with each rock. They glow black for a moment before returning to their usual dull gray, unassuming in their shallow graves. She places her magic into the rocks so that they act as a barrier for the village. It protects them from the chaos she knows too well. Those memories sit like acid in her stomach, bile rising in her mouth.

Birdsong fills her ears, the sun beating on the grassy field. The smoke from the fire she lit earlier taints the air.

"Damn it, the fire's too big. We need to go back."

Rafe runs ahead of her, back to the fire that billows smoke atop the hill. His enormous but sleek figure darts through the tall grass. When they get there, the husks are nothing but ash and dust. The orange flames eat at the remaining bits of cloth from the tabards as ashes float through the breeze. Estrid crouches next to Rafe, watching as the blaze consumes the final bits of evidence of them being here.

Estrid's thoughts are disrupted as she leaps up as a raspy voice yells, "Oi, what are you doing?"

An old man with a limp carries a pitchfork, walking toward her, but stops when he sees Rafe at her side. The sight of the wolf, whose head reaches Estrid's waist, with his jet-black fur and piercing blue eyes, has him raising his pitchfork. His weathered brown eyes dart between her and Rafe.

She needs to scare him off. He can't tell the villagers she's here. They can't find her.

She calls on her magic; the inky black streams flow from her hands—a warning.

Recognition and horror fill the man's eyes. "D-Dark Witch," he croaks out as his hands tremble.

Estrid winces at those two words. The redemption she felt from killing those soldiers melts away at his look of fear. Shame and guilt come crashing back, but people don't know her. She's changed. Made a vow not to hurt innocents anymore. To only protect them from a greater evil.

Not taking her eyes off the man, she whispers to Rafe, "Let's run for it. We're done here."

"Stay away, witch!" the man yells after her.

Her legs feel heavy from the earlier pursuit, but she doesn't dare stop until they're hidden. Though the man didn't follow, it doesn't mean he won't send others after her. She's had a village mob chase her before, and it nearly killed her.

They run until the familiar sight of the Dark Forest greets them. The tree line feels like a border to another world. Gnarled roots and twisted branches leap out of the ground.

Once they reach the trees' safety, she brushes her hands against the rough bark, feeling their welcome greeting. Rafe follows her, finding a cool rock nearby to lie on.

A brisk breeze flows through her hair, catching on the little chimes she's built that hang from the trees. Husks from soldiers she's killed before hanging from hooks alongside them. As they sway in the wind, the faces are frozen in horror, eyes wide, mouths open in permanent screams that can never escape. They warn those outside the forest not to enter or they'll be swallowed by the darkness.

To her left, Rafe stretches out on the rock. The shadows of the trees make his dark fur a deeper black that can swallow someone whole. Estrid smiles to herself at the sight of her relaxed familiar. She hates to disturb him, but more work must be done.

"Come on, Rafe. Let's go hunting."

He lifts his head and gives her a yawn; his long white canines flash in the thick of the shadows. With a sideways glance, he ignores her and puts his head back down.

The smile on Estrid's face morphs into an annoyed scowl. It's always a negotiation with Rafe. You'd almost think he was human.

"We need to go hunting, Rafe," she says, urging her familiar to move as she retrieves her bow and arrow from behind a tree. Fallen autumn leaves litter the forest floor, crunching under her feet. "We have to stock up our food stores before winter sets in."

He doesn't move.

With a sigh, Estrid says, "I'll give you the biggest bone if you come now."

At the word *bone*, Rafe propels himself up like a bird taking off. He looks at her expectantly, but when he realizes there is no bone, he takes his time, stretching his long limbs and shaking himself out before trotting over to Estrid.

She rolls her eyes at his attitude, giving him a scratch behind the ear before setting off.

They move deeper into the woods, the shadows fading. Sunlight pierces through the thick canopy. Trees tower over the small evergreen plants that carpet the floor. Well-trodden paths from Estrid and Rafe's daily comings and goings lead further into the gloom, like veins under the skin. Her boots squelch on the damp ground. Mossy rocks and rotten leaves line the path they take. The air has a musty, earthy smell, masking their scent from predators and prey alike.

Rafe trots in front of her, his ears twitching from side to side as he listens for the sounds of potential game. The forest is noisy, as multitudes of birds chirp. Insects buzz and hum, at times so loud it can be deafening to a person during the summer. Without Rafe's precise hearing, hunting would be much harder for Estrid.

They continue down the trail when suddenly Rafe stops. He crouches low to the ground as if ready to pounce.

Estrid creeps further down the path and kneels beside Rafe, her bow out with an arrow notched. A cool breeze flows through the forest, whispering to her as it catches on the loose strands of her dark brown hair. She draws her bow and waits.

With near-silent footsteps, a deer steps out of the bushes. It stares straight at her and Rafe but doesn't run. Her brow furrows.

Why's it just standing there?

The animal continues to stare, unafraid. Not wanting to waste the opportunity to hunt, she aims and then looses her arrow. With a familiar thud, the arrow finds its mark, and the deer thumps onto the forest floor, birds resuming their steady chirping.

Estrid looks expectedly at Rafe, who hasn't taken his eyes off the deer, and shakes her head.

"Lazy dog, you're only in it for the bone."

Slinging her bow over her shoulder, Estrid approaches the fallen animal. Its deep brown eyes have glassed over as it stares into nothingness. Her arrow sticks out from its chest. The familiar metallic smell of blood permeates the air.

Kneeling next to the body, she thanks it for giving its life. Nothing goes to waste on the hunt. She'll strip its hide and take the meat, the good bits of offal, and some bones to give to Rafe. The other bits will be left for the forest. The forest will use everything.

The light amongst the trees dims as Rafe sits to her right, his eyes focused on the hand with the knife that strips away the parts of the deer that they need. She'd like to think it's about obedience, but the long string of drool from his mouth suggests he's here for his bone.

There's a change in the air as she's removing the last pieces of meat. A sudden stillness settles over the forest like it's holding its breath. Rafe lets out a low, rumbling growl. The forest descends into an eerie silence again.

Thump.

Thump.

Thump.

Thump.

The sound of her heart in her ears. *Something's not right. First the deer, now this.* She grips her knife tighter, her nerves on edge. Estrid hurries to remove the last bits of meat from the animal. Her blade is slippery in her hands, coated in sticky blood.

Rafe lets out another growl, making the hairs stand up on her arms. He takes a step forward. Before she can utter a word, he bolts into the thickets; his black form disappears through the dense and shadowed landscape.

"Rafe!"

Estrid fumbles with her knife as she jumps up and races after him. The heavy satchel of meat and hide bangs against her hip as she crashes through the bushes and trees. The air whistles in her ears as she uses her arms to push tree branches out of her way.

After a few minutes, she stops, looking around her. The dark green of the woodland surrounds her in every direction. It would disorientate anyone, but her time in the forest has taught her the trails.

"Rafe!"

Estrid closes her eyes and listens. Rafe lets out a menacing snarl in the distance.

She follows the pathway to the east, the fallen leaves muffling her footsteps. She stops over bare, damp ground and spots his pawprints in the mud. Claws have slashed deep grooves into the soft dirt. Looking down, she sees leaves dotted with blood next to the prints. The sight makes her freeze, panic rising. She bends down, inspecting the bright green leaves with veins spread like a spider's web.

On high alert, she pulls her bow and arrow out, drawing the string back, poised to take down what's ahead. The beating of her heart floods her ears as she waits for whoever's blood is on the leaf to come out. Another growl reverberates through the forest, making Estrid's stomach drop.

"Rafe!"

She breaks into a sprint, leaping over rocks and logs toward the source of the haunting sounds. They grow louder as a tearing and ripping sound joins them. *Come on, Rafe. Please be okay. Don't you dare fight a bear again.*

She bursts through the dense forest into a small clearing where Rafe has latched his jaws onto a man's leg. The sight of the stranger sends a jolt of fear through her. There's a person in her forest.

A protective instinct to save a life shatters her shock and confusion. Estrid lunges for her familiar, tackling him to the ground.

"Rafe, no!"

She lies on the forest floor, arms and legs wrapped around Rafe as he wriggles to break free. His chest vibrates with a chilling, frenetic snarl.

"Rafe, stop!"

She places her head on his chest, silently pleading with him to relax. They sit in silence as minutes tick by. Rafe's breathing evens out, and the tension in his body eases. They look at the stranger. He isn't moving. Blood oozes from the holes in his flesh where Rafe's teeth punctured it.

Estrid takes in his slumped form. Long, sandy blond hair falls forward over sun-kissed skin. Despite his slumped figure, he's tall and well-built, with broad shoulders and muscular arms. His clothes are good quality, the kind only people with high standing can have. A deep red stain spreads across his stomach.

Estrid scans the forest for clues to his appearance. *Who are you? Why are you here?* Uncertainty coursing through her, she chews the side of her cheek, unsure whether to approach or leave him. *Come on, Estrid, you can't just leave him here!*

Checking to see if he's breathing, she looks at his chest. There's no rise or fall.

Moving closer to the man, she brings her forefinger and middle finger together, checking his neck for a pulse.

A bolt of electricity jolts through her as she touches his warm skin. *Shit!*

A groan escapes the stranger's mouth, and Estrid crab crawls back a few more paces. Rafe lets out another rumble and bares his teeth again.

Someone saved her all that time ago, but saving him could risk everything.

"Is this your idea of redemption?" she says to no one as she looks up through a gap in the trees to the clear blue sky above.

CHAPTER TWO

A deep rumble reverberating through the air is the first sound Zain's ears pick up. His eyes flutter open. His head feels like lead. As he regains consciousness, he realizes he's lying down. Looking up, he sees a roof made of thatch as the haze in his vision clears.

The surrounding scents are an unfamiliar combination, and yet, somehow, they're comforting. Wildflowers and thyme calm his racing pulse. His stomach grumbles in response to the savory smell of stew or soup as it wafts through the air.

Where am I?

He tries to remember what happened, but his mind is too fuzzy.

That menacing rumble comes from somewhere near him again.

He moans, lifting his hand to run it down his face. His skin is coarse with stubble from not shaving.

The growl in the room becomes louder, and Zain's heart picks up its pace. He knows that sound. It's one he's faced many times in the depths of battle. In the darkest places of the world.

He turns to see a pair of enormous ice-blue eyes set in jet-black fur. They stare directly at him.

"What the . . . shadow wolf!" he shouts in surprise, but it comes out as a dry rasp.

He moves to scramble away but is stopped by a searing pain in his stomach. He collapses down to the bed, hitting his head against a wooden wall.

The beast steps forward, baring its gleaming white canines.

Zain searches for something to protect himself with but only finds a woolen blanket covering him. He's stuck in a small room with a shadow wolf. Its muscular body towers over him, black claws protruding from its large paws as they grip the floor.

The wolf's teeth gleam as it peels its lips back in a snarl. He holds up his hands, hoping the gesture will keep the creature from tearing him limb from limb.

Tense moments tick by as they stare each other down. The animal continues to bare its teeth but doesn't attack.

Why aren't you attacking me?

Zain sighs, looking around for something familiar. Something that will tell him where he is and why there's a shadow wolf next to him.

"What's going on?" he groans.

The wolf lets out another low growl at his question.

He winces as he tries to push himself up in the small bed he's been put on. Through one eye, he sees the wolf continue to stand guard near the door.

"Where's your master, beast?" he says, shifting on the lumpy straw mattress. *Can a shadow wolf have a master?*

He looks around the cozy, rustic cottage. In the diagonal corner, two windows allow natural light into a simple kitchen. Through them, he can see the dark green of trees fluttering in the breeze. Birds sing, but their songs seem foreign to him.

He's used to luxury, with poster beds and lavish furniture in large, opulent rooms. The last time he slept in such basic conditions, he was out with the Summer Court Army, training and checking the borders.

The furniture is minimal but enough for the space. A small dining table with two chairs sits just in front of a plain kitchen. To his left, in the center of the wall, a fire roars in the hearth, warming the small area. In the left-hand corner is a single armchair with a small wooden bookshelf next to it.

He squints, trying to read the titles embossed in gold on the tattered leather spines. *Tales and Myths of Faery. A History of Humans and Fae. A History of Solian and Nordia.*

Solian? Nordia? Humans?

The realization of where he is sets in.

How did I get to the human world?

He tries to sit up again, but that piercing sensation in his belly stops him.

His hands drift down his stomach, settling on a gauzy cloth that's keeping some paste pressed against his skin. He lifts the gauze to see a deep gash bordered by angry red blisters. *Iron.*

With a gasp, Zain's memories come flooding back to him. He remembers what happened and who he left behind. He suddenly thinks of his brother, Alvey, and cousin, Del. They didn't make it through the portal.

"I need to go back," he says, wincing as he sits up.

The gesture has the fierce animal stepping toward him, its teeth fully bared.

"Be quiet, wolf. Either attack or don't, but stop the snarling and get out of my way."

The creature huffs in response to Zain's comments as he pulls his legs over the side of the bed. With a groan, Zain stands up, wobbling on his feet as the door to the cottage opens.

"What are you doing?"

Zain pauses, staring at the woman before him, trying not to fall over from the pain.

"What are you doing? You shouldn't be up," she says, striding toward him.

Unsure, he looks around again for a weapon, but she takes his arm, guiding him onto the bed. Her touch sends a jolt of electricity through him. *What was that?* It stuns him enough that he finds himself back on the bed before he can protest.

"I need to leave. I have to go back," he says with urgency to the mystery woman as he tries to get up again, which sends his head swimming.

"You aren't going anywhere. You've been injured and need rest or you'll be useless," she says, grabbing the blanket at his feet and placing it over him.

He lets out a frustrated sigh. He hates feeling vulnerable.

The shadow wolf sits at the foot of his bed, almost smirking at his futile attempts.

Zain's frustration ebbs away as he regains his focus, taking in the woman.

She has deep brown hair that's almost black. It's braided to one side, loose strands sticking to her face as a thin layer of sweat glistens on her olive skin. Her eyes take Zain's breath—golden brown, like the color of rich honey. The khaki brown cotton trousers and white cotton shirt show only a little of her figure off, but the leather belt around her waist accentuates her curves.

He sits there, transfixed. She isn't like any of the women in the Summer Court. They are delicate, hair and faces made up, wearing fine dresses that leave little to the imagination—unlike the mystery woman staring at him.

With a shake of her head, she brings him out of his stupor, walking to the fireplace. "How are you feeling?" she says, placing the logs in a pile by the fire.

Zain takes a moment to register what she's asked. "Alive, thanks to you, I assume?"

She nods, watching him.

"How bad was it?" His voice is still raspy. Until now, he hadn't noticed how dry his throat was, like rough sandpaper.

"Here, let me get you some water." She walks over to a pitcher and cup on the small wooden kitchen table. He doesn't know this woman, but something stirs within him.

"Well, it wasn't a pleasant sight. Your cut was deep, and you'd lost a lot of blood. I brought you here. If I hadn't, you likely would have died," she says, handing him the water.

"Where am I exactly?"

"The Dark Forest. I found you slumped against a tree about two miles from here."

Behind her, he can hear the low grumble of the shadow wolf. The woman glances over her shoulder, giving the animal a commanding look. It lets out a huff and lies in front of the fire.

With a grimace, Zain takes the water, struggling to sit up. The mystery woman hesitates before bending down to help him drink. Her touch is tender, sending another hum of energy through him. He furrows his brows in confusion as he gulps down the water.

"Easy. . . ." She draws the cup away from him. "You'll be sick if you drink too much right away."

She gets up, putting distance between them. Disappointment hits him as she steps away; his brows furrow at the odd feeling. She sets two more logs on the fire, the warm orange light making her skin glow.

He clears his throat. "Thank you. What's your name?"

"Estrid. What's yours?"

"Zain. How long was I out for?"

"About a day."

"What? I have to go," he says, moving to get up again, the pain from his wound making him flinch.

"No, you need to rest." She lays a firm hand on his shoulder to push him down.

"You don't understand. I have to go. There are people who need my help," Zain insists, that feeling of vulnerability coming back, uncomfortable and unfamiliar.

"You'll be no use to them if you don't heal. Your stomach wound could have killed you, and the one on your leg from Rafe . . . ah, sorry," she says, looking sheepish.

An awkward silence descends on them. The crackling of the fire as it takes hold of the wood is the only sound to break it.

Before thinking about what he's saying, he asks, "Who's Rafe? Your husband?"

"No, he's my dog." She dips her head in the shadow wolf's direction.

He scrunches his brow. He looks to Rafe, who lounges by the hearth, one eye open, staring at him.

Zain half coughs and half laughs, the pain from his stomach taking his breath away. He points to the huge shadow wolf who takes up a large amount of space in the small cottage. "Him? A dog?"

Estrid cocks her head to one side. "Yes. Why?" she says in a distrusting tone as she moves to the hearth.

Interesting. Why is there a shadow wolf in the human world? Should I say something?

Instead, he keeps his eyes locked on the creature. "Where did you find your, ah, dog?"

"In the forest. He rescu—I mean, found me one day, and we've stuck together ever since."

Zain eyes her suspiciously, but decides to drop it to try and learn more about her. "I suppose I should say thank you, wolf."

"Wolf?" she says, moving a bubbling pot away from over the fire, lifting the lid and stirring the contents as steam rises and curls around her. The smell of a rich soup quickly reaches him through the small room; the comforting scent of aromatic herbs, vegetables, and meat makes his mouth water.

Zain changes the subject back to learning more about her. "Do you live here alone?"

He observes her; there's an underlying energy surrounding her. Using his own ability to detect other kinds of magic, he hones in on it. The air around her is different—darker, smoother. *She has magic! But what kind? How does a human have magical abilities?*

"It's just Rafe and me," she says, oblivious to his probing magic.

The revelation sprouts new questions about Estrid, her magic, why she lives in a forest alone, why a human has a shadow wolf and the events that led to this situation. He's intrigued by her. Their whole encounter has been strange, and yet he wants to know more, but he's still cautious, having learned the lesson of being too trusting with those around him.

Zain's thoughts swirl in his head. His memories become clearer as he recalls his pain as the blade his friend wielded sank into his abdomen.

"Bastard," he curses at no one.

Estrid looks at him in surprise as she catches what he says. "Excuse me?" she says, getting up and stepping away from him, clutching the wooden spoon.

"Not you. Sorry."

Zain looks away from her, thinking about the events leading up to this moment. Guilt slices through his chest at the thought of Del and Alvey left behind.

He can feel her eyes waiting for him to say more.

Who are you? I don't know you, or trust you.

Looking up at her, he sees she's just as uncertain of him as he is of her, knuckles white as she clutches the wooden spoon. If she wanted to harm him, she would have had the opportunity to do so. But there's a curiosity he has toward her.

He releases a heavy sigh. "The, ahh . . . man who did this to me. He's the bastard. He's my uncle and he betrayed me, attacked my home, and conspired against my family," Zain explains, recalling the battle that raged at his home before he portalled himself out, leaving Del and Alvey behind.

Rage courses through his body, his cheeks heating at the thought. Rafe growls at him from where he lies by the hearth.

Calm down, Zain. The wolf has no problem ripping you to pieces.

He takes a deep breath in, centering himself. "He used a close friend and mentor to try to kill us. I tried to portal out with my brother and cousin, but they didn't make it through."

Zain curses himself for letting slip his magic abilities, but Estrid doesn't flinch. He notices that she isn't surprised and saves that question for later. Right now, he needs to focus on returning to the Summer Court.

"Thank you for saving me. I need to get back home. I should have healed by now, but . . . they used an iron blade," he says, looking down at the gauze-covered wound, remembering the telltale blisters on his skin. Inside, he feels like something is missing; his Fae powers are depleted.

It'll take days for me to heal enough to be useful. What will happen to Del and Alvey? What will happen to my home?

Estrid interrupts his thoughts. "Iron's deadly to Fae, isn't it?"

He takes a moment to realize what she's asked; she knows he's Fae, yet she's human. He nods as she continues to look at him with curiosity. Those golden eyes are searching.

"How did you know I was Fae?" he asks.

"Well, your ears are a giveaway, but I've read a lot about the Fae," she says, her eyes focusing on his dressed wound.

"I know what it's like to be betrayed by someone close to you," she says with a sigh, looking down at Rafe and scratching the wolf's head.

Something stirs in Zain, a familiarity. This stranger understands what he feels more deeply than he realized. *Who betrayed you? And why? Who have you left behind? I have more questions about who you are.*

His eyes sting and blur as a wave of fatigue washes over him. He's too weak now but vows to get back to Faery as soon as he's recovered.

Estrid's face softens, her brow furrowing as a look of pity and sympathy crosses her face.

With a sigh, she gets up, reaching the door. "If you want to get back home, you need to rest. I'll be back soon," she says, leaving Zain alone with Rafe.

✦ ✦ ✦

CHAPTER THREE

Zain jolts awake to the pain hitting his abdomen. His hand flies toward the cause of it, latching on to a small wrist. He opens his eyes, seeing a woman's honey-gold orbs staring at him. A warmth radiates in his chest as he recalls her name—Estrid.

"What are you doing?" he croaks, pulse racing as he tightens his grip on her arm.

Trust her, Zain. She wouldn't have saved you if she wanted to harm you.

"Your wound needs redressing," she says, holding up the wet cloth with faint smears of dark red blood. "It's okay. I won't hurt you."

Zain exhales, loosening his hold on her and giving her a slight nod. In his peripheral vision, he can see Rafe standing on high alert, focused on where Zain touches Estrid.

She twists out of his grasp, resuming her work. She perches off the side of a small bed that his broad frame takes up, his feet dangling off the end.

A trickling sound draws his attention to her hands as she wrings the water out of the cloth. When she brings the material to his stomach, she hesitates, silently asking for his permission to proceed. He gives her another nod, holding his breath in anticipation.

The warmth of the cloth and her hands pressing gently on his mid-section send arousal through him. His cheeks flush with embarrassment at his reaction to her simple movements.

He works to control his breathing, willing the hardness in his pants to subside. She keeps tending to his injuries, oblivious to his inner turmoil. His eyes flutter as she continues to stroke his torso.

The pain of his injury overruns the pleasure coursing through his veins. Embarrassed, he tries to shift his body to hide the evidence of his arousal under the woolen blanket. He releases a grunt as her touch dips lower down his belly.

"Am I hurting you?" she asks, furrowing her brows in concern. Those captivating eyes draw him into her.

"Not really. . . ." He adjusts himself as she strokes him, but the movement is too much.

He grabs her hand, stroking it with his thumb, and she leans into him. *For Dagda's sake, you need to stop that, Estrid.* Their gazes lock on to each other as he caresses the slight calluses that mar her skin.

The moment's lost, though, as she breaks contact, stumbling away from him. She nervously fiddles with the fabric in her hands, her cheeks flushed. He wonders if she felt what he was feeling.

Clearing her throat, she hands him the cotton cloth. Without another word, she bustles out of the room, giving him privacy.

What was that? Why did you scare her off?

Zain finishes washing his abdomen. It feels nowhere near as good as before, but he wills himself to keep control. Once he's finished, he lies back down, thinking about Estrid. He knows nothing of her, but his curiosity is piqued.

Using his sensitive Fae hearing, he listens for her movements in the room that shares the other side of the wall with his bed. There's a creak, like something closing, followed by footsteps on the wooden floor. He straightens up just in time as she walks back into the room.

"Here, take this. I washed it as best I could," Estrid says as she hands him his cleaned cotton tunic. "I had no other clothes to fit you, so I tried to repair it. The high-quality fabric hides the poor patch job."

Zain takes the shirt from her, giving her a nod of thanks. She blushes when their fingertips graze each other. He tries to shuffle himself into a seated position, wincing as his wound sends a jolt of pain throughout his body. He can feel her staring at him.

The straw mattress dips as she comes to sit next to him, gently placing the shirt over his head. Her fingers brush his neck, sending a shiver down his spine. The smell of wildflowers and thyme wraps around him; he breathes her scent in deep. Her face is mere inches away. The warmth of her breath dances across his skin.

She clears her throat, and the moment's lost like ice water being thrown on him as he lies back down on the lumpy pillow.

Every time her touch leaves him, he feels like warmth is leaving his body and wants to reach out to draw her back.

Get yourself together, Zain. You have more questions than you do answers about her, and yet you're acting like a confused youngling.

"Thank you for helping," Zain says, watching as she busies herself. She averts her gaze as her cheeks flush, though there's a small smile on her lips.

"Where are you from?" he asks, curious to know everything about her.

"Where in Faery are you from?" she replies, staring at him intently.

"I asked first," he says with a smirk. This game of cat and mouse intrigues him.

"Why do you want to know?"

"What if I want to get to know you?" He lets his words linger between them.

The tug of a grin appears on her face. His smirk grows a little when she doesn't protest, his spirits buoyed by her flirtatiousness.

"Where in Faery are you from?" she asks again, staring at him, watching him.

As much as he wants to tell her everything, she's holding stuff back from him.

"The Summer Court. Your turn."

"Far away from here. My home is here now," she says, a slightly nervous smile on her face. Zain deflates at her cryptic response.

Careful, Zain. These books have told her about Faery, but she doesn't know about you, and she clearly doesn't want you to know more about her.

"I've read about the courts in Faery. There are six, aren't there?"

"No, only four courts. Summer, Spring, Autumn, and Winter."

"One of my books said there were two more . . . ," she says, getting up and pulling out two bowls and a plate from a cupboard in the kitchen, the air growing lighter as the conversation shifts off her.

"There are only four courts that rule over Faery," Zain says in an abrupt tone. The thought of mentioning the Shadow Court puts him on edge.

"How did you portal into the human world?" Estrid asks, sensing a change in the atmosphere.

"Why do you want to know?" Zain counters, nervous about how much he wants to tell her.

"Maybe I want to get to know you," she jokes, a smirk mirroring his own on her face.

"Ha, well, since you asked so nicely, how can I refuse?" He's still enjoying the light-hearted flirting, but her cryptic response makes him pause. It momentarily takes the weight off his chest from his goal of returning home.

"Well . . . to be honest. I'm not sure how I ended up in a different world. It's never happened to me before, but here I am. Lucky to land where I did," he says, smiling, but it hides his own uncertainty about how he got here. *Can my magic even get me back home? I can't be stuck here. Can Estrid help understand what brought me here.*

Estrid concentrates on serving up the food, but she gives a little chuckle. "Luckily indeed. It's strange that your magic brought you here, but I'm glad it did. It's nice to have company for once."

Her eyes widen as though her words caught her by surprise. Clearing her throat, she perches on the side of the bed with a bowl full of soup. "Let me help you eat," she offers, lifting a spoonful.

"No, you eat first," he insists, an unexplained primal need to see her taken care of dominating his thoughts.

She doesn't leave his bed and lifts a spoon with the warm liquid from the bowl closer to him. "I'll eat later. Besides, you're the wounded one who hasn't eaten in over two days."

His stomach rebels against his thoughts and lets out a loud rumble. A smirk forms on her face at the sound.

"Okay," he concedes as he watches her lick her lips. Hunger for food isn't the only sensation he's feeling; his nerves prick with excitement at her nearness.

By Dagda, why does she do this to me?

They sit in silence as she helps him eat before he asks, "Why do you stay here on your own? Surely there's a village close by."

"I've done terrible things, hurt innocent people," she says, giving him a knowing look. "I should be alone." A sad smile takes over her face.

What could you have done that's so bad? Everything about you seems so good and yet you hide yourself. More questions that should worry me, but I can't seem to think there's something more to this. Something bigger at play.

She turns and looks at the shadow wolf, who's finished his dinner and is now lying in front of the dying fire. "Besides, I like it this way. And I have Rafe."

She clears her throat and changes the subject before he can ask more. "How long before you're fully healed?"

"I'm not sure. A few days, maybe more, and then I'll return home," Zain says as his body feels heavy again. The effects of the iron still drain his energy. With a full stomach, a warm bed, and the comforting scent of this woman, his eyelids grow heavy.

✦ ✦ ✦

Zain regains his strength in no time, thanks primarily to Estrid's excellent knowledge of healing.

The weight to return home grows each day as he feels his strength returning, but he can't help being intrigued by Estrid. Over the days, he's gotten to know her more, but they still only speak in half-truths about their pasts. With each question, another piece falls into place, but the bigger picture is still incomplete.

He often wonders what terrible things she's done to warrant being alone, with only a shadow wolf for company. The wolf trusts him even less than Estrid does, but he's grateful she has Rafe's protection.

Zain has tried to get her to open up, but she skillfully dodges the topic each time, reverting to questions around Faery instead.

He's learned that Estrid is an independent woman, relying on no one. She's built up her winter food stores by being a skilled hunter and foraging. It's clear that because of her, he's healing better than expected.

At night, they have long discussions about culture, music, art, and reading—things he wasn't expecting but show she's from a highborn background too. His attention hangs off her every word; there's no pretending. He can speak freely with her, giving honest opinions without fear of it being manipulated or used against him. She has no agenda with him, doesn't want him for what he can give her—she expects nothing of him but companionship. The simplicity of their relationship draws him further to her.

Often, when Estrid's not looking, he observes her. She picks at the sides of her fingers when she's nervous. She looks to the left when she doesn't want to answer a question. Her eyes soften in affection when she's near Rafe. Zain can't get enough of her little habits; they mesmerize him, but he knows he can't get attached.

It's been almost a week since she found him. *You need to get back to Del and Alvey. They need you,* he says to himself with more frequent urgency. Though he can't help but want to learn more about her. It's impossible for him to resist.

While they've fallen into a simple rhythm, it's like an artificial bubble world. Their time is spent doing chores, hunting, and preparing for the upcoming winter months. The simple nature of being with someone has him captivated.

✦ ✦ ✦

As Zain lies in bed one evening, he mulls over how to return home now that he feels fully healed. The fire emits a warm orange glow as the crackles and pops of the wood die down. The nocturnal forest creatures hoot, screech, and play their soothing evening melodies outside the little cottage. He can hear Rafe's heavy breathing as he lies by Estrid's door, always guarding her.

His thoughts turn in his head. Tomorrow he'll go home. But will his magic be restored enough to portal? What will he face when he gets back? How is he going to save Del, Alvey, and his people? How can he defeat Balius?

Despite having only known Estrid for a few days, he regrets that he has to go. His time here has been some of the most peaceful and content moments in his life. Something so simple has left a significant mark on him.

Zain's ears pick up a low groan from Estrid's room; he can hear her moving in her bed, her breathing picking up pace.

"No! Stop!" she cries as she thrashes about.

In an instant, he's out of his bed. Rafe jolts up, his hackles raised as Zain looms over the wolf.

"Get out of my way, wolf!" he says, balling his fists, ready to fight Rafe if he doesn't get out of the way.

Rafe's right ear twitches as Estrid lets out a shout of pain, spurring the wolf to move with a clatter of claws.

Zain throws open the door as Estrid shouts, "No, please! Stop killing them!"

He rushes into her room. She struggles violently, fighting some invisible force. Sweat beads on her forehead. Her sheets are twisted around her.

"Estrid, wake up! Wake up!" Zain says, panicking. He grabs her by the shoulders, bringing her into his arms. She fights him as if he's attacking her, screaming while using all her strength to get away.

"Stop!" she cries. "Stop it, please! You're hurting them!"

Zain holds her tighter. "Estrid, wake up!"

Inky black ribbons start to leech out of Estrid's hands; they float through the air as if searching for the threat that's terrorizing her.

Zain's eyes widen in shock at the strange sight. *Her magic! What in Dagda's name does it do?*

Rafe lets out a booming bark to stop the chaos. It reverberates across the space, shattering the unseen hold on Estrid. Her body relaxes in his arms. Her strange magic reseeds back. Zain and Rafe are still on high alert, their eyes darting across the room. Zain strokes her head, whispering that it's okay. She stirs, the rising and falling of her chest evening out.

"You're okay, Estrid. What happened?" Zain whispers, the loose strands of her hair tickling his nose.

He can feel her tense up. She pushes away from him, sitting up on her own.

"I-I'm sorry, it was just a . . . a nightmare. I'm fine," she says, her head bent down, weak from the fight.

Nightmare? That was more than a nightmare.

A soft whimper comes from Rafe, looking at Estrid and then at Zain as if asking him to help her.

"It's okay, Rafe. Just another nightmare. I'll be fine," she whispers, swaying slightly as she sits there. Zain moves to catch her, setting her down and straightening the covers.

"I'm fine," she insists, trying to get up.

"Stop saying you're fine. You're not fine. What was that?" he asks, stroking her cheek until the furrow in her brow disappears and her breathing deepens.

"What in Dagda's name was that?" he says, looking at Rafe.

The wolf doesn't take his eyes off her. The soothing peace of the evening takes back over, chasing away whatever plagued her.

With a heavy sigh, Zain grabs the blanket from his bed to sleep on the floor beside her. He's not abandoning her. Not tonight.

Zain wakes up just after dawn, his back stiff from sleeping on the hardwood floor. Morning light streams in from the sole window in the room.

Remembering what happened last night, he jolts up. He panics when he sees Estrid's empty bed. *Where is she?*

There's a clang of dishes coming from the kitchen. As he enters, he sees Estrid making something to eat.

"Morning," he says.

When she turns around, he notices the dark circles under her eyes. Her skin is pale, and her eyes are dull compared to their usual golden shade. The look on her face is defeated, crushed, and sad.

I can't leave her now.

"Are you okay?" he asks, curious what she'll say about what happened.

She doesn't meet his eyes, looking out the kitchen window.

"I've made you some breakfast. I'm heading out for a few hours. There's . . . something I need to do," she says as she grabs her bow and arrow near the front door.

Zain takes her wrist, rubbing his thumb across her smooth skin, enjoying the familiar hum of electricity on his skin from touching her.

"After last night, I'm coming with you. I want to make sure you're okay," he says.

Come on, Estrid. Let me in.

He can sense her inner turmoil, her jaw clenching and unclenching, but with a heavy exhale, she nods.

✦ ✦ ✦

Trekking down a forest path, they reach the ridgeline, where the trees end and rich, lush grass fields begin. In the distance, Zain can hear a village: laughter, heckling, like any small town in his kingdom. He's about to take another step when Estrid stops him with her outstretched arm.

"Keep low to the ground," she says as she crouches in the grass.

Without a word, Estrid moves out further into the field, keeping low in the tall grass. Rafe trots behind her, his ears darting around, on alert.

The sun warms Zain's back as he follows, nearly tripping over Rafe as he stops. The wolf lets out a low growl in warning.

Oh shut it, wolf. He gives Rafe a deadpan look.

Crouching down, Zain puts his hand on the soft ground, moist from the morning dew. He touches something hard, a stone embedded into the earth. He goes to pick it up.

"Stop."

He freezes at the command.

"Leave it where it is," Estrid says in a hushed voice as she moves further away from him. He's about to ask why when she closes her eyes and takes a deep breath.

When she opens them again, they're dark as night. The tendrils of black magic come from her hands and seep into a large river rock she's holding. Zain stumbles back at the sight.

What. Kind. Of. Magic. Is. That? he thinks but is so stunned, the words fail to come out.

He saw a glimpse of her magic last night but didn't expect this, whatever this is. He's unsure what to do. He's never experienced anything like this before, yet somehow, it calls to him.

"Estrid, what's happening?" he finally manages.

She doesn't answer him as more magic seeps into the large rock. It glows black before returning to its usual soft gray.

"Estrid, what's your magic doing?" he asks, his senses on edge from the surrounding air that's charged with energy.

Moments go by as she continues to funnel her magic into the stone. Her eyes eventually return to their honey gold, and Zain sighs with relief, staring at her, waiting for an explanation.

Estrid gets up, beckoning him to follow her as she walks, crouching down low. They crest the top of the ridgeline. In the near distance is a village, small and simple. It's not unlike the villages in the Summer Court.

He's curious why she comes to this place with dirt roads and thatched-roof houses. "Why do you come here? What was that you just did?" His eyes dart between her and the village.

"I come here to protect these people, to keep them from facing the same fate as other villages have in the past. I've embedded my magic into that stone, which acts as a power source for others strategically placed around the perimeter."

"Protect them from what?" he asks, unsure what dangers she's referring to.

"Soldiers, spies, bandits, and anyone who means them harm."

"Why? What does this place mean to you?"

Her beautiful facial features turn sad as she stares out at the little town. The breeze dances across the grass that they're kneeling in, whipping the dark strands of her hair from her face.

With a heavy sigh, she looks at him and says, "In my past, I was destroying villages not dissimilar to this one. I've done things I'm not proud of." She takes a deep breath to collect herself. "I have to protect these people, Zain. Not just for them but for my conscience."

Zain's unsure what to make of this confession. He's not a stranger to killing and death. He's fought in many battles and wars in his lifetime, each taking more lives than he can count. Her eyes don't move from his, searching for any signs of revulsion or disgust. He doesn't give it to her. "Why did you destroy them?"

Estrid looks down. The indecision of whether to answer him is written on her face, but she ultimately gives in. "People have used my magic for their own gain in the past. Manipulated me for my magic, betrayed me. It's why I hide in the Dark Forest, where they can't follow."

Silence hangs between them as she waits for his reaction, but he doesn't give one. He can't judge her, when others have used him for his power too.

Before he can ask another one, she moves again. "Come, we have more work to do," Estrid says over her shoulder.

They circle the village from a distance, keeping low to the ground. After a few moments, he pulls her to a stop.

"Wait, Estrid, what does your magic do?"

The wind around them picks up as the grass rustles. The edges of their green blades tickle his bare arms. Her expression is reluctant at his question.

Small birds flit around them, diving into the tall grass to pick up insects for their meal. Estrid doesn't take her gaze off him as she stretches out her hand. As she strikes a bird in mid-air, her black magic squashes its chirp.

A small, sand-colored husk floats down, the wind almost carrying it off. Zain turns back to Estrid, who has a grim expression on her face, as they track the tiny floating carcass to the ground. They walk to the spot where the small husk has landed. Estrid bends down to pick it up, cupping it in her hands.

"This," she says, cradling the remains of the little bird. "This is what my magic is. It's death."

Zain doesn't know what to say. He feels the weight of the burden Estrid has to carry, the once-chirping bird now silenced.

The horror that her power must cause sinks in, but it doesn't repulse him. He takes her hands in his, offering what comfort he can.

She looks up at him, eyes brimming with tears.

Before either can say anything, their hands glow with a soft light. Warm magic grows around them like a flame chasing off the cold. A chirp comes from the bird in her hand. It tilts its head back and forth, fluttering its brown wings.

Estrid's eyes go wide as the little bird flies off in the wind, and they both sit there in shock.

"How?" is all she says, searching Zain for an answer, but he has none. He has magic that's aligned with the Summer Court. He can wield fire and help things grow, but he can't bring back the dead.

That evening, as they get ready for bed, and Estrid lets Rafe outside to do whatever a domesticated shadow wolf does. Zain still finds the pair's dynamic at odds with the vicious beasts he knows from Faery.

From his bed, he watches Estrid slip out the front door into the frosty night. Curious, he follows.

When he steps outside, his breath mists and his skin prickles as the frigid evening air hits him. His eyes adjust to the darkness, where he finds Estrid sitting on a stump of wood.

She's bathed in moonlight from a break in the thick tree canopy. The cool blue shine of the moon makes her skin flawless. The forest has a rhythmic song of crickets, owls, and evening creatures that create their symphony. With quiet footsteps, he approaches her.

"Rafe likes the moon. He goes out for the night every full moon," she says.

He tips a bucket upside down to sit next to her. She looks up at the sky, her long brown hair cascading down her back, and his breath hitches at the sight. He turns to look at the pale blue ball in the sky before turning to Estrid and asking, "And you? Why do you come out here?"

"It's peaceful. Calm. And I like the moon too," she says, smiling as she sighs. She turns to him, and his stomach flutters.

You are beautiful. The words almost leave his mouth as her face lights up with her smile.

"Not going to turn into a wolf, are you?" he jokes, trying to distract himself.

She giggles at him, dipping her head his way. "And what if I did turn into a wolf? What would you do?" She cocks her eyebrow as she leans toward him.

He smirks. With a shrug, he says, "I'd probably give you a pat on the head, like Rafe. How big of a wolf are we talking about here?"

"Enormous. Six feet high, vicious fangs. Not the petting type," she says with a chuckle.

Zain laughs—*really* laughs. It's the first time he's laughed freely like this in as long as he can remember. His days are usually spent putting on a façade and being careful about what he portrays.

That freedom is short-lived as the purpose of him following her out here comes to the front of his mind.

"Estrid." Zain takes her hand. "Thank you for everything you've done for me . . . but I have to go tomorrow. When my parents died, their responsibilities fell to me. People are waiting for me, depending on me. I hope you know I'll never forget what you did for me."

The smile on her face dies as she gives him a sad nod, her own mask slipping into place.

"I don't know how I can ever repay you for what you've done for me," he continues, looking down at her hand in his. It feels so right, but it can't be. He has to get back home at all costs.

She slips her hand from his and says, "When you leave here, do not mention me, where I live, or what I do for the village to anyone. There is no debt."

I wish I could stay with you. He wants to say it, but it's not the reality of their situation.

Zain raises his hand to cup her smooth, warm cheek. "I promise not to speak of you or where you live."

He doesn't remove his hand from her face, dragging his thumb over her soft lower lip. A fire ignites in him as the need to do more than touch her lips consumes him.

She leans closer to him as he guides their mouths together. The world stops with a kiss. He feels the press of her warm lips against his, jolts of electricity sparking through him as her scent enfolds him.

Estrid breaks the kiss, resting her forehead against his.

"I can't." Her breath is warm against his mouth. His are short and shallow with need. Defeated with reality.

With a sigh, they both turn to watch the shadows around them dance in the moonlight. The eerie sounds of the forest at night hide the strained silence between them.

"Is there somewhere I can take a proper bath? I want one before I leave," he asks, closing his eyes against the evening light. There's no hiding it anymore. He's fully healed, so his time here is done. He needs to move on.

"Yes, I use a pool not too far from here. I'll take you in the morning," she says, disheartened.

There's a shift between them, both disappointed as the moment ends but neither pushing for it to continue.

Zain sighs as Estrid gets up and walks back to the cottage.

✦ ✦ ✦

CHAPTER FOUR

Estrid enters the cottage, her pulse racing, her stomach doing somersaults. Her mind spins like a top, wobbling to stay up.

He's leaving tomorrow, Estrid. It's for the better.

She tries to ignore the memory of his lips on hers.

She pops two more wood logs on the fire before going to her bedroom and shutting the door.

As she gets undressed for bed, her mind won't stop reliving that moment in the moonlight. Ever since she came across Zain in the forest, she's had a companionship that she hasn't had since she was a young girl.

In the days that have passed, they've gotten to know each other and enjoyed each other's company, but it never occurred to her that it would come to a kiss.

She's kissed other men, but she knew they all had an agenda with her: get to her father and his power. With Zain, there's no agenda. She's found joy with him. She's never felt as comfortable and at peace with anyone.

There have been many times that she's had to stop herself from letting down her walls, letting him see the real her. It's not something she can afford to do. Not when they are out there causing havoc in the world.

He's leaving, she reminds herself, trying to banish the desire to kiss him again. *He has others he needs to get back to. Others in his life.*

In her drab sleeping shirt, she gets under the covers, blowing out the candle that sits on the side table.

Sleep doesn't come to her as she lies there for what feels like hours. The sounds of the forest usually help her drift off, but tonight, she can only listen for Zain. She hasn't heard him come in yet.

The bed blankets feel itchy and heavy on her sensitive skin. That kiss has done something to her body, awakening a need she never knew she had.

Tossing and turning, she finally hears his footsteps as he enters the cottage. No growling or claws clicking on the wooden floor, though. Rafe hasn't come back.

With a clunk, Zain's belt hits the ground. It's followed by two thuds of boots and the soft sound of fabric drawn over skin. The thought of seeing him naked makes her ache between her thighs. She closes her eyes, willing the need to disappear, but nothing helps.

What if I just indulged tonight? What harm would it do? He's leaving anyway.

The bed on the other side of the wall creaks as Zain settles into it.

She stands up, padding on the chilly hardwood floor toward her bedroom door. She stares at the round metal handle.

What if it's just for tonight?

Indecision plagues her mind. Something deep down in her says there's no going back if she turns that handle. Doubt creeps in, her walls building back up.

What if he has someone he has to get home to?

The question extinguishes the fire building up in her. She backs away from the door, slipping back into bed and willing sleep to come.

✦ ✦ ✦

The next morning, Estrid wakes, her eyes heavy from what little sleep she had. That kiss plagued her mind while awake and her dreams while she slept. Gone were the nightmares that haunted her the night before. They were replaced by soft lips, hands roaming her body, and ecstasy like she had never felt before.

If only it were real.

The sun's light filters through a small window into her room. She feels a warm sensation stir when she thinks of kissing Zain again. Between her legs, she knows she's wet at the thought of being with him. It's torture.

Snap out of it, Estrid.

With a frustrated breath, she covers her face with the blanket and almost screams, knowing she can't get attached to this Fae. He isn't from the human world. She can't help getting excited at seeing him, though.

Gods, what's wrong with you? He only kissed you. Stop it, Estrid.

"Okay, he's leaving today, and then you can get back to normal life. Deep breath, Estrid. You can do this."

The words spoken out loud steel her nerves as she gets up but pauses at the smell of food wafting in from the kitchen. There's clanking and the scraping of bowls, plates, and cutlery being set on the table. Scents she hasn't smelled in a year seep through the cracks in the door. The sweet aromas of honey and bacon make her stomach grumble.

She sits there in shock. He's making her breakfast! The thought warms her heart but also makes her even sadder that this can't be.

With a groan, she swings her legs off the bed, the rough wood of the cold floor sending a chill up her back as she pulls on her trousers and shirt. Her hands shake with nervousness as she gets herself ready. She retrieves the small brush on the side table, brushing out her long brown hair, leaving the waves to cascade down her shoulders. Once she's ready, she stands at the door, reaching out to grab the handle, taking a deep inhale to calm her nerves. She exhales and opens it.

The common area is warm and cozy from the fire that Zain has stoked back to life. Estrid's eyes go wide. On the round wooden dining table in the kitchen, he's laid out a breakfast for a queen. Fresh berries, jams, fresh bread, honey, and bacon fill the space she usually occupies on her own. There's even a brand-new set of purple and yellow wildflowers, replacing the dead ones she had before.

Zain's shirt sits tight across his back, the strong muscles underneath rising and falling as he works at the kitchen bench. His hair is tied up in a loose bun, accentuating his broad shoulders even more.

Rafe sits by the fire, watching Zain with suspicion. Estrid smiles at the sight. At least he isn't growling, but she suspects food has something to do with it.

Her mouth waters as she looks back at the table filled with the delicious spread. No one has ever done something like this for her. The nerves she tried to steel before entering the room intensify.

"Good morning," Zain says, turning to her. His hungry gaze catches on her long, unbraided hair as he steps toward her.

"Morning," she replies, her cheeks turning pink under his gaze as he drinks her in. Those blue eyes shine as gold flecks dance in them. It's an unrelenting stare.

Estrid clears her throat, gesturing to the table. "What's all of this?"

"You've taken care of me. Before I go, I wanted to say thank you." He gives her an easy smile. "It's time for me to do something nice for you. Come sit." His smile grows wider and makes her weak in the knees.

Taking her hand, he guides her to the chair facing the fireplace. He pulls it out, placing his hand on her lower back. His touch is gentle as it lingers a little longer than needed, sending her pulse skyrocketing. He sits opposite her with a roguish, confident grin on his face. Her eyes track down from his smile to his broad, muscular chest.

Clearing her throat and giving herself a quick shake, she returns to reality. "Thank you. It's lovely, but you didn't have to."

Looking at the feast laid out, she notices that there are things she can't get in the forest. Things you can only buy in a village.

"Where did you get all this food?" she asks, shifting her focus from the table to look at him as he answers her question.

He hasn't stopped staring at her. His eyes spark with hunger.

"I needed to give my magic a go and portal."

Estrid furrows her brow. When Zain first arrived, he mentioned he had portalled into the forest, but they haven't discussed it in great detail.

"So, you portalled to get the food? From where?"

"A small remote village I know at the border of the Summer Court. I needed to see if I could do it after my injury. It's the only way to get home."

Reality comes crashing back to her. *He needed to test his magic because he's leaving today. Don't be stupid, Estrid. This wasn't just for you.*

Disappointment has her heart sinking, but she schools her inner turmoil, keeping her tone light and airy. "Tell me about your magic. You can portal, bring things back to life. What else can you do?"

Zain casually waves his hand at the flowers in front of her. The closed purple and yellow buds bloom as their stems grow taller, brighter, and fuller.

"I can wield fire, help things grow, am stronger and faster than a human, and based on what we saw with the bird, can help bring things back to life now."

Estrid's jaw clenches. His magic is the opposite of hers; it balances her. He helps life, strengthening it.

Zain cocks his head to one side as if sensing her inner turmoil while he spreads a generous helping of a purple jam onto some bread.

"In the stories I've read, it says the Fae are long-lived. How old are you, then?" she asks.

"I'm just over two hundred years old, in human terms."

Estrid chokes on the water she was sipping.

She quickly composes herself, dabbing her mouth on the sleeve of her shirt. Zain laughs at this, handing her a napkin. *Where did you get a napkin?* She takes the white cotton cloth from him and places it on her lap.

The rest of breakfast is uneventful. Estrid tries not to let her nerves show, keeping their conversation focused on anything but her.

"Your hair down suits you," he says as he sweeps his gaze down the waves that flow over her shoulders.

She clenches her thighs together, feeling him undressing her in his mind.

"Thank you." Shifting in her seat, she turns her head to look out the little kitchen window again, trying to get a handle on her body's response to him.

She has to take a deep breath to shake off the need and desire building in her. She remembers that he wanted something today as she tries to distract herself from leaping across the table to kiss him.

"You said you'd like a bath before you leave today, right?"

"Ahh, yes, that would be amazing. While the cold basin washes have been good, I need a proper wash. Will you come with me?"

He lifts an eyebrow at her, waiting for her to bite at his comment. Her cheeks flush.

It's just a bath, Estrid, nothing more.

Not wanting to play into his hands, she stands to clear the table. "Let me get my things. There's a warm pool close to here."

+   +   +

CHAPTER FIVE

Estrid grabs her bow and a quiver of arrows as they leave. Rafe sits by the stump where she and Zain shared their first kiss last night.

"Rafe, stay," she says. She'd like some alone time with Zain without Rafe grumbling in the background.

The wolf gives her a side glance, letting her know he's not impressed with being told to stay behind. With a huff, he lies down near the stump. The morning sun breaks through the trees, catching on his shiny coat. Estrid elbows Zain as he chuckles at Rafe's reaction.

They set off down the forest track. The air is cool, and a light mist hangs over the forest, swirling around their ankles as they walk through it. Birds sing and dart between trees, chasing each other. She can feel Zain observing her—it's like an invisible hand caressing her.

"Who taught you to use that?" he asks, nodding to her bow that sits on her back.

"My father's soldiers."

"I thought only the nobility would have soldiers."

Estrid pauses, wincing that she let slip more information than intended. "Yes, my father's nobility."

Her stomach knots as her unease grows. The familiar feelings of shame and guilt hit home. *He can't know who you are, Estrid. What you've done.*

As she picks up the pace, a small animal darts in front of her, startled by their presence. She halts and Zain crashes into her. An arm snakes around her waist as he steadies her.

He leans down, his lips close to her ear, warm breath on her neck. "Careful," he says.

She stands flush against his body, her beating heart drowning the forest sounds out. She absorbs his warmth before he asks, "Why were you trained?"

The question breaks through the fog that he casts over her. She pushes away from him, quickening her pace and trying to put space between them.

By leaping over a rock with his long legs, he can easily keep up with her. With a sigh, she slows down, resigned to the fact that she'll have to answer. "He wanted me to defend myself with non-magical abilities in case I couldn't use my magic."

"Smart man. Who was your father?"

The question catches her breath. *He can't know.* She doesn't stop moving, focusing on putting one foot in front of the other. Before he can probe any further, they arrive at the pool. Estrid breathes a sigh of relief at the welcomed distraction.

They approach a natural pool fed by a trickling spring. The sun's rays break through like spears of light. The water is a murky crystal blue, steam rising off it. It's surrounded by rocks and a large boulder that offers some privacy. Estrid walks up to the edge and dips her fingers in its warmth, sending goose bumps down her arms.

"How did you find this place?" Zain asks, kneeling and touching the pleasant water with her.

"I stumbled on it one day while exploring with Rafe. The warm water comes from that spring over there. I haven't found the source yet, but it's clean and much better than a cold basin wash."

She can feel him staring at her. His gaze hasn't left her since they arrived at the pool. "You're beautiful, you know." He cups her cheek.

She wants to lean into his touch, but the reminder that he's leaving stops her. Standing, she points to a large boulder to the left of the pool. "I'll go behind there. Call me when you're in the water."

Not wanting to see his reaction, she darts behind the large rock, taking time to undress.

"Are you in?" she yells, hearing water splashing over the sides of the rocky pool.

"Yes! It's amazing!"

Smiling, she folds her clothes and covers herself with her hands. "Close your eyes!"

There's a small silence, and she half expects a witty remark, but he says nothing. Coming out from behind the wall of rock, Estrid slips in gracefully. The warmth of the water washes over her body like a ray of sunshine, easing the tension in her sore muscles.

Sinking in further, she looks at Zain. His back is to her, and his hair is tied up, displaying the many muscles that show off his broad shoulders and taper down to narrower hips. His skin is smooth and unblemished. Water droplets trickle down it, leaving little paths behind them. Estrid's belly grows warm inside, and she squeezes her legs together.

"You can turn around now," she tells him.

He does, and unfortunately for her, the front of his body is more impressive than the back. Intricate light tattoos spread across his chest. The swirls and designs only add to his well-defined muscles. She shifts her gaze up to his, those blue eyes catching hers.

"This is an amazing spot."

They sit there for a few minutes, the silence growing thicker with unspoken words.

Water ripples as he inches closer to her, leaning against the side of the pool and closing his eyes. Estrid watches the rise and fall of the complex designs on his chest with each breath.

"What do your tattoos mean?" she asks.

"When a Fae grows into their power, they get markings that represent it. The bigger and more one has, the greater their power," he says, opening an eye to her.

"Have you got all yours?"

"No, I don't think so. A Fae's power doesn't mature until they're at least three hundred years old or they find their mate," he says, now with both eyes on her. "But since I've arrived here, I think I've gotten more."

There's an awkward pause. *So he doesn't have a mate?*

Too scared to ask, but actually too scared to know the answer, she snaps herself out of something that can't happen.

"We should go," she says, moving to the water's edge near the boulder where she got dressed.

He stops her before she gets out and spins her around, bringing her flush to his body.

"We could just stay here for a while," he says, his face a small breath from hers. He gives her a cheeky smile, keeping her body flush against his.

Gods, yes, I want to stay a while. I want to stay forever.

"We should get back to Rafe. He'll be wondering where I am," she says, trying to sound convincing.

Estrid leaves the water and rushes behind the boulder, trying not to let her nerves get the better of her. Losing heat from the pool and the warmth of Zain's body makes her shiver as a cool breeze weaves through the trees.

As she dresses, her body tingles under her clothes, which irritate against her sensitive skin. She can still feel him against her body as he held her there for just a moment. The butterflies in her stomach are a torrent as she thinks more about it.

Get a grip.

With a tug on her boots, she stands with a wide smile. Despite him leaving, Zain wants her. It's not something she's used to, having been taught to be something dark. Something dangerous.

This feeling gives her hope that one day she can have a normal life.

The forest quietens down, and her smile fades. Birds cease their happy chirping, the hum of cicadas halts, and even the breeze has stopped.

It's never quiet here.

She scans the surrounding area. Tall trees stand straight like sentries, making it hard to see past them into the distance.

Her eyes narrow to watch for any unexpected things. The silence grows; her heart pounds in her chest. She stills her breathing to hear better as the hairs on the back of her neck stand up.

A faint breaking of twigs echoes to her right. Estrid crouches down. More cracking. Leaves scatter. Whatever the sound is, it's heading toward her and Zain.

Grabbing her weapons as she rushes in the direction of the crunching sounds, keeping her footsteps light, she creeps along the damp forest floor. The air is chilly against her cheeks, her body warm as adrenaline courses through it. Estrid sneaks down the path as low as she can go, avoiding the bushes and branches that litter the trail.

Taking a few more steps forward, she spots two figures. The first is a male with dark blond hair and a stocky build. He looks strangely familiar, but Estrid can't place him. Next to him is a striking female with ash-blonde hair and an athletic physique.

Estrid nocks an arrow and raises her bow, jumping up from her hiding spot in the thick bushes to yell, "Stop! Not one more step!"

With an echoing hiss, the female draws her sword. She steps into a fighting stance, eyes trained on Estrid.

But the blond-haired man stops, stunned for a moment, before he puts up his arms in surrender. "Whoa, we mean you no harm."

It hits her like a slap in the face how much the male looks like Zain, though his jaw is squarer and his features are soft, giving him a gentler look compared to Zain's angular features. A small, nervous smile crosses his face.

Estrid's eyes track to their pointed ears, and she struggles to keep her composure at the shock of another two Fae in her home.

The female is tall and slender and has a warrior's build. Her eyes are a bright green that offset her warm ash-blonde hair. Unlike the male next to her, her features are sharp. They're both disheveled, their tunics and pants stained with dirt and what looks like dried blood.

Estrid draws her bow tighter as the male steps forward. He takes the sword off his back, laying it down with one hand, continuing to hold the other up. He looks over his shoulder at the woman. "Del, put down your weapons."

The female doesn't lower her blade, scowling at Estrid as she moves forward as well.

Estrid holds her ground, tightening her bow even more. She stares down the arrow shaft, training it on the female's head. Focusing, she engages her magic. It twirls around the arrowhead aimed right at the pair of Fae.

✦ ✦ ✦

CHAPTER SIX

The air chills Zain's skin, helping to get rid of any hardness in his cock. He wanted nothing more than to kiss Estrid again, but her walls were back up.

It's for the best.

Taking a deep breath, he picks up his clothes from a nearby tree. He can't shake the feel of Estrid against his body, no matter how hard he tries.

He's halfway dressed when a shout from Estrid breaks his thoughts. His heart stops at the panic in her voice.

Like a possessed Fae, he runs through the forest, clearing rocks and bushes with long strides. His heart races as dread sets in. The notion of Estrid being hurt drives him forward. He has no weapons, but he's got magic. His palms light up, his fire magic like the sun's warmth on his skin.

Zain breaks through the trees. Estrid's bow is drawn, the arrow pointed ahead into the dense forest. He follows the direction of the arrow, his eyes growing wide as they land on Del and Alvey.

Estrid yells, "Put down your weapons!"

She doesn't spare him a glance as her fingers hang on to the arrow's notch. The black wisps of her magic twirl around the arrowhead aimed at his brother and cousin.

Zain's muscles freeze, his mind trying to catch up to the scene unfolding before him. He stands rooted in the spot like his feet are being held down by boulders.

Del gasps at the sight of him, drawing him into action.

He jumps in front of Estrid, hands raised. "No! Estrid, stop!" He looks straight into her eyes, no longer golden as black flecks dance in them. "Please . . . I know them."

His palms glow, but this time, they're turned on Estrid.

She draws her bow tighter, her brow creasing in confusion. Everything is still and quiet. The darkness grows in her eyes as they dart from his glowing hands to him. His heartbeat pounds in his ears from the tense standoff. Estrid doesn't blink, focusing on him.

"This is my brother, Alvey," he says, glancing at Alvey, who gives a small wave in return. "And our cousin, Del."

Zain turns back to Estrid with his arms still raised, the arrow shaft pointed at his chest. She stares at him, a look of uncertainty on her face. "They won't hurt you. I promise."

The darkness in her eyes recedes as she looks past his shoulder. Hesitant, cautious, she lowers her weapon, peering around him again.

Turning, he can see Del in her fighting stance, ready to cut anyone down with her long sword. By the red in her cheeks, he can tell she's pissed off. Zain takes in their appearance, which is untidy and unkempt. Neither she nor Alvey have probably seen a bath in days.

Zain strides up to his brother, embracing him like it was their last. "I didn't know what happened to you! How did you . . . ?" Zain says, shaking his head in disbelief. *Thank Dagda you're okay.*

He turns to Del, still gripping the blade while giving Estrid a death stare.

"Del, put down your sword," he says, placing his hand on her wrist in reassurance.

She lowers her weapon, placing it back in its sheath.

"Who's she?" Del says, still not taking her eyes off Estrid.

Zain wraps her in a hug like she's an illusion that might fade. Behind him, Estrid huffs at Del's rudeness.

"This is Estrid. How did you get here?" Zain asks, looking back at his cousin and brother in disbelief, making sure they're real.

Alvey winks and waves at Estrid before turning back to Zain. "Well, brother, I see you've been busy," he says, wiggling his eyebrows and pointing to Zain's naked upper half.

"Don't be an ass, Alvey. I was taking a bath—something you need."

Zain turns to speak to Estrid, but she's already walking away. He's about to call after her when a large arm wraps around him. Alvey pulls him into another bone-crushing hug, the dusty and dung-ridden smell of being on the road wafting around him.

"I don't understand. How did you escape?" Zain asks as the grime from the road gets wiped onto his clean torso. "Actually, tell me once you've had a bath. You stink, Alvey. While I'm glad to see you, get off me before I have to rewash myself." He shrugs Alvey's dirty arm off his shoulder.

The trio walk to the pool, the steam rising off the crystal-blue murky water into the dimmed forest light. Zain looks around for Estrid, but she's nowhere to be seen.

He scans the trees for her, worry piercing his chest. *Where did you go, Estrid? Argh, do I go after you or stay with my family?*

He's half-convinced that she's fled after the less-than-friendly welcome from Del. And with the unexpected arrival of his brother and cousin, the need for him to leave becomes more urgent, since they aren't there to protect his people.

Kicking off his boots and stripping off his clothes, Alvey interrupts Zain's thoughts as his sword clangs to the ground. Days on the road have left him covered in dirt and grime.

While Alvey is thirty years younger than Zain, they look like brothers in every way. Alvey is just an inch shorter, with slightly fewer golden tattoos that cover him.

He enters the pool with a splash, sending the water sloshing over the side. "Ahhh . . . I needed this. So do you, Del. You stink."

Del enters a second after Alvey, who lounges against a rocky edge with his arms stretched out as he leans back. "Shut it, Alvey. I smell less like a horse's ass than you do," she says, washing the grime and dirt from her body.

"Where's your friend?" Alvey asks with a smirk on his face.

Zain perches on a stump at the edge of the pool, staring out into the direction that Estrid walked in.

He searches for her, bouncing his knee impatiently, worrying. *Come on, Estrid. Come back. They won't hurt you.* The worry and loss of her presence grows.

"She'll be around here," he says as the forest's rhythmic music surrounds them. It brings a sense of peace to Zain; it reminds him of her.

Del resurfaces after dunking her head under the water to rinse her blonde hair. "Can we trust her?"

Before Zain can answer, Estrid steps out from behind the large boulder. A scowl sits on her face. "I should ask if I can trust you. You've come into my home and bath," she says, keeping her distance from the Fae.

For Dagda's sake, Del, have some tact.

Zain rubs his hand down his face and clears his throat. "Enough, Del! Estrid saved me, and I owe her for that, so you'll stop being rude."

Del huffs and rolls her eyes at him while Alvey snickers. Zain shakes his head but smiles at how good it feels to have his family back.

"How did you get here? I saw them capture you," he says, his eyes darting between his brother and cousin.

Alvey stretches, letting out a deep sigh before saying, "They did. They caught all your guards too. It's a good thing you portalled out when you did. They were planning on using us to get you to come back, but if you'd been taken, we'd all be dead by now."

"Who are they?" Estrid asks in a concerned tone as she leans against a thick tree.

"Balius, our uncle, and his lapdog, Manis," Del grinds out, her jaw clenching and unclenching.

"How did you make it here, though?" Zain asks, still baffled by their unexpected appearance.

"Oh yes, strangest thing," Alvey says with a look of bemusement on his face. "We portalled here. Well, not quite like a portal you can do, but it got us out. That's all that matters."

"What? How?" Zain just about falls over from the answer. "Neither of you has that ability."

"Someone opened a portal in our cell, gave us our weapons, and shouted at us to get through. And, well . . . here we are," Alvey says, gesturing to the surrounding forest.

Wait, what? Zain turns Alvey's words over in his head.

Del wades through the water until she's by his feet and says, "We have to go back, Zain. Balius plans to take the crown for himself, and he's got something planned, but we're not sure what. Your royal guards are still loyal to you if we—"

"You're royalty?" Estrid asks, standing up straight and giving him an angry, hurt look.

"King, actually," Del says over her shoulder, dismissing Estrid's reaction.

Zain winces at the truth being exposed so blatantly.

He groans inwardly. *Really, Del?* He would trust Del with his life, and he knows she means well, but she can sometimes be hard-headed and rub people up the wrong way.

He looks over at Estrid, shrinking his shoulders under her furious glare. *I didn't know if I could trust you,* he wants to say, but the words fail to come out.

"Zain, we need to take Balius out soon," Del says, stepping out of the water, unashamed of her nakedness.

Zain tries to piece together the events leading up to his uncle stealing the throne from him.

"We need allies. The royal guard won't be enough to take the court if Manis has the army behind him," he says, hopelessness threatening to take over him as he weighs up all the options.

Where am I going to find allies? The Winter Court is leaderless, and I don't trust that Autumn and Spring won't get involved in inter-court politics.

Alvey must sense what he's thinking as he asks, "Why don't we ask the humans to be allies? They support us, and in return, we can open up the trade routes between Faery and them."

Del shushes Alvey, nodding in Estrid's direction, who's observing the conversation between them. She hasn't looked at Zain since finding out he's a king, but Del's obviously irritating her.

Zain shakes his head. "We can trust Estrid, Del. Say what you need to say."

"Yes, yes, maybe you can help us, Estrid?" Alvey asks, now getting out of the water himself. Estrid flushes and spins around to avoid the full-frontal view.

"Alvey! Put some clothes on," Zain barks at his brother.

Alvey gives Zain a casual smirk, pulling on his clothes.

Del sits on a rock, choosing a dagger from the many strapped to her leather corset and flicking out the caked-in dirt from under her fingernails.

"What about that human city near where the portal landed us? Maybe we should talk to them," Alvey says, sitting on a tree stump next to Estrid as he pulls on his boots.

Zain can't help but be jealous of his nearness to her. He shifts, fighting the urge to stand between her and Alvey.

"What did the city look like?" Estrid asks, spinning to face Alvey, her cheeks still flushed from her near eyeful of him.

Once he describes the cold, dreary, rocky landscape, Estrid says they landed in Nordia, the Northern Kingdom. Zain watches her grow anxious as they pepper her with questions about Nordia, whether they have allies or enemies, and if they're a prosperous kingdom.

Estrid answers each one with great detail, including a description of the capital, Oberetta. Zain can see her nervousness growing. She shifts on her feet and fiddles with her fingers. Her eyes dart across the woodland as if someone could hear her.

"We need to go. It's getting dark. Your friends are welcome to stay," she says, spinning on her heel and charging back to the cottage.

"She's a little odd," Del says, sheathing her blade in one fluid motion.

Zain stares down the overgrown path where Estrid disappeared. Her coldness, discomfort, and unease don't sit well with him. It's been less than a week that they've had together, but they've formed a bond of sorts. The events of last night and this morning only fueled that bond further.

"I thought we could approach the nobility and make an agreement. We can trade with them again in exchange for their army to use against Balius," Alvey says, standing next to him.

Zain turns to his brother. "It's an idea, but how will we defeat Balius and Manis with just a human army?"

"I've heard that humans have mages who have magical abilities. We can ask that they be included in an alliance. And they also have one thing in abundance that we do not," Del says with a devilish smile, looking at Zain as they walk along.

"And what's that?" he asks, her dangerous tone making him uncomfortable.

"Iron."

At the mention of the deadly metal, Zain shivers. He's torn between the horror of using something like that on another Fae and losing his kingdom.

✦ ✦ ✦

CHAPTER SEVEN

Walking down the forest path, Zain steps over the bushes creeping over the edges. The air feels thick, a musty and earthy smell coating it. The ferns brush against his legs as they follow Estrid's footprints back to the cottage.

Del steps up beside him, tugging on his arm to slow him down. "Something isn't right here, Zain. I don't trust her."

Her whispered comments draw a scowl on his face. "Leave it, Del. She wouldn't have saved me if she wanted to kill me."

"She has dark magic. I can feel it. She's hiding something too. How do we know she won't turn on us?"

"I said drop it, Del," Zain says as he picks up the pace, leaving her behind.

They exit the forest and enter the small area where Estrid's cabin sits. Smoke drifts out of the chimney.

Before Zain thinks to warn his family, Rafe bounds out from behind the house. Del shrieks, drawing her sword with a sharp twang. "Shadow wolf, get down!" she yells.

Del rushes forward, blade held high. Rafe surges for her with a growl, snapping his jaws at the newcomers. Zain runs up to put himself between Del and Rafe.

Estrid stands next to the wolf as he skids to a stop. Rafe raises his black hackles as his lips peel back to reveal sharp, glistening teeth. His predatory gaze doesn't move from Del.

"Del, no! Stop."

His cousin stops mid-swing, a look of shock and confusion on her face like Zain had just slapped her. "What do you mean? He's a shadow wolf, for Dagda's sake," she says.

"Put down your weapon, or I will shoot," Estrid says with her bow drawn, aimed directly at Del's head.

"Put down your sword, Del. He belongs to Estrid," Zain says, reinforcing Estrid's command. Her eyes are dark when he peeks over his shoulder, her dark power coiling around her shaft. Rafe stands unmoving at her side.

Del lowers her weapon but doesn't sheathe it, a bewildered look on her face. Estrid hasn't dropped her bow, her expression fierce as her eyes grow blacker by the second. Black magic snakes its way out of her hands. Del and Alvey look on in horror.

"I told you she has dark magic!" Del says, in a tone that resembles fear as much as fear can take hold of her.

Zain looks over his shoulder again to Estrid, her eyes almost entirely black. He panics, knowing what happens when she releases her magic.

"Del, put down your sword now! Estrid, take your magic back, please!" he pleads with both women.

Zain holds his breath as tense seconds tick by. Relief washes over him as Del finally sheathes her blade, holding her hands up. Estrid draws her magic back in but keeps her bow pointed at Del.

"I don't understand. He's a shadow wolf. What's he doing here with her?" Del asks.

Zain shakes his head, unable to explain it to them. "I don't know, but he won't harm you if you mean her no harm." He keeps a wary eye on Estrid. The tension suffocates the air around them.

With her bow still drawn and gaze fixed on Del, Estrid asks, "What do you mean, he's a shadow wolf?"

Alvey, who's been standing to the side watching the whole situation unravel, stands in front of Rafe. His eyebrows are raised, and a smirk of amusement inches across his face.

To everyone's surprise, Rafe stops growling and starts wagging his tail at Alvey. Zain rolls his eyes at his brother, who is now giving Rafe a pat on the head.

"I don't understand any of this," Estrid says, lowering her weapon in confusion.

"We haven't seen a shadow wolf in decades in the Summer Court. They're usually ferocious animals, capable of taking down entire regiments of Fae soldiers," says Alvey, now scratching Rafe's belly as he rolls over on the ground like a cheerful dog.

Zain can feel Estrid staring at him, knowing the question she'll ask. "I didn't tell you because I didn't want to shock you or cause any fear, but yes, he's a shadow wolf. He comes from the Shadow Court in Faery."

A mixture of confusion and anger crosses Estrid's face. Zain shakes his head, inwardly scolding himself.

Idiot, I should have told her. Now what's she going to think of me?

With a pat on her leg to command Rafe to follow, Estrid turns on her heel toward the cottage.

"Well, he's just Rafe to me. You're welcome to stay out here, or you can join me inside."

✦   ✦   ✦

The small cottage feels crowded once they all enter. Estrid gestures for the Fae to take a seat.

Del looks at the simple settings. They've been on the road for weeks. She probably wanted a bit more space and a comfortable bed instead of a chair near the fireplace.

Rafe takes his usual spot by the fire, much to Del's concern, who visibly cringes at his proximity to her.

An awkward silence fills the room before Alvey cuts the tension. "Is it just you and the wolf?"

"Yes," Estrid says, leaning against the wooden bench in the kitchen.

Alvey sits back in the dining chair, stretching his legs out in front of him, making the room feel even smaller. He looks around the room, noting the little bed by the wall. A grin grows on his face as he nods to where Zain slept for days. "It's a cozy place, isn't it, brother? No wonder you healed so well, having Estrid take care of you."

"Shut it, Alvey," Del says, smacking him upside the head from the seat next to him.

Zain rolls his eyes, wincing at the vulgarity. Alvey means well, trying to take a light-hearted approach to things, but Zain can tell they've won no favors from Estrid today. Her demeanor is cold as she stands as far from them as possible. A façade of indifference slips over her beautiful face.

After getting comfortable, Alvey and Del fall into a whispered conversation about their plans. Zain sees Del's eyes darting around as she scopes out the cottage, making a note of all the windows, doors, and escape routes. Estrid pays them no attention, working on a meal; the rhythmic sounds of chopping can be heard from where she stands in the kitchen.

As Zain sits there, the memories of the last few days run through his mind. He wishes they had more time together. Being around Estrid has relaxed him.

The news of Balius planning something has put urgency back into his leaving. He needs to return, free his guards, and ensure his people are safe.

Something's not right. Balius can't plan anything. How has he gotten the army behind him and staged a coup?

"Zain," Del says in a hushed voice, bringing him out of his thoughts. "We should set out for the human kingdom of Nordia tomorrow. The sooner we gather allies, the sooner we can stop Balius." She leans her elbows on her knees, fixing her green eyes on him for confirmation.

With a heavy sigh, Zain nods.

Estrid drops plates of food on the table, making a louder noise than necessary, interrupting their conversation. He can sense her anger and annoyance, but there's something more there that he can't put his finger on. The plates are filled with cured meat, nuts, fruits, boiled eggs, and the remaining jam with bread. "It's not much, but it will have to do," she tells them.

With no hesitation, Alvey grabs a plate and piles it high with food as if he hasn't seen any in weeks. "Food is food. Thanks, Estrid. Is that lindenberry jam?" Alvey says through a mouthful.

Zain is about to tell him how he got it, but Estrid jumps in. "Zain brought it this morning for our breakfast."

"Where did you get the jam from in the human realm?" Alvey asks with a cocked eyebrow, a smug grin on his face.

"And what for, I might add?" Del adds.

Zain blushes with embarrassment at the lines of questioning from his family. "I had to test my magic after such a severe injury, so I thought I'd try to portal to Venna."

What he can't tell his family is that he had intentionally gotten it as part of the breakfast he made Estrid. Testing his magic was a side benefit.

Estrid stands there in silence at the exchange, arms folded, a frown on her face.

Zain winces internally. *You need to detach yourself from her.* He struggles to believe his own lie. He doesn't mean to hurt her, but it couldn't work between them. With her being a human, Balius and Manis are an even bigger danger to her.

"Estrid, I'm curious how you came to live alone in a cottage in the middle of a forest," Del says as she devours her food and tries to break the silence.

Estrid shifts uncomfortably on her feet. Zain's curious about the answer; he still hasn't heard it himself.

"I was injured when I came into the forest. Someone found me, brought me here, and helped heal me," Estrid says in a chipped tone.

"Who was it?" Alvey asks.

"I don't know. When I was well enough, they were gone."

"Hmm, how odd? Both you and Zain here show up injured in this forest. Seems a little coincidental and strange to me," Del says with some suspicion.

Ever the peacemaker, Alvey clears his throat and suggests they head to bed early after spending days on the road.

Estrid is already in her room, stepping out with a blanket and some clothing. "You take the bedroom. I've set it up so two people can have the bed, and the other has a bed of wool blankets on the floor. I'll sleep out here with Rafe."

She opens the front door, grabbing her coat and weapons again.

"Where are you going?" Zain asks her, concerned that she's heading out in the evening alone.

"For a walk with Rafe," she says, patting her leg to call the wolf to her side.

With a huff, Rafe gets up from his spot by the fire. He stops in front of Del, giving her a growl and snapping his teeth.

She just about bites back, but Zain clears his throat to distract her. He waits for the click of the door before turning to her; his anger is palpable.

"What's your problem, Del? She's fed us and made a warm place to stay, and you can't even say thank you?"

Del schools her expression. "I don't trust her or this place," she retorts.

Standing to loom over her, Zain says, "I trust her. If she wanted me dead, I would be dead. She saved me, and I am in her debt."

With that, he throws open the door to go after Estrid, the blood pounding in his ears from his anger at his cousin's attitude.

Exiting the cottage, he spots Estrid sitting on the little stump where he'd found her the night before. The memories of that kiss come rushing back to him, and he instantly hardens. He curses his body's quick response. This woman has an immediate effect on him.

The night air is frosty, cooling his flushed cheeks. The familiar eerie sounds of the forest after dark surround them. An owl hoots in the distance with a screech from a creature as the crickets play their songs. A delicate breeze rustles the surrounding leaves in the trees, grabbing the loose strands of Zain's hair.

Rafe is nowhere to be seen, but Zain can feel him nearby as he observes Estrid. There's a hidden magical signature to the shadow wolf. It feels like a cool blanket being pulled over his skin, making the hairs on the back of his neck stand up.

Zain walks up and sits down on the ground next to Estrid. "I'm sorry for Del's behavior. She means well, but she can be hard-headed sometimes."

She doesn't acknowledge his apology.

"So, you're a king?" she says in a serious tone.

"Yes," Zain says with a sigh, inwardly kicking himself.

How was I to know we would stumble across Del and Alvey? I was planning to leave quietly.

"Why didn't you tell me?" Estrid asks, a sadness in her question.

He looks down at his feet, feeling sheepish, but he can't lie to her.

"I didn't know if I could trust you, but . . . that was before last night. I'm sorry, Estrid. I didn't mean to hurt you."

She continues to gaze into the shadows of the forest. Her silence makes him nervous. Finally, she turns to him, the moonless night sky hiding her face in the darkness, but he can sense her emotions like waves of water hitting the shore. A mixture of anger and hurt pounds the air around them.

"I'm fine. I don't know you either, Zain. Leave tomorrow and start your plans. There's nothing for you here."

Those words hurt him more than he would like. As she gets up, he grabs her wrist. "Estrid, wait. I'm grateful for everything you did for me. I want you to be happy. You're a good person. Why not go into the village, make friends, and live your life?"

He doesn't want her to be alone, even though the thought of her with someone else almost sends him over the edge.

Estrid rolls her wrist to free herself from his grasp, looking him straight in the eyes.

"Don't tell anyone I'm here. That's all I want from you," she says and then walks away, the shadows of the night absorbing her.

✦　✦　✦

CHAPTER EIGHT

Estrid wakes up early the next day to prepare some provisions for the three Fae. When she came in late last night, the cottage was silent. She slept in the little bed Zain had been using. His smell of bergamot and cedar wrapped around her, comforting her. It was a rare sleep where she wasn't plagued by nightmares, deep and dreamless instead.

Sitting on the edge of the settee, she can hear the faint whispers coming from the bedroom next door.

"I think we should wipe her memories. Did you see her magic? It's dark," Del says as Estrid presses her ear to the wood of the wall.

She rolls her eyes and scoffs at Del's words. *I'd like to see you try. Stupid Fae. I knew I shouldn't have saved him. This is what happens when you trust someone, Estrid. They try to hurt you.*

She continues to listen to the hushed conversation.

"Del! We're not wiping her memories. Just leave her alone," Zain says in a short and defensive tone. It makes Estrid more confident that he'll keep his promise if he's pushing back against his cousin's demand. He also skirts around answering Del about her magic, sending a second wave of relief through her.

"Del, if she were dark, she would have killed Zain when she first met him, and she had ample opportunity to kill us. Or have you forgotten the arrow aimed at your head yesterday?" Alvey teases.

Frustrated at this conversation, Estrid gets up. She walks on the wooden floor with heavy feet and drops logs on the fire with a thud. The whispers stop as she puts a third log on. The flames spark to life with a pop as she enters the kitchen to prepare some trail food for the three companions.

Wrapping up some dried fruit, nuts, salted meats, and flatbread she made with Zain, she places them into a small leather bag. Preparing the supplies, she looks out the window into the forest. The shadows are darker and thicker as the sun hides behind the overcast clouds above the trees. Its absence is felt. The birds chirp less, and there would usually be red squirrels darting between the branches, but even they're hiding away.

She's not sure why she's helping these Fae, but she wouldn't be who she is if she didn't. She knows Zain has to go, as much for him as it is for her. His remarks about her to his family's questions yesterday hurt her, trying to dismiss and cover anything romantic.

Let it go, Estrid. He has to leave, and it's for the best.

Rafe gets up from the rug he slept on last night, stretching out his long body and giving a big yawn that flashes his teeth. Estrid hears Zain in the next room. "Stay here for ten minutes and give me some privacy with her, okay?"

Nervousness shoots through Estrid as she grabs the bag and opens the front door to let Rafe out. She darts outside as well, escaping the conversation she knows is coming.

The fresh morning air brushes against her cheeks. Walking over to her little shed at the corner of the property, she opens it and grabs one of her smaller hunting knives. Her visitors may have swords, but that won't do them any good if they must hunt small game.

She packs the knife, closes the latch, and heads to the cottage. When she turns, she finds Zain standing outside the front door. He's dressed and has borrowed Alvey's leather vest, which is a little too big for his more slender frame. His hair is down and tucked behind his ears, softening his sharp facial features. Zain stares at Estrid, drinking her in from head to toe.

"What are you doing?" he asks her.

"I've packed you some stuff to take on the road. Your journey will be long, and by the looks of how Alvey ate last night, he hadn't eaten a proper meal in days," she says, fiddling with the strap, trying to close it and hide her nervousness. "There's—"

She's about to tell him about the hunting knife when Zain walks up, cups her cheeks, and kisses her.

It takes her breath away. His lips are soft and warm. This kiss is gentle but urgent.

When it ends, she takes a deep breath to refill her lungs. Zain rests his forehead against hers. She furrows her brow. *Why did you do that?*

"Come with me," he murmurs.

The feel of how intense that kiss was still sits on her lips, numbing her thoughts for a moment.

"Estrid, come with me. I know you want to stay here alone, but there's something between us. I feel it, and I know you do too."

As she looks at him, sadness fills those bright blue eyes. The warmth of his hands envelops her, leaving a soothing sensation on her cheeks. But she knows her answer and what she has to say.

"I can't."

"Why?"

Because he'll kill me if he finds me.

He stares at her, the weight of his gaze heavy as he waits for her answer. Unable to meet his eyes, fearing he might know what she's hiding, she looks away.

"Because we both have responsibilities. I am the only one who can protect that village, and . . . you're a king. We enjoyed each other's company, but that's it."

Her heart breaks as the words leave her mouth, and silence fills the air between them. Someone feels something genuine for her, but where they're going, she can't follow.

If her father got hold of her again, gods only know what he would make her do to fulfil his power-hungry desires.

"Don't go to Nordia . . . please," she says, pleading with Zain.

With a heavy sigh, he draws her into a hug. His arms wrap around her, encasing her in warmth. "Why? What other choice do I have, Estrid? I don't have an army to stop my uncle and save my people."

I know, but you're making a deal with the devil.

She places the bag against his chest and pushes him away. "I've packed food and one of my hunting knives for you. It's not much, but it'll help you until you get there."

Zain takes it from her, his hands wrapping around her wrists to draw her back. She twists out of his grip, taking a step back from him.

"Thank you," he says, shoulders slumping, then returns inside to gather his family.

Estrid stands alone outside, contemplating what just happened. The sun has penetrated the treetops and set a warm glow over the air around her, making the dust shimmer. The birds sing away as the wind blows through the trees; their evergreen leaves dance and wave in the movement.

Taking a deep breath, she can still feel their kiss, hungry and demanding yet gentle. The feeling sends goosebumps down her spine. She releases a sigh, looking down at her tattered tunic and pants.

It's for the best, but maybe Zain is right. Maybe I should try to go back into the wider world. Some new clothes would be good, and having butter and jam again would be nice.

The prospect makes her feel lighter and hopeful about the future.

The creaking sound of the door opening gives her a fright as Del steps out. The indomitable female Fae stands there with her arms crossed, her sword belt on her hips, and a sour look on her pretty face.

"What are you doing?" Del says, cooly.

Her look of distrust says everything Estrid needs to know. She squares her shoulders. This Fae won't intimidate her.

"I gave Zain some provisions for your journey," Estrid says, walking back to the cottage. Del blocks her path, but she doesn't cower, meeting Del's stare, a challenge etched on her face.

"Don't distract him. He's a king who has to get his kingdom back. He doesn't have time for a silly affair," Del says, squaring her shoulders when Estrid doesn't back down.

The words infuriate Estrid. She wasn't the one who made a move, but she won't give Del the satisfaction by showing any emotion. She plays along, giving Del what she needs to hear.

"I don't know what you're talking about. I've packed provisions for the three of you, and I plan on saying goodbye. You don't need to tell me not to get attached."

Del sighs with relief, softening her stance. Estrid moves to take a step forward before Del says, "He cares for you, you know. He never shows that he cares for anyone other than Alvey and me. When you're made king as a youngling, your every move is being watched. Waiting for you to fail. Waiting for you to make the wrong decision so they can take everything away from you. That can't happen."

Del's tone is bitter as she admits that Zain cares for Estrid, but there's a sadness to it too. The honesty in her words shocks Estrid, even though it's delivered with venom. But she can't let it influence her, not after what Zain asked her.

"I don't know you, Del. I don't know Zain, and the sooner you're out of here, the better."

The two women stare at each other—a showdown of will. A low growl escapes from the forest as Rafe emerges. He stands next to Estrid, lips peeled back to reveal his enormous teeth, then lets out another low growl. Del doesn't flinch.

The cottage door squeaks open as Zain steps out, pausing at the sight of the standoff between the two women.

"Del! Get ready!" Zain yells at Del, who rolls her eyes and steps into the dense woodland to take care of her business.

"I'm going to miss her," Estrid says sarcastically, watching Del's retreating figure disappear into the shadows.

Alvey emerges from the cottage, stretching with a groan and a grin as he spots Zain and Estrid together.

"Shall we portal?" Alvey asks, reaching into the bag that he grabbed from Zain to pull out a piece of bread.

"How? I've never seen the Nordian Palace before," Zain says, slapping Alvey's hand away.

"How do you explain portalling into an entirely different world?" Del says as she strides back into the clearing. "We'll describe what we saw to you. It should work."

"What can go wrong, right?" Alvey says, winking at Estrid as he starts down the wooded path with Del.

Zain pauses, taking Estrid's hand in his and kissing it. "We'll open a portal away from here in case someone can track our magical signatures. Thank you, Estrid, for everything. I won't forget it. Maybe I can return one day when things have settled down."

She nods, trying to remain as indifferent as she can, ignoring the tingling from where his lips touched her skin. She watches as he follows his brother and cousin, the forest quickly swallowing them.

✦ ✦ ✦

CHAPTER NINE

The whirring sound fades as the portal shuts behind them. Zain takes in his new surroundings. The temperature has dropped as he stares out across a harsh landscape.

Bony brown bushes replace the greens of the forest as they pop out of the hard, rocky ground. Snow-covered mountains run on either side of them. A fierce wind that whistles over the plains replaces the vibrant birdsong.

"Where did you bring us?" Alvey asks, half-joking, half-serious, as he stares across a monotonous landscape.

Where did I bring us? Zain shivers as a cold gust of wind bites through his tunic.

A small town sits at the mountain basin, smoke drifting out of the stone chimneys that jut from the roofs.

"Come on, we need warm clothes and horses," he says, heading toward the village.

After bartering what they could for thicker woolen clothes that cover their Fae ears and saddled horses, the three Fae set off for the Nordian capital.

Who knew Del's descriptions could lead us so close?

Since arriving in the human world, Zain's powers to portal have changed. He's no longer bound by only portalling to places he's been. Del's accurate details got them to within a two-day ride of Oberetta.

On the roads to the Nordian capital, they encounter all sorts of humans. Most are merchants and tradesmen going to and from the capital's markets.

That night, they camp off the road, keeping a low profile and to themselves. Zain gets a whiff of wild thyme as he drifts off to sleep. He dreams of Estrid, her touch, kisses, and how she felt in his arms. It seems so close, yet the ache in his chest for her feels like a chasm has opened, releasing something dormant inside him.

The next day, the landscape doesn't change, but in the distance, the familiar sight of the spires of a castle breaks the horizon. It's a relief to Zain; the need to get back to his kingdom is weighing on him with greater urgency.

Even though it's only been a day, the cold and barren horizon is unchanging apart from getting drier and duller. It was becoming maddening by the hour. Summer Fae are used to sunshine, rolling green hills, and bright landscapes.

"Look over in the distance," Del says, standing in the stirrups of her saddle.

Zain and Alvey track the line she points to. A gray stone castle is surrounded by stone and wood buildings with dragon heads on each corner.

Zain has to agree with his cousin and brother. The sight is odd, given that dragons have never existed in the human world.

"That's the capital we spoke to you about."

"Thank Dagda! This dull landscape was driving me mad," says Alvey, nudging his horse and setting off into a trot.

Zain and Del follow his lead, all eager to get off the dusty path. Del trots beside Zain as they near the city gates.

"What's your plan when we arrive?" she asks.

"I'm not sure. I've never interacted with a human noble, but if they're anything like the Fae nobility, we'll need to find out what they want first and then bargain."

✦ ✦ ✦

The sun sits low in the sky as the three Fae approach the stone outer walls of the Nordian capital. They're four stories high, and atop them stand guards who observe the countless pedestrians coming and going. The large oak gates are open, allowing a free flow of people and goods.

Inside the gates, the cobblestone paths of the city bustle with people buying and selling. The houses vary from well-maintained brick structures with manicured entrances to lopsided wooden buildings that give the place a disorientating quirkiness.

As they continue up the capital's main street, they notice the increased presence of officers who patrol in groups of two or more. Their uniforms are the blackest of black with gold trim. The insignia is a golden hand with what looks like plumes of yellow smoke coming off it.

Zain observes a pair of guards as they stroll by the three of them. One is a man with a well-rounded stomach and a blond beard that hides most of his face. The other is solidly built, clean-shaven with dark skin and even darker eyes.

Before they pass the duo, Zain holds out his arm to stop them. "Excuse me, where's your captain? We're visiting from a foreign city and wish to speak to him."

Both guards stare at him blankly for a second before the one with the darker complexion responds, "The captain is based in the building to the left of the castle entrance. Good luck getting to see him. He hardly even talks to his men." Then they continue walking without another word.

Zain stares at them in disbelief that a soldier would undermine his senior officer to a stranger. Discomfort grows deep within him from the encounter.

He looks around, noticing some things that are out of place compared to the Summer Court. Dozens of bodies hang on the walls. They're frozen from the cold, but that doesn't hinder the carrion birds from feasting on them.

Zain's restlessness intensifies at the presence of something strange. He can't put a finger on it, but it doesn't feel right.

He turns to Del and Alvey, shrugging at the odd encounter.

Nudging his horse to keep moving, they continue up the road, arriving at the guardhouse outside the inner castle walls. A group of guards loiters out front, all laughing at something said by an older-looking guard with more gold on his uniform.

Zain decides this is the most likely candidate to be the leader, or at least a high-ranking officer. The group's laughter ends abruptly as they see Zain, Alvey, and Del approach. Zain doesn't jump off his horse—being higher than the men may be more intimidating.

"Excuse me. We're looking for the captain of the guard," he says, fixing his gaze on the man with more gold.

"Who's asking?" A low-level grunt with red hair and pale skin pushes himself off a post to walk over to Zain's mare, who whinnies in response.

"We're visitors to this city and wish to see the king. It's urgent," Zain says, narrowing his eyes.

At the request to meet the king, all the guards burst out with booming laughs, as if Zain had just told them the most hilarious joke. The redheaded male smiles at Zain, his teeth stained yellow and chipped. The leader with more gold in his uniform saunters over to Del, eyeing her up.

"No one is seeing His Majesty," he says, patting Del's horse.

She gives him a sneer and moves to her blade, but Zain quickly cuts her off.

"I'd like you to try, please. I'm sure your king wouldn't want you to turn away a Fae king offering an alliance." He grits his teeth, trying to keep his temper in check.

The guards erupt again with laughter, turning their backs on Zain as they resume whatever conversation they'd been having.

Alvey shakes his head at his brother. Before Zain can demand anything, Del leaps off the back of her horse, transforming herself into a massive brown bear.

People scream at the sight, pots, jars, and glass shattering as bystanders drop what they have to take shelter. Spooked by the sudden movement, the horses rear back, their whinnies frantic. Guards stumble over themselves, their swords hitting cobblestones with a clang.

Del stands on all fours, letting out an almighty roar that reverberates around the stone buildings. Her horse bolts as the soldiers scramble for their weapons.

"Really, Del?" Alvey says as he reaches for his sword.

Zain unsheathes his too. *We're meant to be peaceful, Del!*

A figure steps out of the shadows of the barracks. Scars mark his face, and slicked black hair highlights the extent of it. His black robes swish as they drag along the muddy ground.

"How marvelous," the robed figure says, drifting over to Del and admiring her animal form. She roars in his face, but he's unfazed and claps his hands with delight.

Surprised, Del changes back into her Fae form.

"Who the fuck are you?" she seethes at the cloaked stranger walking around her, observing her as if she were an experiment.

"How rude of me. I was just so impressed with what you did. Forgive me, I am the king's high mage, Neros," he says, giving them a smile that sends shivers down Zain's back.

This mage has a strange magic that triggers a warning in Zain's head. It has an oily, unnatural feel to it.

Neros turns to Zain and grabs one of his horse's reins, pulling it down and forcing Zain to bend lower to see him.

Up close, his face is even more monstrous. It's pockmarked with a green tinge to it. "I was told you would come," Neros says, giving Zain a crooked smile.

Zain's horse snorts in protest as the mage walks away, beckoning them to follow. Del stands next to Zain; her hand sits on the pommel of her sword as they watch the retreating figure.

"Who told you we were coming?" Zain asks, suspicious of the strange mage.

"Why, the gods, of course!" Neros cackles as he turns around, his black robes flicking up the muddy ground. He walks, gesturing them forward. "You wish to see the king? Come with me."

The guard with the uniform that has more gold on it rushes up to Neros, grabbing the mage's shoulder to stop him, his eyes darting between Neros and Zain, a clench in his jaw. "Neros, these are strangers and Fae. They could be a danger to His Majesty."

Neros stops and turns to the man, slapping him across the face. Del gasps at the display while Alvey grunts in disapproval. Zain's eyebrows rise.

Who are these people?

"Shut up, Captain. You'll refer to me as High Mage, and when have I ever wanted your input?" With that, Neros continues walking up the castle's main pathway.

Zain looks at the captain, who stares at Neros, his face purple with rage, hands balled into tight fists.

Alvey shakes his head at Zain, who silently pleads with Alvey to understand what's going on in his mind. *We don't have to like them, but we've no other options.*

With a firm nod, Zain kicks his horse to follow the mage.

✦　✦　✦

CHAPTER TEN

The inside of the castle is not much better looking than the outside. Dark. Cold. Unwelcoming. Tapestries depicting battles line the halls, along with gloomy furniture that looks as comfortable as lying on a bed of rocks.

It smells damp and musty, like a window hasn't been opened in a long time. The air is cold and heavy, adding to the depressive state of the interior. It sends shivers down Zain's back, unsettling him.

The contrast to the light and warmth of the Summer Palace is stark. There's always a breeze from one of the many open windows or doors that lets in the familiar scents of flowers, trees, and nature.

"This place is strange," Alvey says, staring at a tapestry depicting a black-robed figure sending what looks like smoke from their hands into a crowd; their faces are contorted in pain.

Zain must admit the tapestries are more gruesome than the war paintings he's used to in his palace.

"Who are these people?" Del whispers from behind him.

Neros walks ahead of them, their footsteps echoing through the stone hallways. "Your arrival will please King Rodden. It's been many decades since we've seen the Fae in the human realm," he says, gliding further down passages, the air becoming more suffocating as they continue their journey.

The mage makes Zain uncomfortable. This whole place doesn't feel right. It's more than coldness and dampness. Something is rotten and wrong here, a sticky and oily sensation. It's not something he's ever felt before, making him wary of his surroundings.

"Please don't go to Nordia." Estrid's words echo in his mind as they approach two large wooden doors.

They open into a hall decorated with black-and-gold standards hanging from the ceiling of the cathedral-style roof. Torches line the walls, bathing the room in a golden light. The soft glow from the overcast day outside comes in through the enormous circular window behind an black throne, giving it a halo effect as the three Fae approach the king.

Sitting on the imposing seat, King Rodden leers as they make their way down. Servants in tattered clothes cower at his feet, backs hunched and eyes cast down to the ground.

As they get closer, the air around Rodden feels thicker, that same sense of oiliness coating it as it does Neros.

Rodden has gray-black hair and a jowly face that has sagged with age, but his eyes are the darkest of browns. They spark with malice, cruelty, and coldness.

The sight sends goose bumps down Zain's arms, the hairs on the back of his neck standing on end. Refusing to be intimidated by a human, he pulls his shoulders further back, shaking off a strange, unwanted presence that feels like it's constricting him.

Beside Rodden stands a young woman with cherry-red hair. She's pretty, with delicate facial features. By her soft-looking skin and black velvet dress, she's royalty.

The four of them approach the bottom of the dais. Rodden tears his gaze from Zain, tracking Neros as he walks. A silent conversation flows between them, Neros nodding as a wicked smile crosses the king's face.

Rodden returns his cold, dead eyes to Zain. His expression is impassive.

Neros glides up the stairs, turning to address the courtiers who loiter about the room. Hushed whispers and curious glances land on the three Fae.

"Welcome to Oberetta and the Kingdom of Nordia, King Zain of the Summer Court."

Zain freezes. *How do they know which court I ruled?* Shocked and uncertain, he relaxes his features, not letting it show.

As they stand at the bottom of the dais, a putrid odor wafts around the king. Alvey coughs and almost gags, but Zain gives him a look, signaling him to be quiet.

"Neros here has been telling me of your arrival for some time now," Rodden says, straightening his back to sit at the edge of his throne.

Trying not to cough at the stench, Zain approaches the top step of the dais and dips his head. Every instinct in his body is telling him to run.

"Thank you, Your Grace. We are grateful to be in your kingdom."

Rodden holds out a wrinkled hand with several heavy gold rings, his nose turned up at Zain, sending a silent command. The treatment flares Zain's temper, but he swallows his pride and looks at the hand before him.

The rotten stench coils around his nose, invading his senses. He has to fight back the urge to retch as he lowers his head to kiss the royal ring on a leathery, bony finger.

"So, why have three Fae entered my kingdom when they abandoned any hope of relations with humans decades ago?" Rodden asks once Zain has paid his respects.

Straightening back up, Zain says, "We've come in need of help, Your Grace. My kingdom has been attacked, and we need your support. In return, we want to revive the trade treaty we once had with humans."

The surrounding court erupts with chatter at Zain's proposal, echoing off the high ceilings. He's no stranger to these diplomatic conversations that evolve like a chess game. He's played this at his court many times. It's how he's had to survive since his parents' deaths.

Rodden sneers at Zain. "The trade with the Fae was well before my time, but I've read the histories and know how your father betrayed us. Why should I trust you, boy?"

Zain grinds his teeth at the disrespectful and condescending tone that Rodden addresses him with. Beside him, Del grows impatient at this political dance.

"What would show you we're serious?" she asks, taking an aggressive step forward. The room goes deathly silent as everyone holds their breaths.

Rodden narrows his eyes at Del as a smirk emerges on his face.

"I have a daughter who's disappeared. She was one of my strongest warriors. We lost her in a battle against Solian. Neros says she's still alive. He's developed a . . . connection to her, but that connection has been damaged, and we can no longer track her whereabouts. I will support an alliance if you can get her back."

"Where was she last seen?" Zain asks as Neros produces a map. With a wave of his hand, the worn paper floats to them in thin air. It's stretched out over an invisible table.

"She was last seen here in a small Solian village near the Dark Forest. We have intelligence that suggests they had been smuggling stolen goods from Nordia through this village," Neros says, pointing to the area where the town sits.

"Why did you send your daughter and not a soldier? That would have been the logical choice," Zain says, finding it unusual that a king would send his daughter into enemy territory.

"That is none of your concern. The Solians are our sworn enemies. Her special abilities allow us to keep the upper hand with them," Rodden says, narrowing his gaze on Zain.

Alvey clears his throat, breaking the tension in the room. "What does she look like?"

Rodden ponders a moment before saying, "She has a slightly olive complexion. Long hair that's such a dark brown, it almost looks black. She's about the height of your female companion here"—Rodden points to Del—"and has unusual eyes. How can I describe them?"

"They are a honey gold, Your Grace," Neros chimes in.

Estrid! Zain's stomach bottoms out at the realization.

He panics as Del steps forward, opening her mouth to give Estrid away. *Don't you dare say it, Del!* Zain casts her a warning look as he grabs her elbow, pulling her back. He spares Neros a glance, the mage narrowing his eyes at the Fae.

This is what she's hiding from?

He thinks back, all the puzzle pieces now making sense. He thought she might have been royalty from the clues in her education and her training in weapons.

"Yes, excellent description, Neros. She's my only daughter, and I miss her dearly. She was also the protector of our kingdom, loved by all," Rodden says, drawing Zain back into the conversation.

Del breaks his grip on her, asking, "If we bring her to you, will you honor terms for an alliance?"

For Dagda's sake, Del, shut up!

A satisfied hum comes from Rodden. "Of course. All I want is my daughter back."

His words sink in. An alliance. What Zain needs to get his kingdom back.

But Estrid . . .

He needs time to think.

"Your Grace, our journey has been long, and we are tired. May I ask that we get quarters for the evening? We'll take this map with us to discuss all the information you gave us to work through a few plans."

Zain looks straight into Rodden's dark eyes. He notices faint black lines like veins creeping up the king's neck. He stares at the unusual markings. He didn't think humans had such markings.

Rodden clears his throat, breaking Zain's daze.

"Apologies, Your Grace. I'm tired from the long journey and missed what you said."

"Not to worry, King Zain. You are more than welcome to stay here in our guest wing. Neros will show you to your quarters and get some food sent up. If you would excuse me now, I have other matters to deal with," Rodden says, getting up from his throne and gesturing to the woman waiting beside him. "Come, Zella."

They bow their heads and watch King Rodden and Zella depart.

Settled in their quarters, Zain takes in the simple furnishings. The dark décor doesn't brighten the room, only adding to the bleakness of their surroundings. Black velvet settees with plush gold pillows take up the middle of the space, flanked by a square dining table to the right.

Three doors lead to their sleeping chambers at ten, twelve, and two o'clock. The room has a warm orange glow from the roaring fire in the stone fireplace on the center-left wall. Tall black candelabras with a dozen lit candles chase the remaining shadows away.

Zain's nose tickles from the incense sticks of sandalwood. He can feel Del's eyes on him before she speaks.

"She's his daughter, Zain! If we return her, we get an alliance. We need this alliance," she says, her tone short and chipped.

How can I give her up after she saved me? He picks at dry skin on the sides of his nails, a stress habit he's formed. A driving need to protect her grows in him, but Zain's mind is a tale of two halves. *How can I not give her up? We need this alliance. Your people need you, Zain.*

"I know, but she helped me. I owe her," he says with a sigh, rubbing his hand over his face to release the pressure building within him.

In the background, he can hear Del speaking, but her words are muffled as his thoughts drift to Estrid. He needs to understand why she wants to stay away from this place.

"Del's right, Zain. We need this alliance. When we were imprisoned, Balius started stripping lords loyal to you of their titles, charging them with anything to lock them up. He whipped and tortured your followers. He's gone mad, Zain. If we don't stop him now, Dagda knows what he'll do," Alvey says, grabbing an apple from the fruit bowl beside the settee and tossing it into the air. "Plus, I think Neros has a sweet spot for Del. Did you see how he looked at her when he said there were training grounds she could use?"

Zain chuckles at Alvey's teasing. He can always make a joke, even in the most stressful situations.

Del is about to retort when there's a knock at the door.

It creaks open as two servant girls walk in with a platter of food and wine. At the sight of proper food, Alvey springs up, almost elbowing Zain in the head. The two maids lay out the small feast on the dining table that sits off to the right of the room, Alvey already helping himself as they turn to leave.

Zain calls, "You two, what do you think of your king and his lost daughter?"

The young girls clasp their hands nervously. They must be no older than fourteen or fifteen—babies in Fae terms. With their heads down, the slightly older of the two peeks up and looks at the three Fae. Her dress is like a quilt made of mismatched patterns. Her bonnet a muddy brown.

"We love our king and all his family, my lord."

The girl's words are forced, and her voice has a quiver. Zain is about to probe deeper, but they both curtsy and rush to leave.

Frustrated by the well-rehearsed answer, Zain slumps in his chair, his appetite non-existent. He needs a bath.

"Come back in an hour. Fill the bath in the far-left room," he says before they reach the door.

The girls nod and curtsy again as they make for a quick exit, but the younger of the two slows her last two steps, allowing the older one to leave first. She turns to face the three Fae, her deep brown eyes darting around the room nervously.

"The king's daughter is his greatest weapon. He uses her dark magic to attack Solian, taking everything for himself. I hear rumors that without her, his plans to take the Solian are in ruins," the young maid says, her gaze landing on the platters of food she just brought in.

Del lets out a harrumph, a triumphant look on her face. Zain can feel the *"I told you so"* coming from her.

Trying not to roll his eyes at his cousin, he takes in the girl's slight frame. Her cheeks are hollow, her skin pale, and she's clearly malnourished. He walks to the food table, picking up some bread, an apple, meat, and cheese in a napkin. He gives it to the girl, and she hurries after her friend.

They lapse into silence again, only the crackle of the fire echoing in the room.

"We have to give her to him, Zain," Del repeats.

"What if we don't?" Zain says as he returns to the settee. "He wants Solian. What if we can give him an alliance in return? Give him what he wants?"

He needs to try something that doesn't end up with Estrid back here. He made a promise to her, but he also made a promise to his family.

"He wants her," Del says with a huff as she paces the room. If she keeps it up, the carpets will wear through.

Zain lets out a heavy sigh as the decision weighs him down. "I'll speak with Rodden tomorrow."

✦ ✦ ✦

Zain rises early the next morning. The looming conversation with Rodden has plagued his mind all night. Guilt racks his body.

He opens his door to the circular common area to find only Alvey. The warm light from a sunny day shines through the small windows that run along the outside wall. To Zain's surprise, his brother is reading a book.

"What are you reading?"

"I'm not sure, to be honest. From what I gather, it's some historical tale. I had to pass the time while I waited for you two to wake up," he says, nodding toward Del's room.

Zain furrows his brow. "She's not up yet?"

Alvey shrugs while continuing to read his book, unfazed by Zain's confusion. Zain lets out a huff of frustration at his brother's lack of urgency.

"It's almost eight in the morning. Del never sleeps past six," he says as he knocks on the wooden door to Del's room. He positions his ear next to it to listen for any sign that she's in there. Nothing. He turns the knob and enters her room. Her bed's untouched.

"Del?"

✦　✦　✦

CHAPTER ELEVEN

What light there is from behind gray clouds struggles to break through the trees outside the small window to Estrid's bedroom. Raindrops pitter-patter from the thick tree foliage onto the roof of her cottage.

As she lies in bed, her mind is in another place—close to Zain. Constant reminders of him surround her. His bergamot-and-cedar smell lingers in the air. The yellow and purple flowers that he brought back from their wilted form.

She'd known he was leaving, and a kiss shouldn't have changed that. She was not supposed to have let herself get so attached to him. A Fae king on a mission to regain his kingdom with a Nordian alliance would never work.

Nordia. The one place on earth that she can never return to.

The rhythmic pitter-patter of rain continues, background music to her thoughts.

Rafe lets out a low and menacing growl from where he sleeps next to her bed.

"What is it, Rafe?"

His next snarl contains more menace. Estrid slides out of bed and crouches low. Rafe stands and stares at the door, his jet-black hackles raised as he bares his teeth.

A branch breaks outside her cottage.

She closes her eyes and focuses her hearing.

Snap.

Crunch.

More branches break under something heavy.

Estrid reaches for the hunting knife she's hidden under the bed. She concentrates again, listening.

Pitter, patter. The soft sounds of rain continue to hit the cottage roof, but all else is silent. Not a bird, bug, or animal makes a noise.

She opens the bedroom door with a slight creak and creeps into the common room of her cottage. Rafe pads behind her as they cross the wooden floor.

She looks over to her bow and arrow stashed out of reach near the entrance to her home. *Damn it.* Estrid moves with stealth to get them, keeping low.

Halfway there.

Silence.

Stillness.

Then a crash.

The window in the kitchen shatters just before a crossbow bolt smashes into her shoulder. She flies back, her body tumbling into the tables and chairs. Searing pain courses through her.

She lets out a scream at the arrow sticking out of her flesh. Black spots appear in her vision. She looks around for her knife. She doesn't have time to react before her front door is smashed open.

A broad-shouldered soldier rushes into the cottage with his sword raised. Rafe charges the man, who yells out in surprise.

Fight the pain, Estrid. Move. Now.

She grunts, trying to ignore the floppiness of her left arm and that horrifying penetrating weight on her shoulder. Using Rafe's distraction, she grabs her knife.

Moving behind the soldier, she slits his throat. Warm blood coats her hands. The burly man goes down, his sword crashing to the ground. A gurgling sound escapes him as he clutches the gaping wound.

"Get in there, you fool," a gruff male voice yells. His thick northern accent sounds very familiar.

Estrid pales. *No. It can't be.*

Her father's soldiers have found her.

The thought of being taken to him freezes her in place. Panic sets in. *How did they find me?*

Only Zain and his companions knew where she was.

He wouldn't . . . would he?

The pain of betrayal looms over her, making her sick. It cuts deep, threatening to break her concentration on getting out of this situation.

Fear and panic turn into anger. *Focus.* She sucks in a breath. *One. Two. Three.*

She yanks on the arrow, biting down on her lip to stifle her scream. Pain floods her body, sending her head spinning. Blinking once, twice, three times, she tries to clear her blurry vision. The bolt won't budge. She tries again, but the shaft breaks off.

Bracing against the side of the wall, she steadies herself as the agony subsides enough for her head to clear. She turns to Rafe on her right. He lets out another growl. His predatory gaze is focused on the smashed door, lips peeled back to reveal sharp canines.

"When I say 'run,' Rafe, you run. Run for the trees."

"Get in there and get her out, you lazy sods!"

"But, sir . . . she's the Dark Witch. What if she uses her magic on us?" A younger voice this time. The fear in it gives her strength.

"She can't, you idiot. That arrow was iron and magically bound. If you don't go in there and get her, I will cut you down myself," that gruff voice says again.

At the mention of power, she tries to gather it, but the arrowhead in her arm is blocking it. She can feel it draining her energy away. A chill snakes around her body, coiling and strangling her.

She can't fight her way out, but she has to try. This is her home. She knows it better than anyone else. If Rafe can cause enough distraction, she might make it into the thick of the trees and disappear into the forest.

With a deep breath, she steadies herself.

"Ready, Rafe."

Estrid grips her hunting knife in one hand, placing her injured arm onto Rafe's back, her fingers giving his coarse fur a quick scratch in reassurance.

"One . . . two . . . three! Run, Rafe!"

He leaps outside through the broken door. Chaos breaks out, soldiers yelling at the sight of Rafe's enormous wolf form. The wet tearing of flesh follows their screams.

Estrid approaches the exit, gripping her hunting knife so tight that her knuckles turn white. She's about to move when a bolt grazes past the other shoulder. It hits the back wall of the cottage with a thud.

Angry, she ducks as a soldier runs through the front door with his sword raised. She spins and stabs him under his arm—years of combat training have taught her the places where gaps in the chain mail expose soft tissue. He cries out and goes down onto his knees.

She shoves the dagger into his neck in the blink of an eye. Panting, she rips it out, thick, warm blood splashing her clothes.

Smash.

Glass scatters across the floor from her bedroom window. Heavy footsteps crash in behind her.

Estrid spins around just as something solid hits her head. Her world tilts. Her vision blurs. Then she's falling.

Lying flat on the ground, her head throbs with pain. Warm blood trickles down the side of her face.

"She's down!" a man yells, entering her cottage.

She tries to grab her dagger, but her eyes can't focus.

"Bind her!" that same gruff voice shouts as her arms are bound with ropes, the harsh fabric biting into her skin.

"Rafe," she calls as they yank her up. A savage blow throws her head back. Unable to fight it anymore, she loses consciousness at the voices of men laughing at her.

✦　✦　✦

In nothing but her nightgown, Estrid's dragged across the floor. Splinters from the remnants of her door dig into her skin. Her head lolls from side to side as they drag her outside into the cool, rainy day.

Raindrops smack her body. They feel like little razor blades as they hit her open wounds. Her captors come to a halt and throw her down on the ground. Blinding pain bursts in her injured shoulder as the arrowhead is pushed deeper into her flesh.

"Ah!" she yells in agony, rolling onto her side. To her left, she sees a still black body of fur lying on the ground next to a lifeless soldier.

"Rafe!" she screams and tries to get up, clenching her teeth through the pain. She's almost on her feet when the back of a leather-gloved hand sends her head flying to the side. Her cheek burns from the impact, the swelling already making her skin feel tight.

"You're not going anywhere, witch."

The man with the deep voice walks past and kicks her, the force of it pushing all the air from her lungs. Labored gasps escape her. She can't breathe. Her chest fills with pain; she can't get any air.

"Linus, that's enough!"

Estrid knows that voice. It's haunted her every minute of her adult life.

Uncurling herself from the fetal position, she looks up to see Neros's black robes floating over the ground.

Like a wraith, his shadowy figure exits the edge of the forest. He stands above her, looking down at her with a cruel smile. "Hello, Estrid, my darling. I've missed you."

He drags a bony finger down her cheek. His rotten stench invades her nose as that malevolent grin grows to reveal stained yellow teeth.

White, fiery anger burns in her.

"I'll kill you, Neros," she says, clenching her jaw.

Deep down inside her lies darkness, which she keeps locked away like water trapped under a frozen lake. Cracks appear in the ice as the shadows seep through. They grow larger as more of it creeps through, intending to kill those responsible for hurting Rafe.

Her magic fights the effects of the arrow. Pushing it. She lets out a cackle of a laugh, her voice becoming raspy and unearthly.

"I'll kill you," she seethes.

Pulling on what energy she has, she tries to draw her dark power out. It battles against the arrow; she can feel it winning as her body attempts to shrug off the chill.

Warmth starts to return to her, spurred on by her goal.

Neros, her tormentor for much of her life, must die.

"Ah, ah, ah, my darling princess," he says as cold metal manacles are snapped onto her wrists held by the rope. Like something has sliced through her body, her magic is painfully cut off. She cries out at the loss of it.

"Come, my dear. Your father's waiting for you," Neros says.

He mutters a spell, and her world fades to black.

✦　✦　✦

Water dripping on wet stone rouses Estrid awake. Her back lies on a cold, hard stone floor. A damp smell of mildew mixed with blood fills her nose.

The wound on her shoulder is still fresh, painful, and raw. They removed the arrowhead but did nothing to treat the injury. Her head feels dizzy and fuzzy from whatever spell Neros put her under.

Like floodgates opening, she's overrun by an overwhelming sense of loss as the memories of what happened in the forest come back to her.

"Oh, Rafe, I'm so sorry."

Sobs rack her body, and tears flow freely down her cheeks. His still form haunts her memories as she tries to sit up.

Anger at Neros finding her and killing Rafe replaces the pain and sadness. But fear swiftly takes the place of the anger as it dawns on her where she is.

"No, no, no!"

"Shh, be quiet, or they'll come down here," a strange feminine voice snaps out from the cell opposite.

Estrid freezes, stilling her breath as she registers that someone else is down here. She uses her arms to push herself up. Pain flashes through her. Her vision blurs, and a groan escapes her mouth. Metal cuts into her wrists as the thick anti-magic manacles yank on the chain at her waist.

"I said be quiet!"

"Who are you?"

"I'm no one. Now be quiet before they come down again."

The sound of keys rattling against the dungeon doors breaks the silence. Estrid's heart jumps out of her chest with fear. Heavy booted footsteps approach her direction, putting her body on high alert.

Whoever sits in the cell across from her scurries back, their chains scraping along the stone floor. Two guards move to Estrid's cell, forcing a key into the rusty lock. It turns with a high-pitched squeal. They hesitate a moment before opening the door.

"You, get her out," one guard says in a raspy voice.

She can't see his face, but by his untidy look, he's only a jail guard and hasn't served active duty in a while. His round stomach hangs over the belt of his tabard. Next to him stands a slimmer guard, as lean and thin as a rack. There's a pause.

"Well, get on with it. Don't be scared," the more oversized man says, shoving the lanky guard into the cell.

"I'm not scared. I've seen what her magic can do. I don't want to be the one she comes after when they take those cuffs off."

"Just do it, Rem, or I'll get the captain. You'll be on stable duties for an entire month."

The other guard's patience wanes with Rem's hesitation. Rem finally takes one, two, three hesitant steps before stopping halfway into Estrid's cell. She tries to shuffle into the corner to hide herself from them.

"Come on, let's get her to the king."

Pain flashes through her body as they grab her by her wounded arms. Her whimper is quickly silenced with a slap to the face by the other guard. The sting of it makes her eyes water.

"Quiet, witch! Don't fight. I've been told we can use whatever force required to get you to your father," the other guard says as he yanks back a fist full of her hair. She can smell the sour beer on his breath, his face close to hers.

"No. Please, you don't know what he'll do with me."

"I'm not facing your father's wrath or Neros's for a witch who betrayed them."

They drag her outside the cell into the corridor. Through the bars opposite, she sees the shadowed outline of a petite woman crouching against the far wall. Estrid makes one last effort to fight the guards, thrashing against them.

"Stop it!"

She doesn't listen, using all her strength to break their hold, but her injuries have left her weak. The larger guard digs his finger into the wound on her left shoulder. Blinding pain laces through her, and she sees stars, making her dizzy.

"Try that again and I'll make it worse, witch!"

Estrid fights to keep conscious as she's dragged further down the dungeon path.

"Bring her to the king," Neros's creepy voice says.

Heavy doors open before her, and Estrid's eyes struggle to adjust to the light.

+ + +

CHAPTER TWELVE

Zain stands at the bottom of the dais to Rodden's throne, waiting for the king to answer his questions. He has to keep himself from pacing, impatience racking his body.

Rodden lounges on his throne with a blank and bored expression. Zella, the redheaded woman from the day before, stands next to him, her face betraying nothing as she stares down the hall. Courtiers fill the large stone chamber with a high ceiling, preened and loitering with all the pomp of aristocrats.

Zain has spent his morning trying to get Rodden to open up about his plans for Estrid. So far, the man has remained frustratingly stubborn and revealed nothing.

Zain watches as Rodden sits bolt upright. He cocks his head to one side, as if something is whispering in his ear. Then a sinister smile breaks across the king's face. His dark eyes land on Zain, then move to the main doors. The emptiness of them sends a wave of unease down Zain's back.

"King Zain, I think we should continue this conversation later." Rodden stands, dismissing him to join Alvey off to the side.

Curiosity at what sparked Rodden's interest has Zain's stomach churning. He reaches Alvey, who looks vexed at the king's quick dismissal. "Well, that was rude."

Zain peers around the room, trying to figure out what has captured Rodden's attention.

"Wha—" he starts, but then the large wooden doors slam open wide. Their creaking hinges reverberate through the cavernous space.

Zain watches as Neros walks through them, looking confident and smug. His putrid smell punctures the air. The echoing sounds of heavy boots and clanking armor follow the mage.

Behind him, two guards drag in a beaten and wounded figure. Their dark brown hair is matted. They wear nothing but a blood- and dirt-covered sleep shirt.

"Where's Del?" Zain asks before he sees her slip through the crowd of courtiers at the back of the room. Del's eyes meet his, but she quickly averts her gaze. A pit opens up in his stomach.

The guards bring the prisoner to the front of the dais. One grabs a handful of their hair, lifting their head to face the king.

"Your Grace, I present to you your lost daughter," Neros says with a victorious look.

Zain stumbles as he recognizes the beaten and bloody figure.

No. It can't be. How did he get to her?

The world stops. His heart is heavy, sinking at the sight of her.

He steps toward her, needing to go to her, but Alvey places his hand on Zain's chest and shakes his head, whispering, "No, brother. Not here."

A roar of frustration echoes in Zain's head, but he knows Alvey is right. They have to be smart about this. All he can do is watch as Rodden walks down his dais to look at his daughter. Malice fills the king's eyes as his smile turns into a sneer.

"Ah, my dear daughter, how wonderful to have you home. Who's responsible for your return?" Rodden addresses the room, scanning the crowd.

With an eerie drift, Neros walks up to the king, bending down as he approaches. "Your Grace, it was our Fae friends. They came through on their promise of returning your daughter in exchange for an alliance."

The revelation slaps Zain in the face, sending him reeling. *Del!* His head snaps to the space in the back of the room where she was standing, but she's no longer there.

"What just happened?" Alvey leans over and whispers to his brother.

Rodden saunters down to the bottom of the dais, his arms wide open. "King Zain! Thank you for my daughter's return. I've been at a loss without her at my side."

Zain wants to protest, but the words get stuck in his throat as Rodden embraces him. He can't move. He just blinks at Rodden and then at Estrid. Stormy eyes of anger, hurt, and betrayal bore into him.

Rodden releases Zain, guiding him to the center of the room. As he nears Estrid, he hears a faint whisper asking why. Seeing her beaten and injured like this is worse than the pain of any wound he's ever had. Rage soon replaces that pain at his cousin's treachery.

His gaze locks on Del's defiant stare as she comes to stand beside a shocked Alvey. He narrows his eyes at her. Zain takes a deep breath, trying to contain his emotions.

How could you betray me?

Zain watches in horror as Rodden walks over to his daughter and slaps her across the face. With a crack, Estrid's head whips to the side. The courtiers who have gathered around them gasp. Whispers of "Traitor" shoot through the crowd.

"You deserted and betrayed your people, Estrid. You deserted me. Your beloved father!" Rodden's booming voice echoes through the vast room.

Estrid stares at her father with contempt. Zain watches as those golden eyes he loves begin to turn black.

Rodden grips her chin and slaps her again, her head whipping to the other side this time.

"How dare you!" he snaps at her, pulling his hand back to slap her once more.

Something cracks in the façade that Zain is trying to hold together. "Stop this!" he yells.

The guard at Estrid's side grabs his sword and unsheathes it with a hiss.

"You have the audacity to command *me*!" Rodden spins around, spitting the words at him.

Zain could slice Rodden's head clean off with his magic from the rage that roars inside him. He squares off against the aging monarch.

Alvey jumps between the two men, trying to defuse the situation. "Your Grace . . . ah, you see, in the Summer Court, we rarely allow prisoners into the throne room. It is, well . . . unbecoming of royalty. So you can understand why my brother is upset. It isn't done where we come from."

Tense moments tick by. Rodden's face turns from beetroot purple with rage to placid and calm at Alvey's words. The guard lowers his sword.

"Quite. Well, I am pleased that you have returned, my daughter. Our campaign against the Southern Kingdom of Solian has stalled without your abilities. Are you ready to continue your work on our enemies, my dear?" Rodden says.

The room darkens and the torches flicker as a sinister laugh comes from Estrid. People step back, panicking as the sound echoes around the chamber. Her black eyes are fixed on Zain, Alvey, and Rodden, a look of pure hatred on her face.

"I'll kill you, old man. I'll kill everyone in here before I ever do your bidding again," she says in an unearthly voice that makes Zain pause for breath. He can feel Estrid's power radiating off her; he's drawn to it. It beacons him, like a siren, but something is binding it, tamping it down.

Unaffected, Rodden moves with a speed Zain wasn't expecting so he's face to face with his daughter. He grips her chin, forcing her eyes to meet his. She thrashes at his touch, leaning back to spit in his face.

Gasps and shouts of treason fill the court. Rodden doesn't flinch, just leans over, giving her a menacing smile that makes Zain's stomach churn.

"Ah, but that's not true, my dear. You will do as you're told. If you don't, there will be consequences."

Defiant, Estrid doesn't break her father's stare.

"As soon as these chains are off, I will come for you," she says with venom. "There is nothing you can do that can make me do your bidding again. I'd rather die."

A chill creeps up Zain's back as Neros stands next to Rodden. His eyes gleam in delight at the challenge Estrid has thrown at them.

Zain steps forward to intercept the mage, but Alvey clasps his forearm. He shakes off his brother's hand, but Alvey grips him tighter. Zain turns to glare at Alvey, who shakes his head, the unspoken words of *"Be smart"* and *"Not here"* crossing his face.

"Don't forget, Neros here knows more about your magic than you do. We know about the little village you were protecting. Neros has reconnected with your power. We traced your magical signature to it. That village is no more."

At the news of the hamlet being destroyed, Estrid goes rigid. Like a snake, Neros slithers closer to her, giving her a predatory look.

"Oh yes, Your Grace. While Estrid has been away, I have created the most inventive machines and potions to do many wonderful things. Most subjects who tried them died," he says with a casual shrug, "but they were not our Estrid. You remember, Estrid, don't you? While you were dreaming, they died, waiting for you to come back."

The mage twirls a lock of her hair in his fingers. His eyes light up at the prospect of having Estrid in his control again.

Zain growls. He wants to rip Neros's arms off. When Estrid shrieks and kicks in the guards' hold, he barely keeps his anger from boiling over, circumventing rational thought.

Thinking fast, Alvey clears his throat. "Your Grace, might it not be a good idea to take your daughter to the cells so we can begin our discussions on the alliance? We did as you requested and returned her."

Estrid whips her head to the side, her stare boring into Zain at his brother's smooth and even tone.

"You bastard! You broke your promise to me for a deal with a monster. I should have let you die!"

Zain winces at the hurt and anger in her voice. He locks eyes with her. *I'm sorry,* he silently pleads with her as her eyes brim with tears. *I'll get you out. I promise.*

Rodden returns to his throne again, dismissing Neros to take Estrid back to the dungeons. She screams to be let go, the crowd parting as she's dragged away. The guards struggle to keep a grip on her as she thrashes around.

Zain has never felt this angry before or this helpless.

The older guard grumbles something before bringing the butt of his sword down on the back of her head. Estrid's body crumples to the floor with a thud.

Zain tries to step forward just as Del steps into his pathway.

He bends his head to her ear, seething. "What did you do, Del?"

"Don't, Zain. It's done, and we have our alliance," she says, gritting her teeth and trying to keep her voice hushed.

"Get out of my way," he says in a whispered voice filled with contempt, his body shaking with anger at her betrayal. Last night, he said he would speak to Rodden today to buy them some time to find an alternative to handing over Estrid. "You went behind my back, Del. You've betrayed me—your king."

His words seem to shock her; her composed expression falters, a crack forming in her hard exterior shell. Del's eyes flash with hurt before they return to their stoic normal. She turns around, storming out of the room.

"Well, I say that this has been the most exciting afternoon. I'll see you in my chambers for dinner, King Zain. We can continue our alliance discussions," Rodden says with a smug expression.

✦　✦　✦

Zain storms into their quarters. The look of anger and hurt Estrid gave him has him reeling. He struggles to keep his temper in check. The leverage Rodden has over him eats at his control as he yells, "Out! Everybody out!"

The servants scuttle out the door as his voice booms. He runs his hands through his long blond hair, pacing the floor like a madman. His mind is a mess.

The door to their quarters creaks open, and Alvey steps through with Del.

"I told you to leave, Del!" Zain shouts as she meets his angry expression with a challenge.

Alvey positions himself between the pair, trying to put a barrier between them. "Zain, calm down and hear what she has to say."

Zain huffs, throwing his arms up in the air. "What! What can she possibly say that would be an excuse for her behavior? She betrayed me, Alvey! Her king!"

Zain's voice raises an octave with every word. Estrid's bruised and bloody face is imprinted in his memory. Her bloodstained shirt and battered body make him roar with rage.

Del steps out from behind Alvey, taking a step toward Zain. Alvey grabs her wrist, shaking his head in a warning to not get too close.

"I did what needed to be done to get our court back, Zain. I could tell you weren't willing to get your hands dirty, so I did!"

"Bullshit, Del! You did this because you are selfish and narrow-minded. You refused to see her for who she is. She helped me. Your king!"

Del's eyes narrow in suspicion.

"What is she to you?"

"It doesn't matter what she is to me, only that you betrayed me. For that, I am banishing you from my side. You are relieved of your duties."

Del stumbles back. Her eyes wide, she stares at Zain in disbelief, tears threatening to fall as his words hit home. He's hurt her, but the hurt she's caused him and Estrid goes beyond his tolerance.

"Get out, Del. Don't come back," Zain says with one last look at his cousin.

The room dims as the sunlight fades outside, dipping below the castle walls. Del opens and closes her hands into fists, and the muscles in her jaw tic.

"You're choosing a woman you've just met over family?" Del says, her voice shaking with emotion.

Zain pauses. He almost feels guilty, but then Estrid's face resurfaces in his mind.

"No, Del, I'm choosing integrity over betrayal. Don't come back."

Not checking to see if she's leaving and also avoiding Alvey, Zain exits to his room. He needs to devise a plan to save Estrid and his kingdom.

Having bathed and with a plan in place, Zain and Alvey follow a pageboy. Their mood is somber as they make their way down the gloomy hallways. He's come up with a way to help his people and Estrid.

The young attendant opens two large wooden doors that lead into the king's private chambers. Rodden's rooms aren't much different from his own, only more extensive, but there's something strange about them. Something oily and sickly hangs in the air.

Rodden sits on a gold velvet chair. He's dressed in nothing but a partially undone robe, revealing an aging bare chest with wrinkled skin. Like the rest of him, it's an unnatural pale color with strange black spiderweb veins fanning over it.

A naked young woman sits at his feet, holding a bowl of fruit. She has a pretty face. Her body is youthful and supple, but her eyes are vacant and void. Zain shivers with disgust at the sight.

Rodden breaks away from eating whatever fruit she holds to greet them in his raspy voice. "Ah, Zain, Alvey. Welcome."

Zain has to use all his control not to reach out and snap Rodden's neck. He takes a deep breath in and out, focusing on the plan.

"Thank you, Your Grace."

Rodden snaps his fingers, commanding the girl to return to his bedroom. Her dead eyes betray no emotion as she gets up and walks into the room. With her back to Zain and Alvey, they notice deep purple scars mottling her skin. They can't be very old.

The control Zain barely hangs on to breaks further at the vile creature before him. Beside him, Alvey gives Rodden a death stare, his jaw muscles flexing as he works to keep hold of his temper.

Stick to the plan, Alvey. Then we leave this place.

Putting his hand on his brother's shoulder to calm him down, Alvey's jokester demeanor extinguished, Zain clears his throat to break the tension. He wants to get out of here as soon as possible.

"Your Grace, we'd like to complete the agreement of our alliance. We need to get our court back as soon as we can."

Rodden smirks. "Ah, yes, of course. I have heard about the troubles in your court. I assume that's why you need the alliance?"

Zain pauses for a moment, flicking Alvey a look of concern. The Fae have been out of the human world for over eighty years. How does Rodden know about Balius's coup? There have been no open portals between the two realms for such news and information to be relayed.

"Well, yes, Your Grace. As I'm sure you would be in our situation, we're concerned for the people of our court. An alliance with you will support our cause," Alvey says through slightly gritted teeth.

"Yes, yes, of course it would. What's in it for me?"

Rodden gets up from his plush seat and walks over to the large dining table laden with food, gesturing for Zain and Alvey to join him. They sit, but eating with such a foul creature puts Zain off.

Alvey was right. Something is off here.

He notices little things out of place from the opulent black-and-gold décor. A mummified human hand sits on a shelf next to some books. There's a jar that contains what appears to be some small, mummified animal. The grotesque relics aren't in plain sight, but if he looks hard enough, they're there.

Zain's attention turns to Rodden, who's been watching him the entire time. Wine spills out the side of his mouth, running down his bare chest as a slimy grin sits on his face.

Zain attempts to keep his expression neutral, trying not to show the disgust he feels inside. His thoughts go to Estrid, the overwhelming need to have her in his arms.

"Taking down your Solian enemy is important to your legacy as a king. If we are allied, I would be willing to pledge my military to support your campaigns. There are also trade agreements we would put in place to foster longer-term prosperity for both kingdoms, but to strengthen this, I would like to offer my hand in marriage to Estrid to solidify the alliance."

Zain looks directly into Rodden's dark eyes, which flash with spite.

"Hmmm, a military alliance is appealing. I can finally conquer those southern cockroaches who have been a thorn in my side for so long. As for Estrid, well . . . that isn't something I can give you. I have promised her to Neros. He's been my most faithful advisor, and with no male heirs, he would make an excellent replacement for me one day."

You what! Zain almost leaps to his feet to strangle Rodden as Alvey coughs out his wine. His breaths come out thick and fast, lips curling in disgust.

Alvey rests his arms on Zain's shoulder, which goes unnoticed by Rodden, and changes the subject. "What are your plans for her and Solian?"

"They've been trying to take my lands for years. Estrid is the key to saving my kingdom. I will defeat Solian with her," Rodden says in a cocky voice.

Zain's pulse is roaring in his ears. He's under no false assumptions that there's more to this tale than Rodden is spinning. He uses her for his greed. She didn't want to come back. Because of Del, she's here and promised to that disgusting mage.

Zain can hear Rodden's description of her magic—black, dark, and death—and how he'd used her for his campaigns. He scoffs at the notion that Estrid would do this willingly, but he fears what Neros would do to her to make her comply.

"How do you stop her from using her magic on you or your men?" he asks, hoping Rodden's sudden cockiness will make him complacent.

"Neros has many ways to keep people in line. You can see why I must reward him for his services."

Zain sucks in a breath of disbelief at the cruelty of this man. He needs to get her out. The ruse of a marriage hasn't worked. He'll need to buy time to find another way.

"I will grant you an alliance. You've returned my daughter and kept your side of our bargain. I am a man of my word, after all," Rodden says, pouring three goblets of red wine and handing one each to Zain and Alvey.

"A toast to our new alliance," he says, his eyes boring into Zain's as a smile creeps up his face.

Zain raises his cup, bringing the liquid to his mouth. The aromatic scents of berries and leather hit his nose, but there's an underlying sourness to it. He pauses. His eyes meet those of Rodden, who takes another sip, raising his eyebrow at Zain.

Zain's instincts scream at him not to drink the wine, but he takes a sip. The sourness of the liquid makes the muscles in his mouth spasm. The bitter aftertaste tickles his throat. He clears it, giving Alvey a look to stop before he can drink.

"We have an alliance, but I require it to be drafted in writing so it's a formal agreement."

"Very well. I'll have my scribes draft it in two days. In the meantime, go out and enjoy yourselves. Nordia has a lot to offer to young men," Rodden says with a greasy smile.

✦ ✦ ✦

CHAPTER THIRTEEN

Estrid's head throbs, her thoughts fuzzy.

They'd dropped her back onto her cell's cold, hard floor, where she's lain for hours, floating in and out of consciousness. As minutes tick by, she becomes more coherent.

While sitting up a wave of nausea hits her. What little food she had in her stomach comes up as her body sways from the concussion. The acid from the bile burning her throat.

She won't get any pain relief, so she drags herself off the stone floor onto a small wooden pallet. It has a thin mattress of moldy straw and a blanket that's only marginally better than the chilly ground.

The musty smell explodes around her as her body hits it. Drips of water echo throughout the dungeon as her vision blurs again, and she passes out.

+ + +

When Estrid comes to, cool moonlight shines through a window in her cell no larger than a book. It cuts through the bleak darkness that surrounds her.

Her head is still sore, but the nausea has subsided. Staring up at the dark gray stones of her cell's ceiling, she studies the uneven cracks between them.

Drip.

Drip.

Drip.

The water drips of the dungeon persist around her. Little creatures, rodents and bugs, scurry around her, heard but not seen as they search for their next meal.

She replays the events of the last day. Tears run down her cheeks as she recalls seeing Rafe's still form lying outside her house. Estrid sobs and hugs her rough, miffy-smelling woolen blanket tighter around her legs.

"Oh, Rafe . . . I'm . . . I'm so sorry."

She places her forehead on her knees and cries at the loss of her best friend. The hurt hangs like a ball of lead in her chest. Heavy, so very heavy. But then a piercing feeling of betrayal replaces the overwhelming sadness of Rafe's loss.

Estrid recalls her entrance to the throne room. Zain and Alvey standing with her father as he congratulated them on her return.

You betrayed me! You lied to me.

She remembers how they stood by and watched it all unfold. There's a deep ache in her stomach as the betrayal pierces deeper, to the point where it hurts so much that it threatens to make her sick again.

"Are you okay?" a soft voice says from the cell opposite her.

Estrid peers over and sees the young woman's face. Her pale skin is smeared with dirt; her hair looks to have a green tinge to it. Her features are sharp, but her emerald eyes give away her innocence.

"Are you okay?" the woman asks again.

Estrid nods to the stranger as she retreats into the shadows. Moments tick by as the water drips persevere.

Drip.

Drip.

Drip.

Chains scrape on the floor across from her. Estrid is about to roll over on her mattress and go back to sleep when the woman's face reappears in the soft light of the torches that hang off the walls.

"Here, take this. It'll make you feel better."

A bony arm tosses over some bread to Estrid. It lands with a dull thud, the staleness making it more like a stone. An audible rumble leaves Estrid's stomach at the sight.

She gingerly gets up to grab the stale bread, her chains rattling on the hard floors as she stumbles over.

"Thank you. What's your name?"

"Imaya."

"Thank you, Imaya. I'm Estrid."

Imaya's big green eyes widen as she stares at Estrid in awe. Estrid knows that look. When people hear her name, they know she's the Dark Witch. Sighing, she sinks back into the shadows of her cell.

Alone with her thoughts and the incessant water drips, Estrid rests her bruised body against the icy stone wall, the coolness helping to ease the swelling of her injuries. She sits there, contemplating.

I'll get out of prison, and when I do, they'll all die. For you, Rafe. I'll take my revenge for you and all those other innocents they killed.

Her breath hitches in panic when she hears the clanking of keys at the dungeon's entrance. The heavy metal door squeals open.

Estrid tenses, her heart pounding in her ears. She backs herself up as far as she can against the stone wall, pulling her blanket up to her chin and bracing herself.

She can't fight. The cuffs around her wrists block her magic like a muzzled dog. It simmers there below the surface but can't break through, her body too injured to resist the effects. She can't even stand without toppling over from her dizzy head.

Light footsteps dart down the dungeon walkway where torches hang, radiating a dim orange glow.

"Estrid," a female whispers quickly as she approaches Estrid's cell.

She can't make out who's calling her name, but after the betrayal she suffered today, she doesn't want to.

"Estrid! Where are you?" the soft singsong voice says with more urgency. "Estrid! It's Zella. Please, where are you?"

Estrid sees the hooded figure dart past, and hope blossoms within her.

"Zella! Zella! I'm here."

Zella comes to a stop in front of the bars of her cell. Kneeling, she removes her hood. Her cherry-red hair flows out, cascading down her shoulders. Estrid would recognize that beautiful shade of hair anywhere. Relief washes through her at the sight of her cousin.

"What did they do to you?" Zella's voice breaks as she takes in the decrepit place. She reaches a delicate hand through the bars.

Estrid gets up, stumbling to her cousin, her head swimming with dizziness. Her foot gets caught on the edge of a stone, and she falls. The effort of moving is still too much for her weakened state.

"Zella . . . you shouldn't be here! If he catches you, there's no telling what he'll do to you."

"That bastard can do what he likes to me! I'm here to help you."

What little light the torches produce shows the extent of her injuries on her face and body. Zella sucks in a sharp breath as she takes stock of Estrid's wounds.

Estrid can feel that her face has multiple bruises on it. Her skin is tight and hot. One eye's swollen shut from the punch she received, her upper lip is split, and her shirt is caked in dried blood from the arrows.

"I'll kill him."

"Don't worry about me. I've suffered worse. You need to get out of here," Estrid says, worry coursing through her at the thought of what would happen to Zella if she was found down here.

"Don't be silly, Estrid. I'm not leaving you like this. I've brought you a few things."

Zella pulls a sack from under her cloak. The contents of it clunk on the ground. She removes some bread, cheese, dried fruits, and a water skin.

Estrid watches as she removes a glass jar filled with a silvery paste and a small vial containing a white substance. Zella's hands shake as she passes Estrid things through the bars.

Her eyes water. Zella has always been there for her. She'd been the one person Estrid could trust throughout their troubled childhood.

When they were younger, she and Zella were inseparable. They did everything together: shared a room, went to lessons, made dolls, and did combat training.

When Estrid's power came in, Rodden separated her from Zella. He had Neros do many things to her to understand her magic. Those dark times threatened to consume Estrid. Zella didn't give up, though. She would sneak into Estrid's rooms at night and stay with her, keeping the nightmares at bay and comforting her.

"You didn't need to do this, Zella. You didn't need to risk everything for this."

"Yes, I did! You're my family, my only friend in this hellhole of a place."

Zella reaches in and grabs Estrid's icy hand. Tears track down Estrid's cheeks as she gives her cousin a weak smile.

"Zella, I need to get out of here. I have to stop him from hurting more people," Estrid says, unsure how to get out, but she has to try.

"I know. We'll remove these cuffs so you have your magic back, and then we'll kill Rodden. We can make this place a peaceful kingdom once more."

Estrid sighs and tilts her head back against the stone walls as she sits against it. It sounds so easy. But looking down at the heavy metal chains that encase her wrists, she knows it's not.

"How can we stop him? He has Neros, an army, and loyal followers," she says, deflated by the enormity of their task.

"We'll figure that out soon. I promise. Let's get you out of here first." Zella squeezes Estrid's hand in reassurance.

But Estrid can't get her hopes up at her cousin's commitment. Zain's betrayal sits heavy in her stomach, fresh and raw.

The sound of something falling down the hall in the dungeon makes Zella stand up, alert, and place her hood back on.

"Give me tonight. I'll come for you. I promise."

Zella gives Estrid one last look of sympathy before rushing down the dungeon hall, the door squealing shut at her departure.

Estrid sighs heavily and collects the goods to take to her little pallet. Before she can get there, Imaya comes back into view.

"Take me with you," the young girl pleads, the orange flames giving a glimpse of the desperation on her face.

Estrid pauses. She grabs some of the bread Zella brought, tossing it over to the cell and asking, "How did you get here?"

"I came to rescue someone but was caught when I arrived. Somehow, Neros knew I would be here. He captured me, and I've been here ever since. It's been so long. Weeks. Maybe months, I don't know."

Estrid's head pounds as she tries to focus on Imaya's words.

"Why should I take you?"

"Because without me, Rodden and Neros are weakened. I'm Neros's seer. He uses me to see what he needs to keep his power with Rodden." Imaya pauses. "And I want to go home."

Estrid is almost asleep when the sounds of the squeaky prison door make the hairs on the back of her neck stand up. A rotten stench travels through the hallway as the dark-robed figure of Neros steps to the front of her cell.

Two burly guards flank him. Fear grips her as she scrambles to move further away from the creature before her. The guard on the left unlocks the door, and Neros steps in. His overripe scent threatens to suffocate her.

"My dear Estrid, how I have missed you. Have you missed me too?"

The black mage kneels, mere inches from her. This close, she can see the pockmark scars on his face that have disfigured him further from when she last saw him.

Dark lines steal up his neck like a creeper crawling up a wall. He lifts his skeletal hand, and a long gray fingernail sticks out to touch her cheek. She tries to back away but is already pressed hard against the wall.

"I thought I would come down and pay you a little visit. After all, you'll be moving up to my quarters tomorrow. Your father has a small surprise for you, too, but I couldn't wait to tell you," he says, looking at her through russet-brown eyes with a cruel smile.

"Your father is making you my bride."

He cups her cheek, and bile rises in her throat, the acid burning it. Revolted by his touch and the news he just shared with her, Estrid does what any scared animal in a corner would do: she bites down hard on his hand, thick blood dripping from her mouth.

"Ahh, you little bitch," Neros howls, frantically trying to get her to release him, but she won't let go.

A guard hits her. Pain floods her body. Neros backs away and stands over her crumpled figure, the promise of revenge written across his monstrous face.

"You will pay for that. I'm going to enjoy controlling you once more, and this time, your father has given me the keys to the castle—"

A high-pitched laugh comes from the cell across from Estrid's. "You sound like a squealing pig when you scream," Imaya cackles from her cell.

Neros spins around to yell at her. "Shut up, Seer, or you'll be next."

Imaya doesn't stop cackling, making Estrid smile as Neros's shrill shriek replays in her mind.

He turns his attention back to Estrid, a devious smirk on his face. "Guards, make sure she knows that actions have consequences."

The threat doesn't faze Estrid as she lets out a maddening laugh with a sinister smile. Everyone knows the tales of the Dark Witch and her powers. Mother tell their children about her so that they'll behave. They want her to be the Dark Witch, so she'll play the part. Anything to get herself free of his rotten place.

"Why are you laughing?" one guard asks, moving from foot to foot.

"Because I'll kill all of you when I'm done with this place. No one will be left standing."

Both guards look at each other and then step back.

Neros stands at the edge of the cell and yells, "I said make her aware of the consequences of her actions!"

They hesitate, unsure who they're more scared of, Neros or Estrid.

One guard finally steps up and grabs Estrid by her hair.

"I'm sorry, my lady, please know I'm sorry." The punch lands squarely on her face. Her nose crunches, and she crumples onto her pallet, not moving.

Neros huffs out an acknowledgment of the job done and exits the cell, followed by the two men. The one that hit her nervously locks her cell.

Their footsteps fade into silence, and Estrid lies there, unmoving, as the creatures scurry around her.

✦ ✦ ✦

CHAPTER FOURTEEN

Zain hasn't moved from his place on the settee for hours, repeatedly replaying the scene in the throne room in his head. The sun has long set, the candles almost down to their wicks.

Estrid's face haunts him. He can no longer think of their time together in the Dark Forest. He sees only the shock and hurt in her expression at him standing by her father.

"Fuck," he yells, his head in his hands. His chest feels light and fractured. He's at a loss for what to do. Rodden intends to marry her off to Neros. He needs this alliance, but he has to fix this mess with Estrid too.

A loud knock at the door disrupts his thoughts as Alvey walks in. His usual easygoing mannerism is back, with a slight sway in his step.

"Have you figured it out yet?" Alvey slurs, flopping down in a seat opposite Zain. His cheeks are flushed, and there's a sour fruit smell about him.

"How much have you had to drink, Alvey? A barrel?"

Alvey's usually tidy shirt is disheveled. Red and purple stains dot it, as well as what looks like smears of dirt.

Zain raises an eyebrow, watching his sibling sway even though he's sitting down. Alvey's face has his usual cheerful expression, albeit alcohol induced. It's his eyes that give away his true feelings—their typical sharp crystal blue is dulled and sad.

"Yes, I have, brother. What else is there to do when someone tears your family apart?" he says with a hiccup.

Zain winces at his brother's comment. "I had to, Alvey. She betrayed me. I'm her king."

Alvey hiccups again as he says, "Our parents are dead, our uncle has betrayed us, and you just banished the one person we can trust."

"Alvey . . ."

Alvey goes cross-eyed as he tries to focus on Zain, another hiccup escaping him—the wine clearly affecting his thinking.

"Shh . . . you know what? I rather liked her, and that wolf was hilarious . . . scaring the shit out of Del."

Zain smiles. It's rare that something genuinely frightens Del; a shadow wolf did the trick.

His smile soon fades as Estrid plagues his mind again. She consumes his thoughts—Rodden's plans for her, his plans to use her to conquer the south.

Alvey hiccups, his eyes closed. Zain sighs and gets his brother a glass of water, rolling his eyes at Alvey's alcohol-induced state.

Alvey gulps water down, some spilling down the sides of his mouth. "If you don't have a plan, I do."

Zain is about to ask Alvey about this grand plan when there's another knock at the door. Alvey drops the glass to the ground; it shatters everywhere as he races to answer it.

"Alvey!"

Ignoring Zain, he hurls the door open, and Del steps into view.

Zain's face turns hot with anger at her presence in the room. "I thought I told you to stay away from us. Get out!"

Alvey pulls Del through, stumbling over his feet as he closes it.

"Hear her out, Zain." He hiccups out the words. He must have been with Del when he got drunk, considering she pays his current state no mind as she focuses on Zain.

"Zain, I didn't know what she meant to you. Please hear me out," Del says, her shoulders slumped in remorse.

He balls his hands into angry fists, ready to throw Del out if not for Alvey's pleading expression.

Del looks like she's been through the wars: dirt on her cheeks, her usual sun-kissed skin pale and dull. She has a miffy smell to her, like she's been somewhere damp. A hint of another scent lingers on her—wild thyme. Zain takes a deep breath in. Estrid.

"I may have a way to help Estrid, but you need to listen to me," Del says, helping Alvey to stand up straight as he sways further.

"Why should I trust you?" Zain bites out at his cousin.

"Because I'm your family. I'd do anything to protect you and those you care about," she says with desperation.

The realization that Del saw his feelings for Estrid shocks him, he tried to be so careful. He nods and returns to sit on the black settee again, the glass from Alvey's smashed glass crunching under his feet.

The three family members sit down, but a giant gulf lies between Zain and Del. He doesn't sit fully back in his chair but rather perched on the seat, ready to spring up and throw her out again.

"After you kicked me out," Del says, giving Zain a sheepish look, "I wandered around looking for something to take the edge off. After a while, I spied that redheaded woman who stood by Rodden. I was curious to know who she was, why she stood behind him so obediently. Turns out she's Estrid's cousin!"

Cousin? Is she loyal to him?

Zain's surprise must show on his face, as Del eagerly nods at him.

"I know. They don't look even a bit related, but she was bribing a guard to go down and see Estrid in her cell. I followed her and kept to the shadows. She found Estrid, took her food and healing balms, and they're hatching a plan to get Estrid out. That's how we can help her."

Zain stills, his expression stoic as he processes this information. He's torn between wanting to believe Del and questioning her motives after her recent betrayal.

A tapestry hangs on a wall with a forest scene on it. It reminds him of the Dark Forest, his time with Estrid.

"How was she?" he asks.

"I didn't see her, but based on her cousin's reaction?" Del shakes her head. "She isn't in great shape."

Zain grinds his teeth together, fighting to control his rage at Rodden and what he's done to Estrid.

Del casts her eyes down to her feet, sensing his anger as she continues to tell him and Alvey about Estrid's vow to overthrow Rodden.

"Did her cousin say how?" Zain asks, his curiosity piqued by Estrid's vow.

"No, but she said she would do it tonight. They want to usurp Rodden," Del says, giving him a desperate look.

This is your only opportunity, Zain. Take it. For Estrid, you must move on from what Del did.

"Find her cousin, bring her here. We need to get Estrid out. Rodden intends to marry her to Neros," Zain says, the words bitter on his tongue. Every time he thinks about Neros touching Estrid, he feels sick.

Del gives Zain a second look before she springs into action to find Zella, curling her lips up in disgust at the mage's name.

✦ ✦ ✦

Zain doesn't leave the settee with Alvey for what feels like hours. The effects of the wine wear off his brother as the hangover kicks in. Groaning, Alvey rolls onto his side.

"I know why you reacted so badly to Del's betrayal," he says with a smirk.

Alvey observes people, their reactions, and habits and is good at using them. He always seems to interject at just the right moments. Zain's tried to convince Alvey to be a royal advisor, but his brother always says no.

Zain finds this amusing, as Alvey usually portrays himself as a goofy, happy-go-lucky sort, but he's very strategic in his thinking and actions.

"It's not because Del betrayed you," Alvey continues. "It's that she betrayed someone you care about. You have feelings for Estrid, don't you?"

With a heavy sigh, Zain reclines onto the couch opposite Alvey. *Yes*, he wants to answer. Estrid consumes all his thoughts. She felt so right when he was with her. But he's cautious about admitting it.

"She's human, Alvey. Since Mother and Father's deaths, I've been groomed to be the heir. I've been told what to do, who to be with. Everything I do has to be for the betterment of the court. How can something like this work?" Zain says with a sigh.

"Does she need to be Fae? Who says she wouldn't be good for the court?" Alvey asks, one eyebrow cocked.

Being the heir to the Summer Court, Zain hasn't felt like his life has been his own to lead. Since his parents died, he's had a sense to uphold their legacy. That's why he strayed away from what he wanted, thinking it would be betraying them. His father's advisors have placed a lot of expectations on him to maintain and follow.

Estrid was the first wild card in his life that he may have just lost. A relationship that hadn't been built on him being a king. A genuine connection made by two people liking each other for who they are, not what they can gain from each other.

"I don't know," Zain says, shaking his head at the predicament. "That could all be ruined now. She thinks I betrayed her. That I used her."

Alvey sits up with a groan, looking green around the ears as he clutches his head. He stumbles to sit next to Zain.

"Win her back, then."

"Sure," Zain says, laughing. "Win her back, win back the Summer Court. Anything else you want me to do?"

The weight of the tasks that sit on his shoulders is crushing him. For the first time ever, he can't see how to achieve something, and it doesn't sit well with him. He's never not achieved something that he's been responsible for or wanted.

Maybe Del's plan will work and solve the Estrid problem, but how will I win my court back without an alliance?

Alvey continues to babble on about Del's plan as Zain's thoughts float between all possibilities to achieve both goals. Alvey sags against the settee, his eyes becoming heavy. With a yawn, he says, "What if we offer her sanctuary? She's homeless. She can't stay here, can't return to the forest either. It's perfect."

Zain ponders this for a moment.

It could work. Rodden said Estrid has powerful magic, enough to deter an army. It could be a win-win if we can get her back to the Summer Court.

The cords that are binding his chest loosen ever so slightly. Maybe he can win back her trust to help them on this quest, and eventually, he can regain her faith in him to explore their feelings for each other.

"It might work. We . . . ," Zain says, looking down at his brother, who's fallen into a drunken sleep, a snore coming from him.

✦ ✦ ✦

Hushed voices echo in the hallway outside their door before a sharp knock has Zain standing up from the settee. It opens with a slow creak as Del slips in with Zella. Her cherry-red hair pops against her emerald gown. She scans the room, her expression stern and determined.

Looking at her, Zain can't see the resemblance to Estrid. Their hair is completely different colors, and Estrid has sharp, delicate features that almost resemble a Fae. Her cousin has a heart-shaped face with softer, round characteristics.

Zella narrows her hazel eyes, watching Zain's every step with caution as he approaches her. She tenses as he steps closer, ready to pounce at any sudden movement. He doesn't doubt that if Estrid is skilled in combat, Zella would be too.

Zain holds up his palms as he comes near her, asking, "It's Zella, right? You're Estrid's cousin?"

"Yes," she grits out.

There are no formalities. He can tell she's trying to hide her disdain for him. Her hazel eyes narrow further with suspicion.

He takes a seat on the settee, nudging Alvey awake. His brother rouses, a little confused about where he is, but he locks on the newcomer.

"Ahh, you must be Zella," Alvey says, standing to greet her, the sway in his step gone—the effects of human alcohol quickly wear off in a Fae's system.

Zain clears his throat and gestures for Zella to sit on the opposite side. She doesn't move, scowling further at him.

"Thank you for coming, Zella. This is my brother, Alvey. You'll have to excuse him, as he went out drinking this afternoon." Zain shoots Alvey a glare before refocusing on Zella. "Del's explained why you're here?"

"Why would you want to help Estrid, King Zain? You betrayed her," Zella bites back, her expression unwavering as she pulls her shoulders back and stares down at him.

In his peripheral vision, Alvey sits next to him, a smirk on his face as a human holds her own against him. He tries not to roll his eyes at his brother.

Zain opens his mouth to defend himself, but Del jumps in. "He didn't betray Estrid. He never will."

She stands beside the fireplace as it crackles and hisses, the logs disintegrating further into the flames. Zella spins to face Del, giving her back to Zain. Her hand closes on something hidden in the back of her skirt.

"I betrayed Estrid," Del says, her gaze locking on to Zella's arm. The fire pops and spits as the room falls silent.

Zella steps toward Del, clutching something behind her back. Zain doesn't stand up, knowing his cousin can disarm anyone. In one fluid motion, Zella pulls out a dagger, crouching low into a fighting stance, her eyes trained on Del.

"I also betrayed Zain. He trusted me with Estrid, and I broke their trust. I'll make it up to both of them. I swear on that," Del says, her shoulders deflating, but she doesn't back away from Zella.

"How do you intend to make it up to her? She's in a dungeon because of you," Zella seethes, her body tightly coiled to attack.

Del squares her shoulders, taking a step closer to Zella. "We want to help Estrid escape. I followed you when you went to see her, and I know you want to help her too."

Zella's eyes drift between the Fae. She straightens but keeps her knife out, watching their every move.

Alvey clears his throat and approaches Zella, who steps back, holding her blade to him. He stretches out his hand with a warm smile. "Your hair is the most unusual shade of red. It's exquisite."

Zain scoffs at his brother. *Now is not the time to flirt and chase a skirt, Alvey.*

Zella's eyes narrow at Alvey as she ignores his outstretched hand.

"I don't have time for this," she says as Del laughs at Alvey, who throws a small decorative pillow at her. "If we're going to get Estrid out, we need to do it tonight. Rodden plans to marry her to Neros within a day."

No! I thought we had more time. Zain snaps his head to Zella, saying, "How do you know this?"

"I overheard Rodden not long after he spoke to you. Neros is up to something; he's putting pressure on Rodden for a quick wedding. To make Estrid his . . . his . . . to do as he pleases with," she says, a revolted expression on her face.

"So, we do it tonight. What's your plan?" Zain asks, gesturing for Zella to take a seat.

Keeping her knife in her hand, she sits eyeing Alvey, who's next to Zain, while Del stands, keeping watch at the door to the hallway.

"Well, I can get us in by bribing the guard at the internal south-end access point. It's usually only manned by one at a time. What I haven't figured out yet is how I get us out," she says, twirling the knife handle in her hand. "The other doors are heavily guarded, and bringing Estrid the way we came will only lead her back into the castle."

Del starts pacing across the doorway.

"We can help with that. I'll get us all out safely," Zain says, sitting forward on the settee. "I can portal us out from the dungeon to a safe place."

"How can you do that?" Zella asks.

"Fae have magic, just like some humans do. It's how I managed to get into the human world in the first place. It's how I met Estrid," he says, the memories of meeting her for the first time replaying in his mind.

He can feel Zella's calculating gaze on him for several moments.

"I'm not sure. What if Neros tracks it? He can portal too," Zella says, her eyes darting between the Fae.

"How can he?" Alvey asks. "He's just a human mage."

"He uses dark magic to do it. You've seen his face? It has a price. Every time he uses it, it takes from him," Zella says, no longer twirling the knife in her hands but clutching it hard.

"Do you remember any other places in the forest that we can portal to that aren't near Estrid's cottage?" Del asks, looking at Zain.

He thinks for a moment, recalling his experiences with Estrid. They explored every day, but there wasn't anything distinct enough that he can focus his mind on to portal.

Alvey lets out a chuckle as they sit in silence. "What about the pool?"

Zain grins at his brother's suggestion.

"I've never seen a woman so quick to draw a bow and arrow. Aye, Del?" Alvey laughs to himself and throws Del a look that draws a frown from her.

Zella smirks, but a grimace quickly replaces it. "That sounds like Estrid."

Zain can sense the worry and concern on her face; she's holding something back.

"What are you not saying, Zella?" he asks with some suspicion in his tone.

"Estrid's not in good shape. We'll have to find somewhere safe where she has time to heal."

At Zella's confession, Zain's heart drops. He hasn't thought about what state she would be in, only getting her out.

Zella shifts her eyes to the floor before rising and saying, "I should get back to my room and prepare. I have to get into more suitable clothes and pack a few things for the road. Be ready in one hour."

Del opens the door for Zella, who steps through but then stops. She spins on her heels, squares her shoulders, pointing the blade at Zain, and saying, "Don't betray her again. Rodden will kill us both if you do."

The sorrow hidden deep betrays the fierce mask she's put on, which nearly breaks Zain. Zella must have also suffered at Rodden's hand, but likely not as much as Estrid.

"I never betrayed Estrid, and I never will."

+ + +

CHAPTER FIFTEEN

Del, Alvey, and Zain navigate the vast hallways to the dungeon's entrance to meet Zella. They creep along the passages, the castle quiet and darker as the witching hour sets in. The quietness amplifies the sound of the wind howling outside. Their sensitive Fae hearing picks up a few night-duty guards, making their way through the maze of corridors. Their heavy booted steps make a distinct thud against the stone floors.

A guard stands at the south entrance to the dungeon, half-asleep. He leans against the wall behind him, his helmet covering his face, oblivious to the sounds of soft footsteps approaching from the opposite direction to where Zain, Del, and Alvey wait.

With grace and elegance in her step, Zella appears out of the shadows, dressed in a dark cloak that covers her face and unique hair. She has a small sack over her shoulder and another bundle under her arm. She spots Zain peering out from behind the wall and gives him a quick nod.

Zella drops her hood and approaches the napping guard, clearing her throat. He wakes with a startle, agitated at being disturbed.

Using his Fae hearing, Zain listens in on the conversation. The sentry eyes Zella with suspicion, but she plays her part well, batting her eyelashes and pleading in her most helpless voice to let her in to help her cousin. She shivers as she says how cold it is and that she has clothes for Estrid. The man doesn't budge, though, staring at her with contempt.

Zain grows impatient and takes a step forward, but Alvey grabs his arm and shakes his head. He turns to see Zella trying her hardest to plead with the guard, but he won't let her through.

"I don't care if she's sick. High Mage Neros said no one is to see her, and he will do far worse to me than the king," the guard says in a firm tone.

Zain shrugs Alvey's hand off his arm, whispering, "This is taking too long. We have to get Estrid out now or we risk not getting her out before the castle wakes up. If Neros can portal, we need distance between us. Del, are you able to take him out?"

She huffs and raises an eyebrow at Zain with an expression that tells him he didn't need to ask. Without a sound, she unsheathes the third small but deadly dagger that's strapped to her side holster and walks past Zain.

On silent footsteps, she approaches. The guard doesn't hear or see Del step out from behind the wall, too distracted by the argument with Zella. Del throws her knife.

Thunk.

Her aim is true, and she hits him squarely in the neck.

The guard grabs where the dagger protrudes, sliding down to the stone with a gurgling sound. Zella catches his spear before it can topple to the hard floor with a loud clang.

Spinning around, she gives Del a death stare. "Was that necessary? I thought we agreed to knock him out once I was through."

Del shrugs and approaches the dead man, ripping the knife from his throat. Without a care, she wipes the blood on his black tabard.

Zain and Alvey follow her and check the hallway for anyone approaching.

"We need to move him," Alvey says, picking the guard's body up from under his arms and pulling him through the entrance to the dark dungeon.

Zain grabs a torch to help light the darkened hallways. The temperature drops as the four of them move down the spiraling stairs, their breath misting the lower they go.

Soon, they reach an iron gate. Zain's skin prickles as they near the metal, his body all too familiar with the effects it has on Fae. His hand goes to his stomach, recalling the blistering flesh, his magic draining, and the slow-healing wound he got from Manis's blade.

All three Fae cringe and step back at the sight of it.

"What's wrong?" Zella asks as she pushes her way through.

"That's an iron gate," Alvey says, his expression unsure.

Zella fishes the key from her cloak pocket and dangles it from her finger. "We have a key. Nothing to be afraid of," she says, tossing Del the bundle from under her arms to open the door.

"Iron is deadly to Fae," Del explains.

"Oh . . . I didn't know that. Sorry."

The key turns in the lock until a loud click echoes off the stone walls.

Zella pushes the heavy door but it doesn't move. "Argh, this wasn't stuck before," she says with another push. "Something's . . . blocking it."

Zain steps up to inspect the doorway; the closer he gets to the metal, the more his skin crawls at the nearness of the iron. Peering through the bars, he sees a rod fixed to the wall on the other side, stopping the hinges from working properly.

Did they know we were coming for her?

"There," he says, pointing to the rod. "That's blocking the hinges. If I push hard enough, you should be able to slip through and remove it, Zella."

She nods as Zain prepares to push, but Alvey's hand comes to his shoulder. "I'll do it. We need your magic, Zain. It's our only way out," he says, giving Zella a nod as he steps up to the gate. "Ready? On the count of three. One . . . two . . . three."

Alvey grips the bars and pushes, his skin burning and hissing as it touches the metallic surface. The scent of burnt flesh wafts through the narrow hallway, making them all gag. He lets out a grunt of pain as the rod on the other side creaks and bends under his Fae strength.

Zella slips through the gap as the door slams shut, echoing across the castle. They all pause at the sound. The wind howls outside as the palace remains silent.

Alvey lets go, cradling his hands as he sways a little from the effects of the element on his magic. Zain steadies his brother, helping him stand as Zella opens the gate for them. Each of them winces slightly as they pass through it, careful not to touch any part of the deadly metal.

"She's the last cell on the left," Zella says once the Fae are through.

She locks the gate that separates this wing from the main dungeon, placing the rod back against the gate. Zain gives Alvey to Del, rushing ahead down the passage, eager to get to Estrid.

When he reaches her cell, the air whooshes out of his lungs as he takes her in. She lies in the middle of the floor, unconscious, a pool of blood next to her head. Her breathing is short and shallow.

Without thinking, he rushes to grip the bars to open the door, but Del yells, "Stop, Zain! Wait for Zella."

The light clip-clop of Zella's footsteps follows him as she hurries with the keys. She tries each key on the ring as Zain paces beside her. His only thought is getting to Estrid. The sight of her unmoving on the floor has his control slipping. He has to hold on to every thread of sanity not to tear this place apart and kill Rodden right now.

With a click, the lock's undone, and Zella opens the gate, rushing through to her cousin.

"Estrid!" she says, kneeling by an unresponsive Estrid.

Zain rushes in and kneels next to her, trying to clear some of the hair on her face, but it's mattered with blood and sticking to her.

"We don't have time for this. They're coming," Del says from the dungeon's hallway, where she's keeping watch. Muffled shouts from within the castle mount as dogs bark and howl.

Alvey crouches next to Zain to pick Estrid up, but Zain lets loose a low and menacing growl.

Alvey grabs Zain's shoulder. "It's okay. I'm helping you. She'll be okay."

"You can hardly stand, Alvey," Zain says, seeing how pale his brother's complexion is from his experience with the iron.

Alvey opens his mouth, but chains scrape across the stone with a dull squeal. They all freeze, looking for the origins of the noise. It's too dark to see into any other cells.

"I can manage, Zain," Alvey whispers. "We need to get out of here now."

With a reluctant nod, Zain takes a deep breath and stands up. Alvey scoops Estrid up, her body limp and head lolling with the motion. The shouts from the castle grow louder.

"Stand back," Zain says to the group as he prepares to open the portal.

Another clank and scrape of chains, this time closer. A dirty woman from the opposite cell appears in the shadows.

"Please take me with you!" she pleads.

No one moves; they all stare at her in astonishment.

Del whispers for Zain to hurry up, but he hesitates, looking at the woman. She's bone thin and filthy. He meets her eyes, and then she turns her head, pulling her hair back from her ears.

"She's Fae," Alvey gasps, almost dropping Estrid.

Zain shoots Alvey a dangerous look as he steps toward the unknown Fae.

"Please take me with you," she repeats.

"We don't have time for this. Leave her!" Del says a little louder.

"She's Fae, Del! She's one of us. We can't leave her here for these monsters," Alvey says with urgency.

Estrid stirs in his arms. "Take Imaya," she murmurs.

Zain looks from Estrid to the dirty Fae, who nods at her name. Her eyes are fixed on Estrid, her brow furrowed with concern as she takes in Estrid's terrible state.

Zain agrees, and Zella fishes the keys out, trying to find the right one for Imaya's cell.

Seconds tick by. Metal gates squeal as the gates to the dungeon are opened. Footsteps thunder down the stone walkways, echoing off the walls.

Click.

The lock turns, and Zella opens the door with a whoosh. Chains drag and clatter on the floor.

A dirty and skinny Fae with green-tinged hair steps out. She's around five-foot-five, has a frail frame, and is covered in dirt. She nods to Zain and steps back next to the rest of the group. Del looks suspiciously at her, almost snarling, as Zain opens a portal.

He pictures the murky crystal-blue waters of the hot pool in his head, Estrid in his arms, safe and well. With a hiss, a strange light humming sound fills the room as the portal grows wider. On the other side, the pristine blue pool appears.

"Stop them!" someone cries out down the darkened hallway.

"Go! Zella, Alvey, take Estrid and go!" Zain says, holding the portal open, watching the three of them go.

"Del and you next," he tells Imaya as an arrow whizzes past him, hitting the stone wall.

"Open the gate and get them, you fools," a husky male voice orders as the final door squeals open and footsteps come rushing in.

Zain steps through himself. The feeling of going through a portal is like tripping over in a dream—the body gets a minor shock as it emerges on the other side.

Zain closes it with all six of them inside as another arrow follows, slamming into a tree by the pool.

He sighs, but his relief is short-lived at the sight of Estrid's limp form, cradled against Alvey's chest.

Zain rushes over to Alvey, taking her into his arms. Seeing her like this in the cell just about broke him.

Del marches over to their unexpected companion and holds her against a tree by the neck. Imaya can do little to stop her as Del yells, "Who are you?"

The strange Fae flails about, gripping Del's arm as she gasps for air.

Alvey grabs Del's wrist, snarling, "Let her go, Del! She's a Fae, just like us!"

Del releases her hold, and Imaya slumps to the ground, clutching her throat and coughing. Zain can't fault his cousin's mistrust. They don't know who this Fae is.

Alvey rubs Imaya's back as she continues to splutter.

"Are you okay? Imaya, isn't it?" he asks in a much calmer tone.

Imaya nods at him with a mixture of innocence and defiance in her eyes.

"Where are you from, and why were you in a human dungeon?" Del asks. She keeps her distance, but her hand is on her sword's pommel.

"I'm a . . . a Fae seer," Imaya says, massaging her throat. "I had a vision that I had to come here to rescue someone. It was the only path, but Neros captured me. I could only complete half the vision before they stopped me from using my magic to get out."

Del continues to eye her suspiciously. Alvey's expression is concerned as he takes it all in.

"Who did you need to rescue?" Zain asks. Something doesn't add up.

Imaya looks at him before shifting her gaze to Estrid's still form. "Her," she says as they all stare at Estrid. "And you." She nods to Zain, Alvey, and Del.

Del scoffs at Imaya. "In case you missed what happened, *we* just saved *you*."

Alvey helps Imaya stand up. "It was you. You helped us portal out of the Summer Court, didn't you?" He shakes his head. "I knew it wasn't Zain; it didn't feel like his magic. How could you do that if Neros captured you?"

All eyes are on Imaya as the cool wind picks up in the evening air, sending a shiver through Estrid's still form.

"It's a long story, but trust me when I say I'm not your enemy. Something bigger is at play here, and she needs to survive it. They can't get her," Imaya says, nodding to Estrid's unmoving body as the wind swirls around them; leaves rustle and trees creak in its wake.

Zain becomes alert as he realizes how out in the open they are from both the elements and their enemies.

"Alvey, Del, fan out and find shelter," he says, cradling Estrid in his arms, trying to shield her from the icy wind that licks at her face.

Imaya's gaze hasn't left Estrid. He's about to ask why the Fae came to rescue her when Del interrupts him.

"I've found a cave close to us. Come on."

Tucked into a rock face, they put the wood they'd collected en route into a tent shape in the middle of the cave that smells damp and earthy.

Zella takes the pack off her back and rummages through it. Zain hasn't let go of Estrid and stands, holding her close. Zella tosses a blanket to Alvey, who wraps it around Imaya. She throws another over to Zain and nods for it to be put over Estrid. Zella continues to rummage through the bags, cursing when she doesn't find what she needs.

"What are you looking for?" Del asks with an impressed look on her face at the never-ending stash of items from the bag: food, water skins, spare clothes, and stuff to treat Estrid's wounds.

"I'm trying to find my flint," Zella says as she rummages in the other pack.

Alvey comes up to stand next to her and blows in his hand. The soft orange glow of embers grows. Zella stops searching, her mouth open in shock that Alvey has conjured a small flame.

He walks over to the little stick tent and guides the flame into it. As it catches, fire licks at the wood, and the cave walls become more visible as warmth moves through it. It isn't deep, but it's enough that they can all be comfortable and get some rest.

"How did you do that?" Zella asks, her eyes wide with surprise.

Alvey shrugs and wraps the blanket tighter around Imaya's shoulders.

"Remember, the Fae have magic. I should be able to do more, but the iron's hampered it," he says, sitting beside Imaya, who inspects his wounds.

Zella contemplates this before getting back to rummaging in her bags. She hands out the provisions to the group. "It's not much, but it must do for now."

She sits back on her haunches, rolling out another blanket as a makeshift bed for Estrid.

"Can I have a moment with her?" Zain says as he holds Estrid.

The other four nod and leave the cave, Alvey muttering about more firewood.

Zain moves to place Estrid down on the rolled-out blanket, trying not to jostle her too much.

"I'm sorry, Estrid." His voice almost breaks from the thick emotion clogging his throat. "This should have never happened to you."

She lets out a groan of pain as he lays her down. Her injuries are much worse in the cave's light than he thought. Her face is covered in bruises, her nose is broken, and from how her jaw hangs, it might be too.

Fury and nausea collide; he can't bear to think what the rest of her must look like after how she was treated. Rage like nothing he has ever felt before courses through him.

Without thinking, instinct tells him to place his hand over her heart.

Like a rope around his torso, the pull becomes more potent as a light forms between his hand and her chest. He watches her face as it contorts and her body heaves up. Energy starts to drain from him like air being sucked away. When it stops, he's left panting, feeling shaky at the energy loss as he looks at his hands.

What was that? That's never happened before.

A scuffle of shoes from someone standing at the cave entrance has him spinning around to see Del holding firewood. "What was that?" she asks.

"I . . . I'm not sure," he admits.

Zain drags his hand through his hair, his face damp with sweat like he's just run a hundred laps around their training ground. He looks down at Estrid. Her bruises have gone from deep purple to yellow. Her broken nose and jaw are set and straight.

"Whatever it was, she seems better now. I . . . It healed her," he says as he skims his fingers over her face.

"So, you can heal now?" Del asks, stepping into the cave, putting the wood to one side and then adding another large branch to the fire.

"I don't know. No one in our family had healing abilities." He places another blanket on top of Estrid before sitting down next to her. Her breathing has evened out, and the grimace on her face has subsided.

Del takes a seat opposite him, watching Estrid. The flames from the fire dance, making waves of orange light in the cave.

"I've never seen you care for anyone like this other than Alvey and me."

He can't deny it, not to himself or his family. He feels something for Estrid but can't explain what.

Del stares at him, waiting for his answer.

"There's this pull toward her like nothing I have ever experienced. I think it's why I could portal to a place I haven't even been to before." It's his only explanation for how he could get into the human realm after Fae portals between the worlds were shut over eighty years ago.

He stares at the fire, its warmth licking his cheeks. With a sigh, Del looks away before saying, "I've said I'm sorry, but I truly am for what happened to her. They're monsters for what they did."

She stands and walks over to his side of the cave. Bending down onto her knees, she places one hand over her heart and her other hand on his shoulder.

"I promise that for the rest of my days, I will protect and keep Estrid safe, even at the expense of my life."

"Del . . . ," Zain says, trying to interrupt his cousin before she makes an unbreakable Fae promise.

"No, this is something I want to do. Please," she says, looking at him with those bright green eyes.

The cave air gets thicker with magic as she recites the words in the ancient tongue that are needed to seal the oath in magic.

ᛗᚨ ᛚᛁᚹᛖ ᚹᛟᚱ ᚪᛟᚢᚱ ᛚᛁᚹᛖ

ᛁ ᛚᛚᛖᚾᚷᛖ ᛗᚨᛋᛗᛚᚹ ᛏᛟ ᚪᛟᚢ, ᛖᛋᛏᚱᛁᚾ ᛟᚹ ᛏᛟᚱᚾᛁᚹ

ᛏᛟ ᛚᚱᛟᛏᛖᛤᛏ, ᛏᛟ ᛋᛖᚱᚹᛖ ᚨᛏᚾ ᛤᚺᛖᚱᛁᛋᚺ

ᛗᚨᚾ ᛏᚺᛖ ᛟᛚᚾ ᚷᛟᚾᛋ ᛋᛖᛖ ᛏᚺᛖ ᛋᚨᛤᚱᛁᚹᛁᛤᛖ ᛗᚨᚾᛖ

ᚨᛤᚹᛏᛟᚹᛚᛖᚾᚷᛁᛏᚷ ᛏᚺᛖ ᚢᛏᛒᚱᛖᚨᚹᚨᛒᛚᛖ ᛒᛁᛏᚾᛁᛏᚷ

My life for your life
I pledge myself to you, Estrid of Nordia
To protect, to serve and cherish
May the old gods see the sacrifice made
Acknowledging the unbreakable binding

The fire burns more brilliantly, and the little sparks from the firewood dance around the cave.

"It is done. I'll forever protect her."

Del sits on the floor next to Estrid's feet, Zain beside her head.

Her protectors.

✦　✦　✦

CHAPTER SIXTEEN

Estrid's eyes flutter open. The roof above her head is made of stone, but it's different, smooth, and dome-shaped. The stone is more brown than gray.

A warm fire burns next to her. There are no drips of water. No creatures are scurrying around her, and the putrid smell of human waste no longer smothers her senses. Instead, the scent of damp earth mixed with wood fire awakens her, raises her awareness, and she realizes she isn't in the dungeon.

Around her, the dirt floor has been disturbed by footprints that lead out to the mouth of a cave. Water skins, food wraps, and jars full of silver balm resembling what Zella gave her in her cell litter the floor.

A fire in the center of the room pops and crackles as it radiates heat toward her. Little huffs of smoke dance through the air. Estrid's ears prick up to the sounds of voices approaching the cave.

"Do you think she's awake?" a familiar female voice asks, getting closer.

She tries to get up, but she pauses, wincing in pain. She's sore, though less than expected from what she remembered of her treatment by her father and Neros. Not knowing what to do, Estrid grabs a stick that sits in a pile, coming to crouch low into an attack position.

"I hope so," a familiar baritone voice says. "When my magic healed her, I could feel how bad—"

The words are cut off as Zain and Zella come into view at the cave's mouth.

"Estrid! You're awake," Zella says with glee, rushing into the cave. She gently hugs her, careful not to aggravate her injuries.

"What's going on? Where am I? Why is he here?"

Estrid breaks Zella's embrace to face Zain. She holds out the stick she'd grabbed. Her handle trembles as she holds out the stick, pointing it like a dagger at the man who betrayed her. She must look a fright, dried blood on her hair and covered in dirt.

"We're in the Dark Forest, Estrid. Zain, Alvey, and Del helped me break you out. They helped us get here. They won't hurt us," Zella says, kneeling in front of Estrid, her tone calm and soothing.

Zain stands at the cave mouth, rooted to the spot. His face is pinched with a pained expression on it. Estrid doesn't lower the stick she holds as she scowls at him.

"He betrayed me! How can you say they won't? He just stood there while Father hurt and humiliated me."

Zain steps back, holding up his hands and staring at Estrid. She tries not to let the tears in her eyes drop. She swallows down the sob forming in her throat like a ball.

"Zella, it's okay. I'll leave."

"No, Zain, don't go." Zella turns to her cousin. "Estrid, listen to me. Please, let us tell you everything. There's been a mistake. Zain didn't betray you. He helped you escape. He healed you."

If he didn't betray me, then who did?

Zella pries the stick from Estrid's hands, the rough bark scraping against her skin. Estrid falls into silence as Zella guides her to sit down.

The tension is disrupted when Del appears from the side of the cave's mouth. She walks in and looks straight at Estrid, her expression grim.

"I was the one who betrayed you, Estrid."

"Timing, Del! Worst timing!" Zella says, shaking her head at Del's terrible entrance.

Estrid sits in silence, furrowing her brow, looking between the three of them. Her thoughts are jumbled, confused at the events that have just transpired.

"What's going on? I don't understand," she says, wrapping her arms around her middle for comfort.

"We'll tell you everything, Estrid. It's a long story, but you're okay. I promise I won't let anything happen to you," Zella says, drawing Estrid into a hug.

The comfort of being embraced by her family calms her. Zella was always there for her. When Neros ran his dark experiments on Estrid, Zella was there to pick up the broken pieces.

Zain and Del sit at the cave entrance as Alvey and Imaya walk in.

"What did I miss? Is she . . . ?" Alvey looks at Estrid. With a grunt, he's pulled down by Del. Imaya sits beside him and gives Estrid a gentle wave and a small smile.

Zella takes Estrid's hand. "Okay, so let's start at the beginning, shall we?"

Estrid doesn't know what to feel as Zella finishes telling her about their escape. Feelings war for domination. Relief. Anger. Surprise. Grief.

Del betrayed me, but Zain did nothing to stop them from humiliating me. I want to hate them, but I can't. What Del did to me, to Rafe . . .

The thought of Rafe clears the fog over her head, and memories of her capture return. "Rafe!" Estrid says, launching herself at Del.

Surprised by the attack, Del doesn't have time to react as Estrid tackles her to the ground. The pain of her injuries is overtaken by rage.

Estrid throws punch after punch at her as she yells, "Rafe! The village! It's because of what you did!"

Angry tears form and run down her cheeks, taking some of the grime and dirt on her face with them. Strong arms wrap around Estrid as Zain tries to calm her down.

"Let me go, Zain!" she says, fighting him with what little strength she has as he pulls her away.

Alvey curses, rushing over to help a shocked Del sit up, both of them staring at Estrid.

Realizing he won't let go, Estrid slumps down in Zain's arms.

His cedar-and-bergamot scent hugs her. As much as she wants to fight it, it calms her. A heavy sob racks her body as sadness finally overtakes her anger.

Zain strokes her hair, whispering, "It's okay, Estrid. What happened to Rafe?"

Another sob.

"H-He's dead. They killed him," she says, trying to calm herself.

Zain's attention snaps to Del as he continues to hold Estrid.

"What!?" he says, narrowing his eyes on Del, who's still sitting on the ground, holding the sleeve of her shirt up against her split lip. "Rafe's dead?"

"Who's Rafe?" Zella asks, her eyes darting between everyone in the cave.

Estrid wriggles to get free of Zain as she yells, "He was my dog! He was my family. He's dead because you betrayed me!"

She digs her nails into Zain's arms. He releases her with a hiss as she charges over to Del again. She's livid. Murderous.

Zain intercepts her, holding his hands up to calm her down. Those bright blue eyes look at her with sadness and guilt. "Estrid, stop, please! I'm so sorry about Rafe, but we need to calm down."

Estrid uses her energy to push him away, hurt flashing in his eyes. That crack in her chest that she felt in the dungeon is back. She's reliving her suffering all over again. Her breaths become shorter. The tightness in her chest constricts, tightening around her lungs. The darkness stirs in her, but she's too weak.

"Get away from me! All of you, go away!"

None of this would have happened if I didn't save you.

Her legs wobble as she shakes with anger. "I want you out!"

Zain flinches as her words hit their mark. It should feel like a victory to Estrid, but the words hurt her as much as they do him. Estrid steps forward but stumbles, falling into a heap on the floor.

"Estrid!" Zella yells and comes to her aid, wrapping her arm under her.

Estrid stares at the dirt floor, her tears dripping down onto it. She can hear Zain stepping toward her, but he stops.

"She needs to rest," Zella says, grabbing Estrid's arm as a wave of tiredness takes over.

✦ ✦ ✦

Creatures of the night wake Estrid from a dreamless sleep. She looks around the dark cave, the fire having turned the piled logs in it to ash.

She can make out where the others were sleeping in its warm glow. Zella is next to her. Alvey and Del are beside each other at the back. Zain and Imaya are nowhere to be found. The outlines of where they should be asleep are barely visible.

Estrid sits in silence as the events of the last few days run through her mind. She winces as her words from earlier that day flow back to her. A low howl comes from outside, breaking her spiraling thoughts. It seems so familiar. She knows that sound.

Sitting up, she closes her eyes and focuses on the haunting howl. Like bone snapping back into place, Estrid realizes it sounds like Rafe.

She creeps over Zella and the others, careful not to rouse them, wincing at the dulling pain in her body.

Then she runs outside into the night.

"Rafe!" she whispers, trying not to wake the others. Silvery light spots dot the forest floor from the full moon above the canopy, allowing her to see enough not to fall over rocks and roots.

The howl continues, followed by the forest's evening sounds. The whoosh of owls' wings rushing through the trees, the odd screech, and the rustle of little creatures scurrying around.

"Rafe! I'm coming, Rafe!"

Estrid gets to a clearing, breathless. The howling suddenly stops. A deep silence follows it. The little hairs on her arms stand up.

She stops running and takes in the clearing that she's just stumbled into. Trees surround a large pond. Its flat, glassy surface reflects the clear night sky above, the water so still that it amplifies the haloed light from the moon and stars. Steam rises off it, giving an eerie feel. There's a soft trickle of water flowing upstream into the pond. It seems so familiar, but it's not. It's bigger than the little spot by her cottage. There are no boulders to hide behind, and the trees seem more imposing.

Estrid calls out for Rafe, but there's no response. Listening to the evening sounds as another creature cries far away, she waits. She knows this forest, the Dark Forest. She sighs in relief, finding comfort in being back home.

Looking down at her blood- and grime-encrusted body, she undresses and wades into the waters, the comfort of the warm water outweighing the uncertainty. Her hands and feet tingle within its warmth. It soothes her aches and bruises as she dips her head underneath.

When she resurfaces, Imaya is sitting on a rock beside the pool, the radiance of the moon bathing her in its cool light. Her skin almost glows under it.

Estrid watches her with suspicion. She may have been in the dungeon with her, but Estrid doesn't know her. She's had little luck with strangers lately. The pair regard each other as Imaya sits there, watching her.

"Why are you all still here?" Estrid asks.

Imaya stares at her and then lifts her head to the sky until the moon lights her face. Her long locks fall over her shoulders, and the pointed tips of her ears are visible from under her green-tinged hair.

Estrid gasps in surprise. Water splashes as she puts distance between herself and the strange Fae.

"Estrid . . . stop," Imaya says, her emerald eyes locking on Estrid.

"You're Fae. You're like them. Why haven't you left with them?" Estrid says, looking at those pointed tips.

Imaya nods in understanding, uncrossing her legs and sticking her feet in the warm water.

Estrid's been bombarded with many stories over the last few days. She doesn't want to stick around for whatever Imaya has to say. She heads to the pool's edge to get out, but Imaya is suddenly standing before her with lightning speed. Her face is no longer on the moon. The shadows in her sharp features make her look almost devil-like.

"We need to talk. This is important," Imaya says, taking a step back to give Estrid room to leave the pool.

Estrid eyes her cautiously, covering herself with her hands, but Imaya takes no notice. The cold air licks at the drops of water on her skin, making her shiver.

"Are you with Zain and his family?" she asks, calling on her magic to defend herself if she needs it.

"No," Imaya says, glancing down at Estrid's magic as it coils around her hand.

"Then why are you here?"

Imaya holds out Estrid's shirt for her. The Fae don't seem to have a big problem with nudity. When she met Del and Alvey, they were happy to strip down in front of her.

"I'm here for you."

The admission shocks Estrid as she pulls the tunic over herself. She steps back, twigs and leaves crunching under her feet as she crouches into a defensive stance, calling her magic out again.

"I won't hurt you. You were the person I was at Rodden's castle trying to rescue, but I failed," Imaya says with an embarrassed smile. "Instead, I got myself captured—for how long, I don't know."

Estrid regards Imaya as she hands Estrid her pants.

"I can help you find your true power and defeat Rodden," Imaya says, stepping back again to give Estrid space.

"What do you mean?" Estrid says, nerves bubbling in the pit of her stomach.

"I can't tell you more than that right now. You need to follow me to a tree in the Dark Forest. It's far to the north of here. If we find it, you'll find the truth behind your power," Imaya says.

Estrid is stunned into silence. *Aha, just like that, you expect me to believe you?*

She's about to turn away when Imaya grabs her arms. The seer's eyes roll back in her head, her grip on Estrid tightening, to the points that it bruises. In an ethereal voice, Imaya says, "If you don't defeat Rodden and the evil that surrounds him, everything dies. Stop him and save the people, but to do this, you must embrace your power."

Estrid stares at the strange Fae. A mixture of shock, horror, and curiosity floods her.

"Who are you?" she asks.

Imaya's grip loosens on her as her green eyes come back into focus. "I am your friend and ally. You can trust me, but you also need to trust Zain. To defeat what's coming, you must work together to stop the events unfolding."

A branch snaps in the forest, drawing Estrid's attention to its shadows. Something is out there, but she needs more information from Imaya.

When she looks back to where Imaya stood, she's gone.

Estrid pulls on her boot, confused by Imaya's cryptic vision. *What did she mean by embracing my power?*

She looks around her, taking everything in. *This place is strange.* It's the Dark Forest, but it feels different, more alive.

First, the howls that sounded like Rafe, drawing her out here. Then she has an eerie encounter with Imaya. The forest has stayed silent, as if waiting for something more to happen.

She slips on her other boot as another branch snaps. Estrid draws her magic to her. The soft silk of her magic, twirling around her fingers. More twigs break as leaves rustle. Focusing on the part of the woods that she just came from, she readies herself for whatever is coming.

The shadows move as the familiar tall, broad-shouldered figure of Zain steps through the trees, the moonlight driving away the darkness.

Estrid inhales. No matter how she feels about him, his beauty still takes her breath away. The gentle radiance of the moon enhances it. His blond hair turns silver, his bright blue eyes shine, and his skin radiates the light.

He stops dead, taking in Estrid's defensive stance. Then he holds up his hands, his brow furrowed in concern.

"I'm just checking you're okay. I was standing watch outside the cave and saw you run this way. I didn't think you wanted me to follow you, but when you never came back . . ." He drags his hand through his hair, which is loosely tied up.

Gods, I wish I could trust you. I wish you could hold me like I want. Like I need.

"Are you okay?"

No.

"I'm fine. You don't need to worry," she says, shaking herself from his spell.

He takes a few steps toward her but stops as she moves one step back. He sighs deeply, defeated. "Estrid . . . Estrid, I'm sorry . . . for everything."

I can't be near you. Her body betrays her mind every time she is close to him. She wants nothing more than to be in his arms, for him to hold her, ground her, but she's been through too much lately.

"I know it wasn't you," she says.

Zain looks at her and nods. His face is a mix of sadness and anger. "I've dealt with Del. She won't ever hurt you again."

"Apart from Zella, I don't know who to trust, Zain."

"You can trust me. You can always trust me."

He steps toward her. This time, she doesn't back away. He's inches in front of her, but she can't look him in the face. The look of pain in his eyes at her words isn't something she has the strength to deal with.

"I know," she whispers and looks away.

He reaches down and lifts her chin with his finger, looking into her eyes.

"Don't send us away. Let me work to earn your trust. I want nothing more than for us to be as we were before I left your cottage."

Zain moves his hands to cradle her shoulders, but she takes another step back. Giddiness at the thought of his touch sends electricity through her body.

Stop it, Estrid. Get a hold of yourself. Remember, you're angry with him.

He doesn't step away; she doesn't want him to.

"Please don't send me away," he says, brushing his fingers against hers.

"What about your alliance? What about your court?" she asks, stopping herself from reaching out to him.

Zain sighs. "I'll figure that out soon. I couldn't build an alliance with a monster who hurt you."

Argh, why do you say that sort of thing?

"Please let us stay, at least until I know you're safe. You don't trust me now, but I'll earn it back," he says, taking another step forward.

Afraid of what she might do, Estrid darts to the side, moving past him. Before she enters the thick, dark forest, she turns her head to look back. "I want to trust you, but I don't know how to get there."

+ + +

CHAPTER SEVENTEEN

Estrid's figure fades into the thick darkness of the trees. Zain gives a heavy sigh as he turns back to the clearing, his heart sinking at her parting words to him.

The air still carries her smell on it. He inhales, taking it in.

How are you going to get her to trust you?

A plop in the water disturbs him from his inner thoughts. He drowns out the sounds of the forest, tuning his ears to find the origin. Unsure, he slips back into the shadows, scanning the area. Nothing's there.

Plop.

The noise draws his attention to the middle of the pond—the glassy surface ripples. The steam around the pool thickens over its reflection. A stone comes hurtling out of the air and lands with another plop. Zain follows the line from where the pebble originated from as Imaya walks out into the moonlight.

"You know, you're the first Summer Court Fae I've ever met," she says, tossing another projectile into the water.

"You're only the second seer I've ever met in my lifetime. Your kind are rare and highly sought after," he says as Imaya sits at the pool's edge.

"What are you doing out in the forest so late?" he asks, taking in her unusual features, but her green eyes betray how young she is. Despite her age, Zain can feel the power radiating off her.

"I'm here to talk to you. I spoke with Estrid before." She gives him a small smile and gestures for him to come sit next to her. The moon is directly above them, chasing away what shadows linger over them.

Zain obliges and takes a seat beside her, his elbows hanging over his knees. Imaya's eyes glow in the blue moonlight as he waits for her to tell him more.

"What did you talk about?" he asks, his patience wearing thin.

"Estrid's going to need your help. The only thing that will stop what's coming is if she embraces who she is and finds her true power. She'll require you to do that."

Zain isn't sure how to respond to Imaya's words. *Estrid already has her magic.*

His thoughts are distracted when Imaya turns to face him, her eyes rolling back in her head. He moves away from the disturbing sight.

"To get back your court, you will be tied to your enemy forever," she says in a deeper voice that isn't hers. It's no longer sweet and innocent but malevolent and harsh.

"What are you trying to say?" Zain asks, bewildered by the vague tangent she's run off on.

Her eyes return to their regular green color as she gives him that innocent smile again. "Your power will only be enough to stop your uncle if you embrace some darkness."

Zain's mind whirls. *Darkness? Enemy? What are you on about?* He racks his brain, trying to recall his enemies. *Balius? Another Fae court? Rodden?* In his two hundred years of existence, he's made many enemies, too many to think of.

Consumed by his thoughts, he turns to dive into the cryptic message with the young seer, but she's gone.

✦ ✦ ✦

Zain's head is swimming from the strange information Imaya gave him. As he returns to the cave, silver light from the moon slices through gaps in the trees. He jumps with fright as Del emerges from the shadows.

"There's a scouting party of Nordian soldiers about ten miles from us. Neros must have used his magic to get them here. We need to leave," Del says, frowning.

Fuck! I thought we would have more time.

Del raises an eyebrow at him in suspicion. "Where have you been?"

"Checking on Estrid. She wandered out by herself. I wanted to make sure she was okay," Zain says, not stopping to chat. He doesn't feel like explaining any of Imaya's puzzling messages. Del may have made a Fae promise to keep Estrid safe, but she doesn't trust Imaya. Zain senses the young seer's power; it could easily deal with Del if she ever felt a true threat from his cousin.

"Where'd she go?" Del asks, keeping pace with him.

"For a walk in the forest," he says bluntly.

"What's your problem?"

"Nothing. Is she back?"

"She's in the cave. I saw her return, but I stayed out of sight. What happened between you two?" Del asks him as he keeps walking briskly, trying to avoid a deeper conversation with her.

For all her brashness, Del's like a dog with a scent that doesn't give up when there's a hint of something being wrong. He needs to give her something to throw her off interrogating him.

"Nothing happened. I said sorry and asked her not to send us away," Zain says, the warm orange glow of the fire outlining the mouth of the cave as they draw closer.

147

"Why?"

Her incessant questions are beginning to annoy him. Spinning around, he throws his arms in the air, needing her to stop interrogating him.

"We're going with them, Del, and I expect you to follow," he snaps.

Del abruptly stops, furrowing her brow as she tips her head in confusion. "What about the court and Balius?"

Zain takes a deep breath, pinching the bridge of his nose, not wanting to pull rank on her again. *She's trying to help you.*

"He'll have to wait. It's because of us that Estrid doesn't have a home. It's because of us that she was hurt and humiliated. We need to get her to safety, and then we can figure out how to deal with Balius."

Del gives him a single nod.

What, no questions? No argument?

He narrows his eyes, taking a step back from his cousin, waiting for her to object, but she merely nods and walks off.

✦ ✦ ✦

The start of a new day has done little to rid Zain of the revelations he got from Estrid and Imaya. He must cool his nerves before telling Estrid he's coming with her.

He takes a walk to revisit the pool from last night to bathe and clear his thoughts. The sound of trickling water flowing into it contrasts with the usual birdsong in the background. When he first arrived in the Dark Forest, the sounds were unfamiliar to him, but now they hold a special place in his heart, reminding him of the many mornings he woke up in Estrid's cottage.

He bends down to wash his face, the warm water ridding him of the nerves and fog of last night's sleeplessness. Light footsteps behind him have him turning to see Del step up to the water's edge.

"They're getting ready to leave. You need to come now if you want to talk to her," she says.

He looks up at the clear blue sky through a gap in the canopy. The sun radiates down onto the pond, the water so pristine that you can see the details of every gray stone.

I have to go with her. I have to see her to safety.

Del steps back to stand against a tree, watching him debate his approach.

"What's your plan?" she asks.

"No plan. I'll tell her I won't let her walk away."

Del grunts at his answer but doesn't offer an alternative solution; asking for permission isn't something Del has experience with.

They reach the cave as Estrid and Zella are packing the provisions into one of the sacks Zella brought. Alvey puts sand on the fire to douse the flames. Del shared the information about the scouting party with the group this morning, sending Estrid and Zella into a flurry of activity to erase any trace of themselves. The distance Zain put between them wouldn't have lasted forever, especially now that Neros knows Estrid has been living in the Dark Forest.

He takes a deep breath, trying to use the air to bolster up the courage to tell Estrid he's not letting her leave on her own. Stepping forward, taking another inhale, he blurts out, "We're coming with you. Rodden and his men aren't far behind. I can portal us further away and give you more time. Please, I want to make sure you're safe."

Zella and Estrid stop what they're doing and look at him, then at each other, a silent conversation bouncing between them. Zella gives Estrid a slight nod and a smile of reassurance; she's always been an ally for Zain.

While Estrid was recovering from her ordeal with Rodden, Zain got to know Zella better. She's a caring but strong woman who has endured much, like Estrid. There's a certain resilience that makes Zain think she can withstand almost anything. She certainly doesn't need anyone to keep her safe.

Before Estrid can answer, Del walks into the cave. Estrid's eyes flash with shadows before returning to their golden hue at the sight of his cousin. He blocks her view of Del and refocuses on his request.

"Please," Zain says, stepping toward Estrid, his tone more pleading, "just until we know you're safe. You can be done with us after that."

She turns to look at Imaya, who leans against the cave wall; a silent conversation happens between them. Estrid nods at the seer before returning to her packing.

Zella stands up and walks over to Zain to pat him on the shoulder, smiling at her cousin's decision.

"Make sure Del keeps some distance from us. Estrid doesn't trust her, nor do I," she tells him.

Zain tries to hide the smile on his face. He expected Estrid to protest and fight. She didn't agree to his direct request, but somehow, she didn't disagree to it.

Estrid packs the final few items while talking with Imaya. Her injuries have all but gone, her skin back to its sun-kissed tone, and she's smiling again.

Del lets out a little huff behind him, having overheard Zella's request.

"I want you to fly overhead, scout above the trees for Rodden and Neros," Zain says, nodding for her to get out of Estrid's way.

Del stomps out of the cave, grumbling to herself.

"Make sure you don't get a male bird hovering over you again, Del. You broke that poor bird's heart and wing," Alvey calls out after her, making everyone chuckle. He looks pleased with himself at getting a laugh out of the group of ladies.

"I'm glad we're sticking together. I've gotten fond of our little merry band," he says, lifting the mood further.

"I have to admit, Alvey, I would miss your bad jokes and stories far too much," Estrid says, making her way out of the cave.

"Well, for that, my lady, may I carry your bag?"

With a smile, Estrid hands him her pack.

Jealousy flares in Zain at his brother getting a laugh from her, but he locks it back down. He has to earn his way there.

"Where are we going?" Alvey asks the three women.

"To the far north of the Dark Forest," Imaya says without a glance back.

Over the next two days, they portal further north, deeper into the forest, putting distance between themselves and the threat of the Nordians. On the third day, the group steps through another portal made by Zain. The whirring sound of the air stops, like running water when a tap is shut off.

The atmosphere feels thick with magic, like a heavy mist hanging over the ground in the early mornings. The group takes in their new surroundings as they trek further into the dense woods. The familiar birdsong and buzz of insects are there, but sprites and other magical creatures make themselves known as their surroundings change. They zip past them as they navigate the terrain, causing mischief whenever they stop to rest, picking on Del in particular.

Zain can only guess it's because she's the grumpiest of the group. He watches as Estrid takes a bit of joy at his cousin's misfortune, making her laugh.

That night, the forest isn't dark or gloomy; rather, it lights up with plants that give off a luminescent glow. The familiar tunes of crickets, bugs, and owl hoots are joined by sounds of creatures they haven't yet seen. Their hauntingly beautiful songs soothe the weariness of the day and the ever-present possibility that their enemy is close behind. The temperature also lifts, turning warm and humid, despite them moving further north, where it should drop.

They sit around the campfire that night, Alvey trying his hardest to get closer to Zella. Zain watches Imaya as she observes Alvey and his failed attempts at wooing the human princess. The way she looks at him has Zain thinking she wishes it was her he was wooing, but Alvey brushes her off as a young Fae.

In the days since they rescued Imaya, she's regained some of her weight back. Her gaunt and sunken appearance has filled out, although she still has the traditional sharp features of a Fae. What they thought was a mold tainting the color turned out to just be her dark green hair. Since being in air charged with magic, she's developed emerald markings along her cheeks. Zain has only seen symbols like that once before, on another seer he'd encountered over a hundred years ago.

Zain doesn't let the opportunity of Imaya and Zella being distracted go to waste. He tries to get closer to Estrid, breaking down her walls, attempting to redeem himself. She gives him a small smile, laughs at his jokes, and is happy to sit next to him.

Del has caught a few creatures resembling rabbits in her hawk form to roast over the fire. Alvey sits with Imaya and Zella, joking and chatting about the little sprite who hasn't left Del in a few days, despite her shooing it away constantly. It sits on her shoulder, braiding some of her hair into a little cocoon.

"I think you have a new housemate, Del," Zella chuckles.

Del looks down to her shoulder and huffs, the little creature waving to her. Its yellow glow hides its features, but there's a high-pitched hum as it tries to talk to her. Although Estrid is still not on good terms with Del, she giggles at seeing a mighty warrior having such a tiny creature taken with her.

Estrid's laugh is like warm nectar going down his throat. It soothes him but also sends a tingle of excitement in him. There are only a few inches that separate them from touching. When a stray piece of hair escapes her braid, he has to restrain himself from reaching out to tuck it back as an excuse to feel her skin against his. He knows his time to win her over is limited. Imaya has led them so far, but she's never said where she expects to go or how long it'll take them to get there.

"How far away are we from this place?" Zain asks Imaya as Estrid finishes her food. Those honey-gold eyes lock on his. He tries to focus on them, but his attention drifts down to her soft lips. The memory of how well they fit against his is still fresh in his mind.

"Maybe one more portal, and then we should be there," Imaya says, shrugging as she moves her gaze off Alvey to Zain.

"How do you know where you're going?" Alvey asks, sucking on a bone.

"I'm a seer. I see things and use it as a rough guide of where to go, but I never know exactly when or how long it'll take." Imaya shrugs. "If I knew everything, it would all be too easy. That's not the way it works."

"So, how *does* it work? How can we be certain you aren't guiding us toward our demise?" Del says, using her dagger to pick the last bits of meat from the bony carcass of an animal they roasted.

"I told you, I see things, but not the complete picture. I can't see it all, as there are too many variables for change that can impact the ultimate vision."

The group doesn't seem to mind Imaya's answer, apart from Del, who storms off, saying she'll take the first watch, the little sprite following her.

"Is she always grumpy?" Zella half teases as they watch Del disappear.

"I think her sprite friend has softened her and made her extra sensitive," Alvey jokes, looking over his shoulder to ensure she doesn't return to give him a wallop.

The fire crackles, and the forest sings its evening song as the group sits in silence.

"She hasn't always been a grump," Zain says in a sad tone, staring into the flickering flames. "When we were younglings, she had the most infectious laugh. She told the best jokes, but that changed when her parents died. She trusts hardly anyone outside of Alvey and me."

Zain observes Estrid while he says this. She doesn't react or respond; she just stares into the warm fire.

"How did they die?" Zella asks in a melancholy tone.

"That's not my story to tell," he says, thinking back to that day when they were so young.

✦ ✦ ✦

CHAPTER EIGHTEEN

As soon as the early-morning sun breaks through the tree canopy, the group sets out on what they expect will be their last day's travel to an unknown destination.

From how Zain's eyes dart around, Estrid can tell that it makes him nervous, but he doesn't question it for her sake. The forest surroundings haven't changed, but the atmosphere around them has. It feels closer to another world than the one she's grown up in.

Estrid feels calmer and more at ease with herself, her companions, and the surroundings. The hole in her chest from Del's betrayal that led to Rafe's death hasn't closed, but the sharp edges of pain accompanying it have dulled.

She's not sure what to do about Zain. He didn't betray her, but she can't quite bring herself to forgive him yet. Her body responds to his nearness, which she feels is like fighting a losing battle. She's noticed that Zain has been considerate, caring, and observant to her during their travels.

As their party has ventured through the Dark Forest, he hasn't left her side, but he has given her enough space to make her not feel uncomfortable. Now and then, if she slipped or missed a step, his large but gentle hands would catch her arm or support her, the lightest of touches sending electricity through her body.

He walks next to her today, focused on the path ahead. She looks at his face, taking in his beauty. His skin is smooth, his sharp jawline defines his flawless Fae features, and his broad shoulders sit back, strong and proud. She wonders how the tips of his pointed ears would feel against her fingertips.

"Something wrong?" Zain asks, halting her thoughts.

"No, nothing's wrong. I was just, uh . . . just looking."

Her cheeks flush, and she glances away from him, hiding her embarrassment, before clearing her throat and focusing on the path ahead. The broad smile on his face makes her blush.

"I see. Anything worth noting?" he says in a light, teasing tone.

An awkward silence hangs between them. Estrid's cheeks go from rosy pink to what feels like a ruby red.

"I was, um . . . looking at your ears. They're quite amazing," she says, clapping a hand over her mouth as soon as the words tumble out.

At her admission, Zain lets out a low chuckle, the vibrations setting off all sorts of responses in her body.

"You know, a Fae's ears are particularly sensitive," he says, leaning into her.

His breath is a gentle brush on her skin, and she sucks in a shocked gasp, his proximity sending a shiver down her spine and a jolt of lust to her core. She turns to look at him, his gaze heavy with desire.

Completely distracted by him, she stumbles over a rock on the path. Zain catches her arm before she falls.

"Oh! No, I didn't know that," she blubbers, blushing even more with that knowledge as she stares into his eyes. They dance with gold flecks and mischief.

Gathering her composure, she straightens herself up. Zain is about to say something when there's a whistle from the front of the group. Estrid freezes, scanning the forest on high alert. Zain gives a hand signal to Del, who flies above them in her hawk form. She responds with a screech, coming down to the ground. She lands, transforming in one smooth and graceful movement.

"What's going on?"

Neither responds to her question as they all run to where Alvey and Zella are standing. Imaya sits cross-legged on the ground. Her green eyes are completely white, her mouth opening a fraction as she performs a chant in an unfamiliar language.

"What's going on?" Del asks again, looking at Alvey.

He shrugs, as confused as the rest of the group, but concern is etched on his face.

Imaya's chanting gathers speed, the words spilling out faster and faster. The air gets thicker around them. It pops and crackles. The hairs on Estrid's skin stand on end, her nerves on high alert. She's never experienced magic like this. Never felt power like it.

There's a sharp hiss on her right as Zain draws his sword. Alvey reaches for his too.

Estrid goes to pull out her dagger, but the mystical energy in the air grows so thick, it becomes hard to breathe in, like water filling her lungs. Suffocating. Black spots fill her vision. She can't get any air.

It suddenly stops. They all drop to the ground, gasping and choking, trying to suck air back in.

Estrid looks over to Imaya, whose eyes have returned to their normal green, a look of determination on her face.

"We're here," the seer announces to the group, who're perplexed at what just happened.

Estrid glances at Zain. He stares at her, scanning her for any injuries. She nods to him and gets up. Imaya gets to her feet as well, bringing Alvey along with her to the right of where they're still hunched over, recovering from what just happened.

"We should make camp over here," Imaya says matter-of-factly.

Everyone takes in the surroundings of the small shaded clearing she's referring to. It's completely bare; not even the grass seems to grow beneath their feet.

"Okay, so where exactly *is* here?" Del says in an irritated tone, clearly uncomfortable with the experience they just had.

"Not sure, but I know this is our destination," Imaya says, sticking out her tongue as Del rolls her eyes.

The two women continue to silently battle each other as Zain tells them to make camp. The light is fading as dusk settles in, and the luminescent plants surrounding them glow, starkly contrasting the upcoming darkness.

The group assembles a small camp, gathering firewood, erecting a little shelter, and foraging for food. Zella finds berries, nuts, and some apple-like fruit. Del returns with some more rabbit-like creatures to roast over the crackling flames. They huddle near the warm fire, shaken from their earlier experience.

Alvey clears his throat to break the silence. "Want to hear a story about our mighty Zain as a youngling?"

Zain groans at his brother, who has a silly smile on his face, his eyes twinkling in mischief.

Intrigued by Zain as a young Fae, Estrid nods along with the others as they tuck into their evening meal.

"When we were younglings, the three of us used to play pretend battle games against the evil Shadow Monsters. In one particular game, Del dared Zain to ring the bell in the tower in the palace." Alvey gestures to Del, who sits there with a smirk on her face.

"Keep in mind that we were forbidden to go near this bell. But not one to back down from a challenge, our wee Zain went up and rang the damn thing," Alvey says.

Zain shakes his head, but he's smiling.

"Del said it was enchanted and wouldn't work unless I used special words to activate it," he explains, laughing at his brother and throwing his hands up in mock protest.

Del scoffs at him.

Estrid enjoys watching the trio. They're so close, much like her and Zella, but with happier memories. Zain smiles and relaxes, something she hasn't seen him do since their time in her cottage.

"Anyway, Zain goes up and rings the huge bell . . . and sends the entire city—not a town, but a city full of Fae—into a frenzy, as they think we're being attacked! You should have seen Zain's face," Alvey says, almost rolling on the ground with laughter. "He was white as a sheet as the chaos unfolded."

"What happened next?" Estrid asks, the light-hearted banter taking the weight off the day.

Zain catches her eye, rolling his as he smiles at Alvey.

"Well, we were all clipped around the ears by our parents," Alvey says.

"Ah, don't forget that we were made to clean the stables for an entire month as punishment," Zain chips in, throwing a small bone at his brother.

"And I was told to make better friends!" Del says, shaking her head.

"Ah, yes, that's right, Del. Your mother and father thought we young princes were a bad influence on you, didn't they? Little did they know you were the troublemaker amongst us," Alvey says with a smirk as Del protests her innocence.

"Tell us some more," Imaya says, smiling at Alvey.

After a few more stories about the Summer Court and the Fae realm, Estrid gets up, needing to get away from the group and clear her head, intuition telling her to prepare for their next challenge.

She walks into the forest, far enough away that it muffles everyone's voices. She finds a bright spot of tall grassy bushes; the blades' tips glow a vibrant orange as they tickle her hands. The sounds of night surround her, creatures playing their songs as the small ribbits of frogs echo.

Estrid sits down, drawing in a deep inhale, the air refreshing. She listens to the rhythmic noises.

You'll have to use your magic soon, something hidden in her mind says.

The thought of using her power always sets off conflicting feelings within her. Fear of what it can do. Guilt for the lives taken by it. Worry about what her companions might think of her. These emotions war for her attention.

You'll need to use it to set yourself free. Don't be afraid; embrace it. Stop fighting it, that inner voice says.

As these thoughts consume her, she doesn't hear Zain walk up behind her, making her jump.

He pauses, gesturing to the spot inches from her. "Mind if I sit with you?"

Estrid nods and smiles, swallowing down the nerves growing in her stomach. It's the first time they've been alone since her cottage.

He sits next to her, just brushing her shoulder with his. Having him this close to her is comforting; it always has been. His golden hair is half up, half down. She wants to reach out and touch him. Have those lips on hers.

As if sensing her thoughts, he turns to look at her, asking, "What are you thinking?" He shuffles closer to her, their shoulders flush against each other, sending a jolt of excitement down her arm.

She's not ready to admit that she can only think about his kiss or the feel of him caressing her skin.

"Something's telling me to use my magic. I don't know what or why I think I need to do it," she says as a lump drives its way up from the pit in her stomach and lodges in her throat from fear.

"I'm scared one of you will get hurt," she continues, swallowing the tightness down and drawing a deep, shaky breath. It's taking a lot for her to admit this to him, to acknowledge the danger of her magic. She hugs her knees to her chest to form a protective barrier.

Zain unclasps his hands and moves to sit in front of her. "I'm here with you. You won't hurt anyone. If your gut tells you to use it, use it."

She looks at him, those blue eyes staring deep into her soul and not flinching. He holds out his palms for her to take.

"I'm here, Estrid. Nothing bad will happen. I won't let it."

She hesitates before placing her hands in his. They're warm, cocooning hers. They sit there for a minute, not saying a word.

Zain moves in closer and pauses as he dips his head, waiting for her approval to kiss her. She doesn't move away, and he presses his lips against hers, gentle and soft. She pushes forward, cupping his face and deepening their kiss, opening her mouth and inviting him in. His tongue sweeps in, caressing hers as she moves her body closer to his. He doesn't need much of an invitation as he brings his hands to her waist before lowering them to cradle her ass, pulling their bodies together. Their kisses become urgent, having been deprived of their needs since they left her cottage.

Zain pauses their heated exchange and places his forehead on hers. Their breaths come out fast and ragged. There's a rustling of bushes to their left, and they break apart from their hold on each other.

"Oh shit! Sorry, I was coming to check on you," Zella says, turning away as she stumbles through a bush that disturbs a tiny swarm of fireflies. They float through the night with yellow glowing bodies shimmering.

With a sigh, Estrid pulls away.

"We should get back," she says, squeezing Zain's hand as she helps him up.

Once they're standing, she kisses him on the cheek and then walks over to Zella. Estrid knows her cousin's interruption wasn't intentional, but she feels like swatting her anyway for breaking an intimate moment.

Zain stands behind her, rubbing the back of his neck, as she walks to camp with Zella, arm in arm. A smile breaks on her face for the first time in weeks.

"So, you two seem to be better, then?" Zella says, elbowing her cousin as they walk along.

"Better, though it doesn't dismiss what happened . . . but I'm sick of fighting this urge to be near him." Her cheeks flush with embarrassment at being caught kissing someone.

"Well, you're happy. That's all that matters." Zella smiles at Estrid, giving her arm a little squeeze, but her smile quickly fades as they enter the clearing, rejoining Del, Imaya, and Alvey. Del has a deeper-than-usual scowl on her face, her arms folded as she leans against a tree, just staring at Imaya.

"What's going on?" Estrid asks, looking between Zella and the rest of the group.

"We need to find the dead tree," Imaya tells the group casually. She picks up a few nuts, popping them into her mouth.

Zella tilts her head toward Estrid and whispers, "It's why I came to get you. This is stranger than usual. She's been talking about a dead tree since you left."

"The what now?" Zain appears beside Estrid and Zella, and Zella jumps with fright, swatting him for his silent arrival.

"The dead tree. Tomorrow, we need to find it," Imaya repeats with a mouthful of food as Del narrows her eyes.

Alvey gets up and starts pacing back and forth, drawing his hand through his long blond hair.

"Ahh, does no one here have a problem with the fact that she's trying to find a creepy tree?" he says, stopping to look at Zain for some support, but he gets none. Alvey flops back down onto the log he was sitting on.

"I need to use my magic on it," Estrid says to silence the group.

Del pushes off the tree she's leaning against and moves toward Estrid, a challenge in her posture and a look of suspicion on her face.

Zain intercepts her and says, "Don't, Del. Estrid has to use it. She can control it, and we're here to help her."

Del stops just short of going chest to chest with Zain, grunting in response. Imaya gives Estrid a cheery smile and a thumbs up, which draws a heavy breath and a shake of Alvey's head as Zella laughs at him.

"Let's get some rest," Zain says, placing his hand on the small of Estrid's back to guide her to a spot near the fire.

The silence of something to come hangs over the group as they drift off to sleep.

✦　✦　✦

CHAPTER NINETEEN

Imaya rouses the group early the next morning. Her excitement doesn't resonate with the rest of them as she leads them toward the strange and unknown thing. The forest thins after about an hour of walking, exposing a barren area where nothing grows.

In the middle sits a tree that resembles a crooked elm that's ten feet tall and completely black, as if it's been charred and burnt by furious red fire. A pulse of magic radiates off it, like the beat of a heart. Their group stops at the edge of the open space, lost for words at the strange sight. Estrid glances at Imaya for direction, but all she gets is a bright smile.

"Okay, so now what? We chop down the creepy tree?" Del asks.

Alvey gestures for her to move forward, earning him a death stare. "Ladies first, Del."

No one moves, but something calls to Estrid, like a siren drawing her in. The pull strengthens, tightening her chest.

She takes a hesitant step ahead. Then another. Another. Her feet feel like they're weighed down with lead. Once she's standing in front of the tree, she looks up.

Zain comes to stand beside her. He places his hand on her back, reassuring her. "I'm here."

Estrid inhales and digs down deep into herself, unlocking the box inside her that has held her magic. Breathing out, she releases it like a cascade of warm water down her body. She places her palms face down on the bark, willing it to flow from her into the rough surface beneath her palms.

Black tethers leave her hands and press into the dark wood. The group gasps in awe as she burrows deeper, pushing more power into it. Sweat glistens on her forehead as she can feel it leeching energy from her.

The tree absorbs Estrid's power like a plant starved of water. It starts to creak and moan under the pressure. The air fills with the smell of charred wood as it groans louder. She can feel Zain standing beside her, his presence comforting and sure.

"Keep going, Estrid." His hand is unmoving from her back as beads of sweat drip down her brow.

She hears the others move to stand directly behind her. With a final groan, a deafening crack punctures the air, and the tree splits down the middle. Her magic stops, and she peers down. The proud trunk is severed in two, like an axe has cleaved right through it.

The two halves fall to either side. At the bottom of the crack, there's a giant hole in the ground.

Time stops. They all hold their breath.

Waiting.

Waiting.

Nothing happens. The forest calls start again as everyone lets out a breath of relief.

"Well, that was underwhelming," Alvey says, followed by an "Ow" from Del swatting him.

Lost for words, Estrid stares at the unearthly sight. An unending black hole stares back at them.

Shadowy dark tendrils burst out of the cavity like steam overflowing from a boiling pot, knocking Estrid and Zain back. They take a moment to register what's happening.

Then shouts erupt from the group as they jump into action. The sharp hissing of metal being drawn zips through the air as swords and daggers are unsheathed. Black barbs of magic rush at them like spears thrown at an oncoming army.

"Get back now!" Zain yells, stepping back as the dark energy speeds in their direction. More tendrils keep rising out of the hole from the tree into the air like snakes being charmed out of a basket.

Estrid stops moving back, Zain at her side in an instant.

"Estrid, get back!" he shouts.

"No, wait. I can stop it," she says, stepping forward.

The magic abruptly halts around her as if it recognizes her. Its sharp ends turn soft as it caresses her hands and wrists, running up her body and encircling her.

"Estrid!" Zain yells for her, but Imaya grabs him.

The tendrils rush out of the hole in the earth like a geyser erupting. The ground shakes as a dark figure with leathery wings steps out of the mass of shadows that shoots out of the tree. Two piercing, glowing green eyes stare out at the group as the darkness wraps around it.

Estrid can't move, her body frozen, watching the streams of magic making their way up her arms, oblivious to the figure in front of her.

"Shadow King!" Zain yells behind her as he pushes past Imaya and rushes forward with Del and Alvey.

The glowing emerald eyes dart to focus on the trio before the dark magic rushes for them.

"No! Stop!" Estrid says as she rushes to place herself between the three of them and the approaching shadows.

The magic knocks into her body. Her back arches as the power rushes into her. She absorbs it, that warm feeling of running water, much like hers feels, flowing through her. As quickly as the tendrils appeared, they recede, leaving the dark figure standing at the mouth of the broken tree.

"It can't be," the broad-shouldered Fae says as it takes a wobbled step toward her.

Estrid furrows her brow at the foreboding creature, her body fixed to the spot in shock as a seven-foot-tall Fae approaches her. His sharp, angular features soften as he takes her in. She can hear the muffled shouts of Zain and her companions telling her to get back, but she just stares at the massive Fae in front of her.

Transfixed by him, Estrid doesn't move, but she feels Zain's hand grab her wrist. He pulls her into him, wrapping his arm around her. His other hand points his sword at the dark figure.

"Get back!"

"Out of my way, Princeling," the mysterious Fae says, encircling a rope of magic around Zain's arm, holding his blade. It yanks hard, disarming him.

Zain lets go of Estrid, pushing her behind him as he takes another step in the direction of the Shadow King. Another tendril darts forward and slaps him out of the way like a rag doll. The Shadow King emits a menacing laugh.

"Zain!" Estrid shouts, running after him. She helps him get back to his feet, watching as he goes to unsheathe his dagger from a leather holster strapped to his left side.

Before the winged Fae can take another swipe at Zain, Del steps out from the other side of the clearing, her sword raised, her expression set to an angry scowl that promises death.

"I've been waiting a long time to get you back for the death of my parents, Shadow King. Your blood will flow today."

She barrels toward the king when another Fae bursts out of the hole and tackles her to the ground.

The figure is in head-to-toe black leather armor, with wings like the king. It pins her to the earthen floor with the force of its wings. Del's shrieks are frantic as the second assailant traps her.

Alvey, Zella, and Zain run to her aid, swords and daggers drawn to attack. Imaya watches on from one side. Estrid looks at the seer, who gives her a slight nod as the chaos unfolds.

"Stop!" Estrid says, throwing out her magic to the king and his man. It does nothing to them besides making them stare at her in shock. The two Fae exchange a glance and a look of awe.

The king nods to his guard, who gets off Del but doesn't return her sword. The female warrior seethes at him.

Estrid observes the strange Fae. Skin so fair, it's almost translucent. He has sharp, angular features, but his eyes seem so familiar, though she can't pinpoint from where.

Her magic seems to calm the situation, like a tornado easing into a simple breeze. The Shadow King moves to stand in front of her, hands up in surrender. Estrid pulls her dagger, but that draws a deep chuckle from the king as he shakes his head, long black hair cascading down to his shoulders.

"You have your mother's spirit . . . and her eyes," he says, the smile disappearing from his face. A sad frown replaces it.

"Come. We have much to discuss," the king orders before turning around to go back down the opening at the base of the fallen tree.

Estrid stands unmoving in the same spot, shocked. Her heart beats like it's about to jump out of her chest.

What? How do you know my mother? You're Fae. I'm so confused.

She looks at Imaya, who's made her way over to the gap without hesitation. As if she can sense Estrid's uncertainty, Imaya looks over her shoulder and waves for Estrid and their travelling party to follow her.

Alvey goes to grab Imaya and pull her back, but she dodges his grasp and inches forward to the dark abyss. Zain stands near her, dagger still drawn, blood dripping down his head from where he hit a tree after being thrown by the king's magic.

"We're not going anywhere with you! Estrid, don't follow these Fae. They can't be trusted!" he shouts.

A gust of wind blows out around them, sending debris flying in all directions. Estrid yelps in surprise as the Shadow King uses his wings to charge at Zain. The king towers over Zain. Massive wings shroud everyone in a dark shade.

The Shadow King narrows his eyes and lets out a low snarl. "Don't talk to me of evil and trust, Princeling. Your court doesn't have the cleanest reputation."

Zain doesn't back down. Del creeps toward the other Fae, ready to remove her sword and his head if she could have her way. Imaya has one foot in the tree's hole as Alvey and Zella call for her to step back.

Like an itch that won't go away, something tells Estrid she needs to be here. She's meant to meet these Fae.

The seer nods with encouragement to confirm her gut feeling.

Estrid reaches for Zain's arm and gently squeezes it until he looks at her. "This is meant to happen. I need to go with them. Come with me?"

His blue eyes are murderous as he takes in the Shadow King in his black leather armor. "Estrid, these Fae, they're evil. They—"

She squeezes his arm with a little more urgency. The furious look in his eyes melts away, concern replacing it as they soften.

"I'm going to go with them, Zain. You've kept your promise to get me to safety. This is it. I release you from any further obligation," she says, not compromising. The magic she's found here feels like the most normal thing to her, like home. She searches Zain's face, hoping he'll change his mind because hers won't.

The gold flecks in his eyes dance from the power that he's trying to contain.

"Please come with me," she pleads.

Zain's eyes dart from her to the Shadow King.

Please come with me.

He narrows his eyes, face set into a hard-line expression as he turns back to the Shadow King. "How can we trust you?"

The king huffs, giving Zain a look of disdain at the question. He folds his muscular arms over his chest and stares at Estrid.

"You can't, Princeling . . . but you can trust her."

Estrid can feel Zain's eyes shift back to her. There's a muted chink as he sheaths his dagger and possessively wraps his arm around her.

Alvey and Del let out a slew of curses and objections at his decision as Estrid's chest warms at Zain's choice to stay with her.

"We'll go with you, but you need to swear nothing will happen to Estrid," Zain says to the Shadow King.

As if Zain's said the most absurd thing in the world, the domineering king breaks out in a smile. His radiant face is something Estrid can only describe as beautiful. His deathly sharp facial features soften, slight dimples forming on either side of his cheeks.

The king places his hand over his heart. "I swear on my life, Princeling, nothing bad will happen to Estrid or any of her friends."

With that, he turns and gives his guard a nod to step through the hole.

Imaya smiles at them, saying, "This is the right path . . . for both of you," as she jumps through the hole.

Alvey lets out a moan of protest before leaping in after her. As much as the young Fae annoys him, he's protective of her.

Zella follows them, yelping as she disappears through the tree.

"Zain, come on! Don't do this," Del says, standing beside them. She doesn't look angry anymore, just scared.

✦ ✦ ✦

CHAPTER TWENTY

Estrid and her travelling party make it through the hole in the tree, which turns out to be a portal. According to Alvey, long-standing portals like that had been closed from the human realm when his and Zain's father, King Lanard, stopped trading decades ago. This one isn't like Zain's, where she can see her destination on the other side. This portal is like stepping into the dark and waiting for the light to find you.

I don't think I can ever get used to portals. It feels like a heavy veil is being pulled from their faces.

The coolness gives way to the brightness of a large marble room well lit by bright orbs of light. Estrid blinks her eyes, taking in the space they've just landed in. The Shadow King waits for them in a chamber made of stone that's carved with intricate designs and sculpted smoothly.

"Welcome to the Shadow Court. Follow me," he says, gesturing for them to come along.

They walk down a hallway adorned with large chandeliers suspended from the ceiling. Unlike the castle in Oberetta, the walls here don't have lavish paintings or giant tapestries hanging off them. Instead, they have intricate patterns chiseled into them.

The pictures and designs seem to come alive beneath the chandelier light. The shadows between the structures dance and move as the light catches different angles as you walk by.

Estrid studies the hallway in fascination. They soon encounter other Fae who curtsy and bow to the king as he walks past them. He greets them back individually by name, a genuine familiarity in his tone. Whispers follow the group as they weave through the passageways.

Estrid stares at the Fae as they pass. None are alike, nor are they like Zain and his family. One has antlers coming from her head, while another resembles some reptile with patterned skin and slits for eyes. They make their way through a maze of hallways, encountering more Fae who must be servants and courtiers along the way.

Her attention turns to Zain, Alvey, and Del, who look uncomfortably around them. She leans over to Zain, who hasn't left her side, and whispers, "How are they different from you?"

"They're lesser Fae. Be careful; they can't be trusted," Zain says, eyeing the one with reptile-like skin. He takes Estrid's hand, pulling her closer to him.

The Shadow King slows down in front of them, coming to walk next to Zain and Estrid.

"They are Fae, Princeling," he says with an annoyed glare at Zain. "Many choose to live here, where they are more widely accepted for who they are, rather than live in one of the upper courts, where they are dismissed for being lower caste." He smiles at Estrid, his tone dismissive of Zain's comments.

Lesser Fae? What are they? The books said nothing about them.

Before she can ask why, they reach a set of large, dusky, gold, wooden double doors that stretch three stories high. There's no command given as they glide apart, the air getting sucked through.

Estrid lets out a gasp of wonder at the most beautiful throne room she has ever seen. Even Alvey and Del's bickering goes silent as they enter, taking in the enormous space before them. The ceiling is like a delicate spider's web of thin, smooth marble beams that form unique designs and shapes as the group moves through the room.

Despite being in the Shadow realm, the space is lit by a dull light, like a sunset. It streams in from the windows and overhead from the roof. It's empty apart from a throne carved of black stone atop a dais at the opposite end. It's simple, with a high oval back and delicately carved designs.

As they come to the center of the vast space, the Shadow King waves his hand, conjuring a large rectangular table with six chairs on either side and a throne-like chair at the head.

"Please, sit. I've asked for some food and drinks to be brought for you. I imagine you must be hungry," he says, taking a seat in the throne-like chair. He gestures for Estrid to sit to his left but leaves the vacant seat opposite her on his right. She spares Zain a glance and catches a hint of annoyance at being dismissed.

An awkward silence descends over them. The three Summer Fae look on edge. Del's eyes scan the room for all the exits and threats. Alvey leans close to Zella, and Zain fixes his narrowed gaze on the king. The silence is so dense, Estrid can hear the breath of each person in the room.

She can't take it anymore and remembers something the Shadow King said to her when he first found them. "You said you knew my mother?"

He sits on his high-backed chair, his hand on his chin, watching her. His eyes change from a bright shade of green to a darker one at her question, and sadness washes over the room.

"Please, call me Cethin. I knew your mother very well. She was . . . an amazing ruler. Smart. Kind. Fair. She wouldn't suffer fools gladly."

He gives her a sad half-smile that reminds Estrid of the hole in her heart from never knowing her mother, who'd died giving birth to her. That guilt always sat heavily in her heart.

"You look so much like her," King Cethin says sorrowfully.

"You said she was a ruler. So, she was the queen of Nordia?" Zain asks.

"No, Princeling, Eria was no human queen. Estrid's mother was Queen Eria of the Winter Court."

Zain and Del gasp in shock as Alvey chokes on his own breath. Estrid looks at the three Fae in confusion while they stare at King Cethin as if he's dropped a magical bombshell on them.

How? Rodden's my father. She had to be human.

Zella stares at Estrid, her brow furrowed.

"You mean the lost Queen Eria?" Alvey asks, trying to catch his breath. His eyes go wide with surprise as King Cethin nods in response.

Zain reaches for Estrid's hand, squeezing it as she looks at him.

"What do you mean, the lost Queen Eria?" Estrid asks, her thoughts whirling in her head.

"Your mother disappeared from Faery without a trace nineteen years ago," Cethin says, looking at Zain for confirmation.

Zain nods with acknowledgement of this as truth.

"What happened to her?" Estrid asks, a little overwhelmed by Cethin's first admission of her mother.

Because of Rodden, she's always known herself as a royal, but he never spoke of her mother. There were never any paintings or descriptions of her while Estrid was growing up. Whenever she asked Rodden about her, he'd shut down the conversation.

The realization hits Estrid like a wave slapping the shore.

I'm half Fae.

Cethin sits up straight, observing them all, but his attention is locked on Estrid. "To answer your first question, I don't know what happened to her. We think someone in the other courts betrayed her. That's all I know. I've spent decades trying to figure out who did it. To the question you haven't asked, I am your father, Estrid."

Stunned silence hangs over the table. Everyone, including Estrid, stares at King Cethin in disbelief.

What? You can't be. Rodden, he—

Her train of thought stops as Zain drops her hand.

She turns to him. He looks like a bucket of cold water has been thrown on him, his golden skin now a much paler shade.

Estrid's confusion turns to hurt at his reaction. Her gaze bounces between Cethin and then back to Zain.

Cethin smirks as Zain clenches his jaw. Estrid looks around and down the table. Del has a sour look on her face, her lips pressed into a thin line, as Alvey sits there with his jaw gaping open and staring at Estrid.

The deep silence is interrupted by the enormous doors to the throne room whisking open. Heavy footsteps make their way to the table with an echoing thud. Estrid watches Cethin as he turns to look at who entered the room.

"Faris! Thank you for joining us."

He smiles as a warrior approaches the table, dressed in full black leather armor like Cethin's.

The warrior gives him a quick bow. "My king, apologies for being late. There's been some unusual activity around the borders. A portal has opened up for the first time in decades."

The broad-shouldered Fae named Faris sits to Cethin's right, directly opposite Estrid. She looks over the table at him. He has short waves of black-brown hair that sit just above his shoulders. His eyes are a deep, bottomless brown. His skin is a deep shade of olive, making them even more profound. Like Cethin and all the other Fae, his facial features are sharp, but unlike Cethin, Faris has a set of wings covered in jet-black feathers.

"Faris, I'd like you to meet Estrid, my daughter," Cethin says, gesturing to Estrid.

Faris's eyes widen with shock for a moment. Quickly composing himself, he gives her a dazzling smile that makes him look almost boyish. With a slight bow of his head to Estrid, he looks to Cethin.

"How?" Faris says before returning his focus to Estrid. The initial shock of the news washes over him as he relaxes back into his seat. He lounges, trying to be casual, but his eyes betray his cautiousness.

Down the table, someone clears their throat.

"Ah, yes, I almost forgot. These are Estrid's companions. Three of them you are very familiar with," Cethin says.

Faris looks at the other Fae with what can only be hatred. He lurches from his chair, knocking it over and reaching for his sword. "What are they doing here?"

Cethin grabs Faris's arm, pulling him back into his seat. Faris grits his teeth at the Summer Fae, hostility dripping from him.

Estrid looks to Zain, who returns Faris's hostile glare with one of his own, as does Del, but Alvey just glances around the room as if bored by the whole encounter.

"Good to see you again, General Faris. It's been decades since I've had the pleasure of cutting your warriors down," Del says, twirling a dagger in her hand, ready to jump across the table and cut Faris's head off.

Estrid looks to Zain for reassurance. The muscles in his jaw twitch and move with his irritated expression. His knuckles are white from the brutal grip he has on the chair.

She reaches out to touch his arm, but he jerks it away as if he's been scorched by fire.

Zain?

The tension in the room is cut as the clopping sound of servants' footsteps and squeaking trollies enter.

"My king," a bald Fae says, approaching the table with a linen cloth draped over his arm. "Your meals have arrived as instructed. Would you like us to arrange them for you?"

Cethin nods to the butler with an amused look as he returns his gaze to the three Summer Fae and Faris, who continue to throw death stares at each other.

"Estrid, you must be hungry. Please help yourself," Cethin says as enormous platters of foods she's never seen before are placed in front of her.

Her stomach rumbles at the smell of fresh bread mixed with sweet and savory scents wafting past her. There are fruits that have the brightest-colored flesh, breads that are not just brown or white but pastel, along with what looks to be cheese and cured meats.

Unsure what else to do, Estrid helps herself to break from the tension in the room. She lets out a moan of delight as she takes a bite of white fruit with pink flesh, which tastes like a candied apple.

The rest of the group—barring Alvey, who piles his plate high—hesitantly help themselves to food. Everyone eats in silence before Faris clears his throat as he sips wine. His eyes dart around, taking in each newcomer before landing on Estrid.

"So, how did you get here?"

"Estrid opened the portal. Her magic takes after mine, but she's something even more special," Cethin jumps in to answer, looking at Estrid with pride.

Faris lowers his glass, raising an eyebrow and smiling back at Estrid.

"Ah, it's because of you that I've been busy all afternoon," he says teasingly.

Estrid takes another bite, unsure how to answer his question.

The rest of the meal goes on with no further events. Faris updates Cethin on the border skirmishes since the portal has reopened. He carefully selects his words, speaking in code.

Estrid steals glances at Zain, who hasn't looked at her once since finding out that she's Cethin's daughter.

Why is he acting like this? Surely he can't be upset by this. He wanted to come. He wanted to see me to safety.

He pushes food around his plate, sparing glances at Del. There is a silent conversation between them.

Alvey and Zella are deep in discussion; the tone is light-hearted as they smile and laugh. It quickly dawns on Estrid that Imaya hasn't been with their party since coming through the portal. She looks around the table, then casts her eyes across the room, searching for the seer. Nothing.

"Excuse me, King Cethin. We've lost one of our traveling companions," she says, interrupting Faris's latest update.

Faris and Cethin turn to her, both unsurprised by her statement.

"Imaya has dark green hair and markings on her face. Where is she?" she asks.

Faris gives a high-pitched whistle. The butler from before comes trotting up and bends down to listen to Faris, who whispers something into his ear, keeping his eyes on Estrid. The servant turns and scuttles out of the room as they lapse back into a deafening silence.

A moment later, the doors open again, the sound vibrating across the room. Light steps echo as Imaya comes bouncing over to them, giving their group a friendly wave and a smile as if everything is perfectly normal.

"Yes, General?" she says.

At these words, Alvey coughs on the wine he'd just sipped, the liquid coming out of his nose. Cursing under his breath, he reaches for a napkin to dab it up.

Estrid stares at the seer who has become her friend. "How do you know him?"

"I work for General Faris and King Cethin. I'm a seer from the Shadow Court . . . well, a seer in training." Imaya says that last bit with some minor irritation before a broad smile stretches across her face.

Faris lets out another high-pitched whistle, and the clattering of claws hitting stone at speed comes from the hallway outside. It's followed by shouts and screams of "Watch out." Estrid holds on to Zain's hand, stopping him from drawing his sword. The strange noise grows louder before a great black wolf comes into view as it charges through the doors.

"Rafe!" Estrid yells, leaping from her chair and running to greet her friend.

The enormous creature runs to her, knocking her over in excitement. A happy whine escapes him as his giant pink tongue darts out to lick her face, Estrid giggling as she puts up her hands to stop him. In the background, Del and Zella yelp at the sight.

"I thought you were dead!" Estrid says, staring into the wolf's ice-blue eyes as he gives the side of her face one last big lick.

She looks over at Faris, about to ask how, but he knows her question before it comes out of her mouth. He walks over to her, bending down to be the same height as her and Rafe, giving the wolf a scratch behind the ear.

"He returned to the Shadow Court badly injured. He came back to rejuvenate and heal. We weren't able to get him back to you, and he's been a mopey old bugger. Haven't you?"

Rafe gives Faris a giant lick, sending him clattering over onto the floor. Estrid hugs Rafe, his thick black fur tickling her skin. The steady beat of his heart calms her while tears of happiness form in her eyes. Faris stands up and puts his hand out to help her up.

"Thank you! Thank you so much," Estrid says as she takes his hand and hugs him. She feels him freeze for a moment before he wraps his muscular arms around her.

From across the room, a low growl comes from the main table. Estrid withdraws from the hug to see Zain staring daggers at him, the muscles in his jaw so tight that they might snap.

Faris gives him a cocky smile. "Jealous, Princeling?"

Estrid tries to defuse the situation by changing the subject, asking how Rafe was in the human realm to begin with. Cethin stands and walks over to where she stands with Rafe, her hand not leaving him.

"It's a long story," King Cethin says with a sigh. "One I'll tell you in good time, but you must be tired from your travels." He walks toward two glass doors that lead onto a large balcony overlooking the incoming night's sky. With a graceful wave, he motions for the rest of them to follow him.

As they trail the king, Alvey reminds Del of her reaction upon meeting Rafe for the first time, how it's the only time she's ever squealed like a girl. Faris laughs; it's deep, smooth, and seductive, sending a shiver down Estrid's back.

They reach the grand balcony, the evening sky glittering with stars. Now and then, one shoots across the midnight-blue canvas. The air outside is warmer and more humid than in the Dark Forest.

Estrid can make out the faint line of where the tall black palace walls stop and the yellow glowing lights from the houses of a city start. They flicker, each one showing a dwelling or home to someone. She hasn't seen this many houses before. Oberetta was big, but that was counting in the hundreds, whereas this is in the thousands.

She stands there, drinking it all in.

To her surprise, Zain comes to stand next to her and Rafe, who growls at him. Their fingers brush against each other, sending a familiar zing down her body before Zain withdraws his hand again. She furrows her brows at him in confusion, but they're interrupted by Cethin.

"Estrid, this is your home," he says with his arms stretched out. "There is much I need to tell you, but I must deal with a few things that need my urgent attention now that we have an active portal. Will you stay so I can tell you more about your history and your mother?" He looks at Estrid with a hopeful expression on his face.

She nods, a sense of rightness outweighing the need for caution.

Cethin smiles as he claps his hands together with a loud smack. The butler who served them dinner comes trotting back into the room. Now that she's standing up, Estrid can see that he actually trots—he has goat legs. She stares wide-eyed at them as the satyr clears his throat.

"Ramier, will you show our friends from the Summer Court to their rooms? Faris, will you escort Estrid and Zella to theirs?" Cethin says as he moves to Estrid and takes her by the shoulders, drawing her into a hug before bidding them all good night.

The tension grows when Cethin leaves the balcony. With his most charming smile, Faris sticks out his arms and asks Zella and Estrid to join him for a walk to their rooms.

"Estrid is going to stay with us. We've journeyed here together, and we'll stay together," Zain says, stepping forward to take her hand.

Oh, now *you want to take my hand? Really? You pretend I don't exist, and then you're jealous as soon as another male offers me something?*

"Oh, that won't be happening, Zain. Estrid is heir to the Shadow Court now. She will stay near her father and me in the royal quarters," Faris says with a smug smile.

That statement silences Zain. A repulsed expression dawns on his face as Faris continues to goad him.

"Ah, yes, I see you haven't thought this through yet, have you?"

Alvey groans in the background at Faris's observation. It wasn't something anyone was prepared for. None of the news tonight was. The two men clearly loathe each other, and Faris knows what buttons to press to get a reaction out of Zain.

"Zain, let's go," Del says, stepping up to pull him in the direction Ramier went.

Estrid looks at Zain and gets a stony expression back before he turns to leave.

"Come along, Zella, Estrid. Let me show you to your rooms. Rafe, come!" Faris says, holding an arm out on each side for them to take.

Estrid takes his arm but gives Zain one last glance. His sudden change of demeanor confuses her. The entire trip to this point, he's been at her side, trying to get her trust back. Now, with the news that's been shared tonight, he's distant—repulsed, even.

Faris guides them from the balcony down another hallway that feeds off the room. Like the rest of the palace, each passageway and room has stone walls expertly carved into many patterns and pictures. The corridor they walk down has a garden etched into the walls. The flowers are so delicate, Estrid can see the fine prints of the leaves and petals. She continues to mull over Zain and Faris's behavior.

"Why is there so much hostility between you and Zain?" she asks.

"It's a long story, but there's a long-running feud between the Shadow Court and the Summer Court—actually, the Shadow Court and all the other courts in Faery," Faris says as they walk at a leisurely pace.

"Why?" Zella asks.

"It's been that way for millennia, a story King Cethin should tell."

"Millennia? How old is Cethin?" Estrid asks, stunned but curious at this bit of information.

Faris chuckles and says, "You'll have to ask him."

"Do all Summer Fae and Shadow Fae react as you did to each other at the dinner table?" Estrid asks, watching Faris's striking face for a hint of emotion.

"No, your friends and I have a very special hatred for each other," he says with a mischievous smile.

"Why? What happened?"

Faris doesn't answer the question and hurries to ask them what they think of the Shadow Court Palace, trying to lift the mood. Zella quickly chimes in with how beautiful it is and asks him about the carvings on the walls, what they mean, and who did them.

Estrid soon zones out of the small talk.

I'm heir to the Shadow Court. I'm Fae. How is this possible? I don't look like a Fae. I don't have Fae magic.

Her thoughts are interrupted by Zella asking Faris, "How did you become King Cethin's general?"

Estrid watches Faris, a tender expression on his face. His cocky smile fades into a humble but sad one as he looks down at the ground, his brown wavy hair dropping over his face.

"I owe King Cethin everything. When my parents died, he took me in, gave me a home, and raised me as he would his own," he says in a melancholy voice.

"I'm sorry," she says, placing her hand on his and smiling at him. He smiles back, but it's haunted by something.

Their footsteps bounce off the stone walls as they continue winding their way through the hallways, the last discussion having muted the conversation.

After a few moments, Faris clears his throat. "Your father wants to take you to Terebian, our capital city, tomorrow. I'll be here at nine."

They round the hallway's corner and arrive outside two large, dusky, gold doors.

"Here, these are your chambers. We've connected an additional room to the side for Zella to access privately. I'll come to fetch you in the morning," Faris says, pushing open the two doors that are a miniature version of the ones to the throne room.

They reveal a space that is both functional and well fitted. The ladies unhook their arms from Faris and walk in, their eyes taking in the large central room. He gives them a quick tour of their accommodations, letting them know about critical areas of the palace too. Once finished, he comes to stand by Estrid and Zella, taking Estrid's hand and placing a kiss on it. He gives Zella a similar goodbye before exiting the rooms to leave them to get settled in.

Zella plops down on one of the emerald-green velvet loungers.

"So, he's nice, isn't he?" she says, wiggling her eyebrows at Estrid, a tease in her tone.

Estrid rolls her eyes at her cousin's insinuation. *He is good-looking, though. Even I can admit that.*

She looks around their quarters. They're big and spacious—more than needed.

Zella and Estrid sit on lounges in the middle of the room, taking in the space. There's a large desk made of what looks to be onyx in one corner with a chair on either side. Another corner is for reading, with giant pillows spread out on the ground and silk curtains hanging from the ceiling. An enormous banquet table with eight chairs stretches down the other side of the room. Colorful flowers in vases decorate the area. Like the rest of the castle, the walls have expertly sculpted pictures in the stone.

Estrid expected a lot less refinery in the Shadow Court. Her books had always painted this as the dark and sinister realm of Faery. She'd pictured run-down dwellings and shadowy settings that lived up to its name. Instead, the castle has proven to be anything but broken and gloomy. It makes the home she came from in Nordia look like a dreary place.

Aside from the stunning stonework of the walls and ceiling, the furniture is simple and unobtrusive and uplifts the room. She expected eternal darkness but was surprised that there seemed to be sun flowing through the throne room windows.

"Hello?" Zella's voice interrupts Estrid's reflection. "What are you going to do about Zain and the others?"

"Hmm . . . I don't know," Estrid sighs, walking over to the small fireplace with a blue-flamed fire dancing away. "I need to talk to King Cethin." It feels odd to call a man whom she's just met her father. She wasn't close to Rodden, but he was the only parental figure in her life, despite his cruelty to her.

"What about Rodden?" Zella asks.

"It doesn't change that he's a monster. We still have to stop him, but it's just not going to be that hard to do it. Let's get some rest. It's been a long day. I have a feeling tomorrow will be even longer," Estrid says, heading to her room.

✦　✦　✦

CHAPTER TWENTY-ONE

A soft knocking at her door wakes Estrid up. Groggy from a sleep so deep, she has to remember where she is, she sits up as a female Fae walks in, bringing with her what looks to be a fresh set of clothes.

"Good morning, Your Highness," the Fae says, laying the garments over the divider in the room's corner.

Estrid stares at her, her mouth open as she takes in the female's appearance. She has midnight-blue hair and delicate antlers that twirl above her head. Despite their differences from the Summer Fae, Estrid can't help but wonder at the beauty of the diversity of the Shadow Fae.

Dusky morning rays stream in as the Fae draws the curtains back. Estrid sees her surroundings in full light for the first time—last night, she climbed in and fell asleep as soon as her head hit the pillow.

The room is a soft gray color that's lighter than the walls in the hallways. Like the exterior walls of her bedroom, they have intricate patterns of flowers, vines, and trees stretching around it, like a forest. She sighs, feeling at home.

The Fae zips around, opening all the curtains, pouring Estrid a glass of water, and putting away her dirty clothes. She stops at the foot of Estrid's bed, curtsies, and stands with her hands clasped at her front.

"My name is Lena, Your Highness. I'm your handmaid while you are here."

Lena stares at Estrid, waiting for her command or approval. It's been some time since anyone has waited on Estrid. She's almost forgotten what to expect and how to act.

"Ah . . . sorry . . . hi, Lena. Nice to meet you," she says, pulling the sheet up slightly higher to cover her chest. She's wearing a nightshirt, but having a stranger in her bedroom at a vulnerable moment is still an odd feeling.

"Would you like me to assist you with bathing or dressing?" Lena asks, gesturing to the clothes that hang on the divider. She looks at Estrid expectantly.

"Um . . . that won't be necessary, but thank you."

Estrid gets up from the bed, unsure where to go. Lena has a look that shows she'll help Estrid with anything to make herself useful.

Estrid pads into the washroom to take care of her business, leaving Lena to make her gigantic bed. The sounds of pillows being fluffed and bedspreads whipped up in the air follow her into a bathroom that's bigger than her little cottage.

A large copper bath is at one end, sitting under a floor-to-ceiling window that overlooks the foreign landscape. Rich floral scents and perfumes from the soaps, scented oils, and lotions that line the walls wash over Estrid.

Gods, yes, a proper bath.

She's giddy at the thought of soaking in a hot tub after they escaped from Rodden.

+ + +

Exiting the washroom after what feels like an hour, the tips of her fingers are pruned, but her muscles have relaxed after lying in the warm water. Those luxuries are something she had long forgotten but sorely missed.

She enters her room and finds Lena waiting for her. "May I help you get dressed, my lady?"

With a sigh and a shrug, Estrid nods, as Lena comes around to start the process. Her tone and eagerness meant that Estrid won't have much luck with any other answer.

One thing that's been bothering Estrid since arriving in the Shadow Court is the reaction that Zain, Alvey, and Del have had toward the other Fae. They said these Fae are evil and lesser, but she can't see anything wrong with them.

"Lena, tell me about your life in the Shadow Court."

Lena helps her put on a stunning gown made of forest-green silk. The fabric feels soft and washes over her skin like water. It hugs her in all the right places but is modest enough. The color accentuates her features, her eyes brighter and her hair darker.

"Hmm, let me see. I was born in the Spring Court, but my parents fled here soon after that because I was slightly different from the other Fae," she says, pointing to her antlers. "Because of these, my family lost whatever little standing they had in the Spring Court."

Estrid's eyes widen with shock at this revelation. *What? How can they do that because someone looks different? That's so wrong.*

She watches Lena work her way around the dress, primping and pulling to get it sitting precisely right. The more Estrid observes her, the more unique and beautiful she looks. Her skin is a light brown, she has freckles that dust her cheeks, and her eyes are a dark amber.

"My parents heard about King Cethin's policy of welcoming all Fae into his kingdom, no matter how different. So, we fled here, where my father worked in the royal smithy, and my mother was part of the kitchen staff," she says, finishing doing up the back of Estrid's dress.

"Not much to tell after that. I've been in King Cethin's service since I was a hundred and sixteen."

Estrid stares at Lena in astonishment. She still can't wrap her head around the long lifespans of Fae.

Lena steps away to admire her handiwork, giving Estrid a nod of approval. Before she can look at herself in the mirror, Lena plops her down on a black velvet stool.

"Please sit, my lady, so I can do your hair."

Lena wheels over a full-length mirror with gold trimming around the edges. When Estrid sees her reflection, she doesn't recognize herself.

For the last year, she's been used to wearing nearly worn-out trousers and tunics with holes in them. The silk dress makes her look and feel like a lady again, the green bringing out the gold in her eyes, almost making them seem to glow. Even when she was with Rodden, she never wore dresses like this. They usually had her in a black sack that hid everything.

Lena takes no notice of her shock and works on Estrid's hair, weaving it into a half-up and half-down do.

Estrid mulls over Lena's answer. Zain said these Fae are evil, but everything she's experienced has pointed to the opposite. She still can't understand Zain's loathing of these Fae.

"Something else is bothering me, Lena. My companions said the Shadow Court is evil, but from what I can see, there's nothing like that here. Why is that?" Estrid asks. That question has been gnawing at her.

"From what I know, there's a lot of bad blood between the Fae courts, but I don't know the details. King Cethin is the greatest ruler the Shadow Court has ever had. He tried to integrate us back with the other courts. A marriage between your mother and the king may have changed that, but . . ." A sadness in Lena's words perks Estrid's attention up.

"Did you know my mother?"

"No, but everyone knows she and your father were fated mates. It devastated him when he realized she had died and he couldn't get to her. It was years before he finally left the castle and we saw him again."

Estrid's shoulders deflate as the hope of hearing more about her mother fades. Cethin said he would tell her, but she can't help but want to get some answers faster.

Lena grabs a little hand mirror to show Estrid the back of her hair. A smile erupts on Estrid's face with amazement. Lena has created a complicated bun held together by a clip of shiny emerald stones, with delicate gold leaves that bind it to form a flower. It's beautiful.

"Fated mates. What does that mean?" Estrid asks, unsure about the term.

"In the Fae world, fated mates are . . ." Lena pulls a face, thinking of the right words. "It's like . . . your soul is whole."

The banquet table is lined with platters of fruit, freshly baked bread, jams, eggs, and meats as Estrid walks into the common area of her apartment. The comforting smell of spices and sugar makes her stomach rumble and her mouth water eagerly.

A door off to the side of the room opens, and Zella comes dancing in, singing a tune that brightens the entire space. She's also wearing a silk dress, the midnight color making her cherry-red hair stand out.

"Morning!" Zella dances to the table where Estrid has just sat, a grin from ear to ear on her face.

"What are you so happy about?" Estrid asks, smiling to herself at her cousin's joyful mood. Her cheeks are a flushed pink, her eyes gleaming with mischief. "Zella, what have you been up to?" Estrid smirks to herself as Zella's antics lighten the weight she still carries from the revelations given to her yesterday.

"I had the most interesting morning!" Zella says as she flops down into the chair next to Estrid, fanning herself.

Estrid cocks an eyebrow at her cousin.

"I was curious to know what was outside our rooms and went for a walk, and I ran into the most beautiful Fae."

Zella fans herself, while flashing her cousin a cheeky grin as she describes her encounter.

Estrid helps herself to some warm bread, fruit, and jam, smiling as the girlish antics makes her grin and lifts her spirits.

"I came across him in the courtyard near the main doors. Good gods, Estrid, I don't think I have ever seen a more handsome man—or I should say Fae—than him. He was perfect, with a smile that made me weak at the knees, and such a gentleman. . . ." Zella continues to fan herself, recounting her run-in with the Fae. "He asked if I was lost and offered to help me back to my room."

Estrid eats her breakfast, listening with a grin as Zella describes a tall, mysterious, handsome Fae with tattooed skin and brown hair.

Throughout the story, Estrid chuckles as she enjoys her morning meal. Zella was more confident with boys than she was when they were growing up. Part of it had to do with Estrid being the king's daughter and then the Dark Witch, but the other half was that she was never taken with the men at court. They were lacking in something.

A knock at the door has Zella sitting up straight and collecting herself.

"May I come in?" Faris's smooth voice enters the room.

Estrid calls for him to enter, swatting Zella away as she gives her a sly smirk.

The handsome general saunters in with a swagger in his step and a dazzling smile. "How are we this morning, ladies?"

"Fine, thank you," Estrid and Zella answer in unison, making Faris chuckle.

"Estrid, your father has asked if you would come see him in his private quarters before we go on our tour of the court," he says, popping a grape in his mouth with a cheeky grin across his face. She has to admit he's good-looking, and his confidence is attractive.

After finishing her breakfast and saying goodbye to Zella, Estrid heads to the door. Before she exits, she hears Faris telling Zella to behave herself in a playful tone. Estrid chuckles as he follows her out.

They walk down the hallway in silence. Estrid's silk dress swishing on the ground is the only sound between them.

"You look exquisite today," he says, causing her to blush at the attention, but her heart sinks a little as she thinks of Zain.

They exit the passage on their way to the king's quarters, her arm in Faris's as his deep black wings brush her back. Sunlight streams through big windows as they walk, the carved stone walls coming to life.

"It's so strange. I thought the Shadow Court was dark. The name itself implies it, but it doesn't fit."

They stop to look out through the large windows that run the full way down the hallway, giving her a glimpse of the outside.

The sun isn't as bright as in her world. Instead, it has a warm glow to it, like dusk. Dark mountains that spring high into the sky surround the palace, encasing it like a basin. They're a deep green, but there are pockets of color from flowers and brightly colored buildings in the distance.

"Don't believe everything you hear. The Shadow Court is much more than shadows," Faris says, beaming at her as they continue their walk.

That smile . . . you know how to wield it, don't you?

Estrid giggles to herself at Faris's flirtatiousness just as Zain, Del, and Alvey round a corner. Sweat drips down their red faces as two fully armored Shadow Guards escort them.

Faris slows their pace as they approach the three Summer Fae and their escorts. Zain's eyes track down Estrid's body, drinking in the curves that the dress hugs. They lock on her arm linked to Faris's. The muscles in his jaw flex back and forth as his eyes narrow, and he emits a low growl.

Estrid and Faris stop to greet them, but the trio keep walking; only Alvey spins around to give her a wave and then shrugs.

"They asked to use the training ground this morning," Faris says with a shrug of his own and a mischievous smile.

"And you just knew when they would walk back this way?" Estrid says, cocking her eyebrow at him.

"I know everything that happens in these walls, love," he replies, stopping at the two large black doors to the king's chambers. An attendant dips his head in recognition and opens the door for them as Cethin waits just inside the door.

With a salute, Faris leaves as Cethin steps aside for Estrid to enter his room, guiding her through. Walking in, she notices that the décor isn't much different from hers and the rest of the castle. Intricately designed stone walls, natural soft colors, and furniture made of blackened wood fill the space.

"Would you like something to drink?" Cethin asks, heading over to a beverage table filled with what looks to be wine, fruit drinks, and some hot tea.

"I'll have tea, please."

Estrid sits at the large dining table that is almost identical to hers. Cethin pours the hot liquid into a delicate tulip cup. Steam rises off it as he hands it to her, reaching out and wrapping around her. Hints of jasmine, vanilla, and something sweet she can't put her finger on fill her nose.

"I thought we could sit and talk for a while before we head out to see the wider city. I realize that since you arrived, you've received a lot of new information," Cethin says, sitting beside her. The small wooden chair can barely hold his enormous frame, creaking beneath him. He moves with grace and ease that she wouldn't expect from such a large being.

They sit there in an awkward silence, observing each other. Estrid sips her tea. The taste surprises her. To the nose, it's floral and sweet, but the flavor has a zesty citrus hint to it.

"What is this tea? It's very unusual but delicious."

"It's kelpa tea, a type of fruit that grows here in the Shadow Court." Cethin smiles at her, but it soon fades, a sad expression taking its place. "I'm sorry. You just look so much like your mother."

A lump lodges in Estrid's throat. She doesn't know what to say. She's still getting her head around the fact that her mother was a Fae queen, her father is a Fae king, and Rodden is nothing but a villain.

With a meek smile, she continues drinking her tea, unsure how to comfort him.

Clearing his throat, Cethin says, "I want to know more about you, Estrid. Where have you been living? How did you find the portal? And how have you ended up with three Summer Court royals for companions?"

She chews the side of her cheek as her thoughts war for dominance. *I don't know you, but I feel like I do . . . I'm trusting you so I can stop Rodden.*

Estrid sighs and tells him her story from the beginning, from being raised by Rodden, encountering Zain, being captured by Rodden, and then escaping and following Imaya to the portal. The king doesn't speak or break his focus on her, just sits and listens.

She shuffles in her seat beneath his unrelenting stare. His face is neutral as she explains her story. The only thing giving away any emotion is his eyes. They glow when Estrid speaks of her treatment by Rodden, a clear sign of the simmering rage he keeps under wraps.

When she finishes, she fidgets with her hands, unsure what Cethin's response will be.

"I'm sorry, Estrid," he says, looking at her with guilt and anger. "I'm sorry for not being able to save you, get to you, and help you avoid what you've had to endure." He takes her hands, cradling them. His are so large compared to hers, engulfing them like a cocoon.

She stares at them, clasped together. It feels so comforting knowing someone cares for her.

Estrid takes a deep breath, a heavy burden lifted off her chest. A single teardrop rolls down her cheek, leaving a cool, wet track behind it. Another inhale as she wipes away the tear, not willing anyone to feel sorry for her. What she was and what she's endured have made her who she is and led her to where she is today.

She looks up and sees Cethin's warm green eyes searching hers, waiting for a response to his words.

"We need to stop Rodden," she says, looking him straight in the eye.

"We'll stop him, Estrid. Together."

✦ ✦ ✦

Cethin escorts Estrid to a great courtyard in the middle of the enormous palace; its ten-foot walls wrap around it. The castle itself has spires that stretch high into the sky. It makes Estrid dizzy just looking up at them.

On the outside, the building lives up to its name. Unlike the inside, the entire structure is black stone, no warm, neutral colors anywhere to be seen.

The size of the courtyard that it wraps around astounds Estrid. It's long and wide. In the center is a massive ebony tree, similar to the portal they came through. Its vast body resembles a piece of linen that has been twisted and wrung out.

Cethin explains the history of the building and the various purposes of the castle as they walk.

They approach the stables in the far corners of the courtyard. Estrid can make out the figures of Zain, Del, and Alvey standing there looking unimpressed as they wait with Faris, three of his men, and Rafe. At the sight of her wolf, Estrid's heart soars.

Zella stands next to one guard, chatting the hind leg off a donkey, but only gets a still and stoic response. Faris and the guards are dressed head to toe in their battle leathers, armed and painting an imposing picture. His dark hair is tied back, revealing his pointed Fae ears and angular jawline.

"Faris, are we ready?" Cethin asks his general, approaching him as they clasp arms.

Faris nods. "Yes, my king. The Lotnars are saddled and all set to go."

He lets out a sharp, ear-piercing whistle that makes Estrid wince.

From deep in the shadows of the stable, there's a low, vibrating growl in response to his call. Four stable hands emerge, clasping reins attached to beasts that Estrid has never fathomed could exist.

She yelps and steps back, grabbing onto Cethin's arm. The creatures have a body that resembles a mountain cat, but they're the size of a horse. They have well-defined muscles and padded feet like a cat's paw, which she can only guess gives way to sharp claws. Sleek jet-black fur covers them, shining with golden hues in the day's soft light.

Their faces resemble a cat's except that they have what look to be leathery spines that surround their heads, like a mane. Their eyes glow yellow, and large canine teeth protrude from their lips as they bare them to the group.

Rafe gives a growl and a huff as one hisses at him. The first Lotnar brought out is at least double the size of the rest. Cethin walks up to it, patting it on the head as it purrs like a domestic cat.

"Wh-What are those things?" Zella stutters as she peers from behind the Fae male she was talking to.

"This," Cethin says, giving the enormous creature another pat, "is Borg, and he's a Lotnar." He swings his leg over the saddle to sit on Borg.

Everyone in the group stares at him, their jaws hanging on the ground. Alvey clears his throat and starts shaking his head. "Yep . . . no, not going to happen."

He makes to turn around before Zain grabs his shirt and spins him back around. Alvey throws his brother a look of annoyance but heeds the command.

"Estrid, who would you like to ride with?" Faris says to the group as he swings his leg over his own Lotnar while staring at her.

Estrid looks around. She would jump at the chance to ride with Zain, but since arriving here, he hasn't said a word to her. He's ignored her this morning as well and hasn't sought her out once since last night to check if she's okay.

After what they went through and how he promised to stay by her side, she would have thought he would have attempted to see her.

She watches Zain, catching his eyes before he looks away again. Annoyed at him, she says, "I'll ride with you, Faris."

She steps toward him, putting her arm out for him to help her onto his Lotnar.

She hears a growl from behind her, though it doesn't come from a Lotnar. Instead, Zain narrows his eyes at Faris.

The general smirks before barking orders to his team and the group. "Delmire, you're with my second, Evander. Zain, Alvey, you should both be fine riding one alone."

With a huff, Del crosses her arms. Her demeanor and posture beg for a challenge from anyone.

"I can ride on my own, Faris. I don't need your second near me," she bites out, almost snapping her jaws at Evander. The tall Fae with purple ram horns on his head backs away with his hands up.

"Fine. If you fall off, Delmire, no one will pick you up," Faris says, giving a little click of his tongue for the Lotnar to move.

Estrid watches Cethin during the entire exchange. He lets the hostilities play out as if they need to clear the air.

She sits in front of Faris, his arms caging her in as he holds the reins, making her feel uncomfortable at the proximity.

"Would you like to steer?" he asks, opening his hands to give her the reins.

She hasn't ridden a horse in a long time but always enjoyed it—assuming a Lotnar will be like a horse. She goes to take the reins, and Faris intentionally closes his hands around hers.

Another growl and a huff behind them. It's followed by the sounds of padded paws hitting the ground at speed. Zain races past them to walk next to Cethin.

Annoyed, Estrid doesn't shake off Faris. There's no hiding the open hostility between the two men, but Zain can't expect her to bend to him if he won't even talk to her.

"Why do you goad him so much?" she asks, straightening her back, putting a little distance between her and Faris. She may be annoyed with Zain, but she's only just met the general.

"Why not? He's an arrogant prince who's used to getting what he wants. What's wrong with a little competition?"

He pulls her back to sit flush against him, and she gasps as she hits a solid wall of muscle. Faris lets out a chuckle, his hot breath on her ear.

Estrid swats him away, saying, "You know he's a king, right?"

"I know, but where's the fun in calling him king?"

"You're not helping. There's bad blood there, but you're making it worse."

Faris leans down so that his breath brushes her ear and whispers, "I'm sorry, Estrid. If you would like me to stop, just say it."

A shiver runs down her back. She doesn't answer him as shouts of orders fill the air as they approach the outer gates. Like the palace, they're solid black. They look like they must weigh a ton but glide like a curtain blowing in a gentle breeze.

The group comes to a halt, Cethin in the middle, watching as the doors open. A sprawling city comes into view.

"Welcome to Shadow Court, Estrid. Your home," Cethin says, the golden rays of the sun making his green eyes glow as he looks at her.

✦ ✦ ✦

CHAPTER TWENTY-TWO

The tour of the Shadow Court catches Zain off guard. It's nothing like he expected. He's been told his whole life it's a dark place, filled with malevolent beings hellbent on the destruction of the other Fae courts.

What he encounters is a functioning Fae society similar to his own. The only difference is the Fae themselves.

They explore a city brimming with businesses, markets, and shops bustling with customers. As they stroll the streets atop the Lotnars, passers-by are unfazed by the beasts. Zain, Del, and Alvey draw more attention than them; the city's inhabitants stare at them with fear and disdain. Memories of his advisors telling him not to trust the lesser Fae, to round them up and exile them from his court, resurface. His cheeks flush with embarrassment.

They move deeper into the capital city. Terebian is composed of intricately linked stone buildings, as if a giant creature had carved them. The elegant arches between structures weave together like vines of a tree.

What shocks him the most is that it isn't too dissimilar to the Summer Court, which uses trees in the same way. The trees themselves are different too. They're the same black wood as the ones in the palace courtyard and the portal, a striking contrast against the gray stone buildings.

What surprises Zain even more is that King Cethin is a beloved leader among his people. His subjects are smiling, waving, and coming forward to greet him. He doesn't turn anyone away. Instead, he greets everyone by name. He asks them how their families are or if a completed project went well.

The Shadow King has a bloodthirsty reputation. Zain was brought up on stories from his advisors that the Shadow King was a fearsome, ruthless, and evil leader who was blind with hunger for power. To his annoyance, even Faris is well liked.

Zain tries not to look at Faris and Estrid, keeping his eyes focused on his surroundings, but he can't help but steal a glance. The pair talk and laugh, sending Zain's jealousy into overdrive. She looks stunning in the green silk gown, her hair half up, exposing the elegance of her long neck.

A battle rages within him. Before they came here, Estrid was a human royal, nothing of significance to his people. Now, she's the daughter of two courts that are his oldest enemies, one who bares the responsibility for destroying his family. The many warnings and teachings about them from his father's advisors cloud his head.

The Shadow King and his court aren't what he was told they were; it goes against everything he was taught.

Don't trust them, Zain. You need to leave, a foreign voice hisses in his thoughts.

✦ ✦ ✦

After the tour, Del, Alvey, and Zain return to their rooms, each taking a seat in the common area of their quarters. None of them says a word, the shock of their experience today rendering them silent. Zain's mood is especially prickly.

You can't trust her, Zain. Go back to Rodden. They won't help you here, that voice says again as it creeps into his head, louder this time.

A shiver runs down his spine as he tries to shake it off. Despite his best efforts to ignore Estrid and Faris, he couldn't stop himself from watching them, wishing it was him she was riding with.

"All right, I'm going to say it. This place is the exact opposite of what we thought," Alvey says, getting up and walking over to the dining table with wine on it.

Zain and Del follow, sitting as Alvey pours them each a glass of wine. Zain drains his in one mouthful: berries and spice with a hint of leather. Tannins catch at the back of his mouth as the liquid goes down smoothly with no bitterness or sourness.

"There's more to this story. There has to be. Why have we had skirmishes with the Shadow Court? The stories we were told had to have come from somewhere," Zain says.

Alvey shrugs, swishing the wine in his mouth.

Del looks down at the carpet in contemplation as she says, "This place is not what I expected either. Whatever the story is, we need to find out more before we decide. They might help us."

Her diplomatic response stops Zain's thoughts dead in their tracks.

Del's the rash one of the trio, running straight into a decision with little thought. He was hoping she would demand that they leave right away.

He leans back and barely listens as Del and Alvey compare notes on their observations of the court.

Estrid distracts the other half of him. How she looked today, her laugh, and Faris's proximity to her.

That could be him.

She's the daughter of your enemy, Zain. An alliance with Rodden will help you, that strange voice whispers to him.

Yes, he agrees. The thought wraps around his mind like a snake coiling around its prey, suffocating the logic. Deep down, he fights his own thoughts.

"We don't have time for this. We have to take down Balius and take the Summer Court back," he says, interrupting Del and Alvey's conversation.

"What about Estrid?" Alvey asks.

"What about her? She seems to get along fine with Faris. They suit each other, both of the Shadow Court. We need to get our court back, not focus on them," Zain bites out before he can think, making Alvey wince.

"Zain—" Del says, but he cuts her off, annoyed that she's even going to talk to him about this. She betrayed Estrid. Why the sudden moral compass?

That invisible serpent grips tighter around his mind, strangling any other thoughts.

"She's the daughter of our enemy, Del! You remember what we were taught as younglings about these Fae? They won't help us," Zain shouts as he jumps up from his seat.

"Our people have fought against them in battles and wars. Our people have died fighting them! What would they think of us? We must get the Summer Court back. Estrid is fine here. She has Faris and Cethin. She doesn't need us anymore," he says, venom seeping into his tone at the mention of Faris's name.

The words don't feel like his own, but he can't stop them from coming out. His cheeks flush with anger as he paces the room in a huff.

"Don't be jealous, Zain. It doesn't suit you. If you care for the woman, then we'll find a way," Del says in a stern tone.

Her words make him pause.

Don't listen to them, Zain. You need to leave now, that same alien voice hisses in his mind.

"She's the daughter of our two enemies, end of discussion. We're leaving at first light tomorrow."

"Where will we go?" Del asks, throwing her arms up. "We have no court, Zain! We have no alliances!"

Zain faces his cousin. The hard lines of her face soften with concern, and she slumps her shoulders as if defeated. It's something he never thought he would see from Del.

"We'll go to Rodden. He was open to an alliance. We know where Estrid is, so we can use that as leverage," Zain says, flinching as the words leave his mouth like they were forced out by some invisible force.

"You can't be serious, Zain!" Alvey says, throwing his hands up in the air as Zain walks to his room. Del gapes in shock at his words.

Ignore them, Zain. They don't know what needs to be done, that inner voice says.

Alvey and Del shout at him, but he drowns out their calls at him for being a fool, how wrong this plan is, and how what they've seen tonight differs from what they've been told. He slams the door shut on them.

The trio head to dinner with Cethin, Faris, Estrid, and Zella that evening in silence.

They reach the throne room, expecting a small meal between the seven of them, but two of Faris's commanders are seated at the table when they get there.

The first is Evander, the one with the horns who accompanied them on their morning tour. The other is Tore. Like Evander, he doesn't have wings, but he has dark tattoos that go from his neck to the edges of his wrists. They're black as the night but alive. Moving. Blinking.

Don't trust them, Zain, the inner voice says to him, putting his nerves on edge. He can feel their eyes on him. Throughout the ages, he's been taught that the Shadow Army is a bloodthirsty group that has killed countless Summer Fae. These two are especially deadly.

Tore is the leader of the shadow walkers, an assassin force that gained a notorious name for being able to slip through shadows. Tore's use of shadows is something Zain has never seen, but his reputation precedes him.

Evander is a colossal figure who towers over seven feet and has impressive horns that add to his intimidating appearance. As Zain learned yesterday, he is Faris's second-in-command and leads the deadly Lotnar battalions.

Zain eyes them suspiciously, not paying attention as Rafe bounds up to Tore and Evander like a puppy, begging for a pat. Alvey chuckles at the wolf, earning him an unimpressed look from Zain.

The trio approaches the large black marble table decorated with unusual flower centerpieces. Gold-and-silver goblets dot each place setting as platters of food run down the length of it.

Zain's mouth waters from the smells as his stomach protests with a rumble. Unlike their first evening here, when Faris was to Cethin's right, the king signals for Zain to sit next to him. Zain's pleased with himself before he sees Faris next to Estrid in the spot he sat in the night before.

See, she can't be trusted, Zain. She's already moved on, that voice says to him. His mood sours further as it takes every fiber in his body not to challenge Faris.

Alvey gives him a pat on the back and whispers, "Don't be jealous, Zain. Just talk to her."

Zain takes his seat opposite Estrid. Her golden eyes catch his as he sits down, and she gives him a soft smile, but Faris clears his throat, drawing her attention away. Zain already hates the Fae male for all the past reasons, but now even more for the focus Estrid gives him.

Everyone falls silent as Cethin stands with his goblet in hand. His large black wings cast a shadow across the table. He's dressed more casually tonight in a dark linen shirt and pants. Zain has to give it to Cethin—he poses an intimidating figure, even when not on the battlefield.

"A special welcome to our guests from the Summer Court, and to my daughter, Estrid, you are home. I hope you all enjoyed your tour of Terebian. I also hope that the Shadow Court can one day join the ranks of the other Fae courts for all of Faery to prosper," Cethin says, raising his cup in a toast.

See, he wants to take your court, Zain. You cannot trust him. That voice pierces his mind as the Shadow Fae cheer at Cethin's words. Zain acknowledges the toast with trepidation.

He tries to avoid looking at Estrid, the sight of her talking to Faris making jealousy rear its ugly head repeatedly. It's maddening, but something is stopping him from going to her.

He sneaks another look as Cethin talks to him. She catches him eyeing her, her expression concerned. His heart skips, but he breaks the stare to focus on anything else. Faris grins and revels in his discomfort.

Stop staring at her, you fool. She's your enemy. When you have your alliance, you can get revenge on the general, the voice tells him, feeding him images of death and destruction.

To avoid thinking about it, he turns back to talk to Cethin.

"I'm curious. Your kingdom is peaceful, but I've always known the Shadow Court to be violent, hellbent on trying to take over the rest of the courts. The two don't line up," Zain says.

Cethin casts a scrutinizing gaze at him, taking a sip of his wine. "You're very observant. I was not always the king of the Shadow Court. Before me, Aragoth ruled for two thousand years. He was an obsessive megalomaniac whose sole drive was absolute power."

Zain listens to Cethin with rapt attention, not touching his food. The rest of the table goes quiet. He's never heard of this Aragoth before. The history they taught him growing up didn't detail the history of the Shadow King, or that there were multiple kings. They painted him as a long-lived savage beast. All eyes stare at Cethin as he continues his story.

"I was his general for a few hundred years, happy to fight and kill as many as was necessary to fulfil his wishes," he says, looking guilty and ashamed of his admission.

"So, the legends and stories of the Shadow Court general's fighting and abilities were about you?" Alvey interjects, acting like a fanboy seeing their greatest hero.

Cethin smiles, nodding. Many Fae battle strategy books were based on the tactics he created. Zain has lost countless men and women to Cethin's military strategies.

"So, what happened to Aragoth?" Del asks, watching Cethin take a long sip of his wine as if it gives him liquid courage.

"I met Eria, and my life changed," he says, staring at Estrid, the pain of the conversation visible on his melancholy face.

Zain can't help but feel for Cethin.

Don't listen to him, that voice says, quickly snuffing out any sympathy he has for the king.

"I was scouting in the Winter Forest for a planned attack that Aragoth wanted to make. I saw her and was hooked. Somehow, I convinced Aragoth not to invade the Winter Court and instead try to seek an alliance. For years, I tried to catch her attention by winning battles against the other courts. I created this fearsome reputation, but she wouldn't even acknowledge me no matter what I did. When I asked her what it would take, she said, 'Only peace.'"

Everyone stares at Cethin in silence. Zain watches Estrid; her expression gives nothing away, but her eyes shine, showing her sadness.

Smiling, Cethin continues, "Those words upended my world. How can a bloodthirsty warrior be peaceful? It was like she'd lifted a veil from my head. I saw Aragoth for what he was, what he was doing to the Shadow Court and its people, and how much more we could be if we could live harmoniously with the other courts."

Lies. It's what he wants you to think, that voice says.

Zain tries to dismiss it, but the thoughts embed themselves within him nonetheless.

"What did you do?" Estrid asks as the table hangs off his every word.

"I killed him," Cethin says with a tone so casual, it's deadly.

The group is shocked, eyes wide and mouths agape.

"When you have a mate, you'll do anything for them. My brother and I overthrew Aragoth and took the throne. But that wasn't good enough for Eria," he says, chuckling with a sad smile. "She still refused me and said killing one tyrant and replacing him with another wouldn't solve things. So, I spent years building the Shadow Court you see today." He gestures around him, the cavernous hall now feeling small and intimate, knowing the background behind it.

"Where is your brother?" Del asks in a distrusting tone from the end of the table, narrowing her eyes at the king.

"Once we took the throne, Malic became like Aragoth. He wanted more. He thought we were superior and was hellbent on taking on the other Fae courts. It's part of the reason many Fae distrust those of us who look different." Cethin sighs, shaking his head.

See! He would kill his own brother to keep his grip on power. What will he do to you, Zain? Go back to Rodden, the voice hisses at him.

"I said before that you'll do anything for your mate, will forsake anyone for them. They are your everything."

The words hang heavy in the room, digging deep into Zain's soul that fights his mind.

"Malic started a radical group against me, plunging the court into chaos." Cethin pauses, trying to find some courage. "I had no choice but to kill him. He was a danger to Eria. To Estrid and all the cou—"

"So, you killed the previous king, then murdered your rogue brother, but something doesn't stack up here," Del interrupts in an irritated tone.

Zain knows what's coming and lets her continue unabated.

"We've had deadly encounters and skirmishes with the Shadow Court. One of them killed my parents. Why haven't things changed?" Del says, now more aggravated than before.

Her voice cracks with emotion, tears brimming in her eyes. Zain is shocked, as she never displays feelings around an unknown group of people.

Cethin sighs and nods in recognition of her words. "Yes, Delmire. We received word that your mother and father died, and I am sorry for that. When I killed Malic, I could not kill his ideology, and some Fae still believe we have a right to take the other courts. Sometimes, these rogues form strong bands and attempt to seize what they want."

"That's your excuse!" Del yells, standing up and knocking over her chair as she slams her fists on the table.

"Watch your tongue!" Faris bites out at her as he makes to stand, as do his two commanders.

Cethin holds his hand up and shakes his head at his men.

"Delmire, understand that the Shadow Court is three times the size of the Summer Court. I try to ensure my people's safety, and anyone threatening peace is swiftly dealt with." The king's gaze isn't soft anymore.

He kills all in his path to power. He will do the same to you, the voice continues to hiss in Zain's mind.

Cethin doesn't back down from the stare Del gives him.

"My men also risk their lives to keep these rogues contained." Irritation coats Cethin's tone. "Faris's parents were killed by Summer Fae under the order of those in the Summer Court, thinking they were being attacked when they were trying to contain those criminals."

This admission shocks everyone, even Del. All eyes go to Faris, a frustrated and irritated tic in his jaw. Estrid places her hand on his, picking up on his anger.

"I'm sorry," Zain hears her whisper to Faris. This should rile him up, but rather than be angry at the gesture, he feels regret. He knows what losing your parents feels like. The hole it leaves in your life. It's the one thing that he can sympathize with Faris on.

Don't listen to them, Zain. They lie, that sinister voice says.

Zain tries to block out these negative thoughts, but they're like hooks embedded deep in him.

"What happened to my mother?" Estrid asks, trying to change the subject.

"Well, once I killed Malic and created a peaceful and prosperous kingdom, she finally accepted me as her mate. I thought that would be it, but the other courts wouldn't accept any of her attempts to have us be a part of Fae society. She was about to tell them we were mates and with child, but someone close to her betrayed her before she could."

Cethin takes Estrid's hand; his eyes scream murder. Zain watches her as she processes this information, swallowing down the emotion.

"Did you ever try to find out?" she asks.

Cethin shakes his head, long strands of dark hair falling down his shoulder. "Whoever deceived her sealed any way in and out of this court, locking us in. It's a powerful magic that I'd never seen before. It wasn't until you came along and unlocked it that we could go about things as they were before. Fae can leave to visit their friends and families in the other courts now. We can resume trade with those willing," he says with pride. "You've saved us, Estrid."

✦　✦　✦

CHAPTER TWENTY-THREE

Zella and Estrid pick at their breakfast the next morning. The barrage of surprises that Cethin shared with the group last night kept Estrid awake. That and Zain. He still hasn't spoken to her since they arrived in the Shadow Court.

At dinner, he seemed distracted, sparing her glances, but not in the kind and gentle way she knows. Afterward, she tried to go to him, calling after him as he left for his rooms. He either didn't hear her or simply ignored her.

Since learning who her parents are, he's been acting strange, cold and distant compared to their previous interactions. She tries not to get caught up in the mixed signals he sends her, but she can't help it.

She doesn't understand the feuds between the courts, but they can't be so bad that he would turn away from her.

He's not worth it, she keeps telling herself, but deep down, she knows she's lying to herself despite being frustrated and hurt.

Cethin proved that stories of the Shadow Court aren't real, so why is he shunning me? He's hot, and then he's cold. I can't keep up.

"What do you think of Tore?" Zella's voice breaks Estrid's train of thought. Her cousin sits there looking at her, waiting for an answer.

"Huh . . . oh, he seems nice."

She goes back to pushing food around her plate. Her fork scrapes against the dish as Zella rambles in the background about Tore being the mysterious Fae from yesterday morning's adventure. Eventually, Zella picks up on Estrid's distracted and melancholy mood. "Are you okay?"

"Hmm . . . yes. It's all just a lot to take in," Estrid says, hoping Zella accepts that as the truth, but her cousin is perceptive when she wants to be.

"Don't lie."

"It's nothing—" Estrid starts, a sudden knock halting her next words, to her relief.

With a groan and a creak, the door to their chambers opens as Del steps in. Her bright blonde hair is braided to the left, showing off her pointed Fae ears and sharp facial features.

Estrid's eyebrows shoot up in surprise. Del has on a simple blue cotton dress. Even though Estrid has only known her a few short weeks, she's well aware that Del isn't the dress type.

In her armor, she's a fierce and forbidding warrior. Wearing a gown, she looks like a princess, poised and almost friendly, albeit a bit awkward.

Del walks in and sits opposite Estrid, an uncomfortable expression on her face. Something isn't right, even with the strange outfit choice.

"I thought you should know that Alvey and Zain left this morning," she says with a fleeting look of sadness before her mask of indifference snaps back into place.

The news stuns Estrid, her breath hitching.

What? How could he do this? Before we came here, he wouldn't leave me alone. Now he's gone. What the hell has happened?

A fresh wound of betrayal cracks open. She'd opened up to him. Allowed him in even after what Del did to her.

Unlike when Zain went away the first time in the forest, Estrid isn't just hurt. She's angry.

Gods, you are stupid, Estrid. You fell right into it. I kept saying don't get attached, and here we are.

"Where've they gone?" She tries to keep her tone even, trying not to shake with the anger.

"They left this morning. They . . ." Del squares her shoulders. "They went back to Nordia."

Estrid's jaw just about drops to the ground from this revelation. She sways at the news. It's taking everything in her not to panic.

Inhale. Exhale. Inhale. Exhale, she tells herself while her heart thumps in her chest.

Zella doesn't hold back, jumping up from her seat and yelling, "He what? Is he a fucking idiot? How could he go back to Rodden after what he did to Estrid and me?"

Del shrinks under the barrage of curses and insults being flung at her. The fierce warrior in her knows a losing fight.

"Why are you here, Del?" Estrid says in a deadly calm tone.

Del sits up straighter, regaining her usual stoic posture. She looks Estrid straight in the eye, never one to back down from a challenge. The sunlight from the windows makes her hair shimmer like golden spun silk.

"Zain's wrong. We've been misguided about the Shadow Court. After last night, I can see that I was wrong too. Cethin isn't the bloodthirsty king we all thought. He wasn't responsible for my parents' deaths. I believe Rodden is the evil one, and I don't want any part of it," she says, looking at Estrid. "Zain's not thinking straight. Something's not right with him, but I can't follow him with his current plan."

Estrid looks at Del, her jaw clenching and unclenching, unsure what to say. It must have taken a lot for Del to admit that she was wrong, let alone to people she just met a few weeks ago.

Zella clutches her knife, giving Del a death stare. "Tell her the rest, Del."

"What else is there, Zella?" Del throws back in a warning tone.

"Pfft, don't play dumb, Del!" Zella says, slamming her hand on the table. "Tell her about the promise you made him."

Del doesn't respond, narrowing her eyes at Estrid's cousin. Zella smirks back, knowing she's got the Fae. Seconds tick by in uncomfortable silence, neither backing down.

"What'd you promise him?" Estrid says, becoming irritated by the whole thing. She was angry before, but knowing there are more secrets only aggravates her further.

Del doesn't say a word as she clasps her hands, avoiding the two women's gazes.

"What. Did. You. Promise. Him. Del?" Estrid repeats as she stands up from her chair and looms over Del, who purses her lips into a thin line.

To Estrid's left, Zella has gotten up and paces the room, waiting for Del to answer the question. With a frustrated huff, Zella answers on her behalf.

"She felt guilty for selling you out to Rodden, so she made a Fae promise on her life to always protect you. If you die, she dies!"

Estrid looks between her cousin and Del and back again. She can't decide if she's more annoyed with Zella for not telling her if she already knew or by Del's underlying motive to stay here.

"Who told you that, Zella?" Del shoots Zella a stare that could extinguish a fire as she jumps from her seat.

"You're such a fool, Del. You think being a powerful warrior is the only way to get what you want from people. I batted my eyes at Alvey, and he told me everything," Zella says with a triumphant smile.

Del's about to respond, but another knock at the door interrupts her.

"Hell—ahh . . . everything okay in here, ladies?" Faris steps in, stopping dead as he takes in the hostility between the women, his mischievous smile fading.

"We're fine. What do you want, Faris?" Estrid snaps.

Faris retreats, his hands going in the air, recoiling at her harsh tone. He creases his brow and opens his mouth to say something, then thinks better of it. His eyes drift between the three women.

Shaking his head, he says, "Your father wants to see you." He steps toward the door, signaling Estrid to follow.

She gets up and storms out with a huff, leaving Del and Zella to rip into each other.

✦ ✦ ✦

Estrid charges down the decorated stone hallway, trying to walk off the anger that simmers just beneath the surface. It's bustling with courtiers going about their daily business, delivering meals, cleaning, and ensuring the run of the palace.

She dodges and weaves past people, stuck in her own thoughts. *Everyone always wants a piece of me for their own gain. It's the story of my life, and I'm sick of it.*

Faris tries to keep up with her pace, knocking a butler carrying a tray over with his enormous wings.

She can hear him asking what happened, calling for her to wait, but her emotions drive her forward like a galloping horse.

He finally grabs her by the elbow and brings her to a stop. She looks at him, her cheeks red with rage, angry tears threatening to spill down.

Faris furrows his brow, catching on to how livid she is as he takes her by the shoulders. Those deep brown eyes bore holes into her soul. She can't hide from him.

"What happened in there, Estrid? What did Del do?"

"Nothing. She's done nothing. It's not Del," she says, trying to avoid Faris's unrelenting gaze. She won't let him or Cethin see how Zain's leaving has upset her. If he can shut off his feelings for her, so can she.

"It's Zain, isn't it? Where is he?" Faris says, placing his finger under her chin to lift her face so she can't turn away.

Estrid doesn't move, averting her eyes from his. A tight ball forms in her chest as she holds back the tears that threaten to spill. She can't look Faris in the eye.

He bundles her into a hug, his amber-and-leather scent enveloping her. It's masculine and warm.

"Don't let that stupid fool's decision hurt you," he whispers.

"That hasn't hurt me," she says, trying to make the lie convincing for herself and Faris. "I'm sick of people using me. I'm sick of people making a fool of me. I'm done with it. Zain. Del. Rodden. I'm done being used."

Estrid hoped she could have talked to Zain last night about everything they'd learned. Instead, he's left.

They stand there for several moments as Fae rush around them.

Faris finally breaks the hold he has on her, taking her shoulders in his hands.

"Look at me, Estrid." When she meets those deep brown eyes, he says, "You're kind and good. You only want to see the best in someone—something I admire. Your father admires it too. I promise you, I'll never use you. Cethin will never use you. We'll only ever protect you."

Faris flashes her one of his dazzling smiles. Any woman would melt at that smile, one cheek dimpling.

Maybe you should move on, Estrid. He's left you, but Faris is here.

But promises can be broken. Be careful.

"Thank you, Faris."

She hugs him again, moving deeper into his embrace. When they break apart, Estrid feels calmer. Grounded. She may not be over Zain, but having Faris here helps, even if only to take that ache away.

"Let's take the long route to your father's office," Faris says, steering them down a hallway that loops around the palace. They walk in silence for a while, her arm looped on Faris's. Estrid's anger subsiding with each step they take.

"I'm curious, if Zain and Alvey left, why is Del still here?" he asks as they turn down a corridor to cut back into the palace's interior.

Estrid sighs, "She said she doesn't agree with Zain's decision to go back to Rodden."

"He's what?" Faris nearly roars. The Fae walking past jump and scatter as he erupts with anger.

Estrid holds her hand up and shakes her head. She refuses to have this debate with Faris. What's done is done. There's nothing she can do to change it.

"He's made his choice, Faris. Del said she disagrees with it, so she stayed . . . but then I found out that she made Zain a Fae promise after we escaped Rodden to protect me and keep me safe."

As they turn down the final corridor toward Cethin's chamber, Faris saying nothing.

"She's only staying here in case I die," Estrid continues. "If I die, she dies."

She turns to look at Faris as they arrive at Cethin's doors.

"I can't speak for Del, but making a Fae promise isn't something you do lightly. Her disagreeing with Zain, after already going against him once, will probably hurt her too. I think she's made the right choice staying here," he tells her.

"Why are you standing up for her?"

"Because she just let go of her only family to protect mine. I may not like Del, but I can respect her."

Faris hugs Estrid and then knocks on Cethin's door. It opens, and they step into his office. Zella, Del, Tore, and Evander are there.

Faris bends down to whisper, "I thought you might have needed a break to talk to someone."

He gives her a calm smile and squeezes her shoulder. The tight ball in her chest eases, as she's grateful for his attention and company. She's unsure of his goal, but he called her his family. Whatever it is, he seems to know what to do, no matter her mood.

Everyone huddles around a table in the large office as Cethin stands at the giant floor-to-ceiling windows overlooking the vast courtyard below. The morning light streams in, casting him in a silhouette like a winged demon.

He turns to the group, green eyes finding Estrid. "I hear Zain and Alvey have left."

She nods, trying not to let her emotions show. To her right, Del's lips thin into a slight frown. The acknowledgement bores a hole in Estrid's heart.

They've really gone.

Cethin sighs and shakes his head in disappointment. "I'd hoped that things might be different between our courts after everything they saw yesterday and heard last night. Seems I was wrong." He walks over to Del to stand before her. "Delmire, I'm grateful that you're with us. Please make this your home for as long as you need it."

She avoids eye contact with everyone but Cethin, swallowing down whatever emotion tries to break the surface. "Thank you, King Cethin. And please, call me Del. Delmire is for when I'm in trouble."

He chuckles, her light-hearted comment lifting the mood. Her usual serious temperaments and stoic expressions don't allow for jokes.

Cethin takes a seat at the head of a large, circular black wooden table in the center of the room. It's littered with maps, books, scrolls, and parchments. He gestures for the group to sit at the table, Estrid at his left-hand side.

"We're here to discuss how to deal with Rodden," he starts. "He played a part in Eria's death and has tormented Estrid . . ."

Cethin continues speaking, but she's lost in her thoughts.

Tell them, Estrid. They need to know if you're going to use them to help you stop Rodden.

"Imaya gave me a vision when we were traveling here. She said that if Rodden isn't stopped, the human realm will fall . . . but also that Faery will too," she blurts, interrupting Cethin.

The group exchanges wary glances, but Cethin nods in contemplation.

"All the more reason we need to deal with him," Cethin says, looking at her with his bright green eyes that see through her soul, his hands balled into tight fists before continuing. "The question is, how do we stop him? Zella informed me that a powerful mage protects him. Is that true?"

At the mention of Neros, Estrid flinches and shivers like a spider has just crawled up her back. *Please stop talking about him.* Bile rises in her throat.

Cethin narrows his eyes and frowns, picking up on her discomfort. Estrid takes a deep breath to calm her anxiety.

"Yes. His name is Neros," Zella says, catching Estrid's gaze from across the table. Estrid gives her a slow nod to continue.

"Rodden was never a saint, but when Estrid got her powers, Neros showed up and took control. It made Rodden crueler. He's lost his mind and, most likely, his soul to that evil mage. Neros has devised ways to command Estrid and her magic, turning her into a weapon to serve Rodden's greed," Zella explains.

Estrid can feel their eyes on her. Pity. Guilt. Anger. Emotions crowd the study, making her shrink back in her seat. She hates how they weaken her. She's been through so much.

A warm, steady hand takes hers and squeezes it. She looks up to see Cethin staring at her. A tic in his jaw muscles shows how he's barely holding it together.

Faris clears his throat, taking the heat off her. "They will all die, there is no doubt of that, but then what?"

"We place Zella on the throne," Estrid replies without a second thought.

"Estrid, no! It's yours!" Zella says, her eyes wide with surprise.

"No, Zella. You're Rodden's heir now. I'm not his family—or even a human, for that matter. The crown must go to you," Estrid insists, giving Zella a warm smile as she admits to the group that she isn't Rodden's successor.

While she hasn't yet said she's Cethin's daughter, this admission is like a heavy weight has been lifted off her shoulders.

"Zella, you've run that castle since you were five. You've taken care of everyone for as long as I can remember, and you're a force to be reckoned with . . . but you are also a good person. Someone I love and someone Nordians love," Estrid says as Zella blushes under all the attention from the group, tears forming at her kind words.

"It's settled. We kill Rodden and his mage and put Zella on the throne . . . but I have a condition of my own," Cethin says, his eyes settling on Estrid, making her uncomfortable. "You must take your place as queen of the Winter Court, Estrid. We've been locked down here since your mother disappeared. From what Del has told me, the power between the Fae courts is unbalanced. There can only be peace if there is harmony in the courts. I must do that. It was your mother's dream." He looks around the table as everyone nods.

Estrid has grown up in royalty and is used to the thought of having to rule one day, but that was in a kingdom she knew.

I don't know this world. How am I to be queen?

She pulls her hand from under Cethin's, fidgeting with her fingers as her nerves grow, before saying, "What if I can't rule a Fae court?"

To her surprise, it isn't Cethin who responds to her question but Del.

"We'll help you. You're not alone, Estrid. You have our support."

The first day of training starts early. The sun is barely up as Estrid, Zella, and Del make their way to the practice facilities.

A silver lining to being raised by a power-hungry Rodden is that Estrid and Zella have decent combat skills. He was a paranoid man who didn't have any male heirs, so he insisted that the girls learn to attack and defend themselves with several weapons in the event of any assassination attempts and the ending of his line.

The three of them arrive at the training grounds, which are better than Estrid expected, as with everything in the Shadow Court. There's an archery practice area that's fenced off to the left-hand side, with targets staged twenty, fifty, and one hundred feet away. A large sand circle for sparring sits in the middle. The walls are stacked with weapons of all natures, glistening in the morning sun.

Estrid and Zella roam the facility, taking it all in. They've never seen such a large one before.

Del walks alongside them, no reaction or words escaping her, as she goes to grab a long sword from a rack on a wall. She starts her drills with it, whisking it in a figure eight, testing its weight and grip. The blade whooshes through the air with every swing.

Estrid may not like her because of their past, but after what Del said yesterday, she can't help but develop some affection for the Fae.

As they approach the sand circle in the center, Faris, Tore, and Evander enter from an entrance opposite. The three of them seem relaxed and at home in this environment as they laugh and joke.

"Welcome, ladies. I hope the facilities will suit you," Faris says, opening his arms and giving them one of his brilliant smiles.

"They're adequate," Zella replies with a bored stare, receiving a chuckle from Tore.

Faris continues to smile at the three women, a glint of mischief in his eyes.

"If we're going to take Rodden down, we need to plan and train," he says, pacing the circle and rolling up his sleeves. "We know Del's skills very well, but, Estrid and Zella, we've not seen what you're capable of."

Faris draws his sword, the metal scraping against his scabbard as he undoes it.

"Tore and Zella, you'll pair up. Evander and Estrid, you two start together. Del, you said you wanted to fight me. Well, now is your chance."

Estrid looks between Del and Faris as he smiles, receiving a frown back from Del. Since their arrival, both Fae have been itching for a scrap. Worry churns in Estrid's stomach. Given the history of their relationship, she's worried that they might try to kill each other.

Her thoughts are scattered as she jumps in fright from Evander silently walking up to stand beside her without her noticing. For a large Fae, he's quiet. "Come on, Estrid. Let's leave these two to get whatever they need out of their system."

She gapes at him, taking in his enormous figure in greater detail. Up close and standing, he's bigger than Cethin. She cranes her neck to look at him. He doesn't have wings, but he has a set of ram-like horns on his head, adding more height to his already tall stature.

Not wanting to be rude, she gives him a small smile, swallowing her worry at facing a giant.

As they approach their part of the training yard, Evander unsheathes his cleaver-like sword. He gestures for Estrid to pick a weapon from the dozens that line the wall.

She runs her hands over the various blades, their steel cool under her fingertips. There are traditional long swords, swords with curved edges, swords with waves, rapiers, and even swords that are really more like hatchets. She examines all the blades, taking in their detail and craftsmanship.

There's a faint buzzing under her fingers as she glides them over one that's as black as the night. She picks it up, and to her surprise, it's warm to the touch. The weapon is light; the handle fits her hand perfectly. She's about to ask Evander about the strange blades, but when she turns around, he's already in a fighting stance.

Estrid crouches low, putting her dominant foot before her and bending her knees. She extends the black blade out as if it were an extension of her own body.

Estrid attacks first, but Evander blocks her with ease. She spins and tries again and again, but he stops her every time. Despite his hulking size, this Fae is more agile and nimble than she expected. They continue until she's puffing, sweat dripping down her face and back.

Evander grabs two water skins that hang on the wall near them and hands her one.

"You're not bad," he says, taking a long drink, his Adam's apple bobbing as he gulps the liquid down.

Estrid merely huffs in response to his words. She never got close to landing a hit on him.

Opening the skin, she gulps the cool water. It cascades down her throat like a trickling waterfall. Her body is a furnace, the coldness dousing the fire in her as she drinks deeply.

"You're a little out of practice, but your stance and grip are good. You haven't tapped into any of your Fae powers yet, so your speed and accuracy are off," he says.

"How do I tap into my Fae powers?"

"That is not my forte. Faris and Cethin are experts at that." He points to where Faris and Del are going at each other. They're a whirl of speed and blades. The dust from their movements hardly has time to settle before it's kicked up again.

Estrid watches the two warriors in fascination. They're evenly matched; neither is good enough to beat the other. The way they move is fluid and smooth, almost like a dance.

After what feels like hours, Del parries and knocks Faris's sword out of his hand. He hits the floor with a thud, dust exploding around him. The tip of Del's long blade is aimed at his neck, a small drip of blood beading from the pressure.

"Yield!" Del yells through heavy, ragged breaths.

With a smile on his face, he holds up his hands with a grin. "Okay, Del, I yield."

There's a collective sigh of relief from the group. Whatever they needed to work out has been taken care of. Drops of sweat drip down Faris's face and neck, soaking the front of his tunic.

Del looms over him, nearly straddling him on the ground. Her sword stays pointed at him. Faris looks up at her with intrigue, his deep brown eyes locked on her bright green ones. Del clears her throat and stands, offering him a hand up. Some of the tension in her eases as Faris accepts her gesture.

"It's been a long time since I've had a workout like that. Tore, Evander, you're getting slack!" Faris says with a giant grin on his face.

Evander and Tore chuckle together at their commanding officer.

"Won't you do me the honors, Del? Seems I haven't been able to keep our general in fighting shape," Evander says, offering Del a water skin.

She gives him a small smirk, and her cheeks flush as she leaves to follow Evander to the far side of the training grounds.

Faris approaches Estrid, sweat glistening on his face. He takes off his shirt to wipe it off, and his well-defined muscles shine. She stares at the wall of tanned, toned muscle that walks toward her.

"Something you like, Estrid?" he says, smiling at her.

"Ha, nothing I haven't seen before, Faris," she says, averting her eyes, but her cheeks are on fire from being caught gawking at his lean muscles.

He laughs and grabs a water skin, sitting on a bench to the side of the circle before turning it up and taking a long drink. She watches as water trickles down the sides of his mouth. Her thoughts are broken as Faris asks her about her training session with Evander.

"He said I'm out of practice and lack using my Fae powers, something he said you can help with."

Faris looks at her and nods as she comes to take a seat next to him. "I'll teach you some things, but a lot is linked to accepting, understanding, and controlling your shadow magic. Your father must help you with that. Has your power from your mother's side come through?"

Estrid stares at him.

My mother's powers? How can that be? I don't even have pointed ears like a Fae, let alone powers.

"No, I've only ever had shadow magic," she says, slightly worried about what she's missing.

"Well, Cethin is the right person to help you. You'll spend every afternoon with him, and mornings and evenings are with me for combat. Sound good?" he asks her, getting up and offering his hand for her to take.

✦ ✦ ✦

CHAPTER TWENTY-FOUR

One morning, after a deep sleep to recover from the previous day's training, Estrid enters the grounds to find Del, Zella, and Tore waiting there.

"Where are Faris and Evander?" Estrid asks, looking at Tore.

"They had to deal with rogue Fae. They should be back shortly," he says as he picks up a spear from the wall and twirls it.

Estrid grows impatient as time ticks on. Her confidence from the last few weeks has her saying, "Let's pair up today, Del."

Del looks at Estrid with uncertainty. Everyone knows the Fae doesn't go easy on anyone in sparring sessions.

"I'm not sure that's a good idea," Del says.

"Come on, Del. I've been training for weeks. I'm ready," Estrid pleads with her.

After some debate, Tore takes Zella off to the other side of the practice area, giving them space.

"Are you sure about this?" Del asks one more time, cocking an eyebrow as Estrid nods and takes her place in the circle's center.

Both women get into their fighting stances. Estrid attacks first, determined to prove her skills. Her heart races as Del blocks her. The shock scatters her thoughts before she tries again. Del blocks her once more, spinning around and sending Estrid flying across the sand.

She lands with a thump on the ground, the impact knocking the wind out of her.

Come on, Estrid! she thinks as she wheezes, her cheeks flushing with embarrassment from the easy defeat.

Del swaggers over, offering her hand to Estrid.

Show-off.

Estrid gets up, the Fae's arrogance triggering her determination. She takes a deep breath in, schooling her nerves.

Del nods to go again. This time, she attacks first. Estrid blocks and counters but misses. Her heart races as they trade blows one for one. The movements disorientate Estrid. Too fast. She spins to duck out of the way as Del lunges, but she's too slow. Del's sword clips Estrid's unpadded right side.

The world stops. It takes a moment for Estrid to figure out what's happened. There's a warm trickle down her abdomen as a slice of pain hits her, waking her to the fact that something feels wrong. Del's muffled voice doesn't register with Estrid as she runs over to look at the wound.

"Estrid! Estrid! Are you okay?" Del says as she helps Estrid peel off her training gear, blood slowly flowing down her tunic and pants.

"It's going to be okay. Let me get help," Del murmurs as Estrid tries to control her breathing.

Shit! That's a lot of blood. Her breaths quicken as her panic rises.

"Del! What the fuck have you done?" Faris's familiar voice booms into the yard. Del flinches at the sound as he comes running over.

"It's not her fault. We were sparring," Estrid says, swaying a little as blood seeps through her fingers.

I don't feel that great.

Her head spins as the sting of the wound bites. She winces, not from the pain but at the guilt of putting Del in this position.

Faris's expression is furious, his face turning a dark shade of red. His brow crinkles in worry before he turns to throw a gaze filled with daggers at Del.

"Why are you training with her? Tore told you to wait!"

With little effort, Faris picks up Estrid in his arms and makes his way to the medical wing. Del just stands there, her brows furrowed in a mixture of worry, anger, and annoyance.

"It's not her fault," Estrid says to Faris, looking back as Evander tries to comfort Del with a pat on the shoulder, but she storms off.

"No, it's both of your fault!" he seethes.

Estrid flinches beneath his anger, but his eyes give away his concern.

They arrive at the medical ward that sits high in one of the palace towers. Faris places Estrid on a bed as they wait for someone to attend her. There's a violent tic in his jaw. His shoulders are tense. He paces the room, the rhythmic thud, thud, thud of his boots the only noise.

"I'll be fine, Faris. I've sustained far worse injuries than this," Estrid says, trying to hold a smile while her head spins from the loss of blood.

This is not her first wound, nor the worst she's ever received. The day she arrived in the Dark Forest, someone had wounded her to the point of death. If Rafe and the mysterious stranger hadn't saved her, she wouldn't be here today.

"I'm not angry, Estrid. I'm worried. Without your Fae power fully in, your not healing fast enough. Nothing can happen to you, do you understand? I can't bear to see what would become of your father if anything happened to you. It almost killed him when Eria died. You mean too much to him . . . to all of us," he says, his face softening from anger into worry.

Estrid's stomach twists at his words. *Things would have been so different if I had been here.* Regret fills her heart. It's the first time that people have cared about her well-being because of *who* she is rather than *what* she is and how they can use her.

She reaches out and takes Faris's calloused hand in hers. His shoulders relax as he sits in the wooden chair beside her. It looks like a child's seat with his broad frame and giant feathery wings spilling over it.

They wait, Faris's knee bobbing as the minutes tick by.

Estrid looks around the tidy medical wing. It's not much different from the infirmary in Oberetta. Two rows of crisply made beds line either side of the room, and tables used for equipment sit next to each bed.

Unlike Oberetta, however, the space is well lit, with natural light entering from the glass skylights on the roof. Dozens of plants line the walls, giving the ward a forest-like feel and smell.

"This place is more like a greenhouse than a medical ward," she says, trying to distract Faris.

He stops bobbing his knee, looking over his shoulder at the plants. Her comment seems to ease his worrying, his body slowly releasing some of its tension.

"We use many plants for healing. What better way to use them than to grow them near the patients? There's an added benefit as well—we've found that they uplift the room and calm those admitted in here."

Estrid asks about the different flora, not expecting Faris to answer her questions. They're as distracting for her as they are for him.

A familiar shuffling of feet and robes comes down one of the dark hallways that filter into the ward, drowning out Faris's voice. He either doesn't notice or it's nothing to be worried about, as he continues to lounge back in his chair.

The movement grows closer. The brightness of the room filters to the edges of the hallway, allowing Estrid to make out the faint outline of a hooded and hunched-over Fae. As the figure emerges, the sunlight that streams in from the many windows that line the roof illuminates their face.

Estrid inhales in surprise. A heart-shaped face with wrinkled and worn leathery skin peeks at her from behind the black hood. It's the eyes that she recognizes. They're the same murky blue eyes she caught between her bouts of consciousness when recovering from the village attack.

"You," she says with awe.

The old Fae faces her with a small smile that makes their wrinkled skin look even more worn out as the crow's feet scrunch together.

Estrid watches them shuffle to the bedside. They open one drawer and pull out dressings, scissors, and ointments.

"Who . . . who are you?" she asks as her hands are pushed aside by the mystery Fae, who cuts away her shirt. Estrid hisses as her wound is cleansed.

"She's known as the Crone," Faris says, watching everything the mysterious Crone is doing as she silently works away.

She applies a green balm, and Estrid sucks in a sharp breath as a cold sensation hits her wound. Tiny needles prickle her skin as the balm works. A trickle of warmth soon replaces the icy cold over the area, and the piercing feeling fades.

Despite her hands looking like leather wrapped over twigs, the Crone's touch is tender and soft. Estrid stares in awe as the strange Fae finishes her care. The cut has stopped bleeding, an angry red scar replacing it.

Estrid has many questions, but without a word, the Crone turns around and starts shuffling her way out of the room.

Cethin enters as the old Fae steps into the fading light of the hallway. His green eyes shine brightly but dull as they lock on Estrid. He relaxes, the worry ebbing away.

The ancient Fae shuffles past him. She's so short that she only comes up to his waist. He stoops to whisper something to her, giving her a slight nod and a hug as she leaves.

Faris immediately stands up straight and tenses at the sight of Cethin, who walks over to Estrid's bed.

"What happened?" Cethin's tone is commanding and authoritative as he looks at Faris. Estrid swears she sees Faris momentarily flinch at the question, but he regains his composure.

"My king—" he starts, but Estrid quickly interrupts him, not willing for him to take any blame.

"I was sparring with Del. I'm fine. Let's move on."

Cethin raises an eyebrow while glancing between her and Faris. The general is still standing tall, ready to bear any punishment.

Satisfied, Cethin nods and dismisses Faris with a wave of his hand.

Faris's footsteps fade down the stone hall as the bed dips from Cethin coming to sit with her. He seems different today, or maybe the room's light shows the slight fine lines of age on his skin. Estrid's still coming to grips with the fact that Cethin is her father.

"Something bothering you?" he asks.

Her stomach is in knots, and Cethin's observant mind makes her nervous. Her hands are clammy as they sweat. She fiddles with her fingers. She's going to need to ask this at some point—now is just as good as any other time.

"If you could feel I was alive when my mother died, why didn't you come for me?"

The memories of all those years being manipulated, abused, and tortured by Rodden flood her mind. Her eyes sting at the thoughts that have left her broken and scarred.

Cethin shuffles up to sit closer to her, the bed squeaking under his weight. His wings cast a shadow over her. He lets out a heavy sigh. "When your mother died, I tried to leave. I tried to get to you, but powerful magic like I have never felt before was placed across all of the Shadow Court. It nearly killed me trying to break through it. It drove me insane. Then one day, it was like someone had put a hood over my eyes. I couldn't sense you, but I knew you were still alive. I would have felt it in here if you weren't," he says, pointing to his heart.

Estrid continues to listen, knowing Neros and Rodden have something to do with this. *Everything would have been so different.* These admissions bring some closure to her, but there are more questions than answers.

"It wasn't until you must have escaped Rodden into the Dark Forest that I could feel you again. I'll never forget it. I was sparring with Faris. It was the one time that he's been able to beat me." Cethin chuckles before he becomes serious once more. "Estrid, you must understand that I did everything I could to get to you, but we were imprisoned here. Locked in our own home. The best I could do was send someone who isn't bound by magic."

"The Crone?" Estrid asks.

Cethin nods, a small smile on his face. "And Rafe. I felt it when you were hurt, and I sent Rafe to protect you. When he was wounded, I felt your pain even more, so I sent the Crone to heal you both. When she was done, she left Rafe with you. You would have been alone otherwise." He looks down at the ground, unwilling to meet Estrid's gaze. "It's the only thing I could do, but I feel like I've still failed you."

Cethin hangs his head, his long black hair draped over his face. The room grows so heavy with despair and guilt that it almost chokes her.

"I have never felt so helpless as I have with your mother's death and not being able to find you. I tried to get to you. The Crone, Rafe, the books—anything to let you know I was here for you."

Estrid's lost for words at Cethin's open honesty.

"Books?" she asks, curious what he meant.

"I couldn't physically get to you, but I wanted you to have some knowledge of the Fae. Deep down, I knew this day would come. I had a feeling that you would return home, so I asked the Crone to take books about the Fae to prepare you. The magic that bound us here was so strong—until you broke it," he says, giving Estrid that proud fatherly look, but his sad eyes betray his genuine emotions.

"None of this is your fault," Estrid says, giving his hand a quick squeeze. "This is all connected to Rodden and Neros. Rodden used me for his gain and greed. When you felt me almost dying, I was. He sent me into a village to kill innocent people, but they found a way to stop me. It wasn't until I had a crossbow bolt sticking out of me that I realized how I was being used. It was like a veil was lifted, and I could finally see clearly. If you hadn't sent Rafe and the Crone, it would have been too late."

✦　✦　✦

After an arduous night's sleep, Estrid's wounds have healed thanks to the Crone's healing magic.

She makes her way down the winding hallways to join the others in Cethin's office. The morning sunshine trickles through the big floor-to-ceiling window overlooking the training yard. Estrid walks into the room with Zella and Del. The rest of the group is already there, wearing casual outfits.

Cethin and Faris stand over the map, deep in conversation about mobilizing thousands of troops into Oberetta without alerting Rodden.

Zella goes to position herself by Tore. They've become close since their training began, and Estrid notices that Zella's giddy-girl behavior has subsided, replaced by a bond that Estrid can't quite put her finger on. Tore smiles at Zella as she stands next to him, whispering something to her.

Estrid takes a spot by Cethin and Faris, trying to deter Del from following her. Since accidentally hurting Estrid yesterday, Del has stuck closer to her, taking her role of protector even more seriously.

"We can't all go through the portal and walk through the Dark Forest. It will take us weeks to get to Rodden's castle," Faris says, his eyes roaming a single large, worn-out map of the human realm that's laid across the circular table.

"We can't just shadow walk to the front of Rodden's castle either. We need to find a spot where we can discreetly shadow walk our forces in without alerting Rodden. Once we've assembled, then we attack," Evander says, Tore nodding at his accurate assessment.

Cethin looks between the map and Faris's commanders. His eyes roam over the landscape until he pinpoints a location about twenty miles away from Rodden's castle, a spot between the Dark Forest and Oberetta.

"There, that should be big enough for us to land and close enough to the Dark Forest not to have any major villages near it," Cethin says, placing a marker next to it. He looks at Estrid and raises his eyebrows before asking her thoughts.

She hasn't ever been part of battle plans. Rodden and Neros only dictated what targets she needed to destroy. Her role was to wipe out entire towns, not plan battles.

She walks over to the map, looking at the spot Cethin has chosen.

"It's a good spot, but Rodden's a paranoid man. He'll have scouts around most of his kingdom, so you'll need to ensure you track them down before they see us," she says, pointing to their likely positions.

When she escaped Rodden, protecting the village enabled her to identify patterns that his scouts formed. Their strategies became predictable, which was part of how she had successfully taken them down.

"Okay, so we need to make sure we have enough shadow walkers who can portal battalions in as short an amount of time as possible," Faris says, helping himself to some food laid out for them in the room.

Estrid's stomach rumbles. She hasn't eaten since sparring with Del yesterday.

Just as she's about to reach for the lindenberry jam, Del speaks to the room. "What about Zain?"

"What *about* him, Del?" Faris grits out, turning to give her a look that would make anyone else cower.

She returns his scowl, the easy truce between them over the last few days disappearing in a second. At the mention of Zain's name, Estrid's stomach somersaults.

Del clenches and unclenches her fists. "Zain and Alvey are at Rodden's castle. Are you planning to attack while they're in there?" She glares at Faris. While they've been strategizing, it hadn't crossed Estrid's mind that they could put Zain at risk.

"When your cousin left to seek an alliance with that pig of a human, he gave up all rights of us giving a fuck," Faris replies, his words laced with venom.

She's given up her family for mine. Faris's support for Del echoes in Estrid's mind.

Del storms over to him, drawing her dagger with a hiss. Faris doesn't retreat, pulling his own sharp blade out and sending everyone leaping back.

The big room shrinks as the two warriors head for each other. If they fought in here, they would destroy everything.

Come on, Estrid. It's not just about Del. You're worried about him too.

She puts her plate down and walks to Cethin, who seems unbothered by the potential outbreak of violence.

"We need to get to Zain and warn him to get out." She tugs at his hand. "Please, I'm asking you, as my father, to send someone."

Cethin looks down at her with an astonished look on his face. This is the first time she's openly acknowledged him as her father. She also has a feeling that he knows the impact that Zain has on her. He stares at her.

"Please. Now that the portal is open, we could send a shadow warrior to warn them. Rodden's never seen a Shadow Fae. He won't be looking out for one," she continues, all eyes in the room on her.

She may logically agree with Faris's statements, but something is telling her that Zain needs help.

Cethin places a large hand on her shoulder. "Why do you want to do this, Estrid?"

"Zain and Alvey are Del's only family, and . . ." She pauses. *Because I still care for him.* "And it's the right thing to do."

She holds her chin up high, fixing her eyes on her father, trying not to let her nerves show. She catches Del staring at her, a look of amazement on her face.

Cethin searches her face, then nods once. "Okay. If that's what you want, we'll send a shadow walker to warn them."

At his words, Del relaxes. She gives Estrid a silent thank you, stepping back from Faris, who still scowls at her.

Cethin turns to Del and says, "Understand that if he betrays us, I will kill him. Rodden dies, and anyone in league with him will die too. Am I clear?"

Del nods at Cethin's serious tone, leaving no room to be questioned, then sheathes her dagger. The tension in the space dissipates.

The meeting ends with Faris ordering Tore to send a set of warriors to shadow walk to both scout Nordia and warn Zain.

CHAPTER TWENTY-FIVE

As Zain and Alvey portal for Nordia, the hissing voice in his head pulls him back to Rodden, but something deeper inside him tells him to stop, to fight it. As they move across the snowy landscape, they question lords and ladies about Rodden's needs and desires and collect intelligence on him.

Nordia is a harsh kingdom that makes most of its income from trading in precious metals, which are hard to mine and becoming rarer by the year.

Many of their conversations with the gentry say this puts pressure on Rodden's treasury. He overtaxes his subjects, leaving barely anything for them to live off. Nordia's people are resourceful, surviving off hunting and fishing, but there isn't much else through trade or agriculture.

As well as taxing his citizens to the brink of starvation, Rodden's a cruel king who rules through fear. To quell any of the highborn nobles from starting a rebellion, he holds their family members as wards in his court.

Alvey has repeatedly questioned Zain about whether seeking an alliance with the human king is the right thing to do.

Don't listen to him, Zain. You need Rodden for your plans. There is no one else you can trust to help you, that voice hisses in his ear each time his brother brings it up.

The battle causes his heart to ache, a constant dull throb, but they don't have any other choice. Cethin and the Shadow Court are their sworn enemy. This is the only option to get the Summer Court back.

After two days of travel, they reach Oberetta. A variety of colors from banners, standards, and flags blots out the muddy ground. An army of thousands has amassed out the front of the castle.

Zain and Alvey look at each other in confusion as they watch people come and go from the large, heavy wooden gates. Unlike last time, where there was free traffic flow, guards check who enters, who leaves, and what they carry.

"This makes things much harder, Zain," Alvey says as he scans the horizon.

Zain nods, trying to devise a plan.

He's about to say something when a carriage rolls past them. It has a dark maroon color with a golden trim around the edges. Zain recognizes the crest on the door: an elk stag with large antlers. It belongs to one of Rodden's lords whose keep sits farther south. He nudges Alvey's elbow to follow the coach.

Zain leans over to his brother and says, "Pull up your hood and get close enough to make it look like we're swords to hire."

Alvey nods as they both step forward to trail the carriage to get into the gates. It rumbles on, splashing mud up as it rolls over the soggy ground. It's late autumn, and a light snowfall has fallen, but it's still too warm for the snow to stick to the surface. Everything is wet and muddy, making for an even more depressing sight against the gray sky.

The guards at the gate stop the coach and begin talking to the driver. While they're distracted, Zain and Alvey slip past undetected and walk through the castle gate.

During their initial visit to Oberetta, the inside of the keep was a hive of activity in trade, with merchants and prospective buyers haggling over prices. This time, the trading markets are nowhere to be seen.

Soldiers' camps, cooking structures, weapons shelters, and other things have replaced them—enough to support an army. The invasive, bitter smells of human sweat, waste, and filth replace the rich aromas of street food.

"What's going on?" Alvey says to Zain, giving a friendly nod to a soldier who looks like he's about to start a fight.

"I'm not sure. Why is he calling a muster?"

They walk along the outer edges of the road, observing the many soldiers mixing and mingling. They sharpen their long swords and shorter blades around fires, laughing, drinking, and eating.

Zain and Alvey halt as they approach the inner walls. Several Summer Court guards are at the barracks. They stand there casually, watching the human troops and the crowd before them, their golden helmets shiny and bright compared to the dark and dreary castle grounds of Oberetta. Zain and Alvey duck down an alley to avoid being seen.

"What is our army doing here?" Alvey says in a frantic voice.

Zain peers around the corner of the wall, hoping they weren't spotted as they ducked away. The guards haven't moved or sounded the alarm.

"Fuck! I don't know, but we need to find out," Zain says, trying to stay calm, his intuition telling him to get out.

The Summer Court's presence can only mean one thing.

Balius is here.

Cursing at the situation, Zain racks his mind about how this could have happened.

Since his uncle's betrayal, nothing has seemed to go his way. First, he loses his court, Estrid's hurt, and when he thinks he has her safe, it turns out that she's both a Shadow and Winter Court Fae. Ever since leaving Cethin's court, he's had a niggling feeling in his gut telling him to go back, but as soon as the thought crosses his mind, that voice surfaces. The ache in his head becomes stronger if he fights it.

Alvey interrupts Zain's thoughts and pulls him down another muddy alleyway. "Come on, we need a drink."

"Now isn't the time to get drunk, Alvey."

"You want to know why they're here? The best way is through the loose lips of a drunken soldier. I guarantee you that whatever is going on, we can find out easily by just plying some sorry sod with a few drinks."

✦　✦　✦

They dart down the back alleys of Oberetta, sparing a glance behind them every so often while trying to avoid drawing suspicion to themselves. The alleyways are a stark contrast to the well-maintained roads that lead up to the castle.

Their feet slosh in the mud as they dash through the maze of paths, narrowly avoiding the potholes and the occasional chamberpot that barely misses being emptied on their heads, splattering on the ground as it's hoisted from a window.

"Gods, this place is barbaric!" Alvey says over his shoulder, dodging being hit with liquid waste. The ammonia stings their nostrils as rats scurry out of the way. The air feels dirty as they continue their journey.

They stop outside a ramshackle brick building with a sign reading The Black Stag Tavern. Enormous deer antlers hang over the entrance. Alvey opens the door, pushing Zain through before he can protest more.

The establishment has a small set of stairs that go down to a massive hall that smells of stale beer, human sweat, and off cheese. It's well lit by a huge candle chandelier hanging from above, providing light over ten long wooden tables lined with chairs and bench seats.

Zain and Alvey make their way down the steps, hoods up just enough to cover their ears. The space is a hive of activity, filled with soldiers and ladies of the night. Behind the bar stands a lanky man with an oddly shaped bald head, scarred and dented.

Zain scrunches his nose as the barkeep spits on a glass he seems to be polishing. In the far corner, on a small elevated stage, sits a lute player, singing a merry tune that's drowned out by the soldiers' loud banter.

They approach the bar, Alvey signaling the lanky man for three ales. The keep nods as Alvey places his coin down, then turns to observe the messy chaos around them, resting his arms on either side of the counter behind him.

"Now what?" Zain asks, facing the barkeep as he brings their drinks to them.

"Now we find a disgruntled soldier and give him an ale," Alvey says, picking up two mugs and taking a sip from one as he heads toward the lute player.

Across the room is a pair of older soldiers, absorbed in conversation. Neither seems to partake in the debauchery like the others who surround them. Each man has three pins on the shoulders of their uniform. Lieutenants are sufficiently aware of what's going on but low enough not to care to hold their tongue.

One man has a deep purple scar that cuts across his face. The other has rumpled brown hair and a five-o'clock shadow, giving him a dirty, unkempt look.

The brothers sit down next to the two soldiers, greeting them with a nod. Alvey places one ale slightly off to his side while taking a sip from his mug. Zain watches the men whisper to each other, straining to hear what they say over the noise of the bar.

The one with the scarred face gets up with a grunt and departs, leaving his unkempt friend on his own.

Alvey suddenly slams his ale down. "Godsdamn Rafe! He said he would be here. I bet you he's gone and found some skirt to chase and left me paying for his beer."

Zain catches on to Alvey's ruse, agreeing. "Yep, he's always had his priorities mixed up."

The guard next to them eyes the large, undrunk tankard and finishes his own before asking, "Waiting on a friend?"

Alvey nods with a huff, faking annoyance as he scouts the room.

"Care to have an ale?" Zain asks the soldier, who shrugs and takes it.

The three sit in silence, listening to the lute player's merry tune reach its high just as a scuffle breaks out at the back of the bar.

Alvey slides over to the man and holds out his hand. "Remy. This is Xavier." He points to Zain.

"Derry," the lieutenant says, taking a large gulp of the ale he's been given. The amber liquid drips down the sides of his mouth onto his black tabard.

"Place is busier than usual," Alvey says.

"Every tavern is busy today with the entire Nordian army here." Derry takes another gulp, putting the mug down harder than needed. Zain tries to hide his smile at his brother's brilliance.

"Why's that?" he asks, then winces as he realizes his directness. Derry eyes up Zain with some suspicion.

Alvey jumps in. "We've just returned from weeks on the road from the far north. We're hunters, so we only come in when we have meat and fur for trade. It's been a while since we've been in Oberetta, and we're a little out of touch."

Derry shrugs and continues to drink his ale, finishing the last sip and releasing a burp that smells like rotten cheese.

"You've come back at a busy time, that's for sure. We're marching out in a few days to take on Solian," Derry says with a hiccup. "Bloody king's got some alliance, which gives him the forces he needs. All bullshit if you ask me. I just want to earn my coin, survive the fight, and fuck off back home."

Alvey and Zain try to act like the news means nothing to them. Alvey nods as he takes another sip of ale while Zain refuses to drink from a potentially spit-polished mug. Around the room, there's a sea of black-and-gold tabards mixed in with common folk.

"Who's the alliance with?" Zain watches as Derry eyes up his untouched ale.

"Dunno, some Fae lord or king or something. All I know is they showed up a few weeks ago, and the king is mustering his troops."

Derry fixes his gaze directly on Zain's tankard. He gladly hands it over; the soldier nods in appreciation and gulps it down.

"I'll go up and get us another round," Alvey offers, pushing his chair back with a scrape on the stone floor.

As he walks to the bar, four Summer Fae enter the tavern. Alvey stops in the middle of the room and locks eyes with a guard, who points and yells, "It's Alvey!"

No one in the room seems to notice their shouts as Alvey backtracks and comes to the table where Zain and Derry sit.

Shit! How the hell did they find us?

Zain stands up, drawing his sword, the sound earning a few startled looks from those around them.

"It's the princes! Stop them!" a Summer Fae yells as he draws his blade with one fluid motion. The four guards clamber down the stairs, trying to get through the drunken crowd.

Zain plants his feet, ready to fight, but Alvey grabs him, pulling him toward a curtain behind the lute player's little stage. "I know a way out!"

If Zain weren't about to run for his life, it wouldn't surprise him that Alvey knows a secret way to escape.

As they dash across the platform to get to the passage, they can hear the Fae shouting at the bar patrons, who haven't taken kindly to their intrusion or being pushed around.

The sounds of the lute player are drowned out as soldiers grunt and yell before a fight breaks out. Glasses smash, chairs crash to the floor, and fists hit flesh with a dull thud.

Alvey and Zain dart through a small back room, which leads outside to another dark alleyway. With light footsteps, they run, trying not to draw too much attention to themselves. They make it to a doorway big enough to duck into and hide, both breathing heavily as they listen for any signs of being followed.

"How has Balius made an alliance?" Alvey stares at Zain, shell-shocked, breathing heavily.

Zain shakes his head and runs his hands through his long, sandy blond hair. "I don't know, but we need to get out of here."

"And go where, Zain? You wanted to leave the Shadow Court to come here. Where do we go now?" Alvey says as he throws his hands up, trying to keep his voice down.

Zain's furious with himself and the situation he finds them in yet again.

"Fuck, I don't know. We need to find a way out, and then we can figure things out from there."

The shadows and darkness hide them from their pursuers, the shouts and footsteps around them fading as the other Fae run past them. They both let out a collective sigh of relief.

Zain tentatively steps out from behind a doorway. "They've gone. Let's go."

He moves forward and weaves his hands to open a portal, but something stops his magic. It feels like a clamp squeezing around him.

"What's wrong? Why isn't your magic working?" Alvey says in a panicked voice.

Zain shakes his hands and tries again. The clamping feeling grows stronger this time, pinching the skin around his wrists.

"Argh! Damn it, I don't know. My powers won't work. Something's blocking it," he says, searching the small alleyway, his instincts scream-ing at him to run. "We have to head for the gates."

They start to move just as a shout goes up to find them. Footsteps echo all around them as soldiers flood the space.

Zain and Alvey pull up their hoods, hiding their faces as they creep down the alleyways in silence, working their way out of the maze to get out of the main entrance. Heavy boots start pounding on the ground behind them. Zain spares a glance, grabbing Alvey to duck into another doorway. A Summer Court soldier runs past them, pausing for a moment to scan the area. Zain lets out a sigh of relief as they push forward again.

The sun sets beyond the castle's stone walls; shadows grow to keep them hidden. The hustle and bustle of the Nordian soldiers hasn't changed from when they first arrived on the main road, oblivious to the commotion unfolding.

They've just reached the gates when a familiar voice calls out, followed by the sounds of weapons being drawn and notched.

"Zain! Alvey! Not another step," Commander Manis says from behind them.

The brothers freeze. Zain looks ahead of them as four Summer Fae block the exit with their swords held ready. He goes for his own sword, but the sharp edge of a blade digs into his back as the cool tip of a dagger comes to his throat. His eyes dart to the left, finding Alvey in the same situation.

"Turn around," Manis says.

With their hands up, the brothers do as they're told. Someone snatches off their hoods, revealing their faces and ears to the world. The courtyard has gone deathly still as all eyes are on them.

You traitorous bastard, Zain snarls to himself as Manis, the commander of the Summer Court Army and right-hand man to his treacherous uncle, stands before him in his full green-and-gold military uniform. That uniform was meant to serve Zain as king, as it had done for his father before him.

Manis stares at the brothers with a smug look plastered on his face. A dozen Summer Fae surround them. Zain notices the fresh raised purple scar on Manis's cheek from their last encounter, when he escaped the Summer Court, giving him some satisfaction.

"Seems I didn't kill you the last time we met, Zain, but I'm pleased that you've made it so easy to capture you both. Where's Del?"

Rage fills Zain, his blood pumping through his body and pounding in his ears from the adrenaline. The cool steel dagger at his neck digs in. A warm trickle rolls down his skin as blood escapes a slight cut from the sharpened blade.

Manis stands and stares at them, waiting for an answer.

"I'll ask you one more time. Where's Del?"

The blade at Zain's throat digs a little deeper. The bite of the blade stings as it cuts into his skin.

"She's not here. She left us," Zain says, looking around to find any way out.

Manis looks to his right. Zain follows his line of sight; a pricking sensation covers his skin as the throb in his head grows. He lets out a hiss as a figure dressed in black robes steps out from inside a small guard shed next to the gate. Neros nods to Manis and leaves without another word, his heavy robes swishing on the ground.

The smug look on Manis's face fades a little at not having captured Del. He spits down in front of him, looking at Zain with his cold blue eyes.

"Take them to the dungeon."

The soldiers remove the blades from their necks. Patting Zain down, they take all his weapons. Then they're pushed down the muddy road, both fighting the holds that their men have on them.

As they approach the dark prison, the butt of a sword hits Zain's head, and he crumples to the floor.

+ + +

CHAPTER TWENTY-SIX

Cold stone numbs Zain's cheek as he comes around. His head pounds and the familiar metallic scent of blood surrounds him. He lies there, eyes shut, head spinning, listening to his surroundings.

Drip.

Drip.

Drip.

The air is moist and damp. The stale and pungent odor of mildew mixes with blood, assaulting his sensitive sense of smell. Little feet scurrying along the stone floors echo around him.

When he opens his eyes, it's dark apart from the orange glow of the torches in the hallway. He takes in his environment: hard gray stone walls and iron bars.

A groan escapes him as he sits up. "Argh," he says as a sharp pain has him jolting back. The more he moves, the more agony he feels, like a hot poker being pressed to his skin. It floods his body from his ankle.

With great effort, he tries not to move his foot, but it's impossible to get it to cooperate. The sounds of chains dragging on the cold stone floor follow his movement. Iron chains. He feels so weak, his body trying to repair the wound on his head while the metal drains his magic.

Taking a deep breath, he tries to push himself up further. Using all his energy, he drags himself over to lean against the wall. The rough and uneven surface of the stone bricks digs into his back.

Zain's vision blurs from the searing pain in his ankle. Looking around his tiny cell, he notices that Alvey's not with him.

"Alvey? Alvey, are you there?"

Silence. He strains, trying to focus his throbbing head on the sounds of his brother. The only thing he can hear is the constant drips of water echoing off the stone walls.

"Zain?"

Relief washes through him, evaporating the band constricting his chest. Alvey's voice is raspy and weak. Knowing their captors have likely left him in the same condition as Zain.

Manis will use everything at his disposal to keep the brothers subdued. The commander knows their power and skills intimately, having trained them in combat since they were younglings. Zain still finds it hard to believe his mentor and father figure in his life has betrayed them.

"Alvey, are you okay?"

Silence. Chains scrape against the stone floor.

Alvey lets out a grunt of pain. "If you call having an iron cuffs chained to your leg okay, then yes, I'm okay."

"Fuck, I'm sorry, Alvey. What a mess. Something told me coming back here was our only option, but now . . . How did Manis and Balius get here?"

"It's a mess all right, but no one could have predicted that, Zain. The only thing we need to focus on is getting out of here."

Alvey lets out a hiss as he drags himself further along the floor.

The clanking of keys opens a gate out of sight. It screeches open, metal scraping on metal. Footsteps pound the stone floor, reverberating off the walls.

The orange torches flicker at the disturbance in the air as someone walks past. Zain looks to his right as Commander Manis stands before him, his full military attire still on.

"How are your accommodations, boys?" he says with his hands on his hips, the edges of his long green cape dragging on the floor. "It could be more comfortable if you cooperate and tell me what I want to know."

Zain doesn't respond to Manis's taunts, not breaking his gaze on the Fae. Rage simmers under the surface as he forgets the pain in his leg and stands up. He clenches his jaw and grits his teeth as the iron on his ankle bites back. He won't give Manis the satisfaction of his torment.

Squaring his shoulders, he comes to stand face to face with Manis. The man he grew up respecting, his mentor, is no longer there. Instead, a hollow imposter waits before him. His face shows weathering, and his once sun-kissed skin appears dull and pale.

Zain studies Manis. His eyes are drawn to the commander's neck. Out the top of his tabard creep the same black lines as Rodden's, though they're less pronounced, the tips just visible under his tunic. They look like thin vines strangling their host.

"What do you want, Manis?"

Zain takes an agonizing step closer to the cell bars, careful not to touch them. The cuff around his ankle has already depleted his magic; any further contact and it'll knock him out. He tries not to sway on his feet. Tries not to show any weakness.

"Where are Del, the witch, and the seer? You've not made our new ally happy, Zain. It seems you brought his daughter back only to snatch her away again, and you took his precious seer with you. Where are they?"

Zain scoffs at Manis's question, trying to sound as uninterested as he can.

"Del left us, and I don't know where the other two are. Why would we steal a witch and a seer? They're humans," he says, his legs almost buckling from the energy it takes to keep him upright.

Alvey laughs in the cell next to him, drawing Manis's attention. "I wish our father could see how far you've fallen, Manis. The lapdog of his spineless and incompetent little brother."

Zain watches Manis's jaw tic with annoyance. The commander waves to someone on the other side of the dungeon. Three pairs of boots enter, their heavy feet stomping loudly as the metal boot caps clank on the floor.

A burly Nordian soldier steps up to open Zain's cell.

Zain stands his ground as the guard enters, grabbing him by the arm and pulling him through. He doesn't fight it. Can't fight. Next to him, another guard pulls Alvey through into the hallway alongside him.

Zain checks Alvey for injuries. To his relief, his sibling has nothing but the iron manacles on his ankles.

Manis steps in front of Zain, his nose inches away. "Tell us where they are, Zain. I won't ask again; next time, I'll force it out of you . . . or your brother. Neros's spell to bring you back here worked well enough, I see. I'm sure he has other ways of getting their whereabouts from you."

What does he mean by Neros's spell?

Neither Zain nor Alvey responds to Manis's threat.

Zain holds Manis's stare as a cruel smile creeps over the commander's face. He gives a nod to the two burly soldiers who stand beside them.

Zain is pushed aside as the guards grab Alvey's arms. A third looms in front of his brother, waiting for Manis's command.

"Last chance, Zain," Manis says, those ocean blue eyes not breaking their stare.

"Don't give them anything, Zain," Alvey says as Manis gives another nod to the soldiers.

Zain's heart drops to the pit of his stomach. He tries to dig into his magic, whatever will help Alvey, but the iron blocks it like a tight lid on a box.

"Don't touch him, Manis! You want me, not him!"

The first punch flies, hitting Alvey in the abdomen. Alvey grunts, refusing to let his pain show.

"This can be over, Zain. Just tell me what I want to know."

Zain looks at Alvey, who coughs, trying to take in what air he can. He catches Zain's eyes, shaking his head in defiance of what Manis wants.

"Tsk, tsk . . . you were always too stubborn for your own good. Stupid fools," Manis says, yanking Zain's arms to force him to watch as they pummel Alvey.

The sounds of bones crunching echo in the room as Alvey goes down. The guards haul him up again and have him kneel. Bile rises in Zain's throat at the sight.

Alvey's blue eyes catch Zain's as he yells, "Don't tell them anything, Zain!"

Another heavy punch gets him head-on. Alvey crumples to the floor; this time, he doesn't stand up.

Zain's stomach churns. He stumbles forward to get to Alvey.

I'll kill you for this, you bastard. You won't live for long once I'm out of these cuffs.

Zain thrashes in Manis's tight grip as he roars with anger. Manis grabs Zain's hair, forcing him to look at him.

"This can stop, Zain. Just tell me where they are," he says, wiping a splatter of Alvey's blood from his cheek.

The assault on his brother stops as soldiers drag a barely conscious Alvey back up again. To Zain's surprise, Alvey chuckles as he raises his head awkwardly.

Zain meets his brother's crystal-blue eyes. They're set with determination and flicker with defiance. With a huff, Manis signals for the guards to resume their work.

Each punch feels like a piece of Zain's soul is being stolen. He stops counting the number of punches Alvey takes. The wet sounds of flesh hitting flesh leave him unrecognizable.

The punishing noises stop when Manis holds up his hands and instructs the soldiers to take Alvey back into his cell. The commander pulls Zain into his cell once again, a vicious sneer on his face.

Manis shuts the gate with a click. "I will break you, Zain. You may think you can endure this, but I'll crush you."

+ + +

Zain sits in the damp, dark dungeon after Manis leaves. A pit grows in his stomach as he barely makes out Alvey's breaths. They're wet, wheezy, and labored. The silence stretches for hours, leaving Zain with nothing but the water drips, rats, and his thoughts for company.

He replays the last few days in his head. Why did he leave Del, Estrid, and the Shadow Court? When he found out Estrid was half Shadow Fae, half Winter Fae, his natural reaction was that she was his enemy.

Years of his advisors telling him that the other Fae courts can't be trusted have made those thoughts stick in his mind, deeply embedded like hooks.

Even when Cethin took them on a tour and spoke the truth of the Shadow Court's past, his bias persisted.

That voice.

The one instructing him not to trust them, not to trust her. Embedding those hooks deeper.

It's done nothing but lead to his capture, Alvey being beaten to within an inch of his life, and alienating his cousin. He can't even fathom what Estrid must think of him. He was wrong, so very wrong, but he won't let Alvey suffer.

A groan comes from Alvey's cell. Muffled, garbled words follow it.

"Alvey, are you okay?"

More jumbled phrases. His brother wheezes as chains scrape on the ground.

"What are you trying to say?"

"I . . . argh . . . I'm fine, Zain."

Alvey's not fine, but it doesn't stop a relieved sigh from escaping Zain.

"I'll get us out of here, Alvey. Hold on, okay?"

"Zain . . . say nothing, okay? Don't give them what they want," Alvey says, struggling to get the words out.

Zain's emotions are all over the place. Fear for Alvey. Anger at Manis. Anger and shame at himself.

Alvey interrupts his thoughts. "Zain, do you hear me? Don't hand over Estrid or Imaya. Im-Imaya gave me a vision. Estrid . . . she's the key to unlocking it all for you . . . me . . . for all of us. No matter what happens to me, protect them both."

Zain absorbs Alvey's words before saying, "Why didn't you tell me you got a vision?"

"Give me your word, Zain," he wheezes, not answering the question.

"I wasn't planning to give them up, brother . . . but I will get us out of here. Just stay with me."

The dungeon door squeals open, sending Zain's heart racing. Manis's threat surfaces in his mind; his body tenses. Placing his hands on the cold, dirty floor, he pushes himself up, ready to take whatever punishment is coming his way.

There are no heavy footfalls that follow the gates being opened. Instead, the rustling sound of fabric dragging on the floor flows down the dungeon hall.

The orange torch flames flicker again as his uncle, Balius, stands in front of his cell. He's slightly shorter than Zain, and signs of aging mar his tanned skin. Thick, rich green velvet robes pool at his feet. A crown of gold vines and leaves sits on top of his mousey brown hair.

His father's crown.

His crown.

Zain lets out a snarl at the sight. *Get. That. Off. Your. Head. Traitor!*

His body shakes as rage fills him at the sight of his uncle. Balius is unaccompanied. No Manis. No lapdog guards.

"Well, well, it is interesting to find you here, Zain. I must admit that a dungeon in the human realm was the last place I thought I'd see you, but one must take every opportunity. When Neros told us he'd cast a spell on you, just in case he needed to control you, how could we refuse? It persuaded you back here."

Balius looks smug and victorious, giving Zain a wide grin that makes the wrinkles of his face grow deeper. His uncle is over seven hundred years old, five hundred Zain's senior. Despite his age, Balius has always been the weak brother of Zain's father, King Lanard.

"How did you do it, Balius? How did you, the most useless Fae I've ever encountered, usurp the throne? You're never organized. You've never shown any ambition. You've only ever coasted off the greatness of others. So, how did you do it?" Zain says, trying to get a reaction out of his uncle.

Balius doesn't take the bait, giving Zain a smug smile as he cranes to peek into Alvey's cell.

Zain lets out a low growl, visualizing the day he can rip off this Fae's head.

Balius tuts as he shakes his head at Zain. "He's always been loyal to you. Too dedicated for his own good, actually."

Zain grinds his teeth together, barely holding in the rage that makes him want to roar at his uncle. If he didn't have these manacles on, he would incinerate Balius with his magic. Just like he did to the guards as he escaped the Summer Court.

"What do you want, Balius?" Zain balls his fists, trying to keep his fury bottled up. The temptation to reach through the iron bars is too easy, with a steep price.

"I thought I would come talk some sense into you, you stupid boy. King Rodden has informed me that you helped his prized daughter and seer escape. Now that I've aligned the Summer Court with the Kingdom of Nordia, my duty as king is to ensure that any crimes

252

committed against my ally are righted . . . and those involved are punished."

Balius paces outside the cell door, his robes swishing as they drag at his feet.

"Rodden's a pig who the Summer Court will never be an ally with. I'll cut the both of you down. Mark my words," Zain seethes, watching his uncle pace. His eyes follow every movement with a predator's focus.

Balius chuckles at the threat. "You'll never leave this cell, Zain. Rodden will kill you, and I won't stop him. Just like you didn't stop your parents from being murdered."

Those words halt whatever protest Zain was about to make.

How does he know?

The memories of that night come flooding back.

He was a youngling, reading in his parents' room as they were getting ready for bed. The soft glow of the orbs of light that dot the space gives it a warm feeling. The smell of his mother's perfume fills the air—cherry blossoms.

There's a loud crash as a scuffle breaks out. He's about to get up when something solid hits the back of his head, and he passes out. When he wakes up, the bodies of his mother and father lie in deep red pools of blood. Panicking and not knowing what to do, he runs into his chambers to hide.

Shame and guilt have dogged him his whole life. When he took the throne, he made a promise to himself to fulfil his father's wishes. Keep his legacy. Listen to the advisors who had served his father, even though he didn't always agree with their policies.

Like he's seeing the world through fresh eyes, the pieces click into place for Zain.

"You!" he shouts. In a pure rage, he runs to grip the iron bars of his cell, trying to get to the man he knows is behind his parents' murders.

The flesh on his hands hisses and burns. He lets go as it drains him.

Balius doesn't flinch at Zain's show of aggression. "Me? What are you talking about, boy? I was saying that the Summer Court and Nordia have mutual interests. There is no stopping this alliance."

Zain tries to piece things together. His parents' murder, Balius's betrayal, and the alliance with Nordia. The iron affects not only his body but also his mind. Zain looks at his uncle in confusion.

Balius has only ever seen humans as lesser than Fae. When Zain's father shut the trading portals with the human world, Balius hailed the decision as a win for the Fae.

Zain scoffs, "What do you have in common with a human kingdom, Balius?"

"You'd be surprised. Your father never saw the full opportunity for a trade agreement with the humans. He missed the big picture."

Trepidation fills Zain's mind as he watches his uncle. The familiar, sickly stench of rotten fruit permeates the air as Balius's robes swish through it. It makes him gag. He knows that smell.

Neros.

"Rodden and I both see an opportunity in taking Solian. He wants their land, and I want their people."

Zain scrunches his brow at his uncle's remark, racking his brain as to why Balius wants Solian people. All the answers he can think of terrify him.

"What do you mean, you want their people?"

Balius stops pacing, coming to stand a hair's breadth away from the bars of Zain's cell.

"The Fae are a superior race. We can elevate ourselves further in our daily lives, leaving mundane and menial tasks to humans," Balius says as an evil grin breaks on his face.

Slaves. Human slaves.

Zain's jaw drops to the floor at the sickening realization of his uncle's plans. *How can you be so evil to enslave another race?*

"You're sick, Balius! I will get out of this, and I will kill you. You have my promise on that."

Balius gives Zain a bored look, the threat washing right over him. With a flick of his wrist, he summons three guards, pointing them to Alvey's cell.

Realizing what he's just done, Zain lurches for his uncle. His hands hiss as he grips the bars tight, the iron burning his flesh.

"No! Balius, no! Leave him alone!"

✦   ✦   ✦

CHAPTER TWENTY-SEVEN

A sword comes for her head. It slices the surrounding air, the cool steel blade missing her cheek by less than an inch.

Estrid pivots, drawing her power to her. A dark shield of shadow erupts from her splayed-out palm. It's so thick, the next strike can't penetrate it. Sweat beads on her forehead as she pushes her magic out, repelling the sword. She can feel the weight of the blade in the darkness she's controlling.

"Good, Estrid! Now force me out. Use your power!" Faris yells as he thrusts his weapon further into the shadow.

"Argh," Estrid says, gritting her teeth. She takes a deep breath in, stilling her mind. She wills her shadows to grow and extend beyond her own strength. As they expand, tentacles dart out from beneath her shield.

"Don't hesitate, Estrid. Use your magic and take me down! Your enemy will never hesitate. Do it!" Faris yells at her from the other side of the wall of darkness she now commands.

She concentrates her energy to disarm him, imagining his sword flying from his hand. With one last scream, she unleashes. Letting go of the fear she has of her power. Letting go of the fear of herself. The release flows through her body, but instead of depleting her energy, it sores to new heights.

Behind her shield of darkness, the weight of Faris's weapon lifts, followed by a loud clanking of swords toppling from the wall they sit on. Estrid withdraws her magic at the sharp sounds, the shadows evaporating at her command.

"Faris!"

She looks around the sparring circle to see Faris steadily getting up from where she'd tossed him aside like a rag doll. Dread spikes in her chest at his slow pace. Running to him, she stops as a low chuckle escapes him. Her friend stands straight, dusting himself off.

"Yes! Estrid, yes!" he says, drawing her into a hug.

Relief chases away her worry. She can't decide whether she wants to hit him again or hug him tighter.

"Why are you laughing? I could have hurt you!"

"That's the best I've seen you use your magic! If you fight like that, no one can stop you," Faris says, pulling away from her, that dazzling smile back.

She can't help but grin at the proud look on his face. Since training morning and night with Faris and harnessing her power with Cethin, Estrid's abilities have grown beyond what she thought she would ever be capable of.

She's become closer to her magic. Her combat skills have made it harder for Faris to even land a blow. She's faster, her senses sharper. The unfortunate accident in the sparring session with Del feels like a distant memory.

Faris tosses her a water skin as they wind down from the evening's training before dinner. The breeze from the cool early-evening air brushes Estrid's flushed cheeks. Faris resets the rack of swords that she threw him into. Each has its place on the wall.

Estrid moves to grab hers when his shoulders go rigid. He spins his head toward the main entrance of the yard, brow furrowed. She follows his gaze to the walls at the edge of the training grounds.

"What's going on, Faris?" she asks, coming to stand next to him.

She's about to ask again when a guard flies in their direction, his reptile-like wings catching the sun behind him. The soldier reaches their group, saluting Faris as his breath comes out fast and heavy.

"General, the shadow walkers are back from the scouting mission. They have news of the human king and the Summer princes."

The world stops momentarily as Estrid's heart speeds up at the potential update of Zain. *Please be okay.*

She seeks Del, who's talking to Evander. Their eyes catch, and Estrid tries not to let her worry show through.

"Where are they?" Faris asks as he hands off the remaining weapons to the guard to put away.

"The king's study, sir. His Highness told me to come find you and wants you all there now, sir," the soldier says, trying to salute while juggling the multiple swords Faris has given him.

Estrid and Faris glance at each other, unsure of what to expect, then make their way to Cethin's office.

✦ ✦ ✦

They enter the study, where Cethin paces in front of his window, his hands clasped behind his back.

Estrid lets out a yelp when two shadow walkers pop out of the shadows as she takes her seat. Dressed in head-to-toe black armor, they blend in perfectly with the dark walls and floors.

The rest of the group sits down at the table that has become so familiar to them. Cethin waves for the spies to come closer, saying, "Tell them."

Moving stealthily, the first shadow walker steps forward; his movements are light and deadly, like those of an assassin.

"General, my lady." He nods to Faris and Estrid. "We slipped into the Nordian castle thanks to the many shadows that hang over it. We were shocked to encounter the Summer Court Fae meeting with Rodden—"

"You mean my cousins?" Del interrupts, the group on edge at the slow delivery of the news.

Cethin raises his palm to silence her, encouraging the messenger to continue his story.

"No, my lady, not the princes. We found that Balius has allied with King Rodden. They intend to conquer Solian together."

The shadow walker pauses as Cethin raises his hand in thought. The group hangs on to every word that's being said.

"Why would they want to take Solian?" Cethin asks in a calculated tone.

"Rodden wants the land, but Balius intends to capture the Solian humans as slaves, Your Highness. We slipped into a few shadows in Rodden's war chambers. Their armies move out in two days."

Gasps of horror ring out around the table. Estrid feels sick and reaches for Zella's hand, seeking comfort from the disgusting news.

Del stands from her seat. "What about my cousins?" Her face is pale, her tone panicked, her eyes pleading for good news.

The soldier looks to Faris with concern, as if telling Del will put them in danger. Faris gives him a nod to continue.

"They've been captured and held in the dungeon, my lady."

The shadow walker steps back after delivering the updates, waiting for Del to fly off the handle. She doesn't move at the information, but her face displays how heartbroken she is.

Estrid can feel the bile in her stomach creeping up the more she thinks about it. Standing up, she places her hands on the table. "We have to act now. We can't allow them to do this. Zain and Alvey aren't part of this." She looks around the group for support, landing on her father and Faris.

They spare a glance at each other before Faris says, "Why should we waste resources to get them when they left?"

"Because I was their prisoner once too. I know what it's like. They're more twisted and evil than we thought. If we leave them there, they will most likely die. That's not something I can live with," Estrid says, noting the nod of approval from Cethin.

With a sigh, Faris nods, waving for the shadow walkers to leave. "Tore, set up a rotation of spies on Rodden and Balius. We need to know their every move. Our best opportunity to break Zain and Alvey out is when their armies have left."

Tore nods before disappearing into his shadows that carry him to his troops for their orders.

Cethin stands at the head of the table, taking them all in.

"Call up the Shadow Army, Faris. We're going to war."

✦ ✦ ✦

After the orders to start the muster have been given, the group sits there, contemplating the depravity of the news they just heard.

The faces of the villagers Estrid protected flash before her. She feels numb, both at the new depths of evil Rodden has sunken to and because Zain is there.

She glances at Del. Her knuckles are white as she grips her chair tightly.

Faris is the first to speak as he pulls out a large map. "This changes our plans," he says as he places it down on the table that Evander had cleared.

He moves the stone figurines representing their army down to the drawn Solian border. "It could be an advantage if we can ally ourselves with the Solians and meet Rodden and Balius on the battlefield. They won't be prepared for an alliance between the Shadow Court and Solian."

"How long do we have before they reach Solian?" Cethin asks, scanning the large document that's sprawled over the table.

"Two weeks, if that. They'll have to go on foot unless Rodden or Balius have the power to portal entire armies," Faris says, looking at Estrid and Del for answers.

Del shakes her head at Faris. "Only Zain and Alvey can portal. Our court doesn't possess magic like that."

Estrid lets Del's answer soak in.

The memories of that book she read in her small cottage return. Each Fae court's magic aligns with a natural element. Winter is air, Autumn is Earth, Summer is fire, and Spring is water. Since shadow and light cannot physically affect the world around them, they align with their names.

"Only the Shadow and Light Courts can possess those kinds of power." She pauses, thinking. "How do we know the Light Court isn't helping them?"

Cethin stands, pacing at his window again. "We don't need to worry about the Light Court. They were destroyed a long time ago by Aragoth. It was one of the last orders I carried out before I met your mother and sought to change," he says, his words heavy with regret.

Faris clears his throat, bringing them back to their task at hand. "Does Rodden possess any portalling capabilities that can move two armies?"

"No. Neros can portal small groups around, but not an entire army. The magical toll on him would be too great," Estrid says, watching as Cethin stops pacing.

"All right, we have a few days before we need to meet them on the battlefield. There's a lot to do in that time," Faris says in a commanding tone.

"Evander, see to the muster. Bring every available warrior here to Terebian and get them armed and kitted up." He faces Cethin. "Your Grace, we must start a dialogue with the Solians as soon as possible. How do you want to approach it?"

Cethin turns to the group, walking to Del, who hasn't sat down since she learned of Zain's imprisonment. He towers over her, cradling her shoulders.

"Send a shadow walker to scout their territory. Our priority is to get your family back, Del. I won't let you lose them. I've felt that pain, and it can be too much to bear. As soon as word arrives that their armies have cleared Rodden's castle, we will rescue them."

Estrid watches the touching encounter. If Del were any other woman, she would be in tears. The only sign of emotion is the small bob of her throat.

Del nods to Cethin. "Thank you, Your Highness, but I want to be the one to collect them."

"I'll go with her. I know that castle well and can help navigate it once inside," Estrid says as Cethin turns to her. He pauses before giving her a nod.

✦　✦　✦

CHAPTER TWENTY-EIGHT

The castle has grown quiet over the past few days. The drips of water and the scurrying of rodents are more noticeable in the absence of heavy boots in the halls.

Since their capture, Alvey has been used to torment Zain, who's forced to watch his brother receive daily beatings as the pair refuse to give up Estrid's whereabouts.

He isn't sure how much more he can take of hearing his brother's bones break or flesh being torn. Zain speaks to him while asleep, so he's not alone.

He listens to Alvey's soft breathing. *I'll kill them all,* he repeats over and over in his head, rage building deep in his chest. The thought of what pain his brother must be in drives him insane.

Drip.

Drip.

Drip.

With a sigh, Zain thinks of a story to uplift the heavy burden that sits in his heart.

"Remember when we told Del's new lady-in-waiting to tell Del to wear a dress? Del's reaction scared her so much that she resigned from her role that day."

He chuckles at the happy memory that he shares with Alvey. They were always up to mischief when they were growing up. Playing tricks on Del was their favorite pastime.

His heart sinks as Alvey doesn't respond—a wet and wheezy breath is the only reply.

A sudden gasp next door interrupts his thoughts before they spiral back to revenge.

Zain scrambles to his feet, his chains rattling on the stone floor. In the orange glow of the torchlight are the silhouettes of four figures. His chest tightens when he recognizes Estrid, Del, and Rafe. The large Fae with them is unmistakably Tore.

"Alvey!" Del drops to her knees, her sword falling with a clang that reverberates through the cells.

"Del! What are you doing here?" Zain whispers, trying not to alert the castle to their presence.

Estrid rushes over to his cell, Rafe at her heels.

Seeing her before him eases the darkness that has been dominating his thoughts. Those golden eyes are something he's never forgotten. They feel like home.

You came for me. A mixture of relief, joy, and other happy emotions washes over him.

Estrid scans him, searching for any sign of injuries, her brow etched with worry and concern. "Are you hurt?"

Zain shakes his head, wanting nothing more than to reach through the bars and drag her into his arms. He must look and smell a sight to her. Disheveled, dirty, and ashamed of his stupidity that he was so easily taken by one of Neros's spells.

"Help Alvey. I'm fine," he says as his voice breaks. His throat feels like a tight ball of emotion. He can't hide the feelings swelling up at the thought of Alvey, but also at his relief of getting him out of here.

"What happened to him?" Del looks helplessly at Alvey, who's lying in his cell unmoving.

"Manis. That fucking bastard beat him every day to get me to talk," Zain says with malice.

Estrid furrows her brow, searching Zain's face for an answer.

"They want you, Estrid. We refused to give you up, and they took it out on Alvey. Please help me get him out of here."

Del lets out a string of curses at this admission, picking up her sword.

Estrid's eyes widen in horror. She needs to know that they'll stop at nothing to capture her.

Estrid quickly composes herself, reaching the Shadow Fae standing guard at the end of the hall. "We need the keys. Tore, can you shadow walk me to the main castle?"

He nods at her. Shadows leap from the tattoos on his arms, but they stop short and wither.

"What the . . . ?" Tore says, looking down at his hands. "My shadows, they aren't working. There's . . ." He closes his eyes and concentrates as if listening to something.

Zain watches Tore, a sense of urgency building in his chest.

"There's a ward in place; I can feel it. I can't shadow walk us out. We need to find and destroy it if we want to leave here alive," Tore says, looking to Estrid for help.

She stares down at her hands, shaking them as if trying to remove some substance. She grabs a torch from the wall.

"It's affecting my power too. Neros's magic is dark and requires a sacrifice. He's probably strung up something or someone to put the ward in place. I think I know where to find it, but we need the keys first."

Estrid gives Del a nod to stay with Alvey. Zain wants to reach out and grab her, but as his hands get close to the iron bars, they pulse with their deadly effects.

Estrid, Tore, and Rafe are making their way to the entrance when they stop. The hiss of swords being drawn echoes through the chamber.

Del jumps to her feet, her knuckles white as she clutches her sword.

The four rescuers step back. They pause as a familiar voice reverberates throughout the dungeon. The hairs on his neck stand on end, anger surging through his veins. It's the same person who's tormented him for days.

Manis.

"Where do you think you're going?" Manis says, stepping into the dungeon's entrance. He's flanked by a dozen Summer and Nordian soldiers. They filter into the room, fanning out and circling the group.

Zain looks on from his cell, helpless to do anything.

Let me out!

"Del, how nice to see you again," Manis purrs. "And you must be the lovely Estrid who Neros has been talking too much about."

Del takes a step forward, but Tore stops her, shaking his head at her advance.

"I'm going to kill you, Manis!" she seethes, barely heeding Tore's command.

Manis lets out an otherworldly laugh. It slithers through the walls of the dungeon, sinking into Zain's bones.

"Del, you're outnumbered, and your magic doesn't work. The wards we have in place are strong. You won't kill me, and you won't be going anywhere either," Manis says, stepping back. With a nod of his head, the soldiers engage.

Zain watches, horror filling him as the enemy descends on his friends.

Be careful! Get me out! Come on, Tore!

Swords clash. They hiss and clang, their sounds jarring over the stone walls. Screams accompany them as bodies fall.

"Get me out of here!" Zain yells to the group as they fend off the attackers who clamber deeper into the dungeon.

Tore fights two guards off; he ducks and whirls around the strikes from his attackers with ease and grace. He slices through one guard, picking his keys off his belt with the edge of his sword and throwing them at Estrid.

"Free Zain! Go!"

The iron keys hit the floor with a crash. Estrid runs to grab them as a big silver blade comes for her.

Nooo!

Del intercepts the killing blow just in time.

"Hurry, Estrid!" she yells, then ducks as another soldier aims for her head.

Estrid rushes to his cell, holding the keys with the edge of her tunic. She scrambles to get the right one into the lock.

Come on. Come on. Come on! Hurry! Zain's fear and panic are palpable, though he's trying not to rush her.

In the background, he can hear Tore and Del holding off the chaos that pushes deeper into the dungeon. Screams mix with the metallic smell of fresh blood, assaulting his senses.

There's a familiar click as the latch turns, and Zain breathes a sigh of relief. The door squeals open, and he steps through to look at Estrid. He wants nothing more than to bring her into his arms, but there's no time as she unlocks the manacles that hold him.

"Zain! Catch!" Del calls out to his right as he moves out the door. She tosses him one of her blades.

The steel soars through the air. He catches it as Estrid gives him a nod, and they rush into the battle. He explodes with the rage that has been bottled up in him in that cell.

He doesn't think, just slices. Warm blood from those who meet the edge of his blade splatters his face. To his left, Estrid blocks and evades strikes, bringing her weapon down on their heads.

Rafe lives up to his ferocious name, working in tandem with Tore. His enormous jaws wrap around a guard's head, squashing it like a piece of fruit as the guard tries to dart away from Tore.

They work their way back up to the dungeon, where Manis waits. His blade is drawn, eyes locked on Zain. A sneer on his devilish face.

As the last soldier hits the ground with a thump, Tore sheathes his sword to get the keys to Alvey's cell.

Del and Zain circle Manis. Estrid and Rafe move behind them to end any soldiers who are still alive.

Del lets out an inhuman growl at Manis. With the only outcome death, she charges the commander. Their blades crash as they dance back and forth.

Zain stalks them. He watches Manis with a predatory gaze, not engaging. Not yet. Del needs this. She needs to take her anger out on him.

He also wants to prolong Manis's fear. The smell of it permeates the air. It's like rotten citrus fruit, sharp but pungent.

A dark side rears its head in Zain's mind, wanting to draw out Manis's desperation before he inflicts his last punishment on him.

Del spins and hits Manis in the nose with the pommel of her sword. His bones crunch, and he drops his blade as blood streams down his face.

Zain circles him, kicking his knees in. The commander falls to the ground with a thump.

Del stands off to the side, her chest heaving. Zain looks at Manis sitting on the back of his heels, clutching his nose. Zai raises his fist to inflict more pain, but pauses.

"Del . . . Zain . . ." Alvey's quiet voice comes from behind them as he slumps while Tore tries to hold him up. He groans in pain as Del hugs him.

The sound lets the beast loose in Zain, and he unfurls a barrage of punches on Manis. He's about to lay another down when a soft hand squeezes his shoulder.

CHAPTER TWENTY-EIGHT

"We need to find the ward and get out of here. Alvey needs help."

Estrid's voice clears the fog in his head. He nods, picking up Manis by his hair and making him look at him. His mentor's eyes, which were once warm and friendly, are cold and dead.

"Where is it, Manis?"

Manis smiles at Zain, choking out a laugh between blood and broken teeth.

"You've never been very clever. Things happen within plain sight of you, and you pay them no attention until it's too late," he says with a smug look, his eyes flicking to Alvey.

Zain's patience is wearing thin. He's ready to beat the information out of Manis like the guards did to Alvey.

"I think I know where the ward is," Estrid says, walking into Alvey's cell. There's a crash as bones come scattering out of the entrance.

Like a veil of chain mail has been lifted, Zain can feel his magic return, but it's weak from the shackles that have clung to him for days. It's warm and comforting. He feels whole again.

Manis's smirk fades as his eyes dart between Zain and Estrid, his expression turning sour. "You won't stop him," Manis says as Zain grips his hair tighter.

I will stop Balius. You'll just be the first to fall.

"You're done. Taking your head will not only give me satisfaction but will wipe your legacy from all records," Zain says, letting go of Manis's hair and stepping back.

He brings his long sword down. A soggy thud echoes around them as Manis's head rolls across the floor, his body slumping to the icy stones.

Zain walks to where the rest of the group waits for him, his chest heaving from the adrenaline coursing through him.

A cold, wet nose nudges his hand as he stands next to Estrid. The sensation breaks the tension in his body.

Rafe gives his palm another nudge. Zain smiles at the gesture from the wolf, giving him a pat on the head as Tore's shadows engulf them.

✦ ✦ ✦

The shadows deposit them back in the Shadow Court.

Zain takes in their surroundings, his pulse still racing from the adrenaline running through his veins after their battle. Rows of hospital beds line either side of the room, which has a warm glow from the Shadow Court's dusky sun. At the head of the chamber stand Cethin, Faris, Imaya, and a weathered-looking old Fae.

Tore and Del move to put Alvey down on a bed. The dirt and blood from their days in the dungeon immediately turn the crisp white sheets into a filthy brown.

Zain moves to Alvey's side, his breath hitching. The daylight shows the full extent of the damage done to him. His face is a patchwork of blue, purple, and yellow. His left shoulder sits at an awkward angle. What skin is showing is scarred and pink. Dark brown and bright red bloodstains cover his tunic and pants.

Del kneels next to him, holding his hand as she whispers to him.

Zain takes Alvey's other hand. "I'm sorry, brother."

They're both pushed out of the way as an old Fae and Imaya move to take care of Alvey. They cut his shirt off him, revealing his bruised and broken chest. Del lets out a scream of anger and storms out of the room.

Beating Manis wouldn't have been enough to work out her rage.

Zain turns to face the rest of the group. He meets Cethin's bright green eyes, expecting some irritation at his stupidity.

"You're safe here. Alvey will be well taken care of. Get cleaned up. Imaya will see to any injuries you have," Cethin says with a sigh.

Zain nods, still angry and embarrassed that a necromancer's spell so easily swayed him.

The Shadow King gives him a single nod, then turns and leaves with Faris behind him. Zella wraps her arms around Tore as they depart, whispering to each other.

Imaya and the old Fae work on Alvey, applying balms, herbs, magic, and many other things to help him heal, as Zain seethes in his thoughts.

Estrid walks up to him, placing a hand on his shoulder. He can't look at her, too overcome by anger and shame.

"Thank you for saving us, but please leave," he grits out.

"Zain, you're safe. It'll be okay," she says.

Grinding his teeth, he grabs her arm and walks her to the other side of the room. "It's because of you that he's like this! He refused to give you up. Just go, Estrid!"

Her worried expression turns into anger. Her eyes narrow as she steps up to him, her fingers inches from poking him in the chest. "You're the one who left! It's because of *you* that Alvey is like this, not me!" She throws her hands up in frustration. "Argh, you know what? I'm done with you."

No words come out as Estrid turns away from him.

He watches as her back fades into the shadows of the hallway, swallowing down his temper. Annoyed with her—and with himself—he returns to watching Imaya and the old Fae care for Alvey.

The bruises that marked his body have faded, his bones are set at the right angles, and the color is returning to his cheeks. The old Fae, whom he's found out is called the Crone, shuffles toward him.

Zain looks down at her. She's not much taller than his waist. She gestures for him to move, and his anger flares again. "What? What do you want?"

If his tone insults her, she doesn't show it or say anything, just signals for him to leave again. He moves so there's enough room for her to get past. She doesn't budge. He lets out a huff in frustration.

"She wants you to clean yourself up. You're filthy and making our ward dirty," Imaya says with a hand on her hip. By the disgruntled look she's giving him, she must have heard his conversation with Estrid.

"I'm not leaving Alvey," Zain says, keeping his feet in place.

Imaya sits on Alvey's bed; it squeaks under her weight. She reaches for the water bowl beside him on the table, wringing out a cloth and then wiping the dirt and blood from his face.

"You can't help him anymore, Zain. He needs rest. Go. I'll watch him," she says, the emotion in her voice thick as she cleans his brother.

There's another swat from a hand to his side, and he looks down. The Crone is there, pushing him to move along.

✦ ✦ ✦

After a bath, Zain feels fresh and somewhat alive again. He hasn't seen Estrid since she stormed away from him, nor does he want to. He hates himself for all of this.

Stupid. Why did you push her away? The thoughts replay repeatedly in his mind.

As he turns down the stone hallway in the direction of the medical ward, voices trickle into earshot. Zain lets out a low growl when he hears Faris speaking.

"Why didn't you give Estrid up? What's in it for you, Alvey?" the general says.

"I told you, Imaya gave me a vision before we arrived here. She said that if Rodden found Estrid before she was ready to face him, we would lose," Alvey says, sounding irritated with the third-degree questioning from the general.

Alvey's tone has Zain leaping into action. He strides into the medical ward, the sun's glow almost gone from the room as Faris stands at the end of his brother's bed. Faris cocks an eyebrow as he enters.

"Alvey needs rest, Faris. Leave," Zain says, his words edged with annoyance.

Faris doesn't move, folding his arms over his chest. His stance says, *Try me.*

"It's fine, Zain. I was debriefing Faris on Nordia. You don't need to coddle me."

Alvey's harsh words make Zain flinch. His brother has been lucid since they arrived, but their time in the dungeons has taken its toll on him.

The purple bruises on his face may have healed and faded, but his eyes have lost their sparkle. That hint of mischief that made Alvey warm and light-hearted is now replaced by pain and anger.

Faris gives Zain a smug grin.

"Alvey . . ." Zain turns to look at his brother.

"No, Zain. Faris needs to hear what went on in there."

Zain clenches and unclenches his fists. *I don't want you to know how they used a spell on me. How they weakened me . . . but I need your help.*

"Fine," he says as he moves to leave.

Faris cocks an eyebrow at him before saying, "Have you apologized to her yet?"

"That's none of your business, Faris," Zain says, but as he utters the words, Faris leaps into action, pushing him to the ground.

It takes Zain by surprise, and he struggles to get the upper hand. Fury fuels what little strength he has after being kept for weeks in a weakened state. A sharp thud hits the side of his jaw, the pain slicing through the fog in his mind.

"Stop!" a feminine voice shouts from behind them as a small hand comes to grab Faris by the ear and yanks him off Zain.

Imaya stands over him, the old Fae beside her holding the general by the ear like a naughty youngling. Faris stares at Zain, a promise that this isn't over.

Imaya steps over Zain and walks to Alvey. He's tried to get up and has ruptured some wounds on his stomach.

"Will you two idiots stop? Alvey has to rest. He's just gotten back, and while our healing is good, he needs time. His magic is too depleted for self-healing," she says, helping Alvey into bed. She smooths his sheets before facing Zain and Faris with a vengeful stare. "Now, you can either behave or leave. Which do you want?"

Faris mumbles that he'll behave, and the old Fae drops the tight grip on his ear. He massages it, shooting the Crone a wary glance.

Zain nods at Imaya, perplexed by what just happened. With a nod, the two ladies exit, Imaya warning Zain that if he upsets Alvey, he'll face her wrath.

With the room silent again, Alvey focuses his gaze on Zain. "Faris, Cethin, the Shadow Court—they're not our enemy, Zain. You are your own enemy if you don't let them help us. Faris sent his own commander to rescue us—"

"Actually, Estrid wanted to save you," Faris interrupts. "I was quite happy to let you lie in the bed you made."

Alvey lets out a sigh of frustration. "Not helping, Faris! But it's nice to know that the Fae I took the beating for was at least the one to help me." He turns to his brother. "Zain, I know you're ashamed that Neros's magic so easily overtook you, but it could have been any of us. You can't blame Estrid for that or what they did to me. They want to drive a wedge between us by having us fight amongst each other. Blame them. Blame Neros, Rodden, and Balius," he says, wincing as he sits up.

The realization of his last words to Estrid comes crashing back to him. Blaming her. Telling her to leave.

"What do you mean, he blames Estrid?" Faris says, his eyes darting between Alvey and Zain. He moves one step closer to Zain, who meets Faris's gaze that promises pain.

"I heard him lay into Estrid for my injuries. Blame *them*, Zain. Not her," Alvey says. His tone is sad and scorned.

Zain's world tilts as the truth of it all hits him.

Fuck, I'm an idiot. Too fucking blind, proud, and stubborn.

Faris takes another step toward him so they're chest to chest. "Ha . . . you are the world's biggest fool, Zain. Estrid was the one who convinced

Cethin and me to send shadow walkers to you. She volunteered to be there to help rescue you. I can see why your uncle usurped you. You're nothing more than a spoiled prince."

Zain doesn't back away from the hit Faris is likely to land on him.

It doesn't come as the general sidesteps him and leaves.

+ + +

CHAPTER TWENTY-NINE

Estrid stomps toward the training yard. She's a tempest of rage as Zain's words echo in her head. *"It's because of you that he's like this."* He has the audacity to blame her after she asked her father to send the shadow walkers to warn them? After she volunteered to be part of the rescue group?

The hole in her heart from being apart from Zain is now a chasm from being blamed and villainized by him.

I'm done.

When she enters the yard, it's bathed in the sun's last warm glow. The familiar thuds of a sword hitting one of the wooden dummies echo through it. Del hacks at one off to the left, her swings powerful and deadly, sending large chunks of wood flying.

Estrid needs to blow off some steam too. Find a release for her anger. Jogging up to the wall filled with weapons, she grabs a random silver sword. The cool steel of the curved blade feels good in her hand; her fingers grip tight around the pommel. She flicks her wrists into a figure eight, feeling the even weight as she moves it.

Whoosh.

Whoosh.

Whoosh.

She pivots and ducks while maneuvering the weapon. In front of her, Del hacks at the dummy. She stops when she sees Estrid walking toward her.

"Want to spar?" Estrid says, stepping into the sparring circle next to the mannequins.

Sweat glistens off Del's face. The loose strands of her fine ash-blonde hair stick to her skin. Her chest heaves.

"Come on, Del. You want to work off some steam just as much as I do . . . or are you afraid? I've got a lot better since our last encounter."

Del's eyes narrow at the challenge Estrid's just set.

Probably not the best idea to goad her, but at this point, I don't care.

"Humph, sure. It's about time we sparred again. Let's go, witch," Del says, swinging her long sword as she steps into the ring.

Estrid smirks at Del's own simmering need to release the rage that burns underneath her skin. She walks to stand in front of the Fae warrior. Nerves briefly overcome her anger as she takes in Del's feral state.

Just don't get stabbed again.

Locking down her nervousness, Estrid attacks first. Their blades clash head-on. Steel on steel grinds and echoes through the quiet yard. Estrid's still no match for Del's experience and skill, but she refuses to back down. She uses her rage as fuel, blocking hit after hit while delivering some of her own. Her dark magic flares as a shield from Del's punishing strikes.

The dying light makes it harder to see Del's blade, but she digs into her Fae powers to guide her senses. Estrid spins just out of reach of Del, the near miss sending adrenaline through her veins. She ducks down on one knee as Del comes to strike down. The seasoned warrior stops dead in her tracks.

Estrid looks straight into Del's piercing green eyes. She moves her gaze down to Del's chest, down the long body of the sword. Its tip sits less than an inch from Del's heart.

"Finish it," Del says, tracking Estrid's blade.

"No," Estrid says as they stand there, neither moving.

At one point, Estrid would have loved nothing more than to slice Del open. The Fae betrayed her. But a lot has changed since then. Del has stuck by her. Left her family to stand for what she saw as right. They may not be friends, but they respect each other.

"I want to hate you, you know. Blame you for Alvey, for Zain, but . . . but I can't. Without . . . without you, they wouldn't have been rescued. Without you, my family might be dead," Del says, dropping her sword in defeat. Her shoulders slump.

Estrid can't help but pity her.

"Ha, you may not blame me, Del, but Zain does. He's made that clear, and I'm done," she says, putting her blade away and turning to leave.

She's halfway out of the training yard when Del says, "I'm sorry that Zain has taken his anger out on you. Sometimes, it's easier to take it out on someone else than to hate yourself. I said I wanted to hate you, Estrid, but I can't. I'm more in debt to you than you know."

Estrid feels calmer as she winds down the hallways of the palace, giving herself a mental pat on the back for besting Del.

Staff and courtiers greet her by name as she passes them by. While there has been no official ceremony naming her as the Shadow Court heir, many bow and curtsy to her.

At first, she tried to make them stop, but there was little point. Now, she gives them a respectful nod back, trying to take a leaf from Cethin's book and recall their names.

She rounds the corner to her rooms and bumps into Lena, who looks flustered, sending her basket of clothes crashing to the floor.

"Lena! Are you okay?" Estrid says, helping her lady's maid pick up the bits of washing that are strewn across the ground.

Lena scrambles to her feet. "Y-Yes, my lady. You have a visitor in your chambers. I'll make sure you're not disturbed," she says, grabbing the basket and scurrying off.

Estrid furrows her brow in confusion before a knot forms in her stomach. She was just with Del, and Faris had said he's debriefing with Tore and Cethin. While it could be anyone, the growing tangle of emotion tells her it can only be one person. Squaring her shoulders, she walks the last few feet to her room.

She throws open the door, finding Zain standing by the fireplace. Despite their argument earlier, she has to control the urge not to jump him. He looks back to his normal handsome self. The glow of the fire's warm flames helps return some color to his skin after their dramatic rescue.

The composure she worked up while sparring with Del slips, and her heart races.

Get a grip, Estrid. You're done, remember?

With a deep breath, she tries to regain her mask of indifference.

"What are you doing here?" she snaps, walking to the drinks cart and pouring herself some wine. Liquid courage. Downing it in two quick gulps, she doesn't bother offering the male who drives her crazy a glass.

"I'd like to apologize," Zain says, rubbing his hand down the back of his neck. "I'm sorry for what I said in there." He tries to close some of the distance between them. "It wasn't okay. I shouldn't have taken it out on you."

Estrid takes a step back, maintaining the space she needs from him. She wants to scream in frustration. Their relationship, if you can call it that, has been one that's been torn apart, then put back together, only to be ripped up again.

"Thank you. You can leave now," she says, moving to her bedroom, but Zain rushes to stop her. The touch on her arms is featherlight, but it sends jolts of electricity through her body. She doesn't want to look up. She can't look up, or it'll be the end of her trying to stay away from him.

Zain drops his hands from her arms. "Please, Estrid, can we talk?"

Her emotions are at war with each other. She could so easily give in and hear him out, but equally, she should walk away. But fates, it's not that easy. Those ice-blue eyes stare back at her with regret.

With a sigh, she gives him a single nod but doesn't move closer. This needs to be quick or there will be no returning.

"I didn't know you were the one who asked for the shadow walkers to come check on us. I didn't know you volunteered to join the rescue party." Zain sighs, placing his hand on her arm. "I thought you were my enemy, but . . . but I was wrong."

The sincerity in his words gives her pause, but she doesn't want to fall for them. Flutters of butterflies grow in her stomach as she intertwines her fingers. She fiddles with them, the nervous habit coming out again.

Zain says nothing, cocking his head to get a response from her.

She bites the side of her mouth, pushing down the dizzy feeling of having him so close to her. Steeling her nerves, she takes a step back. "What do you want me to say, Zain? 'It's okay. I'm fine'?"

All the old emotions for him resurface. The warmth in her body from lust and desire. The sharp pain in her chest from the hurt and anger. The giddiness in her heart from those fleeting happy memories in her little cottage.

"You should leave."

"No, not until we sort this out," Zain says, moving back into her space.

Frustrated, she moves away from this man who is beyond infuriating.

Zain grabs her arm, but she spins around and strikes him on the cheek with a loud slap. His head barely budges at the blow.

"You don't get to touch me, Zain! You want me, don't want me, want me—my head is spinning from the whiplash I get from it! Just leave!"

Zain doesn't move; the muscles in his jaw tic.

Estrid lets out an annoyed huff and marches to the door of her room. If he doesn't leave, she will.

Estrid opens it, but it's pushed shut as Zain cages her in against it. She can feel him against her back, sending a thrill down her spine.

"I won't let you go until you've heard me out." The warmth of his breath brushes against her ear, extinguishing the anger and replacing it with desire.

Estrid swings around, ready for a fight, but it fizzles out as her eyes lock on his. There's a deep hunger in them.

"I was wrong . . . please," he whispers to her.

"Zain, please."

He steps toward her, his broad chest so close that the familiar bergamot-and-cedar scent envelops her. She places her hands on him. It's taking all her control not to run her fingers across the hard planes of his muscles.

"No. I'll never stop with you, Estrid. Never again. I was wrong. So wrong about everything. I never truly appreciated what you went through with Neros. When I left, I wasn't myself. I didn't realize it then, but I should have."

Estrid furrows her brow in confusion. "What are you talking about?"

"When I was in the dungeons, I found out that Neros used his magic to draw us back. He wanted you." Zain sighs. "And I wasn't strong enough to fight it. I'm sorry about it all, about saying it was your fault when it was me who was weak."

His shoulders sag at the confession; he bows his head down to rest on her shoulder.

Estrid doesn't breathe. *How did he do it? Why didn't you say something earlier?* The questions swirl in her mind. She knows it could have been much worse if Neros's magic was involved.

She leans into him. "Lashing out at me isn't okay, but I know all too well how violated you must feel. Neros's power is . . . dark, and it consumes you," she says as he pulls back, searching for confirmation.

Everything stops around her. Zain moves for her again; she doesn't back away this time. His warmth radiates, calling for her to come closer.

Taking a step forward, she brushes her lips to his. Soft, supple, and warm.

He retreats for a breath before crashing his lips to hers. Heat courses through her as his mouth moves down. He nips and kisses down her cheek, then neck. Spikes of excitement follow every caress.

Lost in his touch, her back hits the door as she tilts her neck to the side, giving him better access. He groans, slipping an arm around her waist and devouring her. She won't let this argument go, but she's too caught up in desire. She needs this.

"We're not done talking," she says through heavy breaths.

Zain stops his caresses, looking at her with a smug smile.

"We are . . . for now," he says, their mouths colliding once more. Their kiss is urgent, driven by something insatiable.

She opens her mouth to him. His tongue sweeps in, teasing her. She moans as her core turns molten, wrapping her arms around his neck, drawing him in closer.

He groans and sweeps her legs around his waist, cupping her ass. In two strides, they're on the settee. There's nothing gentle about this. Anger still bubbles underneath the surface, but it's overruled by the desire that's been there since she first met him.

She flips him over, straddling him, breaking their kiss. "I mean it. We're not done, but right now, I want you," she says, whipping off her tunic.

Zain's hands move to her breasts, rolling her nipples between his fingers before taking one in his mouth.

Estrid moans as she fists his hair, rocking her hips, creating friction between them. Zain's hard length strains against his pants.

He groans as he slips his hand beneath the hem of her trousers. What he finds has him groaning. "Gods, you're so wet. . . . These need to come off now."

With that, he flips her and pulls them off in a blur. Then he takes off his tunic, followed by his trousers.

Estrid licks her lips, taking in his naked form. Hard lines of muscle define his body. His cock is jutting up, hard and ready for her. She opens for him, and he groans at the sight of her.

"What are you waiting for, Zain? I thought you said we were done talking," she teases, goading him as she runs her hand down the inside of her thigh, down to her slick folds.

He doesn't need an invitation as he lunges for her. His touch is gentle but brutal in all the right places. With a single thrust, he enters her. She cries out as he fills her, stretching her walls.

The settee creaks and slides on the stone floor as his pace picks up. Estrid's orgasm builds as Zain doesn't hold back. Their sex is angry and desperate from depriving themselves of what they feel.

Zain moves to play with Estrid's clit. Her walls tighten around him as the extra friction sends her over the edge. She cries out his name, digging her fingers into him to hold on as he finds his release.

Their chests heaving, a hand comes up to cup her cheek, drawing her lips to his.

"I could only think of you, Estrid. I could only reflect on how wrong I was. I'll never stop being able to make it up to you," Zain says as his muscular body cages her in.

Estrid looks up into those blue eyes, gold flecks dancing in their depths. They have to have a proper conversation, but the need in her body is overwhelming any rational thought. Reaching up, she returns his lips to hers, swiveling her hips again.

Zain chuckles against her mouth as he hardens once more.

CHAPTER THIRTY

Estrid slips out of bed as the sun peeks through the windows of her room. Zain's deep breaths come from the steady rise and fall of his chest as he sleeps off their time together. Neither got any sleep throughout the night, as they took their time to orientate themselves with each other's bodies.

What am I going to do about you? This thing between us . . . it feels so natural, but something is holding us back.

Her body is sore in all the right places as she gets dressed. They still haven't fully spoken about Neros's magic over Zain, what happened while they were there, or why he did an about-face on blaming her and then seeking her forgiveness. The Fae confuses her, but she can't stay away.

Unsure about her feelings, Estrid makes her way to the only place in the city that feels like a sanctuary.

The black palace gates stand open, towering above her as a hive of activity from the call to muster troops flows through them. Fae filter in and out, giving her a nod of recognition.

Since being in the Shadow Court, she's explored Terebian several times, getting to know the community. It's small enough that she can walk to different sections of it between her training sessions and explore.

284

She's found a few favorite areas that she's frequented on more than a half-dozen occasions: gardens, markets, shops, and places to eat. But there's one spot that holds a special place in her heart.

A bookstore sits off the edge of the central market. It's not just the books that call to her, but she's made a friend in the owner, Merial. The Fae has become a confidant but can also make the best cup of tea.

Estrid's emotions are all over the place. Her body is tired, and she can't shake the feeling that this is the last moment of peace she'll have for some time.

Consumed by her thoughts, she aimlessly walks toward the bookshop.

The morning sun settles in as sellers line the market roads and buyers haggle early for prices and bargains. Now and then, someone calls out to Estrid, waving her over to their little stall. She makes her way further around the market.

One of the local butchers calls her over and gives her a bag of bones that he keeps for Rafe. Knowing how much he loves them, she walks over and accepts them.

"Morning, Estrid. How's that Rafe?" Landon, the butcher, says, handing her a rather large package.

He's a short and stocky Fae with a bald head and spiked horns tracking down from his crown to his back. He gives her a toothy smile with canines that stick out. When he first smiled at her, she almost ran off in terror. But the stout Fae has taken a liking to Rafe.

She smiles, accepting the bones that she knows will make Rafe happy. "He's good. Thank you, Landon, but you spoil him. He's going to be so excited when I return with this treasure. How much do I owe you?"

Estrid knows he'll refuse her money, but she still offers to pay.

The people she's encountered in her adventures are filled with kindness and warmth, showering her with praise for Cethin's exceptional leadership. Many credit her father with the court's prosperity despite being trapped by an unknown power. They often give her things as a sign of thanks for breaking the barrier on their court. While trade with the other courts hasn't started, families and friends are reunited since her magic dropped the barriers.

Arriving at the bookshop, she sighs in relief, her nerves already relaxing at the sight of the haven. It doesn't look like much, but there's a special magic that sits around the shop with planter boxes that have blooming colorful flowers under the windows.

Estrid opens the door and steps in, taking in a deep breath. The savory smell of books mixed with sweet spices and floral scents fills her lungs.

A calmness settles over her. The walls of the shop are dark green with gold trim, giving it an almost forest-like feel. They remind her of her home in the Dark Forest. Taking another deep inhale, all the sensations in the store hit her at once, relaxing her and drawing her in like a siren's call.

Merial appears from the storeroom carrying an enormous book. Her half-moon glasses rest on her delicate nose. Unlike the Shadow Fae, the bookshop owner appears more like Zain and Alvey.

Merial pulls her strawberry hair back from her face in a gold claw clip that gleams in the light. She has sharp but elegant features that are dusted with freckles. She looks up as Estrid enters her store. Her yellow eyes shimmer as a broad smile spreads over her graceful face.

"My dear, I wasn't expecting you today. Come in." Merial glides to Estrid, her yellow gown floating behind her.

When she comes to give Estrid a hug, she wrinkles her nose at the sack of bones in her hands. "I swear, Landon gives you those knowing you're coming straight here. Here, give them to me to keep out back. I won't have my shop smelling like a butcher's block."

She takes the bag of treats for Rafe and disappears into the storeroom.

Waiting, Estrid browses the many bookshelves. Reading has always been a love of hers. It helped her escape.

When she was with Rodden, Zella would bring her books about romance, heroines, and epic tales of adventure. They helped her forget—where she was, what she did. They helped her hope for a happy ending.

Merial appears again, this time carrying a tray of tea. The spiced vanilla-and-cinnamon smell wafts through the store, cocooning Estrid in warmth and calm. "You look tired. Sit. Tell me, is Faris being a tyrant and training you too hard?" she asks, pouring the warm liquid into delicate tulip-shaped cups.

"No, Faris is fine. I just needed a break, some time to myself. We got some bad news from the human world. My fa—Rodden is marching on Solian with the help of Balius, Zain's uncle. We also rescued Zain and Alvey yesterday," Estrid says, trying to avoid her friend's gaze that seeks to draw all the truth from her.

"Ahh . . . did the rescue go well?"

Estrid nods, taking the tea. The little cup's heat radiates against her skin. She blows on the hot liquid and takes a sip. A moan of satisfaction escapes her as her whole body gives in to the sweet tea that has a warm hint of spice.

She lets out a sigh. "Alvey was in terrible shape, but Zain was okay." She pauses a moment, staring down into her teacup. "I'm so torn by him. He left us. He thought I was his enemy, but . . . argh, no matter what, I'm drawn to him."

"I see," Merial says with a touch of understanding in her voice. She walks over to a little drawer under her desk and pulls out a book.

She glides back to Estrid, handing the soft brown leather piece with intricate designs embossed on it to her. "Read this. You might find it interesting," she says, giving Estrid a knowing smile and topping up her tea before floating to the back of the store.

Estrid traces its ridges with her fingers before she opens it. The first page is a dirty cream color, the pages worn. With a little gasp, she sees her mother's name written on the front of the book. It's a diary.

"How did you get this?" she asks.

Merial sticks her head out from behind the counter, giving Estrid a coy smile. Her yellow eyes glisten with mischief. "Your father, of course. He thought with Zain's arrival, it might be useful to read. To give you strength, courage, and . . . some perspective."

✦ ✦ ✦

Estrid is so engrossed in her mother's diary that she loses track of time. The warmth of the morning sun fades as it dims, early evening setting in.

As she reads more about her mother, a clear picture emerges. She has golden eyes, like Estrid, but with white hair and pale flawless skin, like a porcelain doll. It's the closest she's ever felt to her.

There's a hollowness at the thought of never having a family. Estrid fights back a sob as Merial sweeps into the room, getting ready to shut the shop.

"Time to go, dear," she says. "You can't hide out here forever. You'll need to face him at some point."

Estrid stretches, the blood rushing back into her muscles, as her friend switches off the small balls of light that brighten the reading corners of the store.

The little leather book drops from her lap to the wooden floor with a thud.

Bending down, she notices a loose page that's slipped out. It's a hand-painted portrait of Cethin and her mother staring straight at her. She looks exactly as Estrid pictured her. They hold hands, smiles on their faces. Eria has a slight bump visible in her stomach.

The hollowness in Estrid's chest grows wider. Loss of not knowing her mother. Loss of the childhood she could have had. But determination soon replaces the pit of loss. Greed cut her mother's life short. Something she plans to avenge.

She has to stop Rodden.

The bookstore darkens as the final globe of light goes out, the sun dipping to the west.

Merial stands at the entrance, her nose scrunched as she holds out Rafe's bag of bones from Landon. Estrid heads out the door, the cooler early-evening air lovingly kissing her face like a lover's embrace.

The markets have ended, and store owners have packed away the stalls until tomorrow. People have left for the day, leaving behind swept-clean cobblestone paths.

Tranquility has settled upon the once lively streets. Estrid's never known a calm like she has in Terebian.

Keys jingle as Merial locks the bookstore and stands beside Estrid.

"Thank you for my book. You don't know how much it means to me," she says as Merial hugs her.

"It's my pleasure. I hope it helps guide you in what you need to do."

With one last squeeze, Estrid says goodbye to Merial and returns to the palace.

The sounds of crickets and bugs singing their evening songs fill the air as she walks back to the castle, deep in thought.

The diary gave a glimpse into the Winter Court, her mother's rule, and some friends in her life. She read about the first time her parents met. Her mother felt an instant connection to him, but she fought it because of who he was. Because of her own bias.

Footsteps padding on the pavement behind her draw Estrid out of her thoughts. She turns to see a shadowed figure running at her. She whips out her dagger and comes face to face with Zain.

"Zain! You almost gave me a heart attack!"

Butterflies erupt in her stomach at the sight of him. Memories of last night come flooding back, making her blush. The feel of his hard muscles beneath her fingers. His warm breath on her skin as he lavished her with kisses.

He closes the gap between them, reaching out to touch her, but he stops short when she hesitates. "I didn't mean to scare you. You left this morning without saying anything. Are you okay?"

Estrid takes a step back, putting space between them. Her mother's journey to her father rings in her mind. "I'm fine. I needed some time to think after last night," she says, looking around the abandoned streets. "We need to talk."

She grabs his hand, leading him into one of the many small alcoves that line some of the street walls. Vines with dainty white flowers that smell like sweet peas creep up the walls. An orb of light hangs above the entrance, giving it a warm glow inside.

She guides Zain to sit beside her on the stone bench. "Last night was . . . um . . . unexpected. I know Neros used his magic on you to get to me, but you still haven't been the same since learning who my parents are. I'm not your enemy, Zain . . . but I understand why it may be hard for you to overcome that bias," she says, holding up a hand as he tries to say something. "I can't deny that I feel something for you, but I won't let you draw me into any more hot-and-cold mood swings. If you want to act like a child, we're nothing more than friends. Got it?"

Zain's eyes haven't left hers, a smirk growing on his face as she dictates her thoughts to him. Without a word, he takes her lips in his. The kiss is deep, stealing her breath as he presses his mouth against hers. His masculine scent mixes with the delicate flowers in the alcove, sweet and earthy.

He breaks the kiss, leaning his forehead against hers. "I've been thinking about you since I left you. You could never be my enemy, and I was an idiot. There's no excuse. I'll prove that and more," Zain says, kissing her once more.

It takes a lot of effort to push him back, seeking more answers. "I need to understand why there's so much hate from you toward these people. They've been only good to us."

Zain gives a heavy sigh as he takes her hand in his, entwining their fingers together.

"I've told no one this, not even Del or Alvey. It doesn't condone what I've done, but it explains a lot," he says, searching her eyes for confirmation that he can trust her.

Squeezing his hand, she urges him to carry on.

"When I was a youngling, the night my parents died, I was there," he says, glancing away from her. "I'll never forget it. I was in their rooms as they were preparing for bed, reading a book my father wanted me to read. Th-There was a loud crash. I don't remember what happened next, but someone knocked me out, and I woke up on the floor.

"The next thing I remember," he continues, struggling to keep his voice even, "is waking up and seeing them. There was so much blood. I was young and didn't know what to do, so I ran. I ran, Estrid, like a coward. Ran into my room and hid." He visibly swallows down a lump in his throat. His shoulders sag, as if a weight has been lifted.

Estrid rubs his back, moving closer to hold him. "Oh, Zain, it's not your fault. Did they catch whoever did it?"

He nods, leaning into her further. "They charged and executed two lesser Fae from the Shadow Court for it. I'm not using it as an excuse to condone how I've treated the Shadow Fae since we arrived; I've been so wrong about them all. After Rodden captured me, Balius said he knew I was in the room the night my parents died. He had a hand in it; I know he did. I need to find out why."

He takes both her hands, turning to face her, and those blue eyes lock on to hers. "There's something bigger at play here, Estrid. I can finally see that. Whatever it is, I want to be at your side. I want you, Estrid, all of you, no matter what your past is, who your parents are, or if I have a court or not. I just want you."

Desire overtakes her thoughts as she leans into him, his arm wrapping around her waist. Their lips briefly touch before someone clears their throat outside the alcove. They break apart, whipping their heads around to see who's there.

"Please don't make me come in. You're both needed at the palace to prepare to meet with the Solians in the morning," Del's familiar stoic tone sounds from close by. Estrid isn't sure if she's thankful for Del's interruption or wants to slap her.

"Give us a minute, will you, Del?" Zain says, blowing out a frustrated breath.

Estrid stands to leave, but he grabs her wrist, drawing her into one last kiss. "I won't deny it any longer. You're mine, and I'm yours."

✦ ✦ ✦

CHAPTER THIRTY-ONE

Tore's shadow walkers drop the group into a field that's so green it reminds Zain of the Spring Court. Rolling hills of tall, bright green grass and farms stretch far beyond the horizon.

The sky is such a vibrant blue, he finds it hard to believe he's in the human realm. The sun beats down on his back; it isn't harsh and unforgiving but warm and welcoming.

Cethin walks ahead of him toward an enormous black tent that's at least ten feet tall. A large square banner outside the front displays his sigil of two talon-tipped wings. Soldiers line the sides of the tents, armed and alert with spears and swords.

Cethin, Faris, Estrid, Zella, and Zain enter the space one by one. They've kept the group intentionally small. Zain represents the Summer Court in this. Zella is the rightful heir of Nordia, and Cethin, Estrid, and Faris represent the Shadow Court.

Zain enters, his eyes adjusting to the darkness inside the interior. Lush rugs cover the floor, and heavy wooden chairs and a large rectangular table take up most of the space. Tall tables line the walls, covered with an array of refreshments: teas, water, some clear-colored liquids, and amber alcohol.

Cethin sits in a high-backed chair positioned at the head of the table. Faris sits to his right, followed by Estrid to his left. Without hesitation, Zain sits beside Estrid, nodding to Faris and Cethin in acknowledgment for including him.

After speaking with Estrid last night, Zain went to see Cethin to discuss his relationship with her and how they could work together to get the Summer Court back.

Estrid interrupts his thoughts of the wise words the Shadow King gave him when she asks, "Which Solians are we expecting here?"

"I'm told that the Solian king will send some of his generals to meet with us. He doesn't trust us, which is reasonable . . . for now," Cethin says, signaling for water to be brought to them all.

Zain is about to ask how they convinced the Solians to an open dialogue when a Shadow Army runner opens the flaps to the entrance, fixing them to let in the light. With a bow, he says, "The Solian generals are here, my king."

They all stand as Evander approaches with the three Solian generals; they're dressed in their full military armor, red and white with a gold dragon on the front.

Zain catches Estrid nervously shuffling on her feet. *We've got this.* He entwines his fingers with hers. Her hand feels small in his as he gives it a little squeeze. Cethin places a reassuring hand on her shoulder, too, easing some of Zain's worry.

Faris walks to greet the generals as they enter, seemingly dumbfounded at the sight of his large black wings. They hesitantly follow him as he invites them to take a seat.

Their eyes dart around the room, taking in all the various forms of Fae.

A general with shaggy brown hair and a well-kept beard yells, "Witch!" He draws his sword, the metal hissing as he points it at Estrid.

The other two copy their peer into action, drawing their swords out to face the rest of the Fae group.

"What is the witch doing here?" says the general with shoulder-length red hair.

Zain moves his hand to the pommel of his weapon, but Rafe leaps out of a shadowed corner, teeth bared as he lets out a low and menacing growl.

The Fae don't draw their weapons as black smoke from Cethin's hands winds through the tent. It wraps itself around the wrists of each Solian, constricting them. They gasp in shock, eyes wide with terror.

Estrid tries to hide the look of shame at their words, but Zain can see it peeking out from under her stoic façade.

Cethin moves to address the generals. They try to move back from him as his imposing figure towers above them. No one breathes; the only sound is the slight flap of the tent folds in the wind.

"Welcome, generals," Cethin says, taking another step forward to them. "No harm will come to you while you're here. Kindly put away your weapons, and do not threaten my daughter."

Zain's hand hasn't left the pommel of his sword. He narrows his eyes. Focused. Waiting. Watching every move the generals make.

With a clank, all but one general drops their swords.

Cethin returns to his seat at the head of the table, his gaze narrowing on the three humans. "We're here to discuss an alliance, but before that, I need to tell you a tale," he says, then begins the story of Estrid, her mother, and how Rodden has manipulated her.

Zain watches as the generals' shoulders ease slightly, but none fully relax.

As the king finishes his account of the past few decades, the last sword gets sheathed, and each general takes a seat at the table. With stone-sour looks on their faces, they regard Estrid with mistrust.

Cethin continues to talk about the broader opportunities for an alliance now that the portals are open again. Zain has to hold in a growl, as the general with shaggy brown hair hasn't let his gaze drop from Estrid.

He can feel the hate radiating off the man. His peers introduced him as Praxus. He's the youngest of the three.

Estrid shuffles around in her seat. Zain can tell she's uncomfortable with his unrelenting stare.

"General Praxus, is there something you wish to say?" he asks.

Cethin stops talking; the tent goes silent as Estrid turns her head and meets Praxus's murderous gaze head-on.

The oldest general, a man with shoulder-length graying hair named Daros, clears his throat. "Please forgive Praxus's behavior. Rodden and his Dark Witch killed his entire village two years ago. His wife died. His son and daughter were the only ones who survived the attack."

Estrid closes her eyes and winces as the words leave General Daros's mouth. Seeing her hurt like this has Zain wanting to throttle Praxus.

Praxus slams his fists on the table, sending water goblets flying. "She needs to be punished for what she's done!"

Zain, Rafe, and Faris are up in a blur, daggers out as they circle to protect Estrid.

Cethin regards Praxus. Without a word, he stands. His towering figure dwarfs the humans. "We've come here to form an alliance and defeat Rodden. Rodden is to blame for this, not my daughter. He will be stopped, but we need to work together." His tone is calm, his expression neutral, but his eyes say otherwise. The glow that radiates from them is the same furious anger that they saw when he spoke of Queen Eria's murder.

Praxus doesn't back down. Zain's simmering rage becomes a rolling boil as he continues to shout vile words at her. The argument escalates, with all three generals standing up to leave. Zain takes a step forward, ready to cut their throats.

"Wait," Estrid says, getting up and running over to the front of the tent to block the exit. "I'll accept punishment for what I've done!"

No! Zain's stomach drops to the floor. He staggers back as Faris curses next to him. He whips around to Cethin for support, but the king is speechless, slumped back in his chair as Estrid confronts the men.

"Please. I'll accept punishment, but we must stop Rodden together. There is no other way."

Praxus marches up to her; his face is so close that he could slit her throat. "Your punishment will be death, witch! You killed my entire village. My wife!"

Zain is at Estrid's side in an instant. A growl radiates from deep within him as he forms a wall between her and Praxus.

The general puffs out his chest, pushing Zain to the edge of his control. That thread is about to snap when a warm, soft hand finds his shoulder.

He looks down to his left as honey-gold eyes meet his. Shame and sorrow fill those eyes, but they glint in determination. "It's okay, Zain. Please let me talk to Praxus and the other generals."

It takes every ounce of Zain's will to move from that spot. He's finally got her. Finally got over his own pain. And now this.

With a grim expression, he steps aside but doesn't break his stare on Praxus as she approaches the general. "If you swear to align with us and defeat Rodden, I vow that you can take me in to meet whatever justice you see fit for my crimes."

The tent is quiet, apart from Rafe, who gives out a whimper. The three generals stand there in stunned silence, looking at her as if she's sprouted horns.

Praxus's expression is hard, but he takes a breath and nods.

✦ ✦ ✦

After hours of negotiating, they sit around the table that's now littered with maps and pawns.

Zain tries to keep his mind on the strategy discussions, but it feels like an out-of-body experience. He gets drawn back to Estrid's offer. How could he have stopped it? He stares at the map, fixated on the figurines representing Rodden and Balius. Thoughts of what pain he intends to inflict on them are broken as Faris starts speaking to him.

"Zain, are you paying attention? What kind of troops will the Summer Court bring?"

Zain looks between Faris and the map, getting his head back in the game. "If they've found a way to portal their army here, they'll bring infantry and archers at a minimum. They could bring the Nemean lions, but those beasts are big, and without knowing how they're getting into the human world, I can't say whether they can or can't bring them."

"What's a Nemean lion?" Estrid asks, but Zain cannot face her yet; the emotions of her deal with the Solians is too raw.

He clears his throat. "Each court has an animal that represents their court in battle. Winter is wolves, Autumn is bears, Spring is stags, and Summer is Nemean lions. I suppose the equivalent for the Shadow Court is the Lotnars?"

Faris nods at Zain's observation as he starts to discuss the Summer Court.

"The Summer Court has an affinity for the fire element. Some can wield flames like some from the Shadow Court can use the shadows. They'll bring the fire wielders to burn through the front lines."

The group goes silent around him. He knows that sound all too well when anyone mentions the fire wielders, who are next to impossible to stop until they've used up all their magic.

Praxus paces the room; Zain watches his every move. "So, how do we stop them? We can't exactly wield water, can we?" he says, picking up his pace.

"Fire wielders, like all Fae, can't sustain their power indefinitely and will run out at some point. We'll need to distract them enough to burn through their reserves," Zain says.

Faris nods to his right, leaning over the tattered map of the Solian kingdom. "You're right, and we have the element of surprise. Rodden and Balius won't expect the Shadow Court to be here. We can use that to our advantage."

The sun is setting. A golden shine hangs over the grassy hills of Solian as they finish the battle plans. The generals relax as the groups work together. To Zain's astonishment, he's been working very well with Faris, whom he can respect for his strategic thinking.

"Let's go over this one more time," Faris says, looking around the table at everyone while pointing to the map littered with pawns representing the different armies.

"Praxus and the Solian Army, you'll dig trenches in the fields, place spikes in them, and cover them with grass. You'll also form a front line to the south when the day comes." He draws a line on the old parchment.

"Once the fire wielders start their march, you'll release the giant balls of hay and fuel-tainted clay down the hills into their armies. Between that and the trenches, it should slow them down and chew up enough magic that they tire out. Solian archers will fire as the enemy marches forward. We're assuming that there will be cavalry from Nordia and Nemean lions. They'll use them first. Solian pikemen will meet them on the front lines, with infantry to back up those who make it through. When the Nordians and Summer Court engage, you retreat here," Faris says, pointing to a ridgeline that's drawn just behind the front line on the map.

Zain looks at the Solian generals for objections, but each one nods without hesitation.

"Del and Alvey, if he's fit to fight, will be with me, waiting with the Shadow Army to surprise the enemy. The Solian troops will retreat behind us, and we'll engage the oncoming armies. Evander, you'll flank the right with the Lotnar battalions," Faris says and gets a nod back from his second-in-command.

"During that distraction, Cethin, Estrid, and I will use the left flank to get behind their forces to engage Rodden and Balius. Neither of those bastards has enough courage to lead their forces," Zain says with anticipation of meeting the two devils head-on.

"What about Zella?" Estrid asks, taking her cousin's hand. "I want her with me when we take Rodden. He's hurt her as much as he has me."

Zain looks at Cethin, who nods at the idea, knowing full well the cousins would do it with his blessing. Zain must admit that having one more person to fight alongside Estrid brings him comfort.

"Okay, Zella, you're with us. If all goes according to plan, we'll defeat them with minimal casualties on our side," he says, glancing around the room and finding Estrid.

He looks away quickly, unable to take in what the end of the battle means for her.

"Good, then we take the witch and the Nordian crown," Praxus says with a sneer as he glares at Estrid.

Zain is about to jump down the man's throat when Cethin walks to the liquor cart and pours amber liquid into nine glasses. He turns to face the group. The low golden sun from the front flap hits the back of his leathery wings, turning them pink and showing all the veins.

Cethin gives the humans a cold stare. "Let's not talk about my daughter's punishment yet, shall we? As for the Nordian crown, that will go to Zella as the rightful heir of Nordia. Any objections?"

The generals shuffle uncomfortably on their feet.

Their Solian allies leave the black command tent as purple hues of color bring in the night sky. Braziers fight off the cool evening air outside.

With the distraction of forming battle plans gone, Zain fights to keep a tight lid on his emotions.

The atmosphere is heavy with unspoken words about Estrid's willingness to give herself up to the Solians. Rafe senses the tension; his head cradled in her lap, he leans his giant body against her legs as another whimper escapes him.

I can't take this.

Zain gets up and walks over to the drinks table, pouring himself a goblet of amber liquid and drinking it in one gulp. He slams the bottle back down, smashing part of the cart. The muscles in his jaw tic as he paces the tent, agitated and angry. "Why did you do that, Estrid?"

She scowls at him.

Faris strides back and forth on the other side of the room. Cethin hangs his head in his hands, unable to look at his daughter.

Zain's anger is only fueled by the king's lack of response.

"We had no other choice," she says in a defiant tone. "They were going to walk away because of me. I'll do anything to stop Rodden."

"That doesn't mean you give yourself up! We could have defeated them without the Solians," Zain says, looking to Faris for backup.

"He's right, Estrid. We would have made it work," Faris says, coming to take a seat next to Cethin.

Zain throws his hands up in the air with praise from Faris's comments.

Estrid looks like she's about to combust, standing up. "It was my choice! Don't you dare take that away from me. I've killed too many people! Their deaths are a mark on my soul and something I need to atone for. Do not take this away from me," she repeats, hurt tinging her voice.

Zain flinches at her admission. The guilt she must carry every day weighs on her. He knows that, but he can't let this happen. She is his.

"No, I'll take this away . . . because it was not your fault," he says, going over to her.

With a sigh, Cethin stands and walks to the tent's entrance, Faris behind him as he rubs his temples. "Can we continue this lovers' quarrel at the palace? I need to prepare an army to leave in two days," Faris says.

Estrid moves to follow her father, but Zain stops her, grabbing her wrist and turning to Faris. "Keep a shadow walker here. We'll be back soon."

Estrid doesn't fight him, his grip gentle but firm.

Cethin warns Zain, "Talk to each other. Don't turn this into an argument you'll regret later."

The imposing king turns and leaves.

Estrid twists out of Zain's grip, but he pulls her into him so she's flush against his body.

"Let me go, Zain!" she says, digging her fingers into his arm to release her.

With a sigh, he lets her go. "I won't let you do this," he says, chasing after her as he moves to the tent flap.

"There's nothing you can do to change what's been done," Estrid says as she puts space between them.

I won't let anything happen to you. Not after everything we've already endured. Not after I've just made my way back to you.

He takes her hand, spinning her around to face him and drawing her in tight. "I'll never let you go. I'll find a way for you to atone for what you've done, but it won't be by leaving me or anyone else here. We've only just got you back. I've only got you back."

Estrid stops squirming and sinks into his embrace. He pulls back to look at her, eyes shimmering with unshed tears.

Zain crashes his mouth onto hers, the kiss punishing and raw yet tender. It takes everything in him to break away.

Their breaths come out hard and fast, ready to fight each other for either the anger or lust that courses through them.

"The choice isn't yours, Zain. It's mine, and I will see it through if it means that Rodden's stopped."

His temper flares at her words. "So, you'll throw away how we feel for each other like it means nothing?"

"No, but it's the only way," she says, looking at him with determination, but behind the bravado, he can see she's as scared as he is.

He closes the gap between them in two strides and cups her face, keeping his touch light and gentle. "I meant what I said. I will help you atone, but I will not let you go. We'll find a way together."

+ + +

CHAPTER THIRTY-TWO

It's late morning when Estrid gets woken up by Lena. Her eyes feel heavy with the tiredness that dogs her body.

She didn't spend last night with Zain. Instead, she tossed and turned in her bed ahead of the looming battle and her punishment by the Solians. It's been two days since they met with the Solian generals; the time to move out with the Shadow Army has come.

Nerves rock Estrid as Lena helps her get into the black leather armor that Cethin has made before braiding her long dark hair, bringing her food, and packing her gear.

A knock at the entrance to her chambers breaks her thoughts.

"Come in," she says, strapping the last of her throwing knives to her abdomen.

The wooden door opens with a creak as Faris steps in. He's a sight to behold. His black leather armor is fitted like hers, the dips and rises of his broad shoulders and muscular physique leaving nothing to the imagination about how strong he is.

The multiple blades strapped to him twinkle in the light in the room. His black feathered wings make him look more ominous, like an angel of death.

His eyes roam over Estrid's body from head to toe, a proud smile forming on his face. If she were another woman, she may be tempted, but Faris doesn't have that kind of effect on her.

"You ready?" he asks.

"I don't think I can fit another blade on me without stabbing myself," Estrid laughs, patting down her body.

Faris's smile grows as he puffs out his chest like he had something to do with it.

They enter the common room, where Zella and Tore are waiting. They're all wearing armor like hers, fitted to measure and housing just as many weapons.

Zella has two long swords fastened to her back. Her cherry-red hair contrasts with the dark uniform. Tore fusses next to her, checking her weapons and making sure her clasps are strapped on properly.

"New swords?" Estrid says, coming to stand next to Zella. She chuckles at her cousin, who is waving Tore off to wait by Faris at the front door. Their affection for each other warms Estrid; they sometimes act like an old married couple. Zella deserves to be happy.

"Tore had them made for me. Do you like them?"

Zella has lost the demure outer edge she had to keep in place while she was with Rodden. It kept her hidden and alive. Now, it's replaced with an elegant warrior who rigorous training has hardened.

"You look good, like a warrior queen," Estrid says, smiling back at her cousin, bringing her into a hug. They hold each other a little longer than needed.

This is the calm before the storm. Everything will change after today.

The question that hangs over them all is: What will it change to?

They step into the hallways. The palace is a bustling hive of activity, and they weave and dodge as soldiers say goodbye to their families and servants, packing the many provisions that will accompany the army.

Estrid's nerves grow with every step they take toward the central courtyard. The somersaults in her stomach ease when she spots Zain, Alvey, and Del walking in their direction.

Each of them has donned Shadow Court black armor. Her heart squeezes at the sight of their solidarity in wearing the colors of her court.

Her eyes roam Zain's tall and muscular figure, the sight doing many things to her. The leather armor accentuates the hard muscles that her hands have been roaming over for the past few days.

She catches his stare drinking in her own armored body. Desire. Lust. His eyes meet hers with a hungry look, a promise of what's coming should they survive.

She's so lost in that thought that she doesn't see that Faris has stopped and walks straight into his back.

"Sorry," she says, blushing as he looks between her and Zain, a coy smile on his face.

She wouldn't call Zain and Faris friends, but the tension has eased between them since the meeting with the Solian generals. They've joined forces for justice and vengeance.

Estrid clears her throat and moves her eyes to look anywhere but at Zain's distracting figure. She spots Del, who's as fierce as ever.

Like Zella, she has twin swords strapped to her back. Her braided ash-blonde hair shows off her Fae ears. The tips of her shimmering tattoos peek out from her neck.

Estrid's pleased to see Alvey outfitted for battle; she wasn't sure he would come. He's fully healed, but the joyful glint in his eyes hasn't returned after what he went through with Rodden. Imaya used her healing abilities to fix the physical injuries, but the mental toll on him will take years to recover from.

"You're sure you're fit enough to fight, Alvey?" Faris asks, giving the Summer Fae a once-over.

Del scoffs and rolls her eyes at Faris.

"Don't patronize me, Faris. I have every right to be here, if not more so than some," he says, glaring at the Shadow Army general as he reaches for one of his blades.

Zain grabs his brother's hand. "Save it for the battle, Alvey. Faris is not our enemy."

Faris nods at Zain. The words are not lost on Estrid. That feeling of rightness and contentment grows with Zain's admission.

✦ ✦ ✦

The group makes their way to the central courtyard. Courtiers give them a wide berth, wishing them luck and a safe return.

They round the last corner of the familiar carved stone hallways that Estrid calls home. A sea of black unfolds before her eyes. The tall doors open to a view of row upon row of soldiers standing at attention.

The ground shakes and rumbles as thousands stamp their feet at their arrival. Their voices and shouts drown out all sounds around her; it's deafening, like a thousand horses rushing toward her.

Every soldier wears the same black leather armor. Glints of silver twinkle from the myriad of weapons the troops carry or have strapped to them.

The diversity of the Shadow Court is on full display here. Some have wings, and others don't. Some have horns; others have spines and extra limbs. Some sit atop Lotnars, the beasts roaring in anticipation.

Faris nods to the soldiers he passes, each acknowledging their commanding officer with a fist beat on their chest. Estrid blushes as each soldier bows their head in recognition to her. The attention on her makes her uncomfortable.

Come on, Estrid, this is no different to the markets. They're your people.

At the front of the ebony gates stands Cethin, with Evander and Rafe.

The king cuts a regal but magnificent figure. His suit of armor differs from everyone else's. Instead of pure black, he has detailed patterns that are dusted with silver. His leathery wings are tipped with blades at the edges, giving them a demon claw look.

Cethin watches their group approach, his gaze landing on Estrid with pride. He gives her a wide smile as they stand beside him.

In this moment, it strikes her that in her time here, she's been shown more love, care, and support than she's had her entire life. Love for her newfound place in this world fills her, accompanied by a sense of dread.

This isn't just a fight to defeat Rodden but to save her family.

A wet nose nudges her hand as Rafe takes his spot by her side.

Cethin nods to Zain, Del, and Alvey as Tore, Evander, and Faris clasp hands in greeting as they arrive. Faris may be their general, the others his subordinates, but there is more to their relationship. They're as close as brothers, a bond similar to what she has with Zella.

This is her family. This is her home.

"What happens when we get there?" she asks.

"The camp has already been set up. We've had word from our scouts that the Nordian and Summer Court armies are moving faster than expected, no doubt thanks to the mage. When we arrive, we'll go over the plans and start positioning ourselves," Evander says, giving Faris a nod.

Estrid's nerves grow. She shuffles from foot to foot, fiddling with her fingers.

What if they already know our plans? What kind of magic will Neros be using? Gods, this has to work. I can't keep looking over my shoulder.

Faris flaps his wings and launches into the air, blowing on a golden horn. It blasts throughout the area, signaling the troops to move out.

Shadows grow and swell around the courtyard as battalion after battalion slips into them for transportation by the shadow walkers. The cacophony of noise dies down as the last of the soldiers move out.

Faris gives a nod to Cethin. Tore approaches the group, calling in the darkness to transport them. Del looks decidedly nervous as the shadows creep around them.

"Wait, was that all the troops you have?" she asks with a look of worry on her face.

Faris laughs, her question going unanswered as Estrid watches a dark wave of Tore's shadows swallow them.

✝   ✝   ✝

They land in an open field. Beyond the horizon, a ridgeline separates their army to the north. Estrid turns around, her mouth gaping at the sight.

Thousands of Shadow Court soldiers black out the lush, bright green grass of the fields as they camp near the Solian castle. If it were night, there would be little to no distinction between the sky and ground on the horizon. Black armor, tents, and flags cover the vast landscape.

As the troops settle in, smoke from the campfires gives off a low haze. As soon as they land, Faris barks out orders to the surrounding soldiers to get the defenses and watch rotations set up.

Estrid stands rooted to the spot by the sheer size of the Shadow Army operation. None of them expected to see something of this magnitude.

"Holy Ca . . . ," Del says, stunned by the sight.

Faris finishes giving out the last of his commands to a young messenger, coming to stand next to them. His arms folded and a cocky smile on his face, he asks, "Enough troops for you, Del?"

Estrid hides her laugh at his response as the group follows him to the same ten-foot-tall tent they met the Solians in. They pull back the front flap to reveal the same interior. Their battle plans from days ago are still laid out on the rectangular table.

"How are you keeping all these soldiers a secret?" Zella asks as she looks at the maps, figurines, and pawns.

"We've set up a perimeter of Fae to wield a glamour over our troops. No one knows we're here, and if they get too close, they'll have a sudden urge to walk in the opposite direction," Faris says as he reads something and gives another order to a soldier, who scrambles out of the tent.

Estrid can't help but smile at Faris, who's in his element. He's always been the casual, cheeky, and caring man around her. Here, he holds authority. Every soldier hangs on his every word.

Cethin arrives shortly after them, content with Faris running the show.

The group occupies themselves as they wait for the news. Del runs Alvey through the battle plans with Faris. Tore clasps Zella's hands as he whispers into her ear. Estrid scratches Rafe's head to keep herself busy. Zain catches her hand in his, drawing slow circles with his thumb, seeming to calm him as much as her. Cethin looks out over the vast Shadow Army from the front of the tent, its flaps blowing in the gentle breeze.

The shadows move and swirl in one corner as a shadow walker steps through. "Your Highness, sir." He salutes. "I have news of the Nordian and Summer Court armies."

Estrid holds her breath as Cethin nods. Everyone stops what they're doing and looks at the spy.

"We expect they are about a day's ride out. They don't seem to have their Nemean lions with them, but strange magic surrounds them," the shadow walker says, trying not to let his nerves show.

Estrid glances at Zain as concern rushes through her. No doubt Neros's power, but what kind of dark monstrosity is it? She doesn't want to know.

There's no depth he wouldn't sink to for power, she thinks, recalling the many things he did to her.

Faris flicks his wrists, dismissing the shadow walker.

Estrid's nerves swirl in her stomach, making her nauseous. Her past is drawing nearer to her by the hour.

Zain must see the anxiety on her face, as he clasps her hand, bringing his lips to it and tenderly kissing it.

"What kind of magic is it?" Del asks, glancing around the table.

Faris stands to look over their map and plans, his brow furrowed as his deep brown eyes roam over every detail before saying, "Nothing changes. We stick to our plan—"

"I'd like a slight change in plan," Zain cuts in, his eyes flicking to Alvey, who nods.

Estrid narrows her eyes. *What are you planning to do?*

"I have loyal soldiers and guards imprisoned in the Summer Court. With Balius and most of the army here, no major force will be there to stop us from going in. I want a shadow walker to take Alvey and a dozen shadow soldiers to the Summer Court and free those loyal to me so we can take it back with a force of our own when the time is right," Zain says, watching as Faris shifts his attention to Cethin, who looks to Alvey.

Estrid squeezes Zain's hand, ready to jump in and ask her father to support this.

"Alvey, are you up for this?" Cethin asks.

Alvey squares his shoulders and nods in agreement.

"All right, Faris, make it happen," Cethin says with a sigh. "But get in quick and get them out. If you can't free them, you're to come back to the Shadow Court. Is that clear?"

"I can hold down the court while we wait for Zain," Alvey says, taking a step forward.

"Those are my terms. I won't have one of you captured again. We don't know what state the Summer Court is in or what magic is behind all this. Get to the Shadow Court, and when this battle is over, I'll send a whole army to help you get your home back, but right now, I need you all focused and safe." Cethin nods to Faris, who gives Tore the order.

The commander disappears in a whirl of shadows.

Cethin scans their group. "Take the day to prepare yourselves. Go over your part of the plan, visit the troops, check your weapons, and rest."

One by one, everyone filters out of the tent into the warm sunshine rising above their heads. Estrid holds back, watching her father give words of support to each person. Zain, Del, and Alvey take the Shadow King's words in stride, giving him their backing as they all exit.

With everyone gone, Cethin turns to Estrid. "We stick together tomorrow, Estrid. I won't deny you the opportunity to fight, but I won't lose you either, okay?"

She races forward to hug him. The gesture momentarily shocks him before his enormous arms wrap her in an embrace, his leather-and-spice scent encasing her.

"I want you to know how grateful I am for everything you've done for me. No matter what happens, I couldn't do this without you," she says as a tear drips down her cheek.

Cethin breaks away from their hug, bringing her face to meet his. "By the end of tomorrow, the past that's tormented us both will be gone. There'll be only the future to look forward to. Now go rest."

Her father gives her a big hug that calms the storm of nerves that threatens to make her sick. She takes a deep breath and leaves her father.

She needs to find Zain. Needs to be in his arms.

The camp is a hive of activity as all the battalions are brought in and soldiers prepare themselves for the battle ahead. The dulled hiss of blades being drawn against whetstones peppers the merry chatter and laughing from groups huddled around small fires as pink-and-orange hues bring in dusk.

Tonight might be the last for some.

It may be my last.

Her agreement on punishment with Praxus weighs heavily on her. What she could have had is gone. It's now what could have been.

The drive to Zain pushes her through the camp. *One last night before I set things right.*

Entering his tent, she finds it empty. There's a crisply made single bed on one side, a small table on the other, and no armor.

"Zain?" she says, walking up to the table where a little leatherbound book sits. It's a shade darker than her mother's diary, but the pages are white and new.

When she flips it open, it lands on a spot where a dried purple flower lies flat between the pages. It's exactly like the ones in her cottage that Zain brought to her on the morning of their breakfast.

What is this?

"Estrid?"

She startles as Zain comes through the flaps of his tent. He's still in full armor, the edges of his weapons glinting from the small fire he holds in his palm.

"I came to find you. Where were you?" she asks, watching as he blows the flame. He guides the dancing orange orb onto a candle that sits on the table next to her.

"I needed to get everything ready for Alvey's trip. He'll leave before first light," he says, coming to stand beside her. His fingers move up her arm, their brush leaving a trail of energy on her skin.

She inhales as he steps closer to her. "I don't plan on being anywhere other than with you tonight," he says.

He takes her chin between his fingers, tilting her face up and brushing his lips on hers. The warmth of his breath envelops her. Lifting on her toes, she pushes further, their kiss deepening. Zain lets out a groan as his hands grip her waist, eliminating any space between them.

Estrid pulls back, her palm cupping his cheek. She looks down at the little book, the dried flower on display.

"What is this?" she asks.

Zain reaches down and brushes the fragile petals. "After you rescued me, I went back to your cottage to think about us, about how I needed to rethink what's important to me. This was growing outside.

It reminded me of you. Of the first time I met you," he says, dragging his nose along her neck.

Desire and want course through her body as he peppers her sensitive skin with kisses.

Giving in, Estrid tilts her head to the side and arches her back. She drags her hand down the hard planes of his armor, seeking the clasps and straps that hold the barrier between their bodies together. With a clink, they come undone one by one, until his battle leathers part down the middle, revealing a wall of muscle.

"These need to go," she says, pushing them over his shoulders, kissing the soft, smooth skin of his pectorals.

Zain lets out a breathy moan, his hands coming to her hips, gripping them tight.

"If mine go, so do yours," he says as his fingers expertly unclasp each of her straps that hold the tight leathers over her body. Her nipples harden as the cool air meets her skin. Her breasts ache, needing his touch.

When his mouth sucks and licks at her nipples, she can't help but cry out with pleasure. Zain's hand moves to cup her sensitive sex, the friction of it pushing against her remaining clothing, amplifying her reaction.

"Zain, I need you. If this is our last night, I want all of you," she says, grinding against his palm as he lavishes her breasts.

He stands, brushing his nose against hers. "There is no way that I will ever let this be our last night, Estrid. The Solians can get their retribution from someone else. You're mine now."

His hands move down her stomach, reaching down to unbutton her pants. He guides them over her hips, her skin pebbling as it meets the evening air. She bites her lower lip as she stands nude in front of him. This isn't the first time she's been naked with him, but it feels like he truly sees her now.

"You do not know how beautiful you are," he says, stepping back into her space. His fingers trail down her stomach, weaving lazy circles over her skin as they come to her sex. He slips one through her slick folds as she lets out a moan.

As he moves them over her clit, a rush of need courses through her. He pushes two fingers in, thrusting them in and out, curling them to hit that spot that makes her weak in the knees.

"Zain . . ." She traces her hands down his chest and stomach. She brushes the hem of his pants, the strain of his cock pulling them tight. "These need to come off. I want you now," she murmurs, rubbing him.

Zain whips off his bottoms, his hard cock springing free.

Estrid cups his cheeks, bringing her lips to his as he grabs her ass, wrapping her legs around his waist as he takes them to the small bed.

Her back hits the soft blanket, the frame creaking under their weight. Their kisses are needy and wanton. The press of his cock against her skin makes her wetter. She shimmies herself up a little, so his tip just teases at her entrance.

"Please, Zain," she moans at the sensation of it.

He chuckles, leaving a trail of kisses down her neck before nibbling her ear.

"I promise you this won't be our last night, Estrid, but it will be one that we'll speak of forever," he says as he thrusts into her.

CHAPTER THIRTY-THREE

The sun hasn't yet broken the night as the Shadow Army prepares for the looming battle ahead.

Zain sheathes another two blades in his armor, the light leather a familiar feeling from the countless battles he's fought. The soft glow of a candle illuminates his tent.

On the opposite side, Estrid picks up her boots as she gets ready.

He may not want to admit it, but a lot can happen in battle. Knowing it might be their last night together, they made love slowly and deliberately, savoring each moment with each other.

Estrid's braid cascades down her back. Her leathers hug her hips, ass, and waist. Zain has to restrain himself from touching her, knowing where it'll go.

There'll be time for that later, but he just can't resist.

You're mine, and I can't lose you, he thinks as he walks up behind her, drawing her into his body. He dips his nose into the crook of her neck and inhales deeply. The scent of wildflowers and thyme fills his lungs. In and out, he breathes. Each breath grounds him. This woman, her strength, her courage, her willingness to give everything for those she loves—it captivates him.

She tilts her head to his chest, letting him pull her in closer. Neither says anything, just stands there in their embrace. Savoring it.

The squelching sounds of footsteps running through the dewy grass of the early morning draw their attention. There's a yelp of surprise from whoever is out there as they trip over Rafe, and Zain chuckles.

The wolf has stuck close to Estrid's side since arriving in the human realm, unlike in the Shadow Court, where he roams more freely. She had to kick him out of the tent during the night, with the beast mistaking her moans of pleasure for distress.

The entrance flap opens to reveal a shadow soldier. The hilt of a sword peeks up over his shoulder as it's strapped tight to the black leather, a star on his chest noting him as a messenger.

"We're ready to move out, Your Highnesses," he says, bowing to both of them, a flush in his cheeks as he realizes what he's stepped into. He clears his throat and moves on.

With a sigh, Zain kisses Estrid's neck, the loose strands of her hair tickling his face.

"Be safe today. I want to be back in here tonight to pick up where we left off," he says as he squeezes her into his arms.

Turning to face him, she wraps her hands around his neck, flush against his body.

"If that isn't an incentive, I don't know what is," she says, drawing his lips to hers, soft and warm.

Zain lets out a groan, trying to keep himself under control. Outside their tent, someone clears their throat. Zain takes one last look into those honey-gold eyes that draw him in every time.

Del waits for them, wearing Shadow Court black. The leathers have been changed, with three additional sheaths over the ribs to fit her favorite throwing knives.

Only you would need more room for weapons, Del.

Del raises her eyebrow, smirking like she just read his thoughts.

"Good night's rest, then?" she says in a teasing tone.

Estrid chuckles as Zain rolls his eyes.

The sky is awash with warm yellows, oranges, and reds, chasing away the purple of the night. They stroll through the camp, greeting soldiers as they pass through. Each is steadfast as they prepare for war, the tents flapping as the cool morning breeze rolls through. No fires are lit as they make their way to the command tent.

When Zain, Estrid, and Del walk in, it's filled with an electric energy, as battalion leads confirm strategy, friends wish each other luck, and bets are made for the most enemy soldiers downed.

"A red morning sky. A good omen." Imaya joins them at the entrance. She's dressed in leather armor, much like the rest of them. But unlike them, her belt is ladened with wraps, surgical knives, and vials of salves and ointments in place of weapons. The seer walks up to Estrid, embracing her and whispering words of luck.

"You're not going into battle, are you?" Estrid asks, taking in the seer's armor-clad figure.

Imaya laughs and shakes her head, squeezing her shoulders. "No, I'm not, but I find it's better to be in leather if I need to move around fast."

Estrid relaxes at her friend's words, and Zain lets out an exhale.

Thank Dagda. Alvey would kill me if he found out you were going into battle.

The tent flap bursts open behind her as Faris and Cethin emerge, ready to wage war. The soldiers snap to attention, and the chatter dies down.

"Everyone's in position. Zain, Alvey and his team left not long ago. They have their orders, and we'll send a shadow walker back with news," Faris says, handing Zain a note.

His gaze moves down to where Zain and Estrid hold hands. There's an ever-so-small nod from Faris to Zain, like an older brother giving his approval.

Faris moves to the table, distributing parchments of papers to runners and clasping hands with battalion leaders as they move out. Zain wants to roll his eyes at Faris, but he can't help being impressed with the command he holds as a leader.

"Del, you're with me on the front lines. Your Grace, Estrid, Zain, and Zella, a shadow walker will take you to the left flank. There's a small group of walkers and soldiers waiting for you. Remember, do not engage until Evander has flanked the right. It'll distract them enough to ensure your safety to attack from the rear."

The mood becomes more somber as everyone says goodbye and filters out of the tent.

Zain opens the note Faris gave him.

Bring his head back for me, brother, so we can mount it on a pike. I rather liked how the humans added that touch to things.

A

Good luck, brother. He grins as he hands the letter to Del, who chuckles at Alvey's message.

Zain gives her one last hug. The three of them have fought many battles side by side before. This will be the first time they've been separated.

"Don't get killed. We all need you," she tells him.

"Be safe, Del. Try not to kill Faris while you're fighting," he says with a smirk that earns him a clip over the head.

✦ ✦ ✦

Zain stands next to Estrid, Cethin, Zella, and Rafe in a small patch of trees, looking down at the vast empty fields that will soon be consumed in battle.

The light from the morning sun in the east grows, but the ridges and dips of the landscape leave some shadows behind.

In them wait Faris and the Shadow Army. Tore and the shadow walkers grow and extend the darkness to keep their forces hidden until the last moment.

Beyond the ridgeline to the north, out of their sight, stands the Solian Army.

The ground vibrates from the thousands of soldiers marching in unison. The thundering sounds of drumbeats signal the enemy's arrival.

Frantic shouts can be heard from the Solians as they hold their lines. A thrill of adrenaline runs through Zain. He takes a deep breath in to steady himself. The moments before battle can be nerve-racking but equally exhilarating.

Easy, Zain.

His hands itch to reach for his blades, his heart eager for vengeance against those who've harmed his family. Harmed Estrid.

He scans the landscape, catching the black lionlike Lotnars on the opposite flank. The beasts are deathly still, watching the movements with their predatory gaze. He gives Evander a wave and a nod to confirm the position.

Time crawls by, and Zain's body twitches with anticipation.

Whoosh.

Whoosh.

Whoosh.

The familiar sound of fire being wielded and hurled through the air by the Summer Fae.

So it begins.

The shouts and screams for the Solians to hold their lines echo over the fields.

Closing his eyes, Zain concentrates his Fae hearing into the distance, where the battle ramps up.

"Watch out!"

"Move!"

Cries come from the enemy lines, soldiers scrambling to get out of the way as the Solians push their large balls of hay down the ridge into their forces.

Zain smiles to himself. *Ha! Balius, you fool. I knew you'd be lazy and stick to the same tactics.*

There's a screech above Zain's head as a brown hawk soars in the sky. Del. He watches as her bird figure flies over the ridgeline, disappearing.

Relief washes over him as she crests back over. She lands on the front lines of the Shadow Army, moving to speak to Faris. White and black flags wave signals from where the general stands at the front of his forces as Del relays what she saw.

"Any minute now," Cethin says, drawing his blade with a smooth hiss.

The thunderous sounds of stampeding feet grow as Solian soldiers crest over the ridgeline in their retreat. A sea of red and white consumes the fields as they run back to where their allies await.

Zain watches as the Nordian and Summer Court armies give chase to the Solians. A smile breaks over his lips. *That's it. Keep going. Come on, come on.*

His body twitches to jump into the fight. He holds Estrid's hand. The racing thumps of his heart slow and calmness sets in from having her near him.

They watch Tore and his troops lift the shadows that conceal their army. Estrid takes a sharp inhale as the armies collide with an ear-splitting metal-on-metal clang.

Cethin grunts in approval and nods as shouts of surprise come from their enemy as they try to regroup.

The Shadow Army seizes the opportunity and cuts into their lines with brutal efficiency. Screams of the dying fill the air, followed by the roars of triumph from the Solians who regroup and reinforce the front lines.

With a roar of his own, Evander launches the Lotnars from the opposite flank. Both man and Fae alike shriek at the sight of the beasts as they mow people down, the riders on their backs taking heads as their swords rain down hell.

Zain gives Estrid one last look and squeezes her hand. *Be safe. Come back to me.*

"That's our signal," Cethin says as they move.

The dewy grass squelches under their feet as they run. The battle behind them to their right is in full swing, playing its part as the distraction.

Zain glances over his shoulder at the front lines. Those who can fly in the Shadow Army have taken to the sky. They wreak havoc from above, throwing their magic or arrows down on the enemy lines.

Buoyed by their early success, their small group moves along the left flank. They strike down the Summer Fae and Nordians as they make their way to their targets.

Zain wields his sword as an extension of his body. He spares a short glance at Estrid. She hurls out her magic at enemy soldiers who rush her. Their husks are trampled as they keep moving, disintegrating into dust. There's no time to rest.

They keep pressing forward, moving toward the back lines of the enemy. Over his shoulder, Zain can hear the battle's in full swing, too early to understand if one side is winning. Shouts of "Move forward!" and "Hold the line!" can be heard as weapons clash with that all too familiar clang.

As they get closer to their goal, something oily and heavy hangs in the air. It feels wrong, like thick syrup that's seeping around them. Zain pauses, realizing something's off.

The moans of the fallen nearby them die down, and an eerie silence settles over the immediate area. Bones cracking into place raise the hairs on the back of Zain's neck.

Horror and disbelief rock him as a wave of dead Fae and humans rise, the putrid stench of blood and death rising with them.

Screams of fear follow them as the undead attack the living, their jerky movements unnatural but quick.

Shit! Shit! Shit! What's happening?

He thrusts his sword forward, gutting a Nordian as it charges him. The body keeps moving. Zain pulls a dagger from his armor and stabs the creature in the head. Its unnatural movements stop.

A shadow walker next to him screams as two of the undead pull him down. Zain immediately searches for Estrid, catching her as she tries to take down one of the possessed creatures.

"Estrid!" He races for her.

After slicing at the head of an undead Nordian, she turns to Zain. "It's Neros. My magic isn't working on them."

Zain swings to cut down another soulless soldier who's missing an arm. *Where is he?*

He looks at the top of a ridgeline to the north, where Balius and Rodden wait atop their white stallions.

In front of them, Neros has his arms out, his mouth moving as he chants something. The wind picks up behind him.

Cethin flaps his leathery wings, grabbing his sword that's wedged in the ribcage of a body sliced in two and tearing it free. "I've got the mage! Stop Rodden and Balius."

He takes off into the sky, his batlike wings pushing air down on them.

Zain rushes to Estrid and Zella as they fight off more of the necromancer's creatures.

"Estrid! Zella! Come on," he says, waving for them to follow him as the unit of Shadow Army soldiers with them holds against the onslaught of undead.

Zain runs, his heart pounding, legs aching as he pushes forward through enemy lines. His eyes lock on his uncle's, which grow wide at the sight of Zain.

He smirks. *You thought I was still trapped in that depressing dungeon, didn't you, you traitor? I'll do more than just take your head.*

Warm blood sprays over Zain as he charges forward, swinging his sword as soldiers attack him.

Balius leans over and points to where Zain rushes toward them.

Rodden's lip curls into a snarl, and he kicks his horse into a gallop. Balius turns his steed around, taking off to the north.

Zain lets out a roar of frustration. "Balius, you coward!"

A scream has him stopping. He searches for Estrid. Panic grips him like a vice over his lungs. He can't see her.

Around him, the dead remain dead. Cethin sends another barrage of shadow magic out. It barrels into Neros, knocking him down. The necromancer's spell is broken.

Estrid yells to him, preparing to meet Rodden as his horse closes the gap between them. "Zain, go after him!"

The binds that constrict his chest loosen when he hears her voice.

Zain looks around at the chaos that surrounds him. More bodies fall as the battle rages on. Humans and Fae go head-to-head. An arrow whizzes past him, the disturbance in the air altering his senses; he dodges it at the last moment. Angry, Zain throws a fireball in the direction from where it came. Piercing screams answer as it hits its mark.

A Summer Fae charges Estrid, his blade held high. She unleashes her magic on him, the telltale husk drifting to the ground a moment later.

In his peripheral vision, Zain can see Balius putting more and more distance between them. *Shit.* He's torn between going after his uncle and staying with Estrid.

A screech overhead draws his attention, Del's brown hawk beckoning him to follow her. He seeks Estrid out one last time, her magic consuming those around her as she makes her way to Rodden.

Go, Zain, now!

✦ ✦ ✦

CHAPTER THIRTY-FOUR

Husks fall around Estrid, her magic drawing the life from enemy soldiers who cross her path. Zella works with their small group of shadow warriors, the slashing sound as she swings her dual blades with precision filling the air.

Argh, move! Estrid throws out another burst of power, becoming impatient as more soldiers block her path to Rodden. She edges closer, her impatience short-lived as the sound of horse hooves thunders toward her.

Rodden sits atop his white horse, bearing down on the group. A squad of the Nordian king's guard flanks him, shouting to protect the king as they charge down the field.

Estrid's heart races. "Clear the path! Take out their soldiers," she yells to the shadow warriors closest to her.

Whirling around, Estrid finds Zella as she removes her weapon from a Nordian soldier she just gutted, her pretty face sprayed with crimson blood.

"Zella, go to Rodden! I'll draw them away. I'll come soon."

"Be safe," Zella says as they give each other a quick hug and then throw themselves back into it.

Estrid releases more inky black tethers, wrapping them around the Nordians as they try to get to Zella while she hurtles toward Rodden. Her magic pulses through her, taking everything from them.

I told you I'd kill you all one day.

Estrid smirks as she recognizes Linus, the soldier who took her from her cottage. An agonizing scream follows the ropes of her magic as they drain every ounce of life from him. From anyone who dares to cross her.

Shouts to charge turn into screams to run, the Nordians quickly realizing who they're up against. Rafe chases after them, bones crunching between his massive jaws as he snaps down on anyone he catches.

She turns to a shadow warrior fighting by her side. "I'm going after Rodden! Make sure no one gets near us."

The warrior nods and shouts orders to their team as they battle away to create a protected space for her.

This is it!

Estrid races forward, holding out her sword. When she reaches Zella, her cousin's blocking and evading Rodden's powerful blows. He's not quick, but he's strong. The shock of each mighty strike hits Zella, jarring her and slowing her down.

Estrid yells, "Rodden!"

The northern king turns his leathery face her direction, his soulless black eyes narrow as he spots her. "Coming to kill me, Estrid?" he mocks her as he effortlessly blocks another strike from Zella.

Zella circles her uncle to come stand near Estrid. Just like they practiced, the pair set up at four and eight, circling the king.

An arrogant smile appears on his face, and Estrid trembles with rage, the uncontrollable darkness that once was all she was threatening to take hold of her again. It rushes through her body like an energy surge, making every part of her tingle.

Estrid takes a deep breath, refusing to let the darkness take over. She's more than that now. She's in control.

Estrid points her sword at him. "This ends now, you bastard! I am more than just death and darkness. I'll eradicate you from this world."

While all the death in her past haunts her, Rodden's is the one that she will be glad to carry out.

She takes a deep breath. *This is for my mother. This is for me.*

Together, Zella and Estrid charge down their tormentor, Estrid aiming for Rodden's head while Zella goes for his horse.

The beast rears up, tossing him off as Zella's blade slashes its side. With an ear-piercing whinny, it comes crashing down. Zella and Estrid scramble to get out of the way. The animal hits the ground with a heavy thud, dirt and mud flying across them.

"Regroup!" Estrid calls to Zella as Rodden gets up as if being tossed off a horse is nothing.

How are you not down?

He lets out an almighty roar and runs at them, swinging his heavy weapon down. The air ripples around Estrid's head as she ducks just in time.

Moving in tandem, Estrid and Zella strike at Rodden. He parries, deflecting their blows, and thrusts his sword forward. He lets out a low laugh. Estrid clenches her teeth, his arrogance infuriating her.

"You won't stop me, Estrid! You can't even get close to me," Rodden says, pointing his sword to her right. "Once I've killed you, I'll take those Solian pigs and let Balius enslave them all while I take over their precious kingdom."

Sparing a quick glance in the direction of Rodden's blade, she catches Zella clutching her side. Bright red blood seeps from a gash in her armor.

Fear surges through Estrid, but it's greeted by relief as shadow warriors hold their protective barrier around her, taking down Nordians who dare to get close to her and Zella.

A howl in the distance draws her attention to the thick of the battle that rages on. Familiar piercing blue eyes catch hers. He knocks over soldiers as he barrels toward them.

Rodden takes the opportunity and rushes Estrid. She parries, making him stumble as he tries to regain his balance.

"Rafe! Help Zella!"

The tide is turning beyond the wolf. The protective barrier that the shadow warriors created has moved further out, leaving a trail of Nordian and Summer Fae bodies in their wake.

In the distance, shouts of advance can be heard from Faris as he soars through the air, overlooking the battle as he rains arrows down on their enemy. His black armor and wings cast him like an angel of death.

Rodden charges Estrid again. This time, his blade comes crashing down on her with a clang. Vibrations move down her arm as her sword meets his. She struggles to push him back, her feet sliding on the blood-soaked earth.

To her left, Zella sags on the ground, Rafe propping her up. Estrid spares her a glance. Her cousin nods.

Let's finish it.

Estrid takes a big breath in. She digs down into her soul, searching for that hidden box deep inside her, locking away that darkness.

Like opening a box of delicate jewels, she lifts the lid, unleashing her power on Rodden. Black threads of her magic zoom for him, hitting him square in the chest and pushing him back.

The king throws his arms up. His back arches as the darkness moves into his body.

Estrid waits for that pull, that drain of life to come, but it doesn't.

Rodden's gaze fixes on her. A cruel smile erupts on his face as he absorbs her power.

Why aren't you dying? How is my magic not affecting you?

Estrid stands there, confused. Rafe lets out a snarl, but she holds out her hand, a silent command to her companion. *Stay with Zella.*

Rodden looks at his hands, the remnants of her tendrils seeping into him. "You stupid girl. Your magic won't work on me. I made it what it is, and I own it!"

CHAPTER THIRTY-FOUR

He comes at Estrid with newfound energy.

Shocked by her magic not working, she spins out of Rodden's reach. She can feel how close he is as the air ripples near her. He takes the opportunity and swings again. His blade smashes against hers with a force like she's never felt.

A heavy boot kicks her chest, sending her back. She stumbles, fear lacing her as she turns to catch herself before she falls.

Her face meets the wet ground as her sword flies out of her hand. Mud and blood mix to give off a metallic, earthy smell. Disorientated, she looks up, just making out Faris's figure in the air as he picks up and drops a soldier from the sky. The others are lost in the chaos.

Rodden bellows out a laugh behind her. The thud of his footsteps draws closer.

Her sword lies just out of her reach. She reaches down and clasps a dagger strapped on her ribs by her leathers, then flips back over.

The cruel king looms over her, his blade pointed at her neck. "Your magic was the only thing of worth in you. Without it, you're nothing. You can't even defeat me," he spits at her.

Her lips curl up into a snarl. *Fuck you.*

His words renew her determination. She grips her dagger, scrambling back from the tip of his sword.

I need a distraction.

He takes a step forward, that point biting into her neck. Warm blood trickles from the prick it just opened up in her skin.

"Your mother was nothing too. A useless Fae who was betrayed by her own for love. Now, you'll join her."

"Fuck y—"

Warm crimson blood bursts over her face as she's about to surge up and attack.

A sword erupts from Rodden's neck, the silver of the blade coated in the ruby-red liquid.

Rodden's eyes grow wide with shock as he crumples to his knees with a gurgling sound, dropping his weapon to grasp his throat. His eyes roll into the back of his head as his body hits the ground, a deep red pool forming around him.

Estrid looks up to see Zella slumping to the ground behind him.

Swords clank and hiss around them as shouts of "The king is dead!" echo through the enemy lines. Nordians around them try to run but are cut down as they retreat; those who didn't run or surrendered begin dropping their weapons.

Zella sits on the ground, holding her side, her breath coming out in wheezes.

"Zella! No!" Estrid says, running to her cousin. The blood is warm and sticky as it seeps through her fingers.

Zella grabs Estrid's hand and shoves her sword into it. "Make sure he's dead."

Estrid turns around to where Rodden lies. His body doesn't move. There's no rise and fall of his chest.

I'm not taking any chances.

She lifts Zella's sword above her head. Drawing on her Fae strength, she brings it down with a heavy swing.

There's a hatchet sound as the steel slices through flesh and bone.

"I told you I'd kill you, old man," she says, pushing his head away from his body, knowing Neros can bring people back from the dead.

Estrid lets out a laugh as the guilt of killing the man she thought was her father is washed away by relief. Smiling, she feels lighter. She takes a deep breath in. A heavy burden is taken off her shoulders. A dark cloud vanquished forever.

But her smile vanishes as she looks back to where Zella is lying on the ground.

"Get Tore!" Estrid yells to one of the shadow warriors who's rounding up the surrendered Nordians near them. The need for their protective circle is no more, as waves of enemy soldiers drop their weapons at the sight of their beheaded king.

The shadows swell around her as Tore's impressive figure steps out from behind them. His eyes drop to Zella, panic written on his face. "What happened?"

"She needs a healer. Quick, take her," Estrid says, watching as he picks up her cousin. Zella looks up at Tore, cupping his cheek in reassurance.

He nods to the east. "They've all but surrendered. There's still a pocket of resistance over there. Your father's battling Neros. I've got her. You need to get to him now."

Tore's words sink in a second later.

Neros.

+ + +

CHAPTER THIRTY-FIVE

Zain tries not to look back at Estrid as she charges Rodden. Above him, Del lets out another screech in her hawk form, drawing his attention back to the task at hand.

His gaze locks on to Balius's retreating figure as he gallops away atop his white horse. Estrid's message echoes in his mind: *"Go after him."*

Those words spur him into action as he pushes forward. Soldiers cross his path, swiping their blades down. He throws his fire magic at them. The air fills with the smell of charred flesh as the flames take hold.

He swings his sword down on a Nordian soldier who stands ready to take him. His blade slices through the soldier's neck cleanly as his Fae strength propels him forward. It feels like cutting through water, slower but clean and undeterred.

He's about to portal when he sees the shadow messenger who came to get him and Estrid from their tent this morning. He's outnumbered three to one by Summer Fae.

Glancing between Balius's retreating figure and the messenger, Zain lets out a frustrated growl, then leaps into the fight.

His sword meets the edge of a Summer Fae's weapon with a deafening clang as he stops it from taking the Shadow Fae's head.

"Stop! I command you all to stop!" he yells at the three Summer Fae who circle them. Their eyes have a strange glaze on them, like a white film sitting over the top.

Zain shouts again, "I command you as your king to stop!"

His words are met with silence. Their expressions are emotionless as they surround Zain and the Shadow Fae.

"What's your name?" Zain asks over his shoulder to the Shadow Fae as they stand back to back.

"Rolo, my lord," he says as one Summer Fae takes a step forward.

Around them, the battle rages. Shouts, cries, and screams fill the thick air with the metallic smell of blood and ash; their boots squelch in the wet ground.

"Okay, Rolo, on my count, you take the one in front of you, and I'll take the other two. One, t—" Zain says just as one of the Summer Fae charges him.

He parries and slices the soldier's abdomen. The other two take advantage of the distraction and charge.

He can feel the air behind him move as Rolo fights back to back with him. They're a whirl of steel and leather. But the Summer Fae keep coming.

For Dagda's sake, I don't want to have to kill you. Guilt racks him, but they're wasting time.

Frustrated, Zain lights up his left palm. He throws out his fire magic at each of the Summer Fae; their bodies flail around as the flames take hold. Rolo follows, running his sword through them, giving them a far quicker death than being burnt alive.

Giving Rolo a quick nod of thanks, Zain stands over the Summer Fae he took down earlier. Blood trickles from the sides of his mouth. The wound in his abdomen weeps red.

Anger courses through Zain. *You traitor.* He raises his weapon.

"My lord? Whe-Where am I?" the Summer Fae stutters.

Zain's anger is extinguished at the words. He furrows his brow, lowering his weapon. "You don't know where you are?"

"N-No, my lord. Last I remember, I was in the barracks back home. W-We were training with Commander Manis."

Zain shares a confused look with Rolo. *What's going on here?*

"Rolo, take this Fae prisoner. See that he gets a healer. Tell General Faris not to kill any Summer Fae. Subdue them only. Something's not right here."

Rolo shouts to some other Shadow Fae who are giving chase to the enemy as the battle turns in their favor. "Oi! Leave them be and come help me!"

Three Shadow Fae step up to help take the injured Summer Fae away as he groans in pain.

What magic did Balius use to compel them if he didn't know where he was?

The fighting's moved farther east. Shouts of surrender echo all around.

Zain scans the battlefield that's littered with bodies. Most are human from the colors of their kingdoms that lie in the mud. Black and gold of Nordia. Red and white of Solian.

Now and then, he sees the distinctive green and gold of the Summer Court. *How many of my soldiers died today?* A sickening feeling develops in his stomach.

His thoughts are disrupted as Del lands in front of him, the brown of her hawk feathers transforming into ivory skin and blonde hair.

She marches up to Zain. "What are you doing? Balius got away! Why didn't you go after him?"

He shakes his head, picking up the remnants of a charred Summer Court tabard. "They've been compelled to come here, Del. None of our soldiers know what they're doing!"

"What? Balius is getting away! We need to get him!" She's about to take flight again when Zain grabs her shoulder. Her cheeks are splattered with blood and dirt, her hands balled into fists.

"Let him go, Del. He can't go back to the Summer Court. Manis is dead, and Alvey has rescued those loyal to us. He has nothing to fight with. We need to break the spell compelling our soldiers to be here," he says, guilt for those he killed today weighing him down.

Del lets out a heavy sigh and nods. "Okay, but what are you going to do?"

"I have to find Estrid. All of this is connected to Neros. We have to stop him."

✦ ✦ ✦

CHAPTER THIRTY-SIX

odies litter the field. Estrid's boots slip and slide in the mud mixed with both human and Fae blood. The putrid stench of death is heavy in the air.

She scans her surroundings. The Shadow Fae and Solians start gaining as shouts of Rodden's demise spread throughout the battlefield. Nordian soldiers lay down their arms. The Summer Fae scramble as their human allies surrender without a second thought.

In the distance, Faris soars in the sky with feathered wings of darkness. He rains arrows of shadow down onto the remaining enemies while commanding his army. Del fights with him, switching between Fae and animal form to take down as many as possible. The two work well together; their energies and styles are complementary. Their hostility has thawed as they share a common goal: defeating Rodden.

Lotnar roars race through the western flank. Hundreds of the large black-furred animals rip and tear through any remaining enemy lines, their riders taking care of any who manage to escape the Lotnars' teeth and claws.

Estrid scans the battlefield for Zain, but he's nowhere to be seen after running after Balius. Worry builds in her chest, but it's cut short by a roar of pain.

To the east, Cethin battles Neros. Their powers collide. Cethin's is dark, like Estrid's, but there's a sense of light around its edges: shadow. Neros doesn't flinch. His black magic is wrong—there's something distorted and unnatural about it.

Estrid inches her way to Cethin. Drawing nearer, she can see the toll the battle has taken on him. Sweat drenches his brow, his skin a pale gray. One of his wings looks like a rot has set in as it half hangs off.

Dread fills her, but it's replaced by fury as her attention shifts to Neros. His black eyes fixed on Cethin, a cruel smile spreads across his face as he funnels his foul magic toward him.

Estrid creeps forward, carefully navigating through the fallen bodies. Neros is in a trance-like state, fixated on Cethin.

Estrid slips in a bloody patch on the ground, catching herself on a fallen soldier's chest. She recognizes him as a guard from Solian who accompanied their generals to the tent to plan the alliance. His vacant hazel eyes stare at the sky, his lips blue.

She looks up to see if Neros noticed her stumble, but he's focused on Cethin. An oily and sticky sensation corrupts the air, sticking to her lungs. She feels like she's drowning. She calls her magic to her to break the effects of Neros's hold on her.

Her magic wraps around her like black silk, soft, smooth, and cool. It lets the air back into her lungs after the suffocating presence of Neros's power. Determined, she pushes past the sensation, drawing a dagger from the right side of her armor.

She moves to strike, but a cold, skeletal hand grips her wrist before her blade finds its target. Pain shoots through her arm as it's twisted back.

How did you turn so quickly?

Shocked, she drops her dagger.

Neros's solid black eyes focus on her, and panic takes hold of her. He drops his magical assault on Cethin, who lies crumpled on the ground. A prickling sensation creeps up Estrid's body as Neros wraps his magic around her. It feels like a million insect legs crawling up her skin. Sharp. Painful.

"My, my, Estrid. You look divine." Neros licks his lips, bringing her hand to his cheek.

Revulsion has her trying to yank her hand back. His skin feels artificial and wrong. It's hard and waxy. Estrid rakes her other fingers across his cheeks, her nails sinking into his face. No blood follows. Instead, black oozes out.

She recoils at the sight. *What. Is. That?*

Neros doesn't flinch at the claw marks down his cheek. Instead, he lets out an "Mmmm" like he's enjoying the pain. Bile rises in Estrid's throat.

"You were always going to be mine, Estrid. He promised me." His grip tightens on her wrist, her bones creaking as they threaten to break.

She holds down the cry of agony, refusing to give him the satisfaction. "I'll never be yours. I'll die first and take you with me," she says, drawing another dagger with her left hand and slashing at Neros's chest.

The sharp blade opens his dark robes, revealing waxy gray skin over bones. Oozing black liquid comes from the gash she's just opened up.

Neros rears back, dropping her wrist and clutching at his chest. Estrid stumbles back onto her feet. She places herself between Cethin and Neros, picking up the king's sword.

"You'll pay for that, you bitch," Neros says as he straightens, his eyes going black once more as he draws his power to him.

From behind her, Cethin yells at her to get away, but it's too late.

Putrid power slams into the magic she's holding against herself as a shield. It invades the soft silkiness of her magic, tainting it.

Estrid gasps as she tries to keep it together, protecting herself. Drops of sweat bead down her forehead as she focuses her power, willing it to repel Neros's, just like Faris taught her.

Her magic may not kill Neros, but her blade will.

Neros smiles at her, goading her forward.

She grips her weapon tighter and doesn't hesitate, charging him with all her strength.

He disappears, her blade slicing through the air with a whoosh. Behind her, a sinister laugh erupts from where Cethin lies on the earth. Neros picks her father off the ground by his throat, locked in a vicelike grip. She doesn't remember him being this strong.

"Tsk, tsk, did you think I would make it so easy?"

Estrid moves forward, but the mage tightens his hold on Cethin's neck.

No, no, no, no, please. Don't hurt him, she thinks, desperate not to lose the father she just gained.

Crunch.

Snap.

Bones begin to crack and break beneath Neros's punishing grip.

Cethin's eyes roll back in his head from the pressure.

"No!" Estrid shouts. She drops her weapon, not taking another step.

Neros smiles at her. "They say the only way to kill a Fae is by removing their head. Shall I remove his with my hands, Estrid?" His grip tightens on Cethin's neck. "I'll do it unless you come with me."

Anger pulses through her veins. She needs to think. Her mind races for anything that can stop Neros. She needs to stall.

"Okay, okay . . . just let him go."

Neros beckons her over with a bony skeletal finger.

She takes one step and then another before a thunderous roar in the distance in front of her draws her attention.

Zain sits atop a Lotnar, racing toward her. His hands are lit up with white light.

That color brings a memory back to life. The bird in the field. Their magic together can conquer death.

Stall, Estrid. You need to stall him.

"I have one question. Was it me that you wanted or Rodden's power?" she says, faking defeat as she slumps her shoulders forward.

Neros gives her a smug expression. He drops Cethin to the ground, her father's large body landing with a thud.

She lets the tears of anger roll down her cheeks, helping to feign submission while rage boils in her blood.

Neros steps toward her, a triumphant smile on his face.

"Oh, Estrid, I've never needed Rodden for power," he says with a conquering snarl. "I should have tossed the withering fool aside a long time ago. It's you I need, and with you, I'll get the ultimate power. That you are so lovely to look at is just a bonus."

What are you talking about? Estrid thinks, panicking as Neros stalks her like a wraith. His oily black magic mixes with the smell of death that surrounds her. He's so focused on her that he doesn't notice as Zain barrels toward them, the Lotnar aiming for Neros as he dismounts and hurtles for her.

"Zain!"

Neros steps out of the Lotnar's way before it tackles him, drawing his power up.

Zain appears next to her, blood spatters on his face and clothes and a wild look in his eyes as Estrid grabs his hand.

"Remember the bird in the field," she yells.

Zain looks at their joined hands and then nods.

"My magic doesn't affect Neros, but ours together may work." She squeezes his hand, turning to the dark mage.

Neros aims for the pair.

With Zain's hand in hers, Estrid calls up their power.

A blinding white light encased with dark edges hurtles for Neros. The combination feels like the warmth of a flame chasing away the cold. It slices through Neros's sticky, unnatural magic. He leaps out of the way before it can hit him dead on, but it catches his shoulder.

The mage roars as he goes down in a heap of shadowy robes, meters from where he'd been standing.

Estrid and Zain look at each other, then down at their interlocked hands, surprised that it worked. A groan escapes Neros, drawing their attention back to the task.

Estrid stalks toward her tormentor. Nervousness and satisfaction grow at the victory she's about to have. She can feel Zain behind her. His presence is like a solid wall. Unyielding. Ready to catch and protect her if she ever faltered.

"No," Neros says, scrambling away from them. He looks down at his arm, shocked as strange liquid fizzes, bubbles, and oozes out.

Estrid reaches back for Zain's hand, set to strike at Neros again. Before she can summon their magic, Neros opens a portal and dives through it. Only mud mixed with his tainted blood remains where he fell.

Estrid rushes to the spot where he just lay. "Nooo!"

She paces, looking for any small sign of him. Frustration and annoyance send her into a wild state.

Before she can release another scream, the familiar smell of bergamot and cedar envelops her. Zain wraps his arms around her, holding her steady as her breaths come out ragged and uneven.

"We have to get him," she says in a desperate tone.

Zain spins her to face him. His blue eyes shimmer as gold flecks dance through them, his brow furrowed with concern as her words get stuck. He draws her into a hug.

Her raging torrent of anger subsides as she sinks into his arms. They stand there for a moment, the sounds of a victorious battle around them. Cheers go up. Swords clang against shields as calls for victory are raised. Estrid doesn't share the sentiment as tears trickle down her cheeks.

She pulls herself back to look at Zain. "We have to get him, Zain."

"We will, Estrid. We will, but for now, let's take this win."

He brings his hand up to cup her cheek, drying her tears.

A sharp pain stabs her back before she can sink further into his touch. That oily magic surrounds her.

"You will be mine, in life or death," Neros whispers in her ear.

Estrid stumbles and turns to catch the mage, but he disappears. The world fades as agonizing pain takes hold of her. Zain shouts her name, but it seems so distant.

Everything blurs around Estrid. The pain in her back blooms as she can feel the blade Neros stabbed her with. Her legs give out as she crumples in Zain's arms. She stares up at him, panic and desperation clawing at her chest. Her breaths come out shallow.

"Estrid! Estrid, stay with me. Imaya!!" Zain yells. He searches their surroundings, looking for the seer.

Estrid can feel the energy draining out of her as the warm, wet patch on her back grows. Zain continues to yell for help as others come rushing. Her head flops to one side.

A few meters away from her is Cethin's fallen figure. She tries to call out for him, but the words fail her as her strength wanes.

"Estrid, stay with me!"

Footsteps shuffle around her, squelching in the mud and blood from the battlefield. More panicked voices surround her, but she's unsure who they belong to.

Using every ounce of her energy, she lifts her arms to Cethin, trying to get the others to focus on healing him. Zain's voice draws her attention back to him like the sun breaking through clouds.

"Estrid, remember the bird?" he says, jostling her in his arms as he pulls her closer to him.

Yes! Yes, I remember. She's unable to nod as she meets his blue eyes, the gold flecks growing as they lock on to her.

"Now! Pull it out now!" he says, and she feels someone tugging the blade from her back.

Black spots fill her vision as pain floods her body.

Zain, help me! I don't want to die.

She lets out a garbled cry before the dots join together, taking her with them. There's nothing but stillness around her. Unending darkness hangs on to her.

Cold drops sprinkle across Estrid's cheeks, drawing her eyes open. Not drops, snow. Everything is white, covered in a glistening white powder of snow. Her breath mists in front of her as she exhales. There's no more pain. No more blood. No more sound.

"Estrid . . . ," a singsong voice calls out to her. It's familiar yet foreign.

Where am I?

She sits up, furrowing her brow at the lack of pain she should be feeling after Neros stabbed her.

"Estrid . . . ," that voice beckons again.

Estrid jumps to her feet, crouching down and scanning the unfamiliar landscape around her.

Everything blends together, the white hiding in the shadows. She stills as she lands on a pair of honey-gold eyes. They belong to a woman with the whitest hair, fairest skin, and delicate features.

Mother?

Unsure what to make of the creature in front of her, she cautiously stands up and takes a step forward.

"Estrid, my sweet girl, go back. It's not your time. . . ." The voice echoes through the white landscape.

"What?" Estrid says, advancing toward the woman. The figure vanishes before her.

"A great evil is coming. Go back," the melodic voice says.

"Who are you? What do you mean, a great evil?" Estrid says, spinning around, trying to track down the woman again.

"To defeat the evil, you must return to your mate, Estrid. He waits for you," the voice says from behind her.

She jumps back, stumbling in the snow as the female stands a few feet away.

"Mate? I don't understand?" Estrid says, scrambling up.

"A great evil is coming. Together . . . only together can you defeat it," the voice says. Her face softens, and a gentle smile grows as her honey-gold eyes look at Estrid.

"How—" is all Estrid can get out before the woman rushes her, sending her crashing into the snow.

✦ ✦ ✦

She takes a shallow breath in. Then another, and another.

The unending darkness is pierced by a pinprick of light. The warm feeling of a flame envelops her body. It starts slowly and then grows, chasing away the cold, threatening to take her. Her breaths come in deeper. She can feel the light flowing through her body, seeping into every part of her.

The wound in her back knits itself together, one fiber at a time. *What's happening?* She lies there, the sensation foreign but welcomed.

A familiar voice draws her consciousness to focus. It's nothing but a whisper, but it's laced with despair.

"Estrid, come back. Come back to me," Zain says with growing desperation.

It dawns on her where she is. Whose arms cocoon her like she's the most precious thing in the world. Bergamot and cedar fill her nose.

Zain.

She takes a deep breath in. Her eyes flutter open.

Zain rests his forehead on hers, his warm breath brushing her lips. She wraps her arms around his neck, bringing his mouth to hers. Their kiss is tender but passionate.

It draws her mind back to the present.

What happened? Who got away? Who was defeated?

She breaks her kiss with Zain, and her surroundings come flooding back to her. The smells of mud, blood, and death invade her nose. The clanking and crashing of metal on metal are gone, replaced by the pained cries of the injured and dying as carrion birds feast on the dead.

Zain's arms ease around her as she sits up, taking it all in. Fear grips her as she sees Faris pacing over her father's fallen figure. Imaya's eyes are rolled back into her head as her healing magic flows into the king.

"Is he going to be okay?" Estrid asks, her voice coming out hoarse and raspy.

Faris looks up, his brow furrowed with worry. He says nothing as he casts his eyes down to the king again.

"I need to get to him," Estrid says, trying to stand up from where she's cradled in Zain's arms.

He loosens his grip, helping her to stand. Her legs feel like jelly; they wobble under her as she steps toward her father.

Imaya stops her chanting and whips her head to Estrid, saying, "Estrid, stop! You need to step back."

An ice-cold wind whips through her. It wraps itself around her, numbing her skin and freezing the ground at her feet.

Everyone takes a step back with gasps and sounds of shock.

Estrid stops dead. She looks around.

"What's happening?" she says in a panicked voice, reaching for Zain.

He grabs her hand but recoils and hisses as he comes away burnt.

✦ ✦ ✦

EPILOGUE

The darkness is suffocating. Time has stopped, as though it's been absorbed.

At first, he lost his mind to it. The vastness of it is impossible to deal with. He raved. He roared. He fought it, but it always won.

With no strength left, he learned to make peace with it, knowing he couldn't win. Left to exist in nothingness.

Then one day, there was a shift in the surrounding energy, like a ripple of water. Something had changed, but not in here. Out there.

A knock echoes in the void around him. There are no doors here, but someone can still enter.

"Come in," he says, speaking to the cavernous darkness.

Harsh, raspy breaths echo into the vastness as someone enters the room. Only one other can enter here.

"My lord—" The grating sound floats around him, but he cuts them off. The panic in their voice says all that needs to be said. He can feel them squirm under the heavy silence.

"You've failed, Neros," he says when there's a pause in the hoarse breathing.

The silence stretches on.

"My lord, p-please, I will not fail you again. There's another way."
Neros's heart rate picks up, and the thundering sound of it pains his ears.

"I need her to get out of here. Do you understand, Neros?" he says.

He would reach out and strangle the mage, but there's nothing to latch on to.

Not yet.

✦ ✦ ✦

ACKNOWLEDGMENTS

The journey to publishing my first book has been one hell of a ride. My respect for authors and fellow creatives has grown with this adventure. Until this point I never truly comprehended the mammoth effort involved. I am very fortunate to have had the support, care, and love of so many people along this road to achieving my dream. I've made so many new friends along the way, and I am grateful to so many people. To my friends, both old and new, and family, thank you for everything you have done for me. To those that have given me words of encouragement in good times and in bad, thank you. To those who have taken time out of their busy lives to read my book, provide feedback, and give me your honest opinions, thank you. To Megan, who has become a great friend and colleague that has helped support and guide me. To, my kids, for your understanding and unconditional love. To my husband, you've never once stopped believing in me, having my back or giving everything to us. Together we have done this. Together we are a team.

Finally, to you as the reader, thank you for investing in me. I hope you enjoyed this first book in the Binary Souls series. I have one more ask of you, please leave a review. Reviews are critical for the success of authors, without them we don't get to be what we are.

Thank you all xxx
Cat

ABOUT THE AUTHOR

Cat Sirota moved to Middle Earth (known informally as New Zealand) at the age of twelve. The moody, romantic landscape inspired her passion for fantasy novels and would go on to shape her own fiction writing, setting the scene for lush worldbuilding, dark characters, and satisfying plot twists.

Every morning, at 5 a.m., long before her rambunctious household has risen, Cat pours a cup of coffee and gets to work. When she isn't writing and editing, she's lost in the stories of authors like LJ Andrews Penn Cole, and Jennifer L. Armentrout. For Cat, only one thing trumps the magical alchemy of reading, and that is crafting new portals of escapism in her own stories.

If you'd like to escape with me and hear about exclusive up-and-coming adventures, characters, and treats, join my newsletter via my website or my readers group on Facebook. Otherwise, follow me on Instagram or TikTok for general fun and shenanigans.

Facebook: *https://www.facebook.com/profile.php?id=100095441386644*
Facebook readers group: *https://www.facebook.com/groups/463085303369104*
Instagram: *https://www.instagram.com/catsirota_author/*
TikTok: *https://www.tiktok.com/@catsirota_author*
Newsletter: *www.catsirota.com*

BOOKS BY CAT

Binary Souls Series
Forgiving Darkness
Embracing Light—coming soon